Palmer Lake

Other fiction by Thomas C. McCollum III

Tainted Blood

Whipsocket

Palmer Lake

Thomas C. McCollum III

SHOJI BOOKS, Inc.

Charlottesville, VA and Wilmington, DE

SHOJI BOOKS, INC.

2123 Ivy Road
Charlottesville, VA 22903

Shoji and colophon are registered trademarks.

Printed in the United States of America
Cover and text design by Mayapriya Long, www.bookwrights.com
Cover illustration of woman by Duncan Long, www.duncanlong.com
Author photograph by Sandy Jackson Motley
Cover photos from Corbis Images

LIBRARY OF CONGRESS CATALOGING IN PUBLICATION DATA

McCollum, Thomas C.
    Palmer Lake / Thomas C. McCollum III.
        p. cm.
    ISBN 0-9713797-1-8 (alk. paper)
        1. Cryonics—Fiction. 2. Immortalism—Fiction. 3. Billionaires—Fiction.
4. South Dakota—Fiction. 5. Police chiefs—Fiction. 6. Widows—Fiction.
I. Title

PS3563.C3434 P35 2001
813'.54—dc21
                                                                2001054179

1 3 5 7 9 10 8 6 4 2

In respectful memory of Nicole

How I wish you were here to tell your story.

Prologue

~:~:~:

MARCH 2, 1987
IMB CRYOGENIC RESEARCH LAB
ZÜRICH, SWITZERLAND

Light snow was falling when Dr. Ralf Verson left the coffee shop and crossed the narrow cobbled street to his office building. A burly company security guard let him in the front door. Verson headed down the polished marble stairs towards the basement and the restricted area of the cryogenics laboratory, a steaming cup of cappuccino balanced in his right hand. In his left hand he carried a bulging briefcase that was hand-cuffed to his wrist. It was early. Other than the guard he had not seen another employee in the building. The only sound was Verson's own shoes echoing on the hard floor, the noise ricocheting from wall to wall.

Verson absorbed the warm comfort of the building and whistled to himself as he approached the basement laboratory. Oddly, the usually locked door of the lab was ajar. How many times had he chastised the damn maintenance people for being so lax? He pushed open the heavy metal door with his left elbow. He sniffed the air. A pungent smell crept into his nostrils and overcame the sweet aroma of the cappuccino. He stood silent for a moment. All he could hear was water dripping and the whir of a small fan coming from the restricted cryonics area. That's where the smell was coming from, too.

Verson took a small key from his jacket pocket, undid the handcuff from his wrist, and laid down the briefcase full of laboratory secrets. He shook the melting snowflakes from his head and ran both hands through his thick, wavy hair. Then he heard a faint sound as though someone was scratching their fingernails on a blackboard.

His pulse started to race. Was someone in the other room? After all, the lab door had been open. He was ready to call out but stopped himself. What if some kind of small animal had somehow gotten into the room? Maybe a squirrel or a rat? He pushed open a swinging metal door and entered the shadowy restricted cryonics area.

The room was used to store two prototype stainless-steel dewars—protective vaults for bodies that had been cooled to the boiling point of liquid nitrogen. Verson didn't know what to expect, as the scientists had been on a four-day holiday and this was his first day back after a short vacation in Geneva. One of the canister-like dewars sat empty, awaiting a future patient, as yet they did not know whom. The other contained Jutta Kell, a thirty-nine year old physician who had died from sleeping sickness four years earlier after a sabbatical in Central Africa. Her husband, multi-millionaire Suisse banker Hartmut Kell, had her suspended at the IMB research laboratory.

The dewar was a prototype with a full-length Plexiglas window in the front of the pod. Dr. Kell's dewar held only one patient, but it was built to hold as many as three bodies in one hollow unit. (Each body was suspended upside down in the unit in case there was ever a leak. That way the frozen head would be the last to thaw.) The window was riveted to the stainless steel container with fastener bolts one-half inch apart to prevent leakage. The Plexiglas was installed so the research scientists could have a way to view Jutta while she was suspended; they had wrapped her body with gauze, leaving only her head, neck, and shoulders exposed. Over time they would monitor her for any potential physical changes.

During the four years Jutta had been suspended, she had hung upside down in a perpetual frozen state without the slightest change in anatomy, the pale blue liquid nitrogen lazily drifting around her body.

Verson surveyed what little he could see in the semi-darkness. The scratching started again. It was almost inaudible in the distance. His huge palms became moist with sweat. The slow water drip pounded in his ears along with his heartbeat. He took a small step forward and his foot landed with a squish on something soft and boneless. He leapt sideways and bumped into the wall, then groped along the stucco until he found a light switch. Instantaneously the overhead halogen lamps lit the room. In the middle of the corridor lay a large, damp sponge. He almost laughed at his foolishness, but then he looked over at the dewar containing Jutta Kell. The dewar had leaked. A crack from one of the rivets ran about three feet upwards into the Plexiglas. The liquid nitrogen had evaporated as it leaked out, leaving only a noxious odor and a thin film of frost on the interior of the dewar. What Verson saw looking back through the window of the lab door wasn't possible. His massive body stumbled back through the swinging door, which knocked over the coffee, spilling it onto the briefcase.

Jutta Kell was no longer hanging upside down. Her protective bandages and the nylon cord that hung her by her feet in the dewar were lying on the bottom of the pod in a pile like a mummy's wrappings. She was sitting up, her face and hands pressed against the Plexiglas.

She had written in the frost, "HARTMUT, BITTE HILF MIR!"

1

~:~:~:

PALMER LAKE, SOUTH DAKOTA
MARCH 2, 1987 - 12:05 A.M.

Shortly after midnight, the church bells at St. Mark's Cathedral softly clanged for matins. The familiar clamor drifted over the lake.

Will Chase sat in his book-filled study and gazed at last month's cover of Forbes magazine. A television set glowed silently in the corner. Will's feet rested on the edge of his bulky, leather chair and his knees poked through the white and gold bathrobe wrapped around his thin torso. The cover blurb read: *America's Richest Man—MICROMED'S—O. William Chase.*

For once, the cover photo did him justice. The photographer had shot it straight on. Will was wearing wire-rimmed glasses over near-sighted hazel eyes. His tall, lanky frame was bent in a habitual hunched over posture behind a rosewood desk. A silk-screen of Marilyn Monroe by Andy Warhol hung in the background. Will had on a light-gray, Armani suit and a yellow shirt, open at the collar. His unruly brown hair was neatly combed for once, and he seemed to be smirking at the rest of the world. All in all, Will, who hated being photographed, was pleased with the picture.

From a partially opened stained-glass window, the faint echo of a solo church bell floated into the room. Will inhaled a large toke of Turkish tobacco from his pipe, leaned back in his chair, then blew smoke rings towards the frescoed ceiling.

A sudden burst of U-2's "The Joshua Tree" shattered his reverie. The stereo speakers of the Bang & Olufsen TV throbbed with the din. Will jumped up from his worn, comfortable chair. The remote control that he must have sat on fell to the floor. He grabbed it and punched "mute." He didn't want to wake Nina and the children.

"Honey, what's going on up there?" Nina's sleepy voice called.

"It's a televised rock festival on TV. Sorry, it was an accident. Did I wake Stirling or Sophie?"

"They're both sound asleep. Why don't you come to bed?"

"Why don't you come up? Jackson said he'd stop by. We can all have a glass of champagne, and when he leaves, we can fool around a little."

"Get lost. I've got to get up at five o'clock for that school trip to Watertown."

"Aw, come on up anyway."

"Night, William."

Will wasn't the richest man in America because of money. It was the love of his family that made him so wealthy. He glanced out the picture window and watched a blazing white meteor streak across the ebony sky.

At the entrance to Ridgely Heights, Will and Nina Chase's palatial estate, stood a weathered, twenty-five-foot marble statue of Thomas Jefferson holding a copy of the Declaration of Independence. A pigeon roost, as the Chase children called it. He greeted all callers entering the half-mile-long, uphill, Italian cypress-lined driveway. The statue had been placed there over a century before by old man Ridgely, for whom the farm had been named.

Jackson Palmer waved a hello to the guard at the gate from the cab of his Ford Bronco and was let through the metal barrier with no further ado. He drove past the horse pastures to the main house through a good portion of Ridgely Heights' six hundred and eighty acres. This was probably the only private acreage in South Dakota on which no crops were grown, nor any animals raised. The raw land was like a moat, protection against the public's curiosity for the rich.

Jackson stopped in front of a brick, pillared house that Will and Nina had remodeled to resemble the White House—a monstrous bit of construction that everyone thought out of place in Palmer Lake—except Jackson, who liked the house's vulgar majesty.

Jackson hopped out of the truck and walked up the granite stairs to the main entrance. A towering, stone-faced Sioux named War Bird let him in the foyer.

Eggs Benedict, a white and yellow cockatoo, sat uncaged on a metal perch, his head feathers bristling. As Jackson took a step up the red-carpeted, curved stairway, the bird greeted him with an unfriendly peck and a squawk. "DON'T GO UP THERE. DON'T GO UP THERE!"

Jackson scaled the stairs, hearing Tina Turner's soft, sexy singing voice coming from the open study door. He stuck his head in the door of the messy room.

"Top of the evening, Commander," Will said. He handed Jackson a glass of Dom Perignon. "What's up?"

"Not much." Jackson sipped the champagne. "I was out at the cemetery visiting Johanna and Junior and I got to thinking about the upcoming secondary offering. Thought we might kick it around for an hour before I headed home."

Will put his glass on the end table with a crystally clunk.

"Shit, here we go again." Jackson took a breath as if to say something, but Will held up his hand. "Forget the secondary offering for a minute. Don't you think it's about time you let go of the dead? My God, you've been going out to that cemetery four and five times a week the last few years. You can't keep crucifying yourself the rest of your life. Why don't you find somebody new?"

Jackson twisted his fingers around the smooth stem of his glass, then gulped the last of his champagne in one swallow. The bubbles burned his nose. He glanced out the window as if he could find an answer in the darkness. Why couldn't Will understand his loss? Was it because he lived under a golden cloud that had rained nothing but happiness and perfection upon his life? How could Will know his pain? The naive bastard. Jackson turned and glared at his friend. They'd had this discussion before. It wasn't worth an argument tonight. Will never understood anyway.

"Can it, Will. I'm not looking for anyone new," Jackson said, then noticed the cover photograph of Will. Jackson couldn't help but smile.

Will grinned back sheepishly. "Not a bad likeness, eh?"

"No, it's quite flattering considering the subject matter." Jackson laughed aloud and poked Will in the shoulder. "And a damn good article about Micromed. You know, Oswald, we're such lucky bastards." Jackson only used Will's first name to aggravate him, and Jackson was the only one who dared.

A thin haze of tobacco smoke lingered in the air. Will put a stick of mannitol gum in his mouth and puffed his chest. "Isn't that the truth? I feel sometimes I'm beyond life, untouchable, even by death."

"Don't get so cocky. One thing Nam taught me is that just when you think you're invincible, you get your ass shot down." Jackson then extended his index finger like a gun and pointed it at Will. "BAM!"

Will chewed the foul-tasting medicinal gum slowly. He stared at Jackson for a moment and then gave him his irresistible grin. "I was speaking metaphorically. As to the secondary offering, it's all set with Merrill Lynch for May 15th. The two hundred million we raise is to be used only for the development of our erbium laser technology."

"I don't get it," Jackson said. "We've just cornered the world's coronary angioplasty market and now you want to develop technology that'll replace our own catheters?"

One corner of Will's mouth curled in a knowing smirk. "We've got to think of the future," he said. "Catheters only have a life in cardiovascular medicine for another fifteen years. Then it'll all be lasers. So we can corner the market on that as well."

Jackson's hand started shaking as he poured himself more champagne. His nerves had never been the same after his internment during the war. He spilled a few drops on the glass table. "You know that Carl and I disagree with you about this money. No matter how much we agree that lasers are the wave of the future, we feel it's way down the road. We think the company should split the money and put half into development of new inverting catheters for pulmonary medicine."

"Why?"

"Because that market will be huge for the next thirty years. Hell, HIV and AIDS pulmonary catheters alone would account for billions in sales."

"Don't be dumb, the government will find a vaccine in the next year or so for those diseases."

"You're the one being stupid. You know damn well it's not in their best interests to find a vaccine. There's more money to be made by people in the funding of AIDS than there is in finding a cure. So they won't find a cure anytime soon. Mark my word."

"Enough. You and my brother can disagree with me all you want. On this issue, I'm getting my way with the Board."

Jackson threw his hands in the air. "You can always tell a Scotsman—but you can't tell 'em much!"

"Okay, fine. Why don't you and Carl run the operation? I'll just call the shots."

"You obstinate shit. One of these days someone's going to strangle you."

Will grinned. He lit a wooden match over his pipe and sucked the flame deep into the brown tobacco. A red ash soon glowed in its reflection on the window pane.

By superstitious habit, Jackson did not step on any cracks in the sidewalk as he strode towards his truck. He pulled on his thin, woolen gloves and hopped behind the wheel. He punched the FM button to the automatic tuner. Garrison Keillor's nasal voice introduced a Danish accordion player, backed by a trio of washtub and spoon thrashers on the Prairie Home Companion show. Jackson tapped his knee in gleeful accompaniment. His taste in music ran a different direction from Will's.

The cab of the Bronco smelled of leather, cigar, and dog—his black Great Dane named Balthasar. Normally Jackson took him everywhere, but when he went to the town cemetery, he left the dog at home. The giant pooch had a habit of digging things up. A well-used, frayed, Western saddle bounced in the rear of the truck, and a small cedar cigar box, half-full of Padron's, sat on the passenger seat. Jackson put one in his mouth but didn't light it. In case of trouble, or coyotes, a fully loaded .357 Magnum revolver lay in the glove box. An iciness was in the air. Jackson shivered, he could see his breath, but he didn't turn on the heater. The cold embraced and invigorated him.

Beau Palmer, Jackson's great-great-grandfather, had discovered the area in the mid-1800s. There were no borders between South Dakota, North Dakota, and Minnesota at that time. It was wild, desolate prairie. Wolves were king. Buffalo roamed the plains and Indians canoed the rivers and lakes. But Beau was a fearless frontiersman, and a lake and a small river running into it were named after him. Soon after, the town of Palmer Lake was formed. Then in 1874, the gold rush in the Black Hills took off. Nasty, venal gunslingers came pouring through the area on their way to seek buried treasure. Many of them had enslaved Chinese coolies to do the manual labor that lay ahead. One of the worst was Matt Younger, a man with several notches on his guns. He had with him a coolie named Huey Goey Loo, who didn't want to go any farther west. In the middle of the town, Younger strapped him to a horse railing, cut off his pigtail, and, with a bullwhip, whipped him until he was unconscious. Beau tried to intervene and Matt Younger shot him dead. Palmer Lake's first judge, Svend Ronning, had Younger hanged.

Huey Goey Loo lived through the awful beating. When he recovered he stayed in Palmer Lake and worked in the granite quarries; the Chinese were assigned the deep, side-long tunnels beneath the mineshafts where the white man wouldn't go. These tunnels, which yielded the highest grade granite, ran for miles in each direction under and around the lake. Years later, after Huey Goey Loo had hoarded the bulk of his monthly wages, he opened a restaurant, sent for a wife and friends in China, and religiously took care of Beau's gravesite. By his code of honor, he did this until the day he was buried in a plot near Beau. Now, each September 30th the town raucously celebrated Beau Palmer Day at the county fair, culminating with the villagers placing flowers on Beau's and Huey Goey Loo's graves.

Jackson steered the Bronco in the direction of the cemetery. He wasn't angry with Will, only disappointed, maybe even envious of his life. Sometimes it seemed that everything Will had ever done had gone right—never a dark cloud or a gloomy day. He respected Will's inventive ability, but he questioned his business acumen. After all, it was Jackson and Carl who had made the corporate decisions, managed the day-to-day operations of marketing and manufacturing, which in turn had driven the stock to be the darling of Wall Street the past ten years. Hell, Will didn't become a billionaire on his own, and as difficult as it was for anyone to disagree with Will, this time Jackson knew he was right, and he was going to take this matter to the Board and be heard.

Once on County Road 15, Jackson took off a glove, put his unlit cigar in the ashtray, and switched radio stations. As he passed the cemetery, the V8 crooned along with the music of the 1950s and whistling wind outside. As was his usual ritual, Jackson rolled down the window. He waved and yelled. "Good night, Johanna. Good night, Junior."

The moon cast long shadows from odd-shaped, engraved granite tombstones and the howling prairie wind swirled debris through the flat, tree-barren cemetery.

Out of habit, Jackson fingered the dark mole on his right cheekbone. It was the only blemish marring his rugged features. As a man who had studied medicine, Will wanted him to have the growth removed. Johanna had found the mole sexy. It stayed.

The headlights lit up the side of the road in an eerie white. The snow had started to melt in South Dakota, preparing for spring. The plowed earthen fields were partially covered in the crusted snow, and it all glittered off in the distance. Why was Will insisting on jeopardizing the future of the company? Pouring all the new money into unproven lasers. God knows what he'd do next. The Bronco's right front tire skidded, then thumped into a pothole and Jackson gripped the wheel firmly. He saw a large shadow swoop across the pavement in front of him. When he looked up to see the shadow's source, chills shot down his spine. Through the windshield he watched a gliding owl's black silhouette appear against the circular moon.

War Bird had told him that this was the Sioux's symbol of impending death and imminent resurrection.

·   ·   ·   ·

2
᷄᷅ ᷄᷅ ᷄᷅

IMB CRYOGENIC LABORATORY
ZÜRICH, SWITZERLAND

It had taken an hour for the scientists to remove Jutta Kell care-fully from the faulty dewar. Once she was on an operating table, the doctors were surprised to find her body temperature at an abso-lutely normal 98.6 F. Her joints were supple, her skin felt soft to the touch, and she had a beatific smile on her face. She appeared to be alive.

She was not.

Yet, Dr. Verson had seen the writing on the frosty Plexiglas, which proved she had returned to life. He had even heard her. How had she defied the logic of science? Did the mixture of drugs origi-nally given to her for sleeping sickness and the perfusate the lab used create some kind of reaction that brought her back to life? What kind of medical miracle were they witnessing?

Her desperate message, "Hartmut, please help me!", also veri-fied that Jutta had not lost her memory, nor her intelligence, as the message from inside the dewar was written backwards so that one on the outside would be able to read it. However, she was now once again medically dead. How long had she been alive? How could she have survived with a synthetic solution in her system instead of blood? For a brief moment everyone silently watched her lying still on the operating table. Maybe she would move. Maybe there would be a sign.

Verson finally broke the silence and asked his superior, "Should we try and perfuse whole blood into her and see if we can revive her again, or do you prefer we do an autopsy?"

"There'll be no autopsy. Let's try putting her own whole blood that we've stored back into her and see what happens. What perfusate did we use when we suspended her?"

Verson was sitting on a stool next to the perfusionist. With his hand on the patient's arm he said, "It was an animal and insect extract that a scientist in the U.S. at the Izor Foundation developed some years ago. If you recall, he sent us a few gallons some time ago. It's called synthetic arthropoda, but I don't think it had ever been used in a human subject before."

Five pints of Jutta Kell's whole blood were slowly dripped into her unconscious body. Three hours later she became cold. Rigor mortis developed. They decided to remove the blood and perfuse the synthetic arthropoda back into her and suspend her again, this time in the second dewar, as the first one needed repair. When she was hung by her feet in the dewar, they did not re-wrap and bandage her. They wanted to monitor her entire body on a daily basis.

A troubled Verson looked at his superior and asked, "Don't you think it best we contact the authorities or her husband?"

The head doctor, who had saggy cheeks and baleful eyes, said, "No I don't. Cryonics has a bad enough image created by the press. Think of what they would do with this information. Since we can't revive her they'll think we were trying to get publicity. It's best that we have the damaged dewar repaired, then analyze exactly what *transpired today. We could be close to the biggest scientific discovery in all of medical history."*

.   .   .   .

3

JUNE 4, 1987
PALMER LAKE, SOUTH DAKOTA

Due to a minor stroke she had suffered the previous autumn, Ingrid Chase's mouth was tilted at an oblique angle and her lips were puffy. She ran her tongue over their rough surface. Her fingers fiddled with the pins in her hair. She had been so tired the night before that she had forgotten to undo her bun. Yawning, she sat up in bed, propped a pillow behind her back, and for a few minutes thumbed, from back to front, a *Good Housekeeping* magazine, a reading habit she had picked up from her mother.

Today was Ingrid's sixty-ninth birthday. The bones in her body ached, every inflamed joint throbbed with pain. She decided she wasn't going to let it be a bother, and she twisted out of bed. On this day her four boys and Jackson usually had a surprise in store for her. It had become one of life's little pleasures.

Ingrid opened a window to enjoy the fresh morning air. Her

bedroom was on the second floor of her brown and white English Tudor home, which faced southwest and sat on a breezy knoll overlooking the lake. Green buds were forming leaves on six huge, bur oaks, whose branches drooped over the slate roof of the house. Blooming beds of multi-colored hybrid roses were rock-terraced almost to the foot of the water. She attributed this bright location as the key to her yearly success of winning first prize for her Crimson Glory roses at the Big Stone County Fair in Ortonville.

Craning her neck out the window, she could see a hint of low-lying ground fog. The sun, barely over the horizon, winked at her through the whitish steam. The birdbath was full of chattering sparrows splashing in the shallow water, while a single red-winged blackbird warbled his melodious mating song from the base of the circular fountain. On the lake, Ingrid's twenty-foot sailboat bobbed at the side of a wooden pier, lanyards clanging in the wind. Humming a Gershwin tune, she put on her favorite floral dress.

A low, rumbling sound was permeating this serenity and caught Ingrid's attention. She hadn't even noticed before—it seemed muffled, or far away. It was coming from an area near the old, white clapboard garage. It sounded like a motor running. She peered out the window again, but could see no cars or visitors in the driveway. She stepped into her slippers and tottered downstairs to investigate. Her meowing long-haired Persian barely made it through the screendoor and into the house as the door slammed behind Ingrid on her way to the garage.

Ingrid slowly made her way towards the old building. As she approached the garage's side door, she realized the key to that entrance was upstairs, but there was no time to go get it for there was definitely a motor running inside the garage. She stepped gingerly onto the moist grass and made her way along the side of the building towards the double-door entrance.

The garage had been locked since her husband Ian's death five years ago in 1982. To her knowledge, no one had entered the building since. Housed inside was his two-tone, black and white 1955 Crown Victoria Ford. She rounded the corner of the garage. Why were the hasp and padlock hanging open? Was this one of the boys' silly surprises? She cupped her hand over her ear against the double wooden doors. She could hear the loose tappets of a motor. She moved back from the door for a moment, then instinctively grabbed the wooden handle.

The rusty garage door hinges screeched as Ingrid pulled. One of the single heavy doors dug into the dirt driveway. She gave a heave and it opened. A cold blast of pent-up night air shot through her thin cotton dress and a musty odor filled her nostrils along with the smell of carbon monoxide. The Crown Victoria's engine was running. Nervously, she twisted a lace handkerchief in her gnarled, arthritic hands. A leaden haze hung in the air. She put the hankie over her nose and crept softly towards the front of the car. The V-8 hummed rhythmically. She couldn't believe it was still in tune after all these years.

A large spider web hanging from the wooden rafters glittered in the filtered light from the opened garage door. A big black spider scurried up the web in a whir of motion. Metal hubcaps and used auto parts hung from nails that had been pounded into vertical two-by-fours. Hardened bat dung was piled in small batches on the wide, decorative chrome strip that ran over the top of the roof of the car. The slanted rear window reflected Ingrid's image. And then she saw it: a garden hose. It was connected with duct tape to the exhaust pipe and ran up through a small crack in a back-seat window. The windows were covered with fine, filtered grey dust. When she peered in the rear window, her nose pressed to the cold glass, she could see the outline of a body slumped over the steering wheel.

Ingrid looked at the back of the body's head and repressed

an urge to gag. Her tongue moved from side to side, removing the white spittle that had formed on the corners of her mouth. She then rubbed the dust from the window in a circular fashion so she could see more clearly. It appeared to be a man. He had a thick shock of brown hair protruding from a watch cap. His face was lying away from her directly onto the bottom spoke of the steering wheel. His arms were raised up and his hands gripped the top of the wheel. He had on pigskin leather gloves, and a frayed, dark-green Pendleton shirt peeked above the collar of a tattered, black overcoat. She knew she should turn around, go in the house and call the police, but some instinct drove her to open the door and see who this man was.

The chrome door handle was icy cold to her touch, but mechanically loose, and the heavy metal door came open as if the car were still on the showroom floor. Ingrid gritted her teeth as she lifted the head from the steering wheel by pulling up on the back of the man's hair. The effort strained her knotted fingers. The body was partially stiff with rigor mortis. He could not have been dead for long. She maneuvered the head around and looked the man in the face, then let out a scream and fainted.

Ingrid remained motionless for some time, a slight twitch ran down her right arm and her eyelids blinked. A covey of crickets chirped in time with the muffled, running engine. And from the open door, a bright ray of sunlight shot into the dark like the beam from a movie projector in an old theater.

7:15 A.M.

Roberts County coroner, Leonard Bookner, and the city of Palmer Lake's chief of police, George Winter, whose left ear was cauliflowered because he also doubled as the high school wrestling coach, both noticed the stainless steel American Cryonics Society bracelet on the dead man's left wrist. They sat on their haunches gazing at the body slumped over the steering wheel in the still- idling car. Leonard held the stiffening arm of the victim. George stood. The Chief, as he liked to be called, had a jut-jaw that was covered with a day's growth of black beard. He reached in the car and shut off the ignition. "Christ almighty, Will was always a little wacko, but it gives me the creeps to think he'd kill hisself an' then think we're going to freeze his ass so he can come back again some day."

Leonard knew Will had been a pioneer in the field of cryonics, the science of freezing people for future revival. He dropped Will's wrist and snapped at George. "That's an insapory remark and inappropriate at this time. You should be thinking of Nina and the kids. You're going to have to inform them as soon as possible."

"Look, you skinny little turd, you don't have to use them fancy words with me. I ain't impressed." George cleared his throat, coughing into his hand. "I'll call Nina just as soon as I can. An' what about Carl?"

"Before I gave Ingrid a sedative, she insisted on calling Carl. So he knows." In his crouching position, Leonard's left leg was becoming cramped. He straightened it. "The gossip will be all over town soon, so I'll telephone Jackson with the bad news, but right now, let's call the number on that bracelet and honor Will's wishes."

"Listen, if Will wanted to be frozen like a fuckin' popsicle, then you go do it by yourself. I'm goin' to snoop around the garage an' see if he left any clues as to why he wanted to die so rich, an' so young." George tilted back the policeman's cap on his head and muttered to himself as he was walking away, "An' why'd he leave a gorgeous wife an' two beautiful kids."

Leonard looked at George as if the longitudinal fissure between the cerebral hemispheres of the cop's brain had short circuited. He stood to relieve his cramp. His knees cracked. He wiped away a few beads of sweat that were on the top of his bald pate. Tears welled in his eyes when he glanced back at the corpse slumped over the steering wheel.

Lying dead was a man he admired and cared for. A man he had grown up with, a man who was like his brother. All of the Chases had been surrogate family to him. Over the years, Will and Leonard had attended the same schools, from grade school through college, and then into medical school. The only anger Leonard had ever known towards Will was when Will had dropped out of med school during his third year, after he invented his first catheter. Leonard thought he should have gotten his medical degree.

Leonard walked over to the coroner's black wagon. This was not just another cadaver; this was a friend and he was going to adhere to the desires of his pal. The hell with George.

As a pathologist, Leonard was aware that death by carbon monoxide poisoning would at least not have harmed much of Will's body tissues. Will would be an ideal candidate for suspension in liquid nitrogen.

Without disturbing Ingrid, but with her whining cat dashing out the door, Leonard made his way into the kitchen of her house and placed a call to the Izor Life Extension Foundation.

The head physician at the Izor assured Leonard that a plane, complete with a medical team, would arrive in less than four hours. They requested he get the body submersed in ice as soon as possible and start a total body washout (TBW)—a procedure in which blood was removed from a patient and replaced with a perfusate. The perfusate, which could be one of various chemical solutions, would act as an antifreeze for the body that was going to be suspended. Leonard was told this was an essential step in the cryonics process and he would have to get a thoracic surgeon to initiate the procedure.

Time being short, Leonard then telephoned Doc Tragus, Palmer Lake's only ear, nose, and throat surgeon. "Good morning, Doc. It's Lenny. I've got an emergency and I need you over at the morgue in thirty minutes. Can you meet me there?"

Pudgy Doc Tragus was practicing his putting on a fuzzy green mat in his office. He was holding his new Ping putter in one hand and the telephone in the other. He spun the putter in his palm. "Can't do. I've got a tee time in thirty minutes. It's my first day out on the course this year. You'll have to get someone else."

"Sorry, I can't." Leonard sniffled. "It's Will Chase. He committed suicide last night and he wants to be suspended at Izor Life Extension Foundation. They told me they needed a thoracic man to prepare the body for being frozen."

Doc Tragus dropped the putter on the floor. "Well I'll be doggoned. Your pal was always one strange individual, but I never dreamed of suicide."

"No one did, Doc. At least as I can tell."

"I'll be there as soon as I can, Lenny."

George, with his puffy, pork-sausage fingers prying into all of the junk in the garage, found nothing to arouse his curiosity. However, as he was replacing a roll of tar paper in the dark back corner, he noticed a small piece of fabric dangling high up from a nail stud. He examined it. At first inspection, it looked like a piece of Army fatigue material. He stuck it in his pocket. Directly below the nail stud he saw a fresh footprint in the dust on the floor. It was from a very large right foot. George figured between a size thirteen and fifteen, and the sole had an unusual marking, like it was from an athletic shoe.

George knew there could be at least a hundred suspects with size thirteen to fifteen feet living in the county. But he was certain this footprint wasn't the Yeti's. And he was going to find out whose it was. He started by walking over to the car, reaching in, and bending Will's leg so he could examine his feet. Will had on Birkenstock sandals, European size forty-six, which George later calculated to be about an American ten and a half. It wasn't Will's footprint, and it certainly wasn't Ingrid Chase. She had told George no one had been in the garage since 1982.

Then he noticed lying in the darkness of the backseat a bouquet of fresh flowers and a neatly wrapped package with an envelope attached. He reached in the backseat to inspect his findings. Had he found a suicide note? He opened the envelope. It was a signed birthday card to Ingrid. He left the flowers, but put the birthday gift and envelope under his arm to deliver later.

His suspicions aroused, George went to the squad car and took out his large valise, then returned to the garage. He dusted the area and made a plaster of paris mold of the footprint. He thought he might just save it for future reference.

.   .   .   .

4

JUNE 4, 1987 - 8:00 A.M.
IZOR LIFE EXTENSION FOUNDATION
MANKATO, MINNESOTA

NBC investigative newsman Bernard Grable had been in Mankato for five days doing a story on the Izor Foundation. During his short stay, he felt as if the entire staff of the Foundation had adopted him. He knew that much of the network's story had to do with the foundation and Mankato State University each receiving a $50,000,000.00 donation from the university's most famous graduate, O. William Chase.

With the Foundation's permission, NBC hoped to produce a documentary on cryonics. Bernard was in an operating room examining the medical equipment needed for a cryonics suspension when Dr. Peter Sayers received the call from Roberts County coroner, Leonard Bookner.

Visibly shaken, Sayers gave instructions to Leonard as to the protocol that needed to be followed in the upcoming suspension. Then Sayers put down the receiver as if in slow motion. "Bernie, this is bigger than anything we've ever done. Bigger than when we suspended Disney. You're here to do a story on cryonics. Well, here's the opportunity of a lifetime for a reporter to film and see a procedure firsthand."

Goosebumps formed on Bernard's forearms. This was a story that might vault him into prominence at NBC. He was the first black man the network had hired in a news capacity. He was only thirty-three and he felt he needed something controversial. He clicked his tongue against the roof of his mouth and asked, "Pete, what's happened? Is it someone important?"

Sayers cleaned his thick glasses with his smock. He rubbed the material and lenses in little circles, then held the glasses up into the overhead fluorescent lights. He squinted into the light. "The benefactor of this foundation, Will Chase, has just committed suicide."

Bernard's mouth fell open. "What? Did they say how he did it?"

"They found him dead in a car from carbon monoxide poisoning this morning. At least the body will be in good shape when we get there," Sayers said. He picked up a telephone and started organizing his staff.

Bernard smoothed the lapel of his double-breasted blue blazer and rearranged the decorative red hankie in his pocket. What great luck. He would actually get to see a procedure performed. "Is there really a chance I could tag along?"

"If you'd like to bring your film crew and come along, we're leaving in thirty minutes," Sayers said.

Bernard knew it was one thing to talk and write about death, quite another to witness it, especially when it involved seeing a doctor administer the medication that prevented clotting. He hoped Will Chase hadn't opted for a neurosuspension procedure, or a cephalic isolation, where the patient's head is surgically separated from the body between the sixth and seventh cervical vertebrae and then frozen on its own. No way could he handle watching that. He didn't even want to think about such an operation. But it didn't matter. He knew a hot story when it sat in front of him. "Let's go," he said. "I can have my camera man ready in time."

Deep inside the complex in an isolated office, the silhouettes of two men could be seen bent over a large machine that was radiating an iridescent blue hue.

Dr. Kary Duesmann, Nobel nominee in molecular biology, and his associate, Londoner Neville Cruikshank, who was arguably the world's foremost expert in synthetic chemistry, were engrossed in Duesmann's latest invention. He called it an electron tunneling microscope, or ETM. This was a machine that could physically manipulate atoms. It allowed Duesmann a vehicle to perform and monitor construction tasks involving single atoms.

The gaunt, kinky-haired Cruickshank, whose frayed, unbuttoned, shirt collars curled up at the end, stood and reached across the table for a paper towel. He slowly wiped each of his fingers. "You mean to tell me the bloody thing works?"

"Certainly it works," said Duesmann, "but I wanted to wait until I had the right subject in the laboratory before I proved to the world I had a device to repair a cell, atom by atom."

"Does this have anything to do with Sayers' call about Will Chase being brought over here tonight?"

Duesmann rubbed his hands together. "Right on the button. I've been working in secret on this project for two years and now I finally have the right patient."

"I know your machine has the capability to revive a frozen animal, but are you telling me you mean to use it on Will Chase?" Cruickshank was stunned by what his colleague was about to do.

"Got it in one," Duesmann said. His yellow teeth grinned

through his graying, tobacco stained beard. His enormous appetite was legendary, and his gargantuan belly bulged under his lab coat.

Cruickshank sucked air between his spaced buck teeth. It made a whistling sound. "I say, I know we're moving along rapidly in research medicine, but this sounds like science fiction."

"Neville, when you left Oxford and came to Harvard for your graduate work, I know you and your guru, Timothy Leary, dropped enough acid and smoked enough dope to make you think the present world of science isn't reality, but it is." Duesmann burped an odorous burp. "Mark my word, you're going to see a large animal cloned in the next few years. They're damn close to it now in Scotland. Then you'll see the mapping of the human genome, and after that it's a heartbeat away to reviving a frozen human being. So, why shouldn't I be first with my ETM?"

"Jolly well you should be, and I'm all for you, but Will Chase?"

"Might as well start at the top." Duesmann grinned.

"Well, I guess this's the start of nanotechnology."

"Science can call it what it wants. All I know is that I've developed a machine with the ability to assemble atoms according to general specifications. Just like building blocks."

Duesmann took a white porcelain Woodie from his coat pocket, filled it with stringy tobacco, and lit it. A spicy aroma filled the room.

Cruickshank shared a deep scientific bond with Duesmann. For years Cruicksank's only pastimes were taking acid and skiing all the major slopes of the world. No major firm would hire him because he never lied about his use of LSD. He was considered too eccentric, but Duesmann found him reliable and hired him. Cruickshank said, "Does that mean you can assemble any stable arrangement of atoms that could ever be designed?"

"Right again. I can design the atoms regardless of scale or complexity. In a matter of weeks I'll have the ability to synthesize anything!" Duesmann reached over his machine and turned on a toggle switch. "Watch." Green laser beams zigzagged in a glass vacuum chamber the two men were staring into. A fine needle point was positioned by piezoelectric crystals and held close to a conductive surface in the chamber. "When I move the needle close to the surface, electrons tunnel across the vacuum gap. The current becomes very, very strong when the needle's close to the surface and drops off when the needle's further away."

"That's brilliant. But how precise is this instrument?

"I can move this needle to a precision that's a fraction of an atomic diameter." Duesmann inhaled deeply from his pipe.

"So you've got what's needed to build an assembler?"

"I'm certain of it. My assembler will manipulate reactive groups to atomic precision, and this is an instrument that moves a needle around to atomic precision." Duesmann shut off the machine.

Cruickshank gave Duesmann a hearty slap on the back. "My God, if you can do this, it looks like you're close to replicating life. Good show, mate."

Duesmann wiped his beard and nose with a hankie. Long hairs sprang like coiled wires from his eyebrows, nose, and ears; science had long ago become a love that superseded any concern about appearance. "Thanks," he said. "Even though it's not perfected yet, don't ever forget the danger involved with this invention. Can you imagine what the military or the Russians might do with this technology? Programmable germs for germ warfare and so on. This's top secret. It's never to leave this laboratory. If I die prematurely, destroy it."

"Right. In my excitement I hadn't given a thought to anything but productive use," Cruickshank said. "How soon do you think you can start experiments with living and suspended matter?"

Perspiration gleamed on Duesmann's forehead like frost on a bottle of soda pop. "I already have. With hamsters, frogs, rabbits and dogs." Duesmann looked guiltily at Cruickshank.

"Dogs?"

"Yes, dogs. Big mammals, with physical anatomy like humans."

"Your experiments didn't happen to coincide with the disappearance of Elvis a year ago, did they?"

Duesmann's face started turning purple. He took two fingers and loosened his collar. Stale Old Spice cologne wafted from the opening. Bathing more than once a week was not on his agenda. "I assure you, your beagle is in fine fettle," he said. "Come with me into the other room. I was going to wait until your birthday next week to surprise you."

.   .   .   .

5

⌣⌣⌣

IMB CRYOGENIC LABORATORY
ZÜRICH, SWITZERLAND

Dr. Ralf Verson returned breathless to the laboratory from a quick lunch in the company's cafeteria where he had been having a sandwich and watching CNN International. He exclaimed to his superior, "Will Chase committed suicide in the States and he's going to be suspended at The Izor Foundation."

"Verson, are you serious?"

"Yes, it's all over the news."

"This is quite something. He's always been the largest benefactor in the world for our work. How'd he commit suicide?"

"By carbon monoxide poisoning from a car."

"How American."

"At least that type of poisoning should help his chances for revival one day," *said Verson. He paused to think about what he wanted to say.* "But now that we know cryonics works in some fashion, don't you think we should contact the Izor Foundation and share our experience regarding Jutta Kell?"

"No." His superior, a pock-faced man with a Hapsburg lip, whipped around. "What we witnessed must be kept absolutely confidential for the time being. There are millions of dollars at stake— maybe billions. And of course, the prestige of the corporation. We want to be the first to revive someone, not the Izor. We're not going to risk exposing our position until we have more facts on our patient and what happened to her."

.   .   .   .

6

‿:‿:‿:

Duesmann thumbed through the batch of keys on his metal key ring, found the right one, and then opened the locked steel door to his private laboratory. The twosome walked into the depths of the sound-proofed room. The air-springed door closed with a deep thud behind them. From the very rear of the room, Elvis let out a joyful howl from his wiremesh cage.

Cruickshank ran over and fell on his knees. He stuck his face to the dog and received a welcome lick on the nose.

"His condition is remarkable for an animal frozen solid for almost a year, wouldn't you say?" asked Duesmann.

The beagle jumped up and down in his cage and Cruicksank said, "What bloody right did you have to freeze my dog and use him as an experiment?"

"I didn't, he froze himself accidentally."

"Oh, come now."

"It's true. Someone left the lid partially off the liquid nitrogen tank in the lab, and I found him there one morning frozen solid. I knew it would break your heart if Elvis was dead, so I thought I'd keep it a secret. I hope you can forgive me. But it seems fate gave me a chance to try out my theories. Which, by the way, are no longer theories." Duesmannn unlocked the cage, and Elvis joyfully leapt upon Cruickshank's legs.

"It's incredible," Cruickshank said. "He doesn't appear to've suffered any memory loss and there doesn't seem to be any damage to his tissue from freezing. How'd you do it?"

Duesmann extracted a Slim Jim beef jerky from his smock pocket, bit off half of the meat, and threw the rest in the air to the dog, who caught it with an open mouth. "When I found Elvis, he'd fallen in the liquid nitrogen alive and therefore was the perfect cryonics subject, but I didn't know what kind of ice damage had been done to his cells, so I decided to thaw him gradually and inject him with my synthetic arthropoda perfusate and then refreeze him."

Cruickshank was petting Elvis and massaging his long ears. "You mean you synthesized the natural antifreeze that's in the blood of cockroaches?"

"Not exactly," said Duesmann, "I took a combination of natural antifreezes that I found existed in various insects like the cockroach. I mixed that with the concentrate of blood from animals that hibernate in Antarctica and other sub-zero climates of the world by freezing and rethawing themselves annually. None of them had any ill effects by being completely frozen for long periods of time. This's the solution I synthesized as a possible perfusate for mammals."

"What kind of animals?"

"Well, there's Painted turtles, wood and grey tree frogs, and Arctic hamsters, just to name a few."

Cruickshank held Elvis in his lap. The dog was licking his hands. "Did you use any glycerol in the cryoperfusion procedure?"

"No," said Duesmann. "No, I didn't. You see, I've found that most freeze-tolerant animals reach critical minimum cell volume when sixty percent of their total body water is sequestered as ice. My synthetic solute seems to replace over ninety percent of the water in a cell compared to the sixty percent with glycerol."

"How about dehydration?"

"Oddly, I then discovered that freezing had dehydrated Elvis's cells. You know from your own work that the effect of increased extracellular concentration is to draw water out of cells by osmosis. So I tried to protect the cells with the highest concentrate I dared perfuse. It seemed to work."

"Fascinating, but how'd you actually revive Elvis?" Cruickshank asked.

The dog cocked his head as if listening to the conversation.

"I don't quite know exactly how I did it and that's the part I'm working on now," said Duesmann, "After I thawed him, I repaired all of the cellular damage I could find with my ETM; then I used regular CPR and electrical massage to get his heart beating. I really thought there was no hope, especially since he has only a little of his own blood and the synthetic arthropoda in his system."

"And you did all of this with no assistance?"

Duesmann puffed little clouds of smoke from his pipe. He looked heavenward and shrugged his shoulders. "I guess Elvis and forces beyond our powers did the rest. We've got a lot of work ahead of us, Neville. I don't have all the answers, but this is a heck of a start."

"I can't wait to get going." Cruickshank stood and gave Elvis a final pat on the head.

"I've written up the entire procedure and I videoed the freezing and thawing operation. Of course we're going to have to monitor Elvis for a while to see what kind of success he has. By all medical accounts, he shouldn't be alive."

Cruickshank took the black video cartridge and put the papers under his arm. "Kary, you may have advanced cryonics technology by at least fifty years with this machine and your perfusate. I know it won't be that long before you can revive the medical dead."

"Only time will tell." Duesmann walked over to the lab refrigerator and took out a jar of pickles.

Cruickshank, data under his arm, walked out the door. "See you in an hour. Cheers."

.   .   .   .

7

9:00 A.M.
PALMER LAKE

Most people in Palmer Lake knew one another, but everyone in town knew Will Chase. It was a town of eleven thousand people, of which three thousand five hundred were employed by MICROMED. The town owed its economic prosperity to Will's medical inventions, and over the years few people migrated from the area. They had no reason to. Ninety percent of the population was of Scandinavian, German, and Italian descent. American Indians, mostly Sioux, made up the other ten percent. This was a close-knit community, where kids did not wear their baseball caps backwards unless they wanted the crap kicked out of them. People had midwestern values. They went to church each Sunday, they died in the same wars together, they knew their neighbors, supported their families, enjoyed their work, and loved their sports. And, as in most small towns, people did not socialize outside their secular pecking order.

Chief George Winter walked into the morgue, which was located in the basement of the Palmer Lake courthouse, just as Doc Tragus had finished the TBW procedure on Will. Will was now immersed in a stainless steel vat of ice water, his body drained of life and natural fluids, replaced with chemicals that might allow him a chance to renew life one day in the future. As the chunks of ice floated about his body, his face looked at peace with his surroundings.

"Before you sign the death certificate, you ought to know I think there's been some foul play here," George said. "I'm not satisfied this's a suicide."

Leonard raised a thin eyebrow as he looked over at Doc Tragus, then he said to George, "What on earth are you talking about? There's not a mark or indication on this body that would lead us to believe anything but suicide. Have you been over to the Muni drinking on duty again?"

George turned purple from the collar up. He removed his cap, put one foot up on a chair and boomed in an angry voice, "That ain't fair. I've been sober for over seven months. I don't appreciate what you're implying." Realizing how worked up he had gotten, he put his foot on the floor and inhaled deeply, like he had learned at AA. "I called Nina an' told her everythin' we know so far. She's on her way over now. But, damnit, listen to me. We all know Will had no reason to kill hisself. Nina said the same thing." He had lifted his corduroy pants' leg and was scratching the hairy skin above his sock. "An' why'd he have on those weird clothes?"

Doc Tragus pushed his rimless bifocals up the bridge of his pudgy nose. "Will was weird. He was eccentric as hell, we all know that."

"But he had everythin' to live for," George said. "A successful company, a great partner in Jackson, money, a wife an' two kids, his mom, an' three brothers." George pointed towards Will lying in the vat. "Come on you two, look at him. He was in perfect health, yet there was no note, no nothin' from him that he'd kill hisself."

Leonard sighed. He was recovering from the flu, and had had little sleep the previous night. He knew his day was going to be a long one. "As Caesar might have pondered, where's the onus probandi?"

"Watch the French," said George.

"It's Latin."

"Who gives a shit. Speak English, for Chris' sake."

"Sorry, Chief. I just want to know what proof you have that makes you think this isn't suicide."

George gave Leonard and Doc an icy glare. He lowered his voice. "Well, I found some strange evidence in the garage that shouldn't have been there."

Leonard had listened to George Winter exaggerate from the time they were kids in camp together. He rolled his eyes. "Pray tell, Sherlock, what might that be?"

"Piss off. This might be murder. I found a footprint in that garage that shouldn'a been there. Ingrid told me no one'd been in there since '82."

Doc Tragus said, "Chief, I think you've been watching too much Colombo."

"Very funny. I'm tellin' you, there's somthin' wrong here. Do a complete autopsy instead of freezin' Will."

"That's not my department. You know that's for the county coroner."

"What do you think, Lenny?"

"I won't do one unless either Klay Bond or Sasha Maki over at the district attorney's office orders me to do so."

"Aw, come on," George said. "You both know that neither of those two legal eagle teenagers know their ass from a hole in the ground. Hell, they're both just out of law school. I need one of you two to help me out here."

"As long as we don't find any evidence to the contrary, I'm planning on listing this as the suicide it appears to be. How about you, Doc?"

"I've got the lab running blood tests as we speak, and if I hear of something to support George's theory, I'll let him know."

Leonard and Doc Tragus looked at one another, waiting for George to reply. He didn't. The only sound was a scraggly, wire-haired mutt walking by the morgue, who had stopped for a brief moment to yap at his reflection in the small, one-way basement window. George stood staring at Doc and Leonard in furious silence. He purposely held back the fabric evidence and the flowers and birthday present. He needed a card to play later on, and he didn't want people taking away his evidence that he had bothered to look for and find.

Nina Chase's throaty voice broke the quiet. It was harsh, as if she had been smoking a lot, or crying a lot. She spoke from the dark stairs leading down into the room. She had been standing there for some time. "George, thanks for your concern. But I won't allow an autopsy. William had prepared every legal document necessary to make sure that he'd be put in the Izor Foundation upon his death. He filed them with the D.A.'s office a long time ago."

George wondered why she was so intent on bypassing the autopsy.

Nina could see the deep, stainless steel vat in which her husband was immersed in ice. She put two fingers to her lips, then crossed herself. She started down the stairs towards the three men. She had on beaded, leather moccasins and her walk was silent. She walked over to the vat and placed her hand gently on the rail. She seemed more at peace than upset. "Do you think I can be alone with William for a while?"

"Certainly," Leonard said. "We've finished until the doctors from Izor arrive. They should be here in about an hour. Would that give you enough time?"

"Yes."

The men, eyes on the floor, left Nina in the dimly lit room.

Nina was half-Sioux and half-Armenian. Her earth-grounded Sioux side told her to be calm and brave, while her Armenian blood pounded hot in her veins. She was now left alone in the world with two children. She lacked for no material necessity. She and the children were healthy, and she had Ingrid, and Red Cloud and all her friends, but nothing could replace Will. He had been her life. She had loved him since she was fourteen, the day she saw him gracefully playing lacrosse on the reservation with her brothers. That was twenty-six years ago. Her passion never wavered when he departed for four years of college and three years of medical school. She had grown to adore him even more as a husband.

Just the day before, the day of the suicide, they had made love on a padded lounge in the pool room in order not to awaken the children in their bedrooms. Why would the man she loved, the man who loved her, kill himself with no warning?

Nina's straight, silky, black hair was parted in the middle and it came to her shoulders. As she bent down to look in the vat, a thick tide of it fell over her eyes. She held it back with her left hand. With her right hand she moved the ice and glimpsed Will's peaceful face. She had always felt he looked better without his glasses. His normal color was gone. He was a blanched white. The starkness of his flesh contrasted with her cinnamon skin. Warm, salty, tears poured over her high cheekbones and dripped into the cold water. She longed to kiss him. "I love you, my darling. One day I'll find the truth and join you. I promise you, we'll be together again."

With her hand gently on Will's face, she sat down in a chair next to the vat and started humming tribal death chants she had learned as a child on the reservation. Within minutes, a whirring sound, like the beating of breeding monarch butterfly wings in Michoacan, accompanied her. It was her spirit, Wovoka.

In her heart, Nina knew the Indian God would know what to do.

. . . .

8

~:~:~:

From the picture window of Jackson's penthouse, the lake shimmered in the morning light. The waves had tiny white crests on them. Wanting security and isolation, Jackson had moved into the condominium complex shortly after Johanna and his son drowned in the lake during the summer of 1976. To Jackson, the lake never looked as dangerous as it could be.

On this balmy spring morning, Jackson had overslept—something he rarely did. Like clockwork he went to bed at one and woke at six. Today the steady ringing of the telephone woke him from his slumber. Groggily, he answered it. His brown hair was cowlicked in sleepy disarray, and he stood and put an arm through a black, Sulka robe that was hanging from the end of the bed. He peered out the window, listening to Leonard Bookner on the other end of the telephone explain Will's suicide. His first thought was that he and Will were only forty-three. "Does Nina know yet?" Jackson asked in his deep baritone voice.

"Yes, George called her."

Jackson rubbed the short, wiry stubble on his chin with his free hand. "I'll be downtown as soon as I can. Thanks for calling me personally, Lenny."

Normally, if the wind was not up, Jackson could see the reflection of the condo and the steeples of the Methodist and Catholic churches in the lake. In cleaning up during the week after Christmas, the town do-it-all, gigantic, retarded Bruno Tomacelli, had left a silver decoration stuck to the steeple at St. Mark's Cathedral. Father McQueeny didn't seem to mind, and the decoration sparkled each day like a star. The village kids called it "Bruno's Beacon."

A gangling blue heron poked at bullfrogs, while teal, mallards, and an occasional loon floated among the reeds and fed in the lagoon below, known as "Quicksand Swamp." It had engulfed more than one innocent person over the centuries. Yellow Lemon Day and striped Regal lilies were in full bloom along the old highway, separating the lagoon from the main section of Palmer Lake. A few late commuters made their way along the road to the laboratories of MICROMED.

This bucolic setting became a watery haze through Jackson's eyes. He wiped them with the sleeve of his robe, forced back nasty tasting bile that was rising from deep in his stomach, and put the telephone down in its cradle. Will was dead.

Jackson looked at his watch: ten after nine. According to Leonard, Will must have been dead for at least five hours now. Jackson knew Will was odd at times, but suicide? Impossible! They had just played tennis at the club two days before. After the match they had again discussed the upcoming two hundred million dollar-secondary offering of MICROMED stock. Much to Jackson's chagrin, Will had convinced the Board how the funds were to be used. Jackson now felt guilty that after the meeting he had called him a dumb, self-centered bastard. Although at the time it hadn't bothered Will in the least and he had said he couldn't wait to get to New York the next week and ring the bell on the Exchange that day.

Jackson limped slightly as he walked over to a stand-up mahogany humidor. Damn. His bad leg was always stiff in the morning. Around the house he used a walking cane, but he was too proud to do so in public. The leg was something he had learned to live with since he injured himself in the rescue attempt of Johanna and Jackson, Jr. It didn't hinder him in any way. It only ached more as he got older. He lifted the lid of the humidor, took out a Cohiba corona and snipped the end with a cutter. He put a match to the cigar and a small cough accompanied his thick exhale of smoke. Only the loss of his family hurt more than what he had just heard. Now this. He was tired of being lonely.

Balthasar loped in from the roof terrace, his pink tongue hanging out. Jackson sat, then slumped in his favorite chair, a huge, double Lazy-Boy that could accommodate both him and the dog while they watched television. He buried his head in his hands. Tears flowed down his cheeks. The cigar burned smoothly in the ashtray, leaving a nutty but homey odor in the room. Balthasar, at the moment Jackson's only real friend, leaned against his master. At one hundred and sixty-five pounds the dog weighed almost as much as Jackson. Jackson scratched Balthasar behind the ear. "Well, it's happened again, boy. More death in my life."

In June of 1950, his father, Thomas Palmer, had been the first American pilot killed during the Korean War. He was shot down in a stubby-winged jet north of the 38th parallel; his body was never recovered. In lieu of this military oversight, the family received the Distinguished Flying Cross. The conflict seemed forgotten to all but Jackson, who just wanted a father, and the other families who had lost a loved one. When he was thirteen, his mother, who never bore another child, disappeared while walking the shores of the lagoon. Official word was that Quick-sand Swamp claimed another victim, however, no body was ever found. Luckily, Ian and Ingrid Chase had taken him in and raised him as their own son.

As Jackson scanned the living room, he could see the privi-leges of wealth. It didn't seem that long ago he and Johanna used to worry about the monthly gas and electric bills. Nor that long ago when his only dream was to be an airline pilot and take care of Johanna forever. Now he was chief executive officer of MICROMED and a multi-millionaire. Surrounding him were all the material trappings of success: twenty-foot-high, mahogany beamed ceilings, columned windows with flowing Austrian drapes, marble fireplaces, Persian carpets, libraries of leather-bound books from around the world, antique furniture from France, the latest in electronic equipment, and photos of him with dignitaries and celebrities.

But Jackson had never felt so broke and alone. He just wanted to be needed. What good was all of this without sharing it and loving someone in your life?

The living room fireplace radiated a hint of heat from the previous night's coals. Jackson held open his hands to take in the warmth. He looked up onto the mantle at a silver-framed black and white snapshot of his father and mother taken right after World War II. They were holding hands. His father's flying medal was draped over the picture. His mother had written on the back of the photo:

> *Son, people will always find you a mystery, and al-ways be that mystery, but don't worry that you're differ-ent from others. You've got greatness in you. Don't ever forget that, Mom.*

He hadn't. Even though he wasn't sure what his mother had meant at the time. Other than a ragged, hand-written poem from his father, which Jackson carried in his wallet, they had left nothing else behind.

Jackson pulled the lever on the chair and lay back. He turned on CNN news. Will's suicide was the top news story. Balthasar nudged closer. Jackson switched off the TV. The cigar was smoldering and as he took a long drag from it the ashes fell to the carpet. Balthasar licked the salty tears from Jackson's cheeks. Jackson gave him a rueful smile and a pet. The closeness of the animal made him think of his former family. Johanna would have turned forty-two this year. Jackson, Jr. would have been sixteen and ready to start thinking of college. Now all he had were memories. A rustling sound broke Jackson's train of thought.

From behind a potted split-leaf philodendron a small voice asked, "Is everything okay, Mr. Palmer?" It was his maid, Running Fawn, Nina's distant cousin.

Balthasar, who could smell a dog biscuit under a pillow two rooms away, instinctively sniffed the air. He was sitting halfway in the chair, leaning on Jackson. As Jackson stood, Balthasar lunged to the floor and loped back to the roof terrace to enjoy the morning sun.

"I'm okay." Jackson straightened the lapels of his silk smoker robe. "Have you heard about Will?"

Running Fawn stepped out from behind the large, green plant. It was obvious from her puffy eyes that she had been crying. She was fat and was missing a front tooth. She held her hand over her mouth. "Yeth. I spoke with Nina earlier. She's heartbroken. She's called on Wovoka for help. But I don't think our spirit can help 'cause she's putting Will in a big 'frigerator forever. I don' know what to do." Running Fawn started to cry.

"Why don't you go over to her house and comfort her," said Jackson. "Tell her I'll be over as soon as possible. Right now I'm going to get dressed and go downstairs and see Papa Loo."

"Okay, Mr. Palmer. I'll do that." Running Fawn stared heavenward and started chanting to Wovoka as she left the room.

.   .   .   .

9

⌣:⌣:⌣:

PALMER LAKE - 9:30 A.M.

In downtown Palmer Lake, on elm-lined Walleye Lane, the rumors regarding Will's suicide roared through Donna's Donut Shoppe quicker than one of her raised donuts could go stale. In this quiet town, this was now bigger news than Liberace's recent death. Donna's sat on a corner across from Bobby Joe Baker's Used Car Lot, and between Jake Schwartz's Jewelry Store and Pietro Gambinni's Pizza Parlor. Four stories up from the jewelry store was the Borg Investment Counsel office. Overweight and jovial, Kirby Borg handled most of the business interests of the MICROMED employees. He was also Will and Jackson's personal investment advisor and one of their closest friends.

The good ol' boys network of shopkeepers, blue-collar workers, and local farmers who met every morning at Donna's for coffee, pancakes, and bacon and eggs, usually griped about the federal government and the upcoming weather. Each morning they exchanged raunchy jokes within earshot of the waitresses

and discussed who was pregnant, and by whom. Then they
headed off to their daily occupations feeling they had solved
the world's problems.

Jake, Kirby, Pietro, and Bobby Joe were regulars at Donna's.
They all suspected her of being a lesbian. However, on this morning that subject was not even mentioned. Over black coffee and
fluffy pecan rolls, they listened with interest to the latest buzz
in the diner about Will's death:

*"I wouldn't trust that sneaky fag Woody as far as I can throw
him."*
"How about that goddamn Nazi, Carl?"
"Where the hell was Rising Coyote last night?"
*"That crazy fuckin' sister in law of his, Big Bertha, strangled
the rich bastard."*
"Bullshit, old Red Cloud knifed him."

Red Cloud, Will's father-in-law, had indeed threatened to do
just that from the day Nina married Will. Years before Will's
and Nina's union, and long before society accepted interracial
marriage, Red Cloud had run off with Sophie Sarkisian, the History teacher at Palmer Lake Elementary School. But he married
her on the Indian reservation, with an Indian ceremony. To him,
it was inexcusable that Will had married his daughter in the
United Methodist Church in town.

The jukebox played a tragic Merle Haggard love song.

At a formica-topped, chrome-legged table, one of Will's childhood Indian buddies said, "If he didn't die of a drug overdose,
you'd better believe Big Bertha's the culprit."

Across the room, the German and Scandinavian contingent
were dipping their fresh donuts into steaming hot Ovaltine.

"I'm tellin' ya, Per-Olaf, the Mafia strangled Will for trying
to buy into the gamblin' over on the reservation."

"That's bullshit."

A stringy-haired waitress rapped the German farmer on the knuckles with a tablespoon. "Quiet your filthy mouth. I've watched Will gulp huge helpings of biscuits and gravy down his gizzard for years now. He must have just had a heart attack. Once all the commotion dies down, you'll see."

Donna, who had a stumpy body and a long, slim neck like a bottle of Lea & Perrins Worcestershire Sauce, did not voice an opinion, but she, like everyone else in the diner, never considered Will's death a suicide. Nor did she like the rumors she was hearing.

A quarter of a mile down the street, in the soda fountain and grill of Burt's Pharmacy, next door to Huey Goey Loo's Chinese restaurant, the white-collar workers from MICROMED whispered about Will's demise. They were joined most mornings by other town professionals. The town elite congregated and gossiped in Burt's leather booths with their *Wall Street Journals*. Most breakfasted on tea, granola, and yogurt:

"It's unbelievable."
"Is it true?"
"Yes, suicide I think."
"That's impossible."
"What about the children, Stirling and Sophie?"
"I don't know. The poor things."
"There's been talk of drugs and murder?"

Burt, the proprietor, who had the looks and personality of an angry grizzly, shook hands with the long-time county judge, Lars Ronning. "Morning, Judge. I hope you'll accept condolences for the suicide of your friend, Will Chase. He did a lot for this town. What do you think made him do it?"

Following family tradition, every Ronning for a century had been a lawyer or a judge in Roberts County. Lars Ronning had passed out sentences as harsh as the awful tasting medicine Burt dispensed. His fine, corn-silk hair was messed from the breeze and he combed it back with his hand. "At the moment I don't have any facts yet on what happened. Best I don't comment until I get those facts."

Judge Ronning smiled sternly at Burt, sat down in a booth and snapped open his briefcase.

Burt fiddled with the cord of his hearing aid. He always did this when he didn't get the answers he wanted from someone, it was as if the right answers were stuck somewhere in the bends of the wire.

The employees of MICROMED knew that Will enjoyed pot and occasional peyote. Judge Ronning did not. They also felt Will was more than eccentric in his lifestyle. This was a man who had founded their company and had become a billionaire by the time he was forty. Aside from his little personal foibles he was a rock-solid individual. Yet, they all agreed that brilliant people often committed suicide.

Will's older brother, Carl, the chief operating officer of MICROMED, was the only person sitting at a table alone. Carl's white shirts were always so stiffly starched they crackled when he moved. He was engrossed in his morning paper, The Palmer Lake Pride. After his mother had telephoned him, telling him of Will's suicide, Carl had his wife, Dixie, call his younger twin brothers, Woody and Freddie.

Genetically the twins were identical, however, Freddie had only one eye. His wife had poked out the other one in an argument. Other than this eye, they looked as if they were stamped from a cookie cutter: blond, fair-skinned, blue-eyed, and boring scientists. Carl knew they were never cut out for upper management.

Carl had been told that Ingrid was going to be sedated and there was nothing he could do at the morgue to help Doc Tragus and Leonard. Besides, Lute Olsen's prize bantam rooster, who crowed at all hours, had kept him up most of the night. So he thought he might get away from Dixie's tears and have a cup of black coffee at Burt's before facing the onslaught of questions.

But he couldn't. His employees surrounded him with slavish sympathy. So Carl wiped his trim salt and pepper goatee, and excused himself to go see his mother and deliver her birthday present. Of course Will's suicide had ruined his surprise, a roundtrip, first-class ticket to Hawaii. Carl hated always being upstaged by Will. Even in death, his brother's ghost would somehow get the attention. But one of these days he would have a big hit at the tables in Vegas and things would be different.

Judge Ronning peeked up from his legal notes. He found it odd that the victim's brother had been impassively enjoying coffee and reading his paper but said, "You have my condolences, Carl. Is there anything I can do for you?"

"Thanks, your honor, but Leonard Bookner seems to be in command of everything. Good morning." And by military habit, "Sir!"

.   .   .   .

10

In the northern woods of Minnesota and down on the prairies of the Dakotas, lone Timber wolves still roam. One can often see their huge paw prints in the mud flats near Palmer Lake. Tracks of a solitary predator. To the locals, footprints of fear, and the image of glistening green eyes piercing the dark nights looking for food. Maybe children. Yet this misunderstood canine often wanders close to people, not for fodder, but for companionship. On the flat, wind swept prairie, his woeful baying on a moonlit night is often mistaken as a cry of hunger. Mistaken because the Timber wolf, *Canis lupus*, is normally a pack animal—a creature who hunts, socializes, and mates forever. He howls on the prairie only because he's lonely.

Wolves have a pecking order, their hunting, eating, and social habits are organized. Their breeding is selected by strength, not weakness. There is a pack leader, the alpha dominant male, breeding males, and passive and active subservient males; there is an alpha dominant female, breeding females, a lead female for the hunt, and social females to care for the young. They have a rigid order, and to keep harmony in the pack, when a mate dies the survivor leaves or is forced from the pack and becomes a lone predator. It's nature's way of doing things.

Jackson Palmer and Johanna Drexler were lone wolves most of their young lives. Two humans culled from the pack of society by the unfair vicissitudes of life. They were foster children howling for attention, either on the athletic field or in the classroom. In a community as small as Palmer Lake, that same drive for success and acceptance brought them together in high school.

Jackson was the star athlete who captained every team and every student organization he joined. Being the leader kept him separated from the pack. It kept him aloof and alone. An alpha dominant male. Even after his parents were gone and he was taken in by the Chases he didn't feel part of the pack. He was the outsider, a loner. Then he met Johanna. A love grew inside him that replaced his step-family. She made him feel wanted. Loved. He felt he belonged to her—he knew from the moment that he met her this was going to be his lifemate—a bond that was forever. They would raise their own pack.

Johanna, however, had an unusual provenance. Years back, at a retreat on the far end of the lake during a church choir weekend, her mother, a fair-haired Swede, had an affair with a Jamaican gospel singer. She thought he looked like Harry Belafonte. They hit some high notes together and she got pregnant. Palmer Lake was a typical, small-minded, prejudiced midwestern town. Few women had abortions in those days, and none brought home from the hospital a child who was half black. The mother abandoned Johanna to the St. Mark's orphanage and left town with an aspiring actor.

The church home where Johanna grew up never housed more than ten children at a time. They were the castoffs of a mixed breed of humanity from the area. Children are truthful yet malevolent by nature. They create a pecking order where there is none, it's their way of culling the pack.

At the orphanage there wasn't a pure white face to be found and the unwanted mixlings waxed cruel. Being a loner, Johanna adopted the Virgin of Guadalupe as her matron of protection. But she didn't care what the kids said, she always told everyone: color is good. And her color was better than good, it was envied. Her unblemished skin was a light-tan-caramel, like a cube of Kraft candy.

In public high school, Johanna became the smartest in her class, she captained her lacrosse team, and was president of the student council. She became a cheerleader, where she couldn't take her eyes from Jackson in his athletic endeavors. When she was crowned homecoming queen, he couldn't take his eyes from her. She became an alpha dominant female.

The day of November 22, 1963, was etched indelibly in the minds of Jackson and Johanna, for that was the morning Jackson had taken all of his meager savings and bought an inexpensive diamond ring from Schwartz's jewelry store. During breakfast, in a booth at Burt's Drugstore, he had hidden it under Johanna's glass of orange juice. With it he put a poem he had written and a proposal:

Like two light starved saplings,
* whose branches touched,*
their trunks entwined in a gnarled grip,
* forever wrapped in harmony,*
their unity reached the sun in the sky.
* —I'll love you forever.*
Will you marry me?
Jackson.

Johanna thought this the most romantic poem in the world. Who were Keats, cummings, and Browning compared to the man who wanted to marry her? This was almost like what happened to people in the movies. She was just eighteen and Jackson was soon to be twenty, but their youth didn't matter, all that mattered was that she would love him like he loved her. With her eyes shining with tears of joy, she said, "Yes, I'll marry you. And I'll love you forever, too."

They had decided to form their own pack.

When Jackson became a teenager Ian Chase had taught him to fly in a small seaplane that he kept on the lake. Ian's theory was that his boys were safer up in the air than driving down on the ground.

Jackson took to flying like his father. He wanted to one day join the air force just like him. Jackson worked so hard at it that he got his pilot's license at the same time he got his driver's license. The plane was at his disposal on an honor system with the other Chase boys. It wasn't long before he was volunteering for search and rescue work for the fire department and for the state relief agencies.

For part of his engagement surprise Jackson decided to take Johanna on her first airplane ride.

They left Burt's and walked down to a pier on the lake. It was what the locals called a late Indian autumn day, cozy warm at about sixty degrees. Jackson helped Johanna across one of the large pontoons of Ian's seaplane. She was shaking with both excitement and fear. She had never been in an airplane.

Blue-grey plumes of smoke spat from the piston engines when Jackson started the plane. He taxied into takeoff position. As the props spewed jets of water behind them, she crossed herself and wished she had remembered her rosary. They rose into the clear sky. Jackson gave her a confident smile.

They circled the lake with the gulls. A quarter of a mile out the cockpit window a gaggle of Canada geese flew in a V formation heading south. Jackson nodded towards his favorite areas to fish, made up stories about the uninhabited islands below, showed her Quicksand swamp, although he didn't tell her about his mother's disappearance there, and pointed out the most private places to swim.

Johanna said, "I think I'm in heaven."

"I know it's the closest I'm ever going to get. It's so peaceful and quiet up here. No hassles. Maybe that's why I like flying so much."

"You're not very religious are you?"

"No, I guess not. I'm more spiritual."

"You know, I love you, but you're really a mystery to me."

"My mother wrote me that once. So I'll take it as a compliment."

"When we get married are you going to become a pilot and support us?"

"Yep. First I'd like to get married on your birthday. What do you think?"

"I love it."

"Then you can come up to State and join me on that scholarship they've offered you, and after graduation I'll join the air force and learn to fly jets."

"Can we have a baby right away?"

"I'd like to wait until I've got my jet rating and a job first, if that's okay with you. But I'd sure like to practice a lot."

Johanna laughed and squeezed his muscular forearm. "That's okay with me. But I want us to have a son just like you. I dream about that." She felt so proud of her man. As the plane banked she asked, "Hey, what's that big island over there?"

"That's my favorite place in the world to be alone. It's called

Pine Island. Would you like to land and take a quick dip?"

"Can we, really?"

"Yep. And I brought along a picnic basket so we can celebrate."

Jackson put the plane down and lightly skimmed the lake's mirrored surface as he landed. He taxied towards a giant weeping willow, its normal glistening green leaves had turned brown and its long branches touched the water. He threw out an anchor and moored the seaplane in the shallows. They giggled while they took off their shoes and socks, then waded to shore holding hands and carrying the wicker picnic basket. The water was cold and tan cattails jutted from the shore banks and their soft fuzz brushed against them. Jackson took her to the base of the weeping willow. He opened the lid of the basket and removed a red and white checkered tablecloth, which he spread under the shadowy branches of the tree. The gentle wind made a lulling tune as it whistled though the pine boughs behind them.

Jackson ran his hand through Johanna's curled hair. He brushed two long tendrils behind her ears. They lay down and embraced, half on the tablecloth and half in the dried leaves and cool moss under the tree, kissing long and deep.

"I'll love you forever," Johanna promised.

Forever. Jackson let the words seep into the solitude of his mind. He had wanted to hear this from a loved one all of his life. He gently rolled over on top of her. "Me, too." He became excited under his Levi's.

A meadowlark sang on a branch in the reddened sumac.

Johanna broke from under him and stood. "We'll save that for the honeymoon." She grinned and said, "Hey, I thought we were going swimming?"

"We are, but I always go naked out here by myself."

"Well, you're not by yourself anymore, so you're going to have to see what the future's going to be like."

Johanna was facing him, with a tender, inviting look, she slowly started undressing. She removed her blouse, all the while not taking her gaze from Jackson. When she undid and removed her bra, her breasts bounced lightly. Her nipples had dark brown aureoles the size of ginger snaps. She handed her bra down to Jackson. Then she unzipped the back of her skirt and let it drop to the tablecloth. She removed her white cotton panties. The black, powder puff of down that nature had placed between her legs curled above the moist, sweet-smelling area below.

"My God. It's no wonder I love you. You're beautiful."

Johanna darkened with pride.

Jackson couldn't take his eyes off her. He quickly stripped his shirt, jeans, and boxer underwear. His tan athletic body taut with excitement.

Johanna had never seen a man naked before, she thought him beautiful, too.

He grabbed her hand and they ran laughing into the lake. They got knee deep and made an abrupt stop. The water was freezing. They ran back to shore. Their splashing and laughing drove red-winged blackbirds scattering to the sky. Jackson embraced Johanna in another kiss.

It was on the flight home that the plane's radio informed them that President John F. Kennedy had been assassinated that afternoon. Like everyone else in America, they never forgot where they were on that day.

. . . .

11

ZÜRICH, SWITZERLAND

The head office of Credit Suisse sits near the banks of the Limmat River. A black Mercedes limousine waited in front of the financial institution for its passenger. The limo driver gazed across the street at Zürich's City Hall, the Rathaüs. Through the gray drizzle he could make out the towers of the Fraumünster cathedral looming above. The buildings dated back to Charlemagne. A person could learn history just sitting here. The driver yawned.

Arguably Switzerland's richest man, Hartmut Kell was only fifty-five. With his penetrating brown eyes and cherub face, he was considered handsome by most women. When he started balding, he had his hair cut almost as short as if he'd shaved his head. He wore a rain slicker and his hat was pulled down almost to his reddish-grey, bushy eyebrows. He left the bank, and like the cross-country skier he was, made hurried, choppy strides to the car. Once seated in the rear he gave the driver instructions through the open glass partition.

Hartmut had heard on television about the suicide and the up-coming suspension of Will Chase, a man he admired and had met through correspondence when Jutta was suspended. Will had writ-ten him several times inquiring about the facilities and physicians in Switzerland. He had offered to be a benefactor to the cryonics foundations of Europe. Hartmut had the last letter from Will in his jacket pocket, which spoke of Will's desire to be suspended if he were to die. Hartmut wanted to speak personally to the doctors at the IMB facility about Will's suspension in the States. The limo driver expertly wound through the narrow streets of the small city and arrived at the laboratory in thirty minutes.

A security guard opened the glass door of the lab and Hartmut walked briskly down a well-lit hall, then proceeded down the stairs to where the dewars were located.

Ralf Verson was surprised at Hartmut's unannounced visit. "Wel-come, Herr Kell. Please come in and have a seat."

Hartmut removed his raincoat and sat in a metal chair. He started to take out Will's letter from his inner-jacket pocket when he noticed laboratory workers on the far side of the room were removing the Plexiglas window of the damaged dewar his wife had originally been suspended in.

Verson saw the shocked look on Hartmut's face. "We had a small accident sometime back. The dewar Jutta was in cracked. We had to move her to the empty one."

Hartmut stood. "Please tell me nothing happened to Jutta," he said. "None of the liquid nitrogen escaped, did it?"

Verson was speechless. The lab's head physician, who had been standing in the hall, entered the room. In a firm voice he said, "Herr Kell, be assured, your wife is perfectly fine. No gas escaped and we moved her with no problem whatsoever."

.   .   .   .

12

VIETNAM
APRIL 3, 1968

The mountains where Navy flight commander Jackson Palmer's A-4 was shot down were at an elevation of over six thousand feet. The altitude made for cold nights on the floor of the jungle. In the darkness, monkeys screamed, hungry leopards growled, and other nocturnal creatures bellowed their nightly cries. Jackson covered himself with plant leaves and tried to rest. Bugs crawled over him and bit him wherever his skin was exposed. He couldn't sleep. He propped himself against a tree and ate a piece of beef jerky. The jungle sounds reminded him of the Tarzan movies he had seen as a kid. After an hour sitting and thinking of his upcoming rescue, he toppled over and slept.

As the sun rose a steamy mist formed among the towering trees, and the screeching from thousands of birds made it difficult for him to hear helicopters searching for him. He sat up; his body ached, and the vegetation he had covered himself with fell to the ground. He looked up and saw the bright white of his parachute dangling from the branches. At the same time, the glint of a knife blade flashed in his peripheral vision. Suddenly a knee went into his spine, and someone pulled him back by the hair while holding the knife to his throat. As a martial arts expert, Jackson automatically threw his left arm under the arm wielding knife. He pushed it away from his throat, then flipped backwards into the Viet Cong, and in the next motion stuck his .38 caliber into the straw hat of the intruder and shot him in the top of the head. The thick hat muffled the shot and the V.C. fell into his lap. Blood and brains dribbled down Jackson's flight suit.

For an instant, Jackson lost his breath. Other than hunting pheasants and ducks back home, he had never killed anything before. He vomited. Although it was war, and it was self-defense, it was still another human life he had just taken. He was overwhelmed with grief. But voices in the distance made him realize he had to get out of the area he had marked for his rescue.

Using the sun as a compass, Jackson started hiking higher into the mountains. He found sparkling, clear creeks for water and fruit growing wild most everywhere. He picked a papaya and ate the tasty orange pulp. By early afternoon he could hear the choppers looking for him, but he had no way to signal them without giving himself away. As the sun started setting, he wandered towards what he thought would be the Laos border.

During the days that followed Jackson went through his entire supply of ammunition. When he would run into someone who would either scream his whereabouts or try to capture him, he disposed of them. He wandered blindly through the dense forest. When not on an animal path, the terrain was close to impossible to traverse. After he threw his pistol away, he found thin vines hanging from canopied trees and pulled them down, using them as a garrote for anyone who got in his way. In the days to come, he garroted four men. Killing for survival became automatic. He had no regrets, he was just happy to be alive. He didn't know where he was going and soon felt like Sisyphus, pushing his tired body up one hill and falling down the next. During the day he captured sleeping fruit bats, which he skinned and ate raw. Protein rich insect larvae were abundant and he scooped fresh water from banana leaves to wash it down.

The mosquitos and the fungus of the jungle floor had soon infected him. He developed fever and diarrhea. His mind became a blur, he developed a rash beneath his beard, and his toes were swollen three times their original size. It was steaming hot and humid during the day and near-freezing cold at night. Jackson thought of suicide, but the memory of Johanna and home kept him going. He wandered the jungle for a month before he fell into a coma.

Thirty-three days after he had ejected from his doomed fighter, the NVA picked him up and took him to a POW camp outside of Son-la. Without knowing it, Jackson had stumbled within forty miles of freedom in Laos. The Viet Cong nursed him back to health just to torture him and to try and get information from him. Jackson wouldn't talk. They slopped him like an animal and put him in solitary confinement, making him sleep in his own defecation and urine. They took him outside only an hour a day but it was just to beat him for not talking. In his mind he made love to Johanna everyday. He wrote her love notes in the sand, letters that would never be delivered. He visualized having a son with her upon his release. He never doubted her love for him or he wouldn't have made it. The imprisonment and torture continued for three years. The image of Johanna was always with him.

On one of the most humid and oppressive days of his captivity, when Jackson was near the end of his tether in solitary confinement, the V. C. came in early one morning to take him to the outside containment area where the other prisoners were kept during the day. Jackson rubbed his eyes and squinted in the sun. There were twenty-one other POW and they were lined up against a bamboo wall. The V.C. marched Jackson next to them. They were to be executed. Five boyish looking guards armed with AK-47s were thirty feet away—waiting instructions from the officer in charge—a man not much older than his troops. The skinny prisoners looked ominously at one another, a few gave thumbs up signs, a few were crying. Jackson was only angry. As long as he was going to go, he thought he'd jump one of the little guards, grab his automatic rifle and start shooting them before they killed him. He had no opportunity, for the officer in charge shouted instructions to the guards, who took up their guns and aimed at the prisoners. Everyone but Jackson closed their eyes. As they did, a volley of shooting echoed and boomed from behind the bamboo wall. The ten guards were blown to bits by a barrage of gunfire. At the same time, twenty Green Beret troops, led by Commander Carl Chase, jumped the wall, firing at the stunned officer in command and his few men left standing. They were all killed. The thumping of the rotor blades of two Jolly Green Giants was heard in the background about the time the prisoners on the bamboo wall opened their eyes and realized what was going on. In unison they crawled and limped to the landing helicopters.

Jackson walked over to a sweating Carl Chase. "Jesus Christ, with all of the thousands of soldiers in this shit war, I never expected to see you here."

Carl barked orders into a walkie-talkie. He flipped it off. "When we heard in our outfit a fellow South Dakotan might be trapped up here, Joey Gabrelli and I volunteered for the mission."

"Thanks, Carl. I guess I owe you and Joey one."

Time and desperation had made Johanna become pious. Jackson had been gone for almost four years. After she was told he was missing in action, she had prayed to her matron saint for three years. She just knew the Virgin would look out for her missing husband.

Johanna never missed Mass. She lit votive candles each day for Jackson, and she walked the transept of St Mark's Cathedral so often and so late that Father Mc Queeny pleaded with her to go home at night. But it was lonely there. The memory of Jackson burned in her mind and her empty bed. She had never been so forsaken in her life, but she never gave up hope. Then two months *before* Jackson was rescued, Johanna was informed by the air force that Jackson was no longer missing in action, *he had been confirmed killed.*

Dead. Just like his father. Now she would have two medals hanging on photos over the fireplace. She was once again alone— no longer part of a pack. She was no longer loved and wanted. Each evening she would sit in a church pew and cry. Why? She had waited four years for her man. Why did this happen? Was life worth living? Nothing she thought of, or that anyone said, took away her pain.

Three weeks later Johanna went to Pietro's for dinner, where across the room she saw a young pilot in uniform who reminded her of Jackson. He was talking to his friends. The resemblance was more than remarkable. Did God bring him back? Were her prayers finally answered? The tilt of his hat, the stripes on his jacket, his rough, baritone voice, all the bravado of the uninitiated heading for war. She'd heard it all before. The only thing missing was a mole on his cheek.

The pilot noticed her stare and winked at her, she blushed and dropped her gaze. He brazenly came to her table, just as

Jackson might have done, and then ordered a pizza and beers. They talked small talk, he reached over and touched the top of her warm hand as she spoke. He listened to her sad story. He ordered more beer, many more beers and a bourbon shooter or two as the night wore on. Intoxicated by the alcohol and enjoying companionship, Johanna invited him home for the night. She was tired of being lonely.

Once at the apartment she took him to bed unashamedly. She hadn't been with a man in four years, and that man had been her first. But her husband was dead. There was no love making, no tenderness, just the grappling of the lonesome animal she was. She slept with the stranger, crying and pretending to herself that it was Jackson as she did so. She was the dominant, breeding female.

The pilot left in the morning, disappearing that very day into the sky to fight a war in Indochina thousands of miles away.

Johanna never saw him again. She believed she was once again a lone wolf on the prairie, not knowing there was now a new member of the pack growing inside of her.

·　·　·　·

13

JUNE 4th, 1987

Wayne Goey Loo, Huey Goey Loo's grandson, was eighty-seven years old. He told everyone it was easy to remember his age as he'd been born on January 1st in 1900 and he was always the same age as the present year. Then he'd give his little laugh, heh, heh, heh.

Wayne Goey Loo and his wife, who never learned English after coming over from China, had ten children, five boys and five girls, before she died in 1949 fighting a fire in the family restaurant. He now had fifteen grandchildren and three new great-grand children. He remembered each one of them by number, not by name. The years had now bent Wayne Goey Loo over like a question mark; a hand-rolled cigarette always dangled from the corner of his mouth as if he'd been born with it hanging there. He'd spent the entire twentieth century pinching pennies and running the family restaurant. All his long life he had walked everywhere so he could save the fifty cent bus fare, and every dollar he saved he sent to China to bring over more family.

One day after Jackson had come home from the war, he stopped and picked up Wayne Goey Loo as he was walking home carrying a shopping bag full of groceries.

Wayne Goey Loo sat silent for most of the trip to his restaurant. Just as he was departing from the car he said, "You have dark mole on cheek. I have dark mole on cheek. Long white hair growing from this mole, how come no hair in your mole? Mean bad luck."

Jackson never forgot the old man's opening question to him. He was always checking the mole to see if a hair would grow and he would only have good luck. When the old man told Jackson why he walked everywhere, Jackson and Johanna went to the Loo family and found out how many more Loos were left in China. They then sold some of their MICROMED stock and had all nine of them flown to Palmer Lake. When they arrived, Wayne Goey Loo didn't want to lose face to his family. He offered to pay Jackson back, but the only way he could repay him was to offer him all of the free Chinese food he could eat. Along with his friendship, Jackson always felt more than compensated.

Over the years, Wayne Goey Loo and Jackson had shared hundreds of meals and even more evenings of philosophical talks drinking hot tea or Tsing-Tao beer in green bottles. In time, Wayne Goey Loo became the father Jackson never had. They would smoke, talk, and play cribbage, checkers, or chess until the wee hours of the morning. Although Wayne Goey Loo had no formal education, and his pidgin-English was at times indecipherable, Jackson thought him the smartest man he'd ever known. He never could figure out a way to beat the old man at chess.

On Wayne Goey Loo's seventy-seventh birthday, Jackson purchased him a first floor, garden apartment in his building. Wayne

Goey Loo loved the small flower garden in back of the apartment, but he took out most of the flowers and grew vegetables there instead. Tomatoes, onions, snow peas, celery, garlic, peppers, and his famous miniature red potatoes.

Now Jackson gave his special rat-a-tat-tat buzz on the doorbell.

Wayne Goey Loo, was shaking a steaming wok of fried chicken necks, bamboo shoots and snow peas. "Come in, number six son."

"Morning, Papa Loo. Do you have any hot tea?"

Wayne Goey Loo poured a splash of peanut oil into the wok, stirred the mixture with a wooden fork until the flames singed the food, and then turned off the gas. "Papa Loo always have hot water on stove. Put new green tea in big cup for both."

Jackson sprinkled the tea in the bottom of a silver pot. "Have you heard the news about Will yet?"

"I hear news of Will. Much gossip in town. I know my son have problem." Papa Loo's cigarette glowed and smoke poured from his nostrils. He flicked the ash from the end of the cigarette into the empty bamboo shoot can with the long, brown-stained fingernail of his pinky finger.

Jackson let the tea steep.

Across the room he could see a desk piled high with restaurant receipts and an abacus with well-worn black beads sat on top of the stack. A yellow canary warbled from its hanging wooden cage. Porcelain figurines and intricately carved ivory *objets d'art* from the Tang Dynasty were scattered on table tops. Smoke from sandalwood incense rose from the belly of a tubby jade Buddha in the corner of the room. A tasseled scroll painting of the Great Wall hung in a long rectangle over a couch and family photos adorned teak end tables. The odor of good food and old smoke clung to the room. One could just as easily have been in an apartment in Beijing.

"How come your tea is always better than anyone else's?" Jackson tried to make small talk as he poured the hot brew into two cups.

"Distill water. Papa Loo only make with distill water. Never boil. Water just about boil, remove kettle from stove. Pour over tea in pot, let sit. You like? heh, heh, heh."

"Yes. I like."

"You not come see me to talk tea. My son, always many dead people in this small town. Why?"

"I don't know. But Will couldn't have killed himself."

"Agree. Not like him. So, what happen?"

"Again, I don't know. I haven't talked to anyone yet. Lenny just called me a while ago, so I thought I'd come and see you. You always seem to have the answers to everything."

"I old man. Only answer I have—respect family, eat chicken, fish, drink tea, beer, and smoke all time. No enemies. No one want to murder Papa Loo."

Jackson swirled the dregs of the tea leaves around the cup. Some stuck to the sides, most went to the bottom. He read them as Papa Loo had taught him. There was no answer to the riddle of Will's demise in the leaves. "So you think Will was murdered?"

"Must be. Not like man with family kill himself."

"I'll keep that in mind."

"You stay for lunch?" Papa Loo tucked a thin rice paper napkin under his chin.

"No, thanks. I'm going to run upstairs and call Nina and then go down to the police station."

.　.　.　.

14

DOWNTOWN PALMER LAKE

Still hot under the collar, George Winter trotted briskly down Walleye Lane. The tall American elms, which each year miraculously escaped the bark beetle and Dutch elm disease, had sprouted new leaves. On the porch of a Victorian house surrounded by a white picket fence, a baby cried in its crib. For once, George was going to prove Leonard Bookner wrong. He almost bumped into the spinning red and white barber pole at Bollie's. He smirked impishly when Bollie, scissors and comb in hand, waved at him. George had had his hair cut by Bollie from the time he was four. Bollie even nipped his bad ear once or twice over the years.

"Hey, George. Watch where you're going. Too bad about Chase, eh?"

"Yup, sure is, Bollie."

George kept walking towards the police station.

Most of the office buildings in Palmer Lake were two or

three stories and made from red granite brought in from the local quarries. There was only one building five stories high, with lots of glass, and that was the new Radisson Hotel on Beach Street. George passed the 5 & 10 Kresge's store, which smelled of fresh popcorn and chocolate. He peeked at his reflection in the window of Hank Stampf's chiropractic office. The multi-talented doctor was practicing a jazz number on his trombone in the back room. George turned and headed over to Gordy's Sporting Goods with all its hunting and fishing gear displayed in the window.

Gordy, clad in a checkered shirt, hollered out the front door. "Morning, Chief. Unbelievable about Will, eh?"

"Yup, sure is, Gordy."

George walked faster. He passed the smell of oven baked bread at Olsen's Bakery. They made the best pumpernickel bread this side of Oslo.

Rotund Lute Olsen waved and remarked in his Scandinavian accent. "Morgan, Yorge. Awful 'bout Will, eh?"

"Yup, sure is, Lute."

George rounded the corner on Elk Street and walked past the American Legion Hall, where Bruno Tomacelli was unfurling the flags to display for the day.

Bruno's large head appeared lopsided and he normally had a toothpick behind his ear. When he saw George, he flashed his wide grin but didn't say anything, which was unusual for he always seemed to be talking to someone. His limited vocabulary consisted of calling himself "Rumpleforeskin," and shouting, "WOW, YOU'RE A BEAUT."

Bruno had been in the same high school class as Will, Jackson, and Leonard, but he followed Joey Gabrelli and Carl Chase around like an obedient dog. Bruno loved games and he had wanted to win a state wrestling championship like Joey and Carl had. Bruno had tried out for George's high school team, and everyone felt he would have won the championship as a heavyweight, except his I.Q. was lower than seventy and he couldn't stay academically eligible.

Bruno had spent the bulk of his adult life doing manual labor around town. The rumor was that his family, the Tomacellis, headed the state Mafia. It was also rumored they controlled the Indians who owned the gambling rights at the reservation, and the local laundries and linen services.

George waved back and thought Bruno certainly had at least a size fifteen shoe. Maybe bigger. Hell, the guy was at least six-feet-eight inches tall and weighed in the neighborhood of three-hundred and twenty pounds. George wondered if Bruno could be a suspect. But that was absurd; the poor, big lug was harmless. But then, it was perhaps no more absurd than maybe believing Nina did it.

George headed towards Shorty's A & W Drive-in in the distance. Maybe he could dash over and have a quick root beer float. Nah. He sprinted the last fifty yards to his office.

The Palmer Lake police department consisted of six officers and a secretary. Two men worked three eight-hour shifts. There was not a great deal of crime in the village, nor in the county for that matter. Most of the personnel's time was spent solving the usual traffic matters, small altercations, and alcohol problems, especially at the Legion Hall on the weekends when the Indians and the locals got drunk together. But George had kept meticulous files over the years on all crimes and infractions, no matter how minor. On this sunny day in June he headed for his desk and those files and photographs.

Polly Byrd, her blonde hair piled high on her head, looked up when George entered. "Morning, Chief. Is it true about Will Chase?"

"It sure is."

He gave his secretary a cursory inspection.

Polly had on a black silk blouse, a scarlet taffeta skirt, matching lipstick and nails, and black high heels. "Why'd he kill himself?" she said. "I mean, he had zillions. Was it drugs?" Only her spearmint gum slowed her down. "I heard from Bobby Joe Baker this morning that Red Cloud might have killed him, what do you think?"

George took off his jacket, removed his 9mm PPK Walther and holster from around his shoulder, and threw them over a high-backed wooden rocking chair. He went to his huge file cabinet and started pulling out papers and pictures. He knew he shouldn't be telling Polly any of this, but he couldn't help himself. "Bobby Joe's nothin' but a blabbin' used car salesman. Plus, he may be a suspect in murder. The guy's got at least a size thirteen shoe an' he was always flirtin' with Nina. But keep that info under your blonde wig, will ya?"

"You know this isn't a wig. I just use a little coloring, that's all. And you of all people know I can keep a secret." Polly pushed some loose ends of hair into her billowing hairdo.

"Red Cloud didn't have a thing to do with it. His feet're too small an' he was never in the military. There's somethin' here that ain't kosher. I'm telling you that in private. Police business, o.k.?"

Polly snapped her gum. "Got it, but what's his feet and the army got to do with it? He's just a crazy old Indian."

George took the piece of army fatigue fabric from his pocket and sealed it in an envelope. He locked it in a drawer. Then started spreading the photos and files across his desk. "First of all, Red Cloud is no crazier than me. He just thinks like an Indian, that's all. An' don't you ever forget, he's a damn good friend of mine."

"Sorry. But what's his little feet and never being in the Army got to do with Mr. Chase killing himself?"

George looked up. He held photos of four ominous looking men.

"Could you quit chewin' that gum at the office? It drives me nuts."

Polly uncrossed her legs and smiled coyly.

George caught a glimpse of her new sheer panties and broke into a wide grin. You could have put a banana in his face sideways. But right now he had other things on his mind. "Let's stick to business. I'm tryin' to find every size thirteen to fifteen shoe in the county who might've had a reason to kill Will." George couldn't help but look above the top of Polly's stockings. He grinned again. "Trace down the whereabouts of these four thugs, would you? But be careful. Each one of em's got a rap sheet longer than a roll of toilet paper. Also, see if any of 'em served in the military."

Polly took the gum out and stuck it under her chair. "You mean you think someone murdered Mr. Chase and he didn't really kill himself?"

Before he could answer, her telephone rang. "It's Nina Chase."

George pointed at the door with his finger. "Polly, please give me some privacy."

She sashayed out of the room.

George put his feet up on the desk and the phone between his shoulder and ear. "Nina, I'm sure sorry about everythin'. What can I do to help you?"

"I've spent the past hour in the morgue with William and the spirit Wovoka. We did the Ghost Dance. Wovoka says William will live again. But I called to tell you, we don't think he committed suicide."

George was relieved Nina might not be a suspect after all. "Well, what does your Indian shaman think happened?"

"The Messiah thinks William was murdered by someone he knew. And Wovoka and I aren't going to rest until we find out who killed him."

George put his feet back on the floor. "You know, you may be on to somethin'. But let's talk in private at another time. Okay?" He rubbed his eyes. *Holy shit, just what I need, an Indian witch doctor.*

No sooner had he hung up the telephone than it started ringing again. It was going to be a long day. This was probably the first of many reporters calling. Polly had disappeared and the telephone kept ringing. George finally picked it up.

"Chief, it's Leonard. I called to tell you how much I appreciate your efforts this morning regarding Will. The blood analysis just came back from the lab and the only thing we found was an overabundance of peyote."

"Enough to kill him?"

"No, but certainly enough to make him pass out before the carbon monoxide killed him. Come on, you know as well as we do that Will and Nina were always using illegal substances."

"True," George said.

"So I'm officially informing you that I just signed the death certificate, and Doc Tragus witnessed. We both agree Will's death was caused by suicide. *Nil desperandum.*"

"Jus' go screw yerself, you wordy shit."

But Leonard had already hung up.

George continued talking into the receiver. "Aw, hell, you're nothing but a scrawny little faggot."

. . . .

15

ᴗ.ᴗ.ᴗ.

The fences surrounding Ridgely Heights were draped with blooming yellow honeysuckle and Stirling's and Sophie's Shetland ponies tugged at the growth.

Nina's phone had been busy for over two hours. Jackson had tried reaching her all morning. When he finally got through, War Bird answered.

"Red Cloud's daughter not here. She at morgue. Husband dead. I tell her last month about bad omen—owl in moon."

Eggs Benedict was cackling in the background. "BIG BERTHA DID IT. BIG BERTHA DID IT!"

Jackson hung up wondering two things. One, who had been teasing the bird? The other was, how the hell had Nina Rose Sarkisian ever fallen in love with Will as a teenager? She was so beautiful, sensual, and charming. While Will was such a geek in high school. Everyone but Nina thought that. He seemed interested only in basketball, studying medicine, and inventing things. She seemed interested only in him, when she could have had any man of her choice. And, she certainly couldn't have guessed he'd become America's richest man one day. The romance and marriage always baffled Jackson. As much as he loved Johanna, he couldn't swear he wasn't a little jealous of Will at the time. He dressed, walked out to the terrace, and left Balthasar a meal of four large cans of Alpo.

The elevator slid smoothly to the basement garage. Dew drops streaked down the glass windows, making it difficult for Jackson to see the panoramic countryside view. When the elevator came to a stop, musical chimes tinkled, and the silver metal door opened silently. Jackson walked through the near-empty underground parking area. He passed by the Bronco, and, instead, got into his red Ferarri Daytona.

Clusters of people gathered on every corner Jackson passed. He could see their mouths moving, they were all gossiping about Will's death. A queue of reporters and curiosity seekers was blocking the entrance to the police department. Jackson decided to postpone his visit to George until later and go get a massage. He shifted gears and accelerated, heading for the country club.

When he drove up to the entrance, the teenage attendant said, "Good morning, Mr. Palmer. I'm sure sorry about Mr. Chase."

Jackson didn't reply as he climbed out of the car, the engine still running. He might start crying. Once the boy rounded the corner of the building, Jackson heard the motor being gunned, followed by a noisy screech of tires. He managed a small grin. Hell, he had done the same thing at seventeen. Jackson wanted to avoid other club members, so he walked around to the side entrance.

Walter Belsky, the burly Romanian masseur, outfitted in his

starched white uniform and dark blue New York Yankees base-ball cap, greeted him. "I know exactly what you need. A good hot steam and one of my massages."

Walter wore his cap indoors and outdoors, not to play base-ball, but to cover his balding head. An old tape recorder played a Bach organ fugue. Jackson and Walter shared a love of classi-cal music and like most relationships between masseurs, bar-tenders, barbers, and their clients, also shared many of each other's deepest secrets.

"You got it," Jackson said. "But first I want to use the gym. Is anyone in there?"

"Naw, it's too early. I'll be in my office later."

Jackson went to his locker and changed into gray cotton sweats. He put on a pair of thin leather sparring gloves to work on the heavy bag and the speed bag, smacked his fists together in anticipation, then ran into the gym. Hanging from the walls and staring at him were lifesize pen and ink drawings of Rocky Marciano, Jake LaMotto, Joe Louis, and Muhammad Ali.

Jackson poured all the anger, sorrow, and hurt he felt into the heavy bag. He soon was drenched in perspiration. He took a drink of water and then skipped rope. He skipped as only boxers can do with quick movements of the feet, forward and down, feet appearing to never leave the ground and yet with the rope somehow gliding through time and again. He whipped the rope so rapidly that a callus on his left hand bled and dripped down the wooden handle.

After ten minutes, Jackson threw the rope to one side and attacked the speed bag. He hit it so fast and hard he thought it would tear from its mounting and splatter against the padded wall. Mucous ran from his nose and he wiped it on his long sleeve. He was panting. As a kid Jackson had done these drills hours on end, hoping to become the state Golden Glove champion. But he could never beat Indian Danny Whistle. He lost to him in the finals of the regional every year. Jackson was a good amateur boxer as a kid, but nature had never bestowed upon him the skills to be a top pro.

Jackson looked at himself in a ceiling to floor wall mirror. He wasn't in the shape he used to be. He patted his gut and found a hardness few men in their forties could claim. His underwear size had only gone to a thirty-four from the thirty-two of university days. Women still found him attractive, and there had been a few after he lost Johanna, but they were just a diversion. He had known the ultimate in love and to attempt to pursue it further was an exercise in futility. Exhausted, he walked slowly down the hall to the steam room.

The Finnish bath opened Jackson's sinuses and flushed the toxins from every pore in his body. He wrapped a white towel around his waist, put on a pair of rubber thongs, and shuffled over to the massage room. Chopin's Nocturnes now played in the background. The small cubicle smelled of talc and liniment. Jackson lay down on the padded table.

Walter slowly rubbed warm coconut oil on Jackson's back and dug his fingers deep into the trapezius muscles. He worked his way down the spine and into the legs. For years, Walter had given Jackson therapy on his shredded thigh and he knew exactly the right pressure to exert.

"I don't mean to be rude, but there's an ugly rumor going around that Mr. Chase was murdered. Any truth to that?"

Jackson's body stiffened with tension. "You know, there's no poison more toxic than malicious gossip. I wouldn't pay any attention to it."

"I'll try, but it's awfully hard to ignore. Are you sure there isn't something you want to tell me?"

"Zip it, will you Walter?"

.   .   .

For some reason Woody Chase wasn't surprised to hear the words Dixie had just uttered.

"I'm sorry to be the one to inform you, Woody, but Will committed suicide last night."

Woody wondered why Carl hadn't called instead of Dixie. What was that mean bastard up to anyway? Woody ran his hand through his blond crewcut. "How'd he do it?"

"Carbon monoxide poisoning from Ian's old car."

"You mean the Crown Victoria Ford in Ingrid's garage?

"Yes, she found him there early this morning."

"Thanks for calling, Dixie, but I'm sure you know everything Will did was beyond me. I never really liked my brother, you know. I bet there'll probably be rumors going around that I had him killed."

"What?"

"And I'm not going to tell you whether I did or not."

"Don't joke about such things, Woody. What are you going to do?"

"I wasn't joking and I don't know what I'm going to do. Maybe go see Mom, or call Lenny."

"You can't see Ingrid, she's sedated at her house, and Lenny's looking after Will over at the morgue. I'm sure you know Will wanted to be frozen so Nina's making certain they do it."

Woody cradled the telephone next to his shoulder. He picked up the television remote control and fiddled with the buttons until a blaring John Wayne western came on. Stagecoach. He turned the volume down. "Will always told me he wanted to try cryonics if he died. So I guess there's not much I can do. And I suppose you know that goddamn Jackson is probably going to get everything."

Dixie gasped. "What! Not Carl?"

"Not Carl or his other brothers," Woody said.

There was a long silence. Dixie had probably thought she was now rich and wouldn't have to wait for one of Carl's gambling dreams to come true.

"You might as well sit tight until you hear from someone," She said at last. "Woody, I want you to know I feel horrible about this. If there's anything I can do, call me."

Woody hung up without a goodbye. He liked Dixie. She was always kind to him, which not many people were, but she was a snoop. He got up from his chair, turned up the volume on the western, then put a bag of popcorn in the microwave.

Freddie Chase hung up the telephone and cocked his head. He looked at Big Bertha with his protruding good eye. Hawkeye, as she had called him ever since she had accidentally poked it out during a family feud. "Will's dead," said Freddie.

"You're kidding me?" Big Bertha was wolfing down a huge bowl of Wheaties with a tablespoon—all six-feet-six inches of her—milk and cereal streamed from her open mouth.

"No, I'm not kidding. Dixie just told me he committed suicide."

Freddie was pale and fleshy. His baby-blue flannel pajamas hung on him like a clown's suit. "I loved him you know, even if I couldn't understand what made him tick. He was always so good to me."

Big Bertha had left the Sisseton Indian reservation as a teenager to join the Barnum and Bailey circus as the Giant Lady. She was so strong that when business was slow, she took on all challengers in a ring, boxing or wrestling. She never lost. She became known as The Commander. This was the off-season for the circus and she was home with Freddie and her family on the reservation. Like a sitting camel trying to stand, she rose in herky-jerky movements. She had on an iridescent pink track suit and fuzzy bunny slippers. As she walked over to Freddie, she ripped off the thin latex gloves she was wearing. Her hands were red and raw. She picked him up.

"Look, Hawkeye, I'm not sorry your brother's dead. I guess you know that. The son of a bitch thought I was a freak."

"Yes, my dearest, I know that. But he didn't mean it." Her mustache tickled his skin. He liked that.

"The hell he didn't." Big Bertha banged her fist on the table. "I suppose you'll be going over to St. Mark's now to pray to those goddamn statues."

"Don't be so sacrilegious, sweetheart, and be careful of your hands. You know the doctor told you to wear those gloves all the time."

Big Bertha squeezed him hard. Her grip was like a python's. "Hawkeye, your brother hated me."

Freddie loved it when she squeezed him. "Will didn't hate you. He apologized for telling me I shouldn't marry a freak."

"Bullshit," Big Bertha said. "He hated me and I hated him. Hell, I mighta killed him myself, ya know. And don't be calling your mother and whining to her about that either."

"Is that where you went last night?"

"It's none of your damn business where I went last night. It's a surprise." Big Bertha released Freddie and he dropped on his feet with a thud.

"But I'll never tell." He rubbed his bad eye.

God, she made him horny.

.　　.　　.　　.

16

~:~:~:

MANKATO, MINNESOTA
JUNE 4, 1987

The air control tower at Mankato's Municipal Airport vali-
dated the pilot's flight plan and gave the converted DC-3 an
okay for take-off. It was a warm morning with only a few pil-
lowy cumulus clouds in the sky. Pink and white clouds that
kids think are made of cotton candy. Two four-prop Pratt and
Whitney engines whined as the plane gained altitude. Once at
cruising speed, the old aircraft was slow but stable and smooth
riding.

Palmer Lake, South Dakota, was approximately two hundred and twenty miles from Mankato. With visual flight rules,
all the pilot had to do was fly northwest for an hour and a half
following the Minnesota River. Talk about easy. The pilot had
only to pass over the farming communities of New Ulm, Granite Falls, Montevideo, Appleton, and Ortonville, then descend
over Big Stone Lake—the source of the Minnesota River—and

across the South Dakota border down to Palmer Lake.

The plane held a crew of two and eight passengers. The cargo bay had been set up as a hospital operating room. On board were Dr. Peter Sayers, in charge of Will's suspension procedure; perfusionist Dr. Jan Elton; a team of four skilled emergency response technicians; nervous NBC reporter, Bernard Grable; and one of his camera men, Rudy Barrnet.

Bernard had changed into his favorite tan Brioni suit with matching vest, set off with a dark brown tie, a light blue shirt and tasseled loafers. His mother once told him that by an accident of being born the wrong color in a bigoted society he already had a strike against him, so he should always look more than the part. He did.

Bernard turned to Sayers. "I've never been to a morgue before, much less seen an autopsy. Maybe you can give me an idea where I should start my narrative and filming."

Sayers, clad in green surgical scrubs, stopped dictating medical notes into a hand-held tape recorder. "We don't do an autopsy," he said. "Jan and I prepare the body for storage, which can take us up to four hours. It involves some surgery, which I'll explain as the procedure progresses. So you and Rudy can follow us around with your video."

"Have you got that, Rudy?" Bernard asked.

"Got it," answered a sleepy voice.

"Oh, and one more thing," Sayers said. "I like you, Bernie——we've spent a lot of time together these past few days—and I'm thrilled to have you filming. I think the exposure will do marvelous things for the public's understanding and support of cryogenics. But if you and Rudy get in my way with that big camera, I'm going to suspend you by your tasseled loafers."

"Fair enough," said Bernard. "By the way, no offense to Jan, but I still haven't figured out exactly what a perfusionist does."

Jan was sitting directly across the aisle applying a coat of lipstick that matched the color of her hair and freckles. She had recently turned thirty-four and was starting to worry about why she was still single. She worked all the time, that was why. It didn't hurt to try looking good. She retracted the gold tube. "No offense taken, really. A perfusionist is one of those newly formed specialties. Perfusion is simply the passage of fluid through a tissue. Our job is to deliberately introduce fluid into a tissue. We usually do that by injection into the blood vessels supplying the tissue. Then—"

"Let's not get carried away with being too technical," Sayers said. "Bernie, just remember, I can't do this procedure without her. But let me assure you, this operation will be successful. Will Chase is a young man and he'll return one day in the same physical condition we find him."

"Don't you mean Will *was* a young man? Not *is* a young man?"

It was warm in the cabin and perspiration had formed on Sayers brow. He took a Kleenex from his gown pocket and wiped his forehead and his double chin. "Sorry, it's easy to get confused. Let me give you a quick explanation of the issues of resuscitation and death in medicine today," he said. "As you know, the word death is usually taken to mean irreversible loss of life. But medicine has advanced in its ability to reverse formerly fatal conditions, and now the exact conditions determining irreversible loss of life have changed."

"You mean like what you said earlier about reviving heart attack victims?"

"Exactly. Remember, it wasn't that long ago you'd have been pronounced dead after cardiac arrest with no thought of resuscitation. Now it's standard medical procedure. We're trying to convince medical people that when a person is pronounced clinically dead today, their cells and tissue are still alive and can possibly be restored if they're frozen quickly enough."

"So is that why hair and nails keep growing after a person dies?" asked Bernard.

"Right. Ideally, we'd like to start suspension of a patient within minutes of being pronounced clinically dead so we might prevent any ischemic injury."

"What's that?"

"Ischemia occurs during clinical death. It's nothing more than impaired blood circulation. Same as if your arm goes to sleep because you slept on it wrong all night," said Sayers. "Ischemic injury is what we're concerned about, and that's because injurious changes occur in cells and tissue when blood circulation stops due to oxygen loss. Obviously that's the reason for our hasty departure to get Will this morning." Sayers picked up his tape recorder again. "Look, why don't you sit back and relax the rest of the flight and I'll be sure to go through the whole procedure slowly."

The plane's engines buzzed like hornets.

Jan, also in green surgical scrubs, settled back and rocked her head from side to side, getting out the cricks.

The techs were engrossed in getting all of the medical equipment ready for the procedure. Their movements were as precise as a military operation.

Rudy, red bandanna around his pony-tailed hair, faded blue denim shirt open at the collar, was sound asleep with his L.L. Bean boots propped up on his camera equipment.

Bernard couldn't relax and he wandered up to the cockpit. He peeked out the rectangular window over the shoulder of the navigator. "Is that where the Minnesota and Red Rivers meet?"

The navigator had one ear of his headset over the side of his temple, the other over his left ear. He looked up from his sectional map and pointed out the window with a pencil. "Sure is. And that's the end of Big Stone Lake. We'll circle north over that little city of Browns Valley, then fly over the south end of Lake Traverse and cross over the Sisseton Indian Reservation before landing."

Bernard peeked out the window and then looked at the map.

"You can see that between Big Stone Lake and Lake Traverse, the source of the Red River—one of the few rivers in North America to flow north," the navigator went on, "there's a land bridge about twenty-five miles long that separates those two bodies of water. It's about fifteen feet higher than the two lakes, a natural dam of glacial debris. It formed a continental divide after the Wisconsin glaciation period."

As far as Bernard's eye could see, desolate marshes and flatland extended west through South Dakota. The terrain was filled with maple basswood, wild ginger, jack-in-the-pulpit, and Dakota skipper butterfly. The original settlers had called it Coteau des Prairies.

The DC-3 slowly started dropping towards the ground. Palmer Lake came into view. The navigator said, "We'll be landing soon, you'd better have a seat."

The medical team was dozing as Bernard returned to his seat. He looked out the window. He could see the east end of the lake. Palmer Lake was shaped like a huge lady bug. Seven large creeks and Palmer River flowed into both sides of the lake, making it look as if it had legs attached to it. The head was the lagoon and the body was the circular lake, deep and black and about fifteen miles wide. Several small islands dotted the center of the lake, giving an image of spots on a lady bug's back.

The plane lazily descended towards the prairie, making a looping circle over the area, heading for its base leg. They were going to pick up Will Chase, a medically dead man, and try to return him to life one day.

The thought of this made Bernard realize that it was just the past Sunday that he and Sayers had attended Mass at St. Peter

& Paul's together in Mankato. They had stood in the narthex and discussed their religious differences regarding cryonics; they didn't have many, but Bernard had some morality issues he hadn't figured out. He asked, "Where do you think the soul goes if you suspend someone?"

"I've asked myself the same question. I've got to have the same faith in medicine that I have in the church. I assume the soul stays with an individual's memory, because medically if they're suspended, I don't find them dead."

"Then how does your religious belief influence your medical views of freezing somebody?"

"Bernie, I don't have any religious objections to resuscitating someone who's died from a heart attack, nor did I have any objections to the doctors who anesthetized and suspended the Pope for twelve hours during surgery after he was shot by that Turk. Remember, medically he was dead. But suspending him with that anesthesia kept the Pontiff alive. So I don't have an objection to the resuscitation of suspended cryonics patients."

"Yeah, but the Pope's suspension was only for a short amount of time, where a cryonics patient could be hundreds of years." "Everyone tries to make that argument. But it's a matter of putting time in perspective. What's the real difference between a few minutes and a long period of time during an operation—or years?"

Bernard nodded in agreement.

"My point to you, is that life has a purpose here and now, and there's nothing wrong with acting to extend and enhance that life. After all, that's why I became a doctor."

Leonard Bookner had two ambulances and a four-ton Hertz rental truck waiting on the tarmac. Peter, Jan, Bernard, and Rudy got in the ambulances, and the techs loaded their equipment into the truck.

Izor's transport system contained a modified hospital gurney upon which was mounted a heart-lung resuscitator capable of providing mechanical cardio-pulmonary support during initial restoration of circulation and oxygenation; a complete heart-lung machine made up of a blood pump, membrane oxygenator, blood gas/pH monitoring equipment, and heat exchanger; and an independent power and oxygen supply.

.   .   .   .

17

~:~:~:

11:30 A.M.

All the lights on George Winter's switchboard were lit up. He ignored them. His coffee mug sat empty. He jotted down a note to have Danny go over Ingrid's garage thoroughly. He needed to see exactly how high up the nail stud was that had snagged the army fatigue fabric. To the best of his recollection it must have been a very tall person who hooked a jacket on that nail. The morning had been so busy George hadn't had time for a break.

Jackson pushed open George's office door a crack and handed in a cold six pack of Cokes. "Hi, Chief. Anything I can do to help?"

"Mornin'. No, I think Lenny an' Doc got most everythin' under control. I'm sure sorry, Jackson. I know Will was your best friend."

"Thanks, George."

"It's the strangest damn thing, eh?"

"That's for sure. It's hard for me to believe Will could leave Ingrid and Nina and the kids behind, it just isn't like him."

"How 'bout leavin' you behind? It sure wasn't the Will Chase I knew," George said. "He always seemed to have everythin' to live for."

"I'll be damned if I know what to think. I only know suicide just doesn't make any sense."

"It sure don't."

"I can see you're busy. I'll come back later, if that's okay."

"Sure. But where you goin' now?"

"I thought I'd try and find Nina, she seems to have just disappeared. Then I'll go see Ingrid."

"Tell them I'm sorry." George looked at the floor, then peeked up. "Say, by any chance are you missin' any of your old military fatigues?"

Jackson tilted his head to the side. After a moment of silence, he said, "Not that I know of. But I'll look for you. What's so important about my fatigues?"

"I found a piece of fabric in Ingrid's garage that shouldn't have been there." George didn't know why he slipped and said that. He was exhausted, that's why. "Keep that on the Q.T., will you? Police business, if ya know what I mean."

"Don't worry, it's between us. But are you saying there might be some foul play involved with Will's death?"

"No, not yet anyway. I'm just tryin' to do my job."

Jackson walked towards the front door.

George called after him, "By the way, if you're goin' out to Ingrid's, would you mind deliverin' these things to her? Will left 'em in the back seat of Ian's car. Kind of weird, but I know she'd like 'em." He pointed at the presents and the flowers.

"No problem." Jackson picked them up, then put a hand on

George's shoulder. "Be sure to let me know if I can be of any help."

Before Jackson could get out the door, George called out, "Thanks for the Cokes."

George pulled on his cartilaged, cauliflowered ear and then inserted his finger into it. He moved the finger from side to side. Although the ear was numb, it itched. That was always a sign of good luck.

Polly Byrd came barging through George's private office door. "I've got unbelievable news for you on those four guys you asked me to trace down. I've been on this for three straight hours. It looks like we hit the jackpot." Her hands were on her hips and she was smiling. "And to think I might be on to solving a murder."

George rolled a piece of ear wax into a ball, looked at it, then flicked it into a wastebasket. Sometimes he wished Polly would just say what she meant. "Let's have it, Babe."

Her blonde hair was hanging in her face. She tried to blow it up with a puff of air. It fell back down, and she pushed it behind her ears. She was blushing. "I thought we weren't going to call each other affectionate names in the office."

Out of patience, George raised his voice. "Sorry. But dammit, get to the point."

"Okay, okay. First of all, they were all in the military. And suspect number one, Terry Potter, has a size thirteen and a half shoe, hated Mr. Chase 'cause he was rich, and he has no alibi for his whereabouts last night. Likely story!"

George's eyes were on the photos lying on his desk and he was pointing at each man. "Okay, no need to play detective. Keep goin'."

Polly had a mouthful of fresh spearmint gum. She cracked it. George cringed.

"Well, suspect number two, Kris Catlin, has a size thirteen shoe. Mr. Chase fired him from his company for drinking on the job. When we had him here in the drunk tank, he threatened to wipe out the whole lot of Chases one day. He's not home so I don't know if he's got an alibi."

George nodded.

"Suspect number three, Joey Gabrelli, has huge feet. Size fifteen."

"I know all about Joey. He wrestled for me you know. He won state. A tough hombre, but always gettin' into trouble."

"Did you know the two-bit thug really hauls garbage for a living?"

"Yeah, he works for the Tomacellis and flies their little plane around on 'company' business. He's really nothing but a mob front."

"Well, your rastler beat up Will at the senior prom and there'd always bad blood between them after Ian Chase went out and knocked the snot out of the kid." Polly was chewing her gum furiously. "And Joey doesn't have an alibi either. Says he was sound asleep all night. No phone calls. No visitors. Another likely story!"

George raised his head from the desk. "Joey could have thirty Mafioso testify for him in a second. But what about the Indian, Risin' Coyote? He wasn't very thrilled his girlfriend married Will."

"I tried calling his family over at the reservation, but they said he didn't come home last night. They don't know where he is, but his mom said he wears size thirteen and a half shoes. Plus, he's a friend of Red Cloud's. Might be the jackpot, eh?"

George stood and unhooked his holster and gun from the back of his chair. He fastened them snugly around his shoulder, then put his jacket on. He smiled at Polly. "You're not just beautiful, but you got brains too. As the frog policeman said in that Casablanca movie, let's round up the usual suspects!" George pulled his tie up to his throat and cinched it. "Have Danny pick 'em up for questionin'. An' Polly, hav'em see if any of 'em are wearing those new fangled Nukie tennis shoes. I think they're made in Germany."

Polly turned red. "Thanks for the compliment. No offense, but I think it's pronounced Nike and they're made in America." Then she dialed Danny's extension.

Doc Tragus watched the four technicians haul the portable cryonics equipment down the stairs of the city morgue. Sad as he was over the demise of Will Chase, and knowing he had to talk to Dr. Peter Sayers regarding what he had done to prepare the body, he was still longing to get out on the golf course before the day was over. After all, death was part of his daily life. He was used to it.

The crowd outside the city courthouse had grown to around fifty people. They had heard the rumor that Will was going to be frozen and not buried in the United Methodist cemetery. The local news and CNN already had reporters and camera crews waiting. The townsfolk watched the entourage from the Izor Life Extension Foundation arrive, curious about the medical procedure that would take place.

The murmurs, whispers, and pointing fingers of the crowd made Bernard almost forget his apprehension. He nodded and smiled at them. Two blonde Scandinavian girls smiled back and waved. He asked Jan, "Do we follow you or wait here?"

"I'll be downstairs in the morgue. We have to start the procedure immediately. Have Rudy bring his equipment right away and I'll show you where to start."

Bernard's stomach was queasy about watching the upcoming operation. He went back to the ambulance and found Rudy, camera in hand. They quickly headed downstairs.

Peter Sayers, Leonard Bookner, and Doc Tragus had all introduced themselves. They were standing next to the vat containing Will.

Doc Tragus simply wanted to get out of the building. "I followed your instructions as best I could," he said.

"Were you able to do a total body washout?" asked Sayers.

"Yes I was. And during the TBW, I administered DMSO, sodium bicarbonate, Maalox and a solution I use for hypothermic flushing."

Surprised, Sayers raised his left eyebrow like a croissant. "You mean the commercial stuff for storage of transplant organs?"

"Yes, I use it to convey organs from a donor to a distant recipient."

"How'd you circulate the drugs?"

"I performed closed-chest compressions for about twenty minutes. And, as you can see, I packed the patient in ice."

Sayers wiped his glasses on his green surgical smock. Normally, in a cryoperfusion procedure there was some kind of delay at the morticians, either in the pronunciation of the patient being clinically dead or some other legal matter. Fortunately this was not the case here. "I can't thank you enough," he said. "People never realize how important it is to get the body properly prepared. Looks as if you did a splendid job. I'll have my staff ready to take over from here. Thanks again."

Doc Tragus glanced over at Leonard before he left. He waved a sympathetic goodbye. He knew the county coroner had to view the entire procedure and sign the necessary legal papers before the foundation could take Will's body back to Mankato.

The techs had set up the operating table and the heart-lung machine in the middle of the morgue. They wore full-body, water-resistant coveralls, face masks, hair covers and puncture-resistant gloves. They removed Will from the vat and put him on the table. His chest was shaved quickly and prepped for surgery.

Bernard spoke into a recorder and Rudy had the camera running. The techs scrambled about filling syringes, connecting tubes, plugging in equipment and lighting the area over the operating table. Jan filled plastic bags with glycerol. The suspension team had the room prepared in precisely fifteen minutes.

The techs then started cardiopulmonary support (CPS) to re-initiate Will's circulation. In less than five minutes they had him coupled to the heart-lung resuscitator. With the CPS being done mechanically, the techs were free to administer multiple medications that would support the body's metabolism as it attempted to ward off the effects of ischemia. This was done to minimize the damage resulting from re-initiating circulation and oxygenation, called reperfusion injury.

Two of the four techs filled syringes with the slow calcium channel blocker, nimodipine; the anticoagulant, heparin; and a variety of free radical inhibitors. Several other medications that would reduce the damage associated with depressed cerebral blood flow were administered. While this was going on, the other two techs had begun the external cooling. They packed Will in ice water. Each 10 degree Celsius drop in temperature cut his metabolic demand in half. This preface to the cryoprotective perfusion took only about ten minutes.

Sayers pulled on his surgical mask. His voice was muffled as he said to Bernard, "Have Rudy stand on the chair and get an overhead shot of the next procedure. We're going to access the femoral vessels in the groin."

"I thought you started with the heart."

"No, we start here. We use Will's circulatory system for direct control of respiration. It gives us a very efficient method to rapidly `core cool' him."

"How cold does he have to be?"

"We'll cool him to a temperature of 3 degrees Celsius in about fifteen minutes. We use the high efficiency heat exchanger."

"Then do you start the cryoprotective perfusion?"

"Yes."

Bernard watched Sayers make a small incision in Will's groin, then insert a long catheter into the surgical opening. Will was quickly connected by tubes to the blood pump and membrane oxygenator. Bernard's heart pounded. The room spun. He grabbed hold of the side of the gurney. This was his first time watching any type of surgery. He was not a hardened veteran like Rudy, a photographer who had covered the Vietnam War and watched the medics treat the wounded. But Bernard gutted it out. He knew this was just the beginning of his exposure to cryonics.

"You and Rudy can take a quick break while we cool Will," Sayers said.

Bernard noticed that Sayers held a bloody scalpel in his hand. Jan saw Bernard pale. "Come on, Bernie," she said. "Let's go upstairs."

He gave her a grateful look, then yelled up at Rudy, "Pete says you can take a quick break before he starts the open-heart surgery."

Rudy headed upstairs for a cigarette. Bernard and Jan followed, passing Leonard in the corner of the room. He was dictating what sounded like Latin into his tape recorder.

Jan lowered her surgical mask. Her freckles made her look younger than her age. Yet, she worried about the wrinkles at the corners of her eyes. She said to Bernard, "It's amazing, isn't it?"

"Do you mean the operation, or the fact I've made it this far?"

They both laughed. Upstairs, they found an unoccupied bench and sat next to each other.

"You're doing very well for the first time." Jan said. "What I meant is how medical progress continues. It seems there's something new discovered every day. It won't be long before medicine will be able to heal and resuscitate at the level of the cell."

"You mean bringing people back to life and repairing them once you've done that?"

"Exactly. Medicine will mature into a technology capable of the prevention and treatment of all diseases and injuries."

"How about aging?" Bernard said. "People worry about that more than dying."

"Me, too," she said, not forgetting the creeping crow's-feet. "I should've included the changes that occur with aging. Don't worry, medicine will be able to address that, too. Imagine, human lifespans will be measured in terms of centuries instead of decades. But to me the most exciting thing is that it won't be long before we can make these medical advances revive someone like Will Chase."

"Any idea when this will all come about?"

"With the advent of nanocomputers and nanotechnology, I think it'll be sooner than you can imagine."

Just then Peter Sayers, his head covered with a face shield, came up the stairs. "I just spoke with our pilot and there might be a nasty weather front coming in later this afternoon," he said. "If we want to get the patient back to Mankato today, let's get this operation completed."

The surgical team headed back to the body.

Bernard and Rudy assumed their former positions.

.   .   .   .

18

~.~.~.

HAÜS ZÜM RUDEN RESTAURANT
ZÜRICH, SWITZERLAND

The sommelier uncorked Hartmut a bottle of 1969 Puligny Montrachet and poured a small portion of the golden-white Burgundy into a crystal goblet. Hartmut sipped the wine and nodded his head in approval. He spread some cold pate onto a slice of French bread, ate it, and drank the entire glass of wine. Normally he did not dine this early. He preferred eating later, but with Jutta gone he had gotten into the habit of eating whenever he felt like it in the evening. Without waiting for the wine steward he refilled his glass and drank again. Then he sat staring at the Giacometti painting of Christ that the restaurant had hung on the wall. It had been Jutta's favorite.

Something did not make sense over at the cryonics laboratory. What was it? Why were they being so secretive? How did this leak happen? How did they get Jutta moved without disturbing her? Was there any possible harm done to her? Why were they in such a hurry to get him out of the building? Before he could get the next sip of wine to his lips, it struck him.

Jutta was hanging completely naked in the new dewar. How could that be? She was wrapped in medical bandages from her feet to her shoulders when she was originally suspended. She must have thawed in order for the bandages to have been removed from her body—they had been frozen to her flesh. Hartmut pushed his chair back, left a fifty franc note, and ran from the restaurant.

. . . . .

19

~:~:~:

The temperature in the morgue's operating room was a frigid 53F. Because the surgical unit was now rushing to get Will to Mankato, somehow the cold room didn't seem to bother them. But Bernard felt more than chilly.

Jan wore plastic protective goggles. She said to Bernard, "We have to minimize freezing injury, so we're going to introduce concentrations of a special solution into his tissue to reduce ice crystal formation during the cooling to liquid nitrogen temperature."

"How cold is that?" Bernard said, fiddling nervously with one of his cufflinks.

"Minus 196 degrees Celsius.

"What's that in Fahrenheit?"

"Minus 320 degrees."

Fresh scalpel in hand, Peter Sayers started open-heart surgery. He opened Will down the sternum.

Bernard was astonished by the lack of blood. He expected a tidal wave of messy, uncongealed fluids. Instead, the dry incisions reminded him of a butcher carving up a well-hung carcass of beef.

Sayers carefully divided the breastbone medially.

Jan placed cannulae in the atrium and the aorta. She then connected the tubes to the large heart-lung machine.

Rudy was perched on a scaffold videoing every move, while Bernard recorded every sound.

Jan turned to him. "Watch carefully. I'm going to introduce a concentration of glycerol into his system."

Bernard eyed the syringe, which to him seemed as big as a tire pump. "Wow, how much of that stuff do you put in him?"

"A lot," Jan said. "I have to inject it gradually due to the metabolic limitations that inhibit the rapid assimilation of viscous fluid." Her goggles had slipped and she pushed them up her nose. "We try to dissolve the glycerol in water with mannitol and other ingredients. And in the course of the perfusion the concentrate of glycerol in the solution will increase, the water will decrease, but the other ingredients will remain the same."

"How long does that take?"

"About two hours, maybe three. We'll end up replacing over sixty percent of his body water with glycerol."

Within minutes the cryoprotective fluid was being pumped through the heart and body.

Suddenly, a siren wailed. A large red light flashed on the portable computer.

"Quick, give me some help," Jan said. "He's got a nosebleed. Get a tech over here—NOW!"

A tech ran across the room. He swabbed away the blood dripping from Will's nose with cotton.

The warning siren stopped and the red light went dead. The

scene seemed surrealistic to Bernard: here was a dead man, known as America's richest man, with his heart beating, and with tubes and a machine forcing man-made chemicals through his system in order that one day he might live again.

The techs scrambled to check Will's condition and his response to the procedure. One monitored the pressure of the solution. Another monitored the rate at which Will's tissues were assimilating the cyroprotectant. A third checked Will's temperature and bio-chemical status.

Sayers, now with a smaller scalpel in a rubber-gloved hand, made a short incision in Will's scalp. He took a miniature drill and made a hole through the parietal bone of the skull.

The hair stood on the back of Bernard's neck; the noise and smell of drilled bone reminded him of his last trip to the dentist.

The burr hole allowed Sayers to observe the brain surface beneath the dura during the perfusion. This was a highly important step, since brain preservation was of the greatest priority. Sayers finished the procedure and laid the medical equipment down, but his eyes were riveted to the area he had just opened. There were no clots visible. A good sign.

Jan bent over and peered into the small cavity of the skull. She said to Bernard, "Have Rudy focus in on this area for a moment." She was perspiring, and her goggles became fogged. "This procedure allows us to assess the degree to which the brain swells or shrinks in response to the perfusion."

Bernard held back the urge to puke. He tried to remain calm and interested in what he was witnessing. He bent over for a better view of the protruding gray matter and asked, "What's better for the patient, if the brain swells or shrinks?"

Jan stepped back from the operating table and cleaned her goggles. The corners of her mouth crinkled in a smile under her face mask. "Shrinkage of the brain is preferable, this indicates good water removal and replacement in the tissues by the glycerol and the other cryoprotective components."

"And if it swells, what happens?"

"Well, edema is our worst nightmare at this point in the procedure. It indicates fluid accumulation and we'd have to stop and find the fault. Just for precaution, I'll measure the effluent in the burrhole."

Jan took a measuring syringe and aspirated a small bit of effluent from Will's brain. She found they had achieved a high glycerol concentration. Smiling, she turned to Bernard. "This is excellent under any circumstances. Actually it's extraordinary considering the time factor it took us to get here after his suicide. He seems to be responding beautifully."

Sayers had removed his face shield and was scrubbing up at a stainless steel basin. He raised his voice above the commotion and said, "Jan, before we take off again, the techs have to monitor the perfusion for the next hour. Why don't we go over to that pizza place we saw?"

Bernard blanched. How could anyone think of eating? His gut rumbled. He excused himself to use the toilet.

At 4:00 p.m. the cryoprotective perfusion was complete. Will was disconnected from the heart-lung machine and the surgical incisions in his chest and head were closed. Before Sayers closed the cranial opening with bone wax, he gently placed a temperature monitoring probe on the brain surface.

Bernard's stomach growled. He wanted to get back to Mankato and finish editing the video Rudy had just shot. "What does that device do?"

"It monitors the brain surface temperature, the time of freezing, and other events in the cool-down process."

"So, are we about finished?"

"No. Right now we have to remove Will from the operating table and get him ready for the next phase of the cryonics suspension—deep cooling."

The four techs placed Will into two plastic, liquid-proof bags. They evacuated air from the plastic to enable better heat transfer from the bath of cold silicone oil into which Will was now submerged. They would then add small amounts of dry ice to the bath at regular intervals. Will's temperature would be gradually and evenly lowered.

Rudy reloaded his camera and said to her, "How are we doing on time? I'd like to get a couple of shots outside the morgue."

"There'll be time for you to do that on our way out," Jan said. "Once we get back to Mankato, cooling him from the postoperative temperature of about zero degrees Celsius to the dry ice target of minus 79 degrees Celsius takes about forty hours. Then it'll take about five days to cool him to minus 196 degrees Celsius."

"Guess we'll all have plenty of time on our hands for awhile," Bernard said.

The techs carefully loaded Will onto a high-wheeled gurney. They used the freight elevator to transport him to the first floor and secretly ushered him to the Hertz truck waiting in the alley.

.   .   .

After the operation Nina waited for Leonard. She could hear the morning doves cooing on the roof of the courthouse. She was sitting inside on the basement steps hugging her knees. She tried to smile when she saw him. "Did everything go okay, Lenny?"

A throbbing steam radiator belched the last of its winter water through its metal veins. Leonard raised his voice above the noise. "Just the way Will would have wanted it. He's on his way to Mankato and suspension now. Doc Tragus and I figure he must have planned the whole shenanigan."

"What are you talking about? William didn't have any reason to kill himself."

"Please hear me out." Leonard ran his hands over his shiny head and lowered his voice. "I know it must be painful, but let's accept the truth of what's happened."

Nina threw her hair back with a quick motion of her head and looked him in the eye. "Okay, go ahead with what you have to say."

"Our theory is that Will was under tremendous daily pressure with the corporation and his assets. He talked constantly about his hate for the daily grind and his lack of personal freedom."

"That's a bunch of crap."

"PLEASE. What kind of talk is that from a lady? Hear me out."

"Okay. I'm sorry, Lenny."

"Doc and I feel that once Will achieved all of his goals and became the country's richest man, he had nothing left on earth to conquer," Leonard said. "He just wanted his freedom back. So he decided to escape, to test death and become the first man to be revived using cryonics. He'd be free for awhile and he'd be even more famous than he is now when he returned."

"That last part may be true," Nina said, "but you're forgetting the William I knew and loved. And what about his love for Stirling and Sophie? I don't think he wanted to escape to some frozen Nirvana for excitement and release from reality. He's a more rational man than that."

Leonard shuffled his feet and looked down at his brown Thom McAn wing-tips. "We also think he set up the Izor Foundation with a purpose."

"And what was that?"

"His own immortality. You know how he was always chewing that horrible tasting mannitol gum? The reason was, he planned to be suspended one day and he knew that gum worked as a diuretic. It acted like a preservative for his brain."

"But he chewed that gum everyday in case of any type of death," said Nina. "He told me so."

"That may be, but we think Will was a lot more egoistic and nefarious than you care to admit. We think he knew exactly what he was doing and didn't want to upset you by telling you what he was up to. He knew you loved him and you'd figure it all out on your own after he was gone."

"Listen close, Lenny. William might do something strange to me, but he'd never do that to Ingrid. Especially on her birthday. Never!"

Leonard pointed his finger at Nina. "It's you who should listen. This was a preplanned event. There was no sign of anything but suicide. Look, you and Will didn't exactly lead what's considered normal life here in Palmer Lake. Believing in spirits, smoking hash and taking peyote under the guise of tribal and religious reasons never sat too well with the locals." A single tear ran down Nina's cheek. Leonard took a deep breath. "These drugs sway your usual judgment. And Doc Tragus and I know Will's mind was definitely altered by peyote last night. There was a ton of it in his blood."

"What?" Nina said. "That's impossible. When he left the house he was fine. He said he was going to meet the boys for a beer and then drop by Ingrid's."

"I'm just telling you what we found in his body. He even had a birthday gift, flowers, and a signed card for Ingrid in the backseat of Ian's car."

"Well wouldn't that imply that he planned to live? That he planned to deliver the presents?"

Leonard's cell phone rang. "Hello, Jackson."

There was a lengthy pause and Nina motioned that she wanted to speak with him.

"I understand everything you're saying, yes, hold on, she's right here and she wants to talk to you, too."

Jackson felt he knew Nina better than anyone alive. She, along with Papa Loo, had been his saving grace when Johanna and Jackson, Jr. drowned. Now with Will dead, they understood each other's grief like no one else. Besides, in the papers Will had drawn up years ago, Jackson was sole executor of the Chase estate. Will knew that if he died, Nina would need Jackson's strength, or what he had left. Trying to keep his voice even, he said, "Nina, I know there's nothing I can say to ease your pain. But I love you and I'm here for you."

"Thanks, Jackson. You know, William's love was life to me. If it weren't for the kids, I'd join him."

"I know, I felt that way at first with Johanna and Junior, but the ache will go away," lied Jackson. "Remember, Will wants to come back. Maybe we can all work towards that goal."

"Please listen to me, I can't believe this suicide thing. I did the Ghost Dance with Wovoka and he doesn't believe it either. Lenny, of course, thinks I'm nuts. But Wovoka has never guided me wrong before. I want you to give me your word you'll help me find out if William killed himself."

"You have my word."

"That's all I ask. I'm going over to the reservation to see if Red Cloud will let me have a memorial service out there."

"Do you want me to go with you?"

"No, I need to do this myself. I'll call you later. Bye."

.   .   .   .

20

PALMER LAKE

Danny had just left Ingrid Chase's garage. He had measured the height of the nail stud from the floor as the chief requested. It was six feet up from the concrete. Indian Danny Whistle, Jackson's close friend and boxing nemesis, was a former two time upper-midwest middleweight Golden Glove champion. He was five-feet-nine inches tall, and needed to stretch his arms so the tape could reach the exact height.

Danny was cruising up Elm Street in the town's new black and white, 1987 Mercury Cougar police car. He looked in the rear view mirror. Like most macho men, he was vain. Six years of professional boxing had left a few battle scars. However, his well-healed broken nose didn't detract from his good looks. One day he'd have the crooked, flattened cartilage repaired by a plastic surgeon. His radio blared with static. He would have that damn thing fixed, too. He wondered why they'd put the old one in a new squad car.

Polly Byrd's voice finally came through. "Danny, George wants you to pick up Joey Gabrelli over at the garbage dump and Rising Coyote over at the reservation. He wants to know their whereabouts last night when Will committed suicide. And a couple of other guys, too, but I'll have to call those names over later. Just tell these two he wants them for questioning asap. This's on the QT, understand?"

Danny said in an adenoidal voice, "Gotcha. I'll pick up those two scumbags as soon as I find 'em. By the way, tell George that the nail in Ingrid's garage was seventy-two inches exactly. Over and out."

Danny turned on the red dome lights, the siren, and floored the Cougar.

A hand extended to turn up the volume on the short wave radio. It sat on a table next to the television, which was quietly tuned to CNN. The other hand turned down the TV. The wave length on the radio was tuned to the Palmer Lake police frequency. There was static on the old set, but Polly Byrd's message to Indian Danny Whistle was quite comprehensible.

.   .   .

The only noise in Ingrid's bedroom was her snoring. The sedative Leonard had given her had knocked her out. Her wheezing was so loud that her Persian, who usually slept on the bed, was downstairs preening himself.

Carl gazed for a moment at his sleeping mother. He thought she looked much older than her age. She'd had a rough time of it since Ian died. First her stroke. Now Will. The future wasn't going to be easy, for he knew Will had always been her favorite.

Knowing this was now a lost birthday celebration, Carl bent over and gave Ingrid a kiss on the cheek and put the Hawaii plane ticket, which was enclosed in a humorous Peanuts card, on the nightstand next to her bed. Then he got in his Range Rover and drove home. It was only a mile farther down the lake.

As soon as Carl entered the Cape Cod style house with the mansard roof, he wished he had gone somewhere else.

Dixie was still crying, a sound that to him was even worse than her high-pitched laughter. Of all the executive wives at MICROMED, she was the only childless one. Dixie's only solace was her horses, or dressing up in sexy outfits. Her favorite attire was short skirts, black garter belt and stockings. She was the town's equestrian queen, but Carl suspected she occasionally rode two-legged stallions. "Oh Carl, what are we going to do now?"

"Excuse me? Will was my brother, not yours, and he was about the only man in town you never paid any attention to. What do you mean, what are we going to do?"

Carl glanced at his reflection in the wall mirror, then ran his hand through his light-blonde hair. His Weimaraner steel gray eyes stared back at him. At forty-five, short and stocky, Carl was the oldest of the Chase brothers, but he had been the last to join the firm. Although he was a graduate of Harvard and the Wharton School of Business, Ian Chase had never wanted him involved with the company. Since Carl's days as a Green Beret in Vietnam, he was feared more than respected. Plus his father also knew about the gambling. It was a disease with Carl. The only reason he had his job at all was Jackson, who felt he owed Carl a debt of gratitude for saving him during the war. He had convinced the Chases and the remainder of the board of directors that Carl was the right man to administer the corporation. Once he was voted in, Carl ran MICROMED with an iron hand. The company was well organized, efficiently run, and prospered. But Carl knew the employees, and even Dixie, thought he was ruthless, and petty.

Dixie dried her eyes. She wore her brown hair straight back with her trademark headband. "Sweetheart, don't you have any compassion for me, or for anyone for that matter? I still love you, you know."

Carl glared at Dixie. Why had he ever married her? He walked over to the well-stocked bar and started making himself a "Mexican Sunshine"—his personal concoction of two jiggers of Spraggett's 1955 tequila, one-fourth jigger of Martini & Rossi sweet red vermouth, and a small lemon peel. He shook it well in ice and drained it into a stemmed glass. "Yeah, me and half the town."

"That's not true. I just dress sexy and the old town gossips start nasty rumors."

"That's a subject for another time. My brother's dead."

"I know, and that's my point. Will just killed himself and you wander off and leave me here alone."

"Would you like a Sunshine, or are you looking for an argument? Because I'm going to spend the day getting pissed, talking to my buddies on my CB, and doing some target practice in the basement."

He gulped his drink in one swallow and started mixing another. He grimaced as the booze burned the back of his throat. A few droplets had stuck to his goatee.

"I'm sorry I can't stop crying. It's just been too much for me. Pour me a ginger ale, will you?" Dixie wanted to know why he wasn't inheriting Will's money and stock.

So did Carl.

After he made himself another drink and left Dixie's soda on the bar counter, Carl walked over to his gun cabinet. He took out a .357 Smith & Wesson pistol, three boxes of cartridges, earplugs and his shooting glasses and gloves. Without a glance at Dixie he stormed down the basement stairs, his white shirt crackling.

. . .

Nina drove out to the reservation at a speed that should have gotten her a ticket.

Red Cloud was sitting outside on the porch of his hut. He had been peeling an apple with a small penknife. He could peel the entire skin of a fruit in a circular fashion until it hung like a coiled telephone cord. Children were always amazed that the peel never broke.

Red Cloud's face was lined with weather and wisdom. He had put on his tribal funeral costume once he heard of Will's death. He knew Nina would come to him for empathy. When he saw her get out of the car crying he stood. She ran into his outstretched arms. "My daughter, Wovoka will know what to do," he said. "Have you asked for his guidance yet?"

"Yes. We did the Ghost Dance earlier." Her tears quickly dried up, but she didn't let go of Red Cloud. "I want to hold a memorial service out here on the reservation."

"But your husband won't be buried here. I've heard he wants to be frozen."

"That's true, father. He'll be frozen until he returns, but his spirit is still alive, and in my heart he'll live forever."

The old man gently pushed his daughter away and held her at arm's length. "Will was very powerful. He had silent enemies. Many people had reasons to kill him."

"I can't believe anyone would want to murder him!"

"You should believe," Red Cloud said. "The Mafioso and our chieftain disliked Will's meddling in the gambling on the reservation. People think I hated him because you didn't marry within your people. Big Bertha threatened him more than once. Rising Coyote was jealous of him and hated him." He sat back down. "And, I'm sure you're aware that many other men found you rich and beautiful and dreamed of having you."

Nina looked away but remained silent.

"Don't forget, his brothers are greedy, and Jackson benefits monetarily by Will's death, as do many other people, including you."

Nina turned back to her father. "Jackson and I never cared about the money, only William. We loved him."

"This may be true for you, but don't judge others and their desires by the set of morals I taught you," Red Cloud said. "With Rising Coyote around, it'll be difficult to have a peaceful ceremony here at the reservation, but I promise, if that's what you want, I'll see that it's done."

"That's what I want. Thank you, father."

Rising Coyote, dressed in a blue and gold South Dakota State sweatsuit and tennis shoes, stood in the rutted road a few huts down, watching Nina talk to her father. He had a punk haircut that hung to his shoulders like dead fronds on a palm tree. On his biceps there was still a tattoo of a heart with the words, "Rising Coyote Loves Nina." He was six-feet-three inches of sinew. He had played on the 1961 Palmer Lake state championship basketball team with Jackson and Will. Rising Coyote had missed two free throws that would have won the game in regulation; however, it was tall, skinny, nerdy, Will Chase who tipped in the rebound with no time left and won the game. Amid the cheers and turmoil that followed, Nina ran into Will's arms. Desolate and humiliated, Rising Coyote sprinted from the floor claiming he'd kill Will one day.

Danny Whistle came roaring onto the reservation, lights blinking and siren screaming, a plume of amber dust following his new squad car.

Bruno, who was fixing the plumbing in Red Cloud's hut, peeked out the open window. "WOW, DANNY YOU BEAUT. WHERE'D YOU GET THE NEW POLICE CAR? LEMME RIDE WID YOU, PLEASE," he screamed.

Danny skidded to a stop and hopped out the door. "Sorry

Bruno, but I'm here to ask Rising Coyote to come downtown with me. Seems George wants to ask him a few questions."

"YOU BEAUT."

Red Cloud stepped forward and asked, "What's he done, Danny?"

"Keep out of this, old man." Rising Coyote looked defiantly at Nina and Red Cloud. Then he turned to Danny. "Look, suckface, have you got an arrest warrant? Cause I got nothin' to say to George. He can go fuck himself as far as I'm concerned."

"No, but I can get one, smart-ass. So why don't you just come with me, that way I won't have to come back and cuff you."

Swift as his canine namesake, Rising Coyote was on Danny. He swung at the cop. "I'll show you who can cuff who."

Danny ducked easily and brought an upper-cut into Rising Coyote's solar plexus.

Nina ran between the two men.

Rising Coyote started to fall. He swung again, his aim directed at Nina's face, when out of nowhere came a giant arm that stopped the blow with an effortless motion.

It was Bruno. He put a half nelson on Rising Coyote and threw him in the back of the squad car. He gave Danny his lopsided grin. "Now can I ride in the new car?"

"Sure, Bruno. As a matter of fact you can put the cuffs on him so he doesn't get away."

Nina ran back to Red Cloud's arms, crying quietly.

Danny drove Rising Coyote downtown.

Bruno yelled out the rear window all the way. "YOU BEAUTS! OL' RUMPLEFORESKIN'S GOT R.C. HANCUFFED IN THE BACK OF THE CAR."

Danny deposited Rising Coyote with George. "Charge him with assaulting a police officer," he said, then left to find Joey Gabrelli.

Bruno thought he would wander over to Ingrid's and prune all of last year's old wood off of her roses. He had his clippers and gardening gloves in his work overalls.

. . . .

21

ਪਾਪਾਪ

Joey Gabrelli stuffed an olive-colored canvas duffel bag partially full of clothes and put two kilos of cocaine in the bottom. He finished packing the bag with a few Nestle Crunch bars and put a small .22 caliber pistol in his shaving kit. He also stuck two pinches of the white powder up his nostrils, then threw on his old Green Beret fatigue jacket and zipped the bag.

Although Joey had been no more than a lowly private in Carl Chase's Green Beret unit, he was the most efficient sniper in the outfit. A professional killer at six-feet-four inches and two hundred and forty pounds.

Had Old George figured out all that he'd been up to recently, or just that he was dealing drugs? Joey was sure it must be the coke. There wasn't any way the stupid cop could have figured out the other stuff.

He was only making about fifty grand a year from the dope, and he'd salted all of that away down in a bank down in Sioux

Falls. It was a mob bank controlled by his uncle. No trace there.

The boys at the city dump had said Danny had arrived with the lights and the siren on. Of course, they told the detective nothing. Hadn't seen Joey for a couple of days.

Joey had done his biggest deal yet last night. Christ, he was as good as busted. Wanting to get a head start on George, he hopped in his old silver Corvette and headed for the airport.

Danny spotted him about a quarter of a mile from the terminal. He radioed headquarters. There was the usual static. "George, it's Danny. I got a bead on Gabrelli. He's heading for the airport. You want me to get him?"

"You damn well better get 'em."

Danny spun the Cougar around in the middle of the highway. The tires shrieked and left black skid marks on the concrete. He punched the throttle and the two four-barrel Holley carburetors sucked in air. Siren blaring, he made a beeline for the landing strip.

Joey had his gear stored and the Continental engine of the Cessna 172 running when Danny entered the airport. Joey jumped into the cockpit. Danny saw him get in the plane and wondered why Joey had on army fatigues. And what the hell was he was doing?

Joey turned his radio off and taxied towards the main runway. The prop threw up grassy debris. A large DC-3 occupied the take-off position on the tarmac, its engines blasting smoke and its props whining for air.

The tower screamed at the pilot of the DC-3, "We can't make radio contact with a Cessna 172 behind you! Be careful, he's heading right for the runway trying to cut you off!"

Joey pushed the throttle as hard as he could into the control panel. The instruments spun and lit up. The little Cessna scooted around the right hand side of the DC-3 and up the runway.

Danny's squad car came speeding down the runway from

the opposite direction. Danny was yelling on the radio's bullhorn, "Joey, stop, you're under arrest. Stop, or I'll shoot." He screeched to a halt and jumped out of the police car, shotgun in hand.

The tower continued trying contact by radio, "Niner. Niner. Zulu. Yankee. Niner. Niner. Zulu. Yankee. Come in, come in."

Everyone on the Izor Foundation plane was leaning against the starboard windows trying to see what the delay was about.

Danny had crawled on the roof of the squad car and was lying prone, shotgun aimed at the Cessna coming right at him. The light aircraft was about to lift off the ground.

Joey's arm came out the pilot's window of the 172. He aimed the .22 pistol at Danny and fired. The shot shattered the wind-shield of the police car like a spider's web.

Everyone but Rudy on the DC-3 got down on the floor. The photographer had his camera running and his adrenaline flow-ing. This was just like Nam.

With a thousand foot headstart, the small aircraft powered its way up and over the squad car. The force of the wind blew off Danny's cap. He fired both barrels of the twelve gauge at the undercarriage of the high-winged plane. He could hear the pel-lets hit metal and the thud of lead into the tires hanging from the struts. The pellets pinged in hundreds of spots, but the plane kept climbing.

Joey was laughing. They'd never catch him now.

Danny quickly reloaded and fired again.

Joey decided to show off with a chandelle—a steep climb and turn—he was going almost straight up coming out of his loop. Perpendicular to the plane loomed a billowing, white cu-mulus cloud. The engine throbbed powerfully in its ascent. Joey's heart was pounding and he looked down at his pursuer and grinned.

Suddenly the elevator in the tail section blew off and plum-meted towards the ground. The Cessna spun wildly. Some of the twelve-gauge pellets had snapped the wire connecting the cables to the controls. The plane turned nose down into a graveyard spiral. Joey's feet in their Nike tennis shoes fought the rudders. He pulled on the wheel and turned the ailerons.

Nothing.

He thought of jumping out, but the G-forces stretched his mouth and cheeks and kept him pinned to the seat. Like a balloon with the air let out of it, the plane zoomed wildly towards earth. Then at about one hundred feet above the ground it swooped up and leveled off upside down. It floated and lazily spun as if in slow motion towards the ground before it fell softly into an abandoned granite mineshaft next to the airport.

Just after the 172 crashed Danny swore he could hear Joey screaming for help. He ran over to the opening in the ground and stared down the sheer two hundred foot vertical shaft, it felt like looking into the cone of a crater, but there was nothing but silence.

Danny listened closely. Suddenly a muffled explosion rocked the singular shaft the plane had entered. Smoke blew out of the opening like a smoldering volcano and tons of granite debris started crumbling and filling the mineshaft. Danny slowly walked away. He turned around. Was that another scream?

The DC-3 taxied into position. Its passengers looked out at the giant hole in stunned disbelief. Small wisps of smoke lazily drifted up from the opening.

Rudy kept videoing and Bernard described the scene into his tape recorder.

The pilot gave the plane full throttle and took off for Mankato.

·   ·   ·

7:30 P.M.

The sun was setting outside the police-headquarters window. George Winter could faintly make out the twinkle of a star. It was Alkaid, the first star in the handle of the Big Dipper. George glanced over at an exhausted Polly Byrd and a weary Danny Whistle. "It's been a hell of a day. Thanks for stayin' on with me."

"You're welcome," Polly said. "Maybe we can all sneak over to Pietro's and have some dinner later."

"Sounds great to me," Danny said.

Rising Coyote yelled out from behind the bars in his cell. "Maybe you can send some fucking pizza in here. I'm starving! And goddamnit, I want a lawyer. Let me make a call."

Danny walked over to the cell with a portable telephone. He handed it to the prisoner. "Here ya are, R.C.; you got three minutes and I cut you off."

"You're nothin' but an Indian Uncle Tom, you asshole."

Danny walked down the hall to the toilet and relieved himself. The flush of the toilet echoed down the narrow hallway as he returned to the cell and took the telephone back to the office.

Rising Coyote yelled, "I don't care if that rich bastard's dead! He got no right marrying an Indian. And if you think you're going to catch me for killing him, you're nuts."

Danny walked over and closed the steel door in the hallway that connected the jail to the offices. Rising Coyote's complaints became a muffle. "Did that sound like some kind of confession to you?" Danny said.

"Yeah, a little, but if we go back there an' question him more, he'll just stonewall until one of Ronning's boys gets here to bail his ass out." George grinned at Danny. "Since the turd won't tell us where he was last night, let him spend the evenin' with the rest of the crap we got bottled up back there. We can check the rest of his alibi tomorrow."

"Good idea," Danny said, as he rubbed his sinuses.

George tilted back in his wooden chair. "Isn't life strange. Here we are in this little midwest town mindin' our own business. We wake up an' find one person dead an' he wants to exit earth as a bag of ice. We get ready to go home an' another person chooses to exit earth through a mine shaft heading for hell. I'll be damned." He dropped the chair to the floor.

"Chief, you know every piece of evidence Joey might have had went down in that airplane," Danny said. "Think there's any chance that one day we could get to the bottom of that shaft and find anything?"

"Hell, you saw what happened and you know the depth of that shaft. It must be down there a few hundred feet buried in granite, and there ain't nothin' down below that 'cept tunnels leadin' to nowhere." George stood. "I'll send a crane out there to see if we can salvage anythin'. If we can't, we might as well seal it up and let what charcoal's left of him stay down there instead of the city spendin' good money gettin' him out. It's late, let's eat."

· · · ·

22

.·.·.·.

7:30 P.M.
IZOR FOUNDATION -
MANKATO, MINNESOTA

Along a fence row peeking its head out from the protection of a clump of wild camomile, a ring-necked cock pheasant gabbled one last time before settling in for the night. The only other sound was in the distance and it was the raging spring water of the wild flowing Minnesota River banging into the granite boulders below the city of Mankato. Over the centuries these natural monuments had not been moved by the force of the river. They turned the water north, causing it to flow upward to the Twin Cities where it emptied into the Mississippi.

The Izor Foundation's research laboratory and headquarters were located on a bluff above the Minnesota River about five miles north from the campus of Mankato State College. The Foundation was secluded, heavily secured, and sat on two hundred wooded acres. The buildings were engineered shapes of redwood and glass, and the laboratory was as well equipped as any research institution in the world, thanks to Will's endowment.

At the lower floor entrance of the main Izor laboratory, the ambulance that had delivered Will to the Foundation was still parked outside, its rear doors inadvertently left open. A number of Izor medical people scurried about. The techs wheeled in Will's gurney. Peter Sayers, Jan Elton, Bernard Grable, and Rudy Barrnet followed the others into the well-lit building.

10:00 P.M.

It had been a long, tiring day and everyone connected with Will's suspension decided a break was in order. Cokes and cookies sat on a table in the lounge. Bernard, Rudy, Peter, Jan and the four techs grabbed snacks and flopped down on chairs. Jan turned on the television in the corner of the room. They watched the video Rudy had forwarded to station KARE-11 in Minneapolis upon their arrival to the cryonics medical facility. KARE-11 had edited, then forwarded the video via satellite to New York and the NBC studios for the late night news.

As Bernard watched the broadcast and heard his throaty narration, he glowed in delight. The video showed the dramatic escape attempt, the shooting between Danny and Gabrelli, the screams from the control tower to the pilot of the Izor DC-3, the emotions of the passengers during the episode, and the horrendous spinning fall and crash of the Cessna slowly disappearing down into the mine shaft. Bernard's cool voice over captured it all. The nationwide audience was held spellbound. He knew this was going to help him skip a few rungs in his climb up the reporting ladder at NBC.

When the newscast ended, Sayers didn't want anyone to start watching the Tonight Show, so he stood. "Let's get finished and then get a good night's sleep. We've got a lot ahead of us tomorrow."

Earlier that night, Will had been placed in the cooling room. The techs had gradually added small amounts of dry ice to his bath at regular intervals, lowering his temperature evenly. At midnight, an exhausted Sayers asked the techs to hook Will up to a computer that would monitor his descent to minus 79 degrees Celsius over the next few days. Once he arrived at that temperature, he would be removed from the cooling bath and his outer plastic wrap would be taken off. Two sleeping bags would be positioned near the dry ice cooling bath and precooled with liquid nitrogen vapor. Will would be immediately transferred into these sleeping bags, further secured inside a protective aluminum pod, and lowered into a cooldown vessel for the final temperature descent to minus 320 degrees Fahrenheit.

Cooling Will to liquid nitrogen temperature would be achieved by controlled introduction of cold nitrogen vapor into the cooling vessel. Over the next three days his temperature would be slowly reduced to very nearly that of liquid nitrogen, then he would be submerged.

Jan interrupted the techs. "I want to take one more glycerol sample from the burrhole. Peter, would you give me a hand?"

Rudy started videoing.

This time Bernard didn't flinch. He felt like a hardened veteran after all that had transpired that day. But he needed to get back to Palmer Lake to visit with Jackson, whom he had met on his way to the airport. Jackson had even suggested a golf game. "Could you tell me where we are in the procedure and how long you might want me here?" he asked Jan.

She looked up. "Once he's safely submerged in liquid nitrogen, there's but one remaining step in the cryonics suspension procedure," she said. "And that would be the transfer to long-term storage, which consists of moving him from the cooling vessel into a dewar that's also filled with liquid nitrogen, his new home until revival."

Rudy took his eye from the camera viewfinder and said, "Let's hope it's soon."

Sayers walked over to Will with a syringe and started aspiration of the brain. He took his sample, measured the filled syringe and snapped the tube with his finger. "Wouldn't it be wonderful if it happened in our lifetime?"

"Wouldn't it, though?" Jan said. "But realistically we're probably looking at another fifty years." She turned to Bernard. "Rudy can video Will being put in the dewar if you need to get going."

Thank god. Bernard longed to get to bed, yet he didn't want to miss anything. "That'd be great," he said. "I need to get back to Palmer Lake and talk to Will's friends and family. But one last thing before I hit the sack. Could you explain to me how the dewar works?"

"Later," said Jan. "I'm tired, too. Although I'm glad you're so interested. But answer me this: how can you be so perfectly groomed after sixteen hours of debilitating work?" She drank the last of her Coke with a noisy suck of the straw and put her hand on top of Bernard's.

Bernard grinned. "All part of the job," he said.

"I've simply got to go to bed. Good night all." She headed out.

Bernard watched her until the lab door closed. He was amazed by her energy and enthusiasm. The subject of cryonics was never boring when she spoke about it. She was attractive too, and she seemed to like him. No wedding ring either. He wondered if she'd ever dated a black man?

The others cleaned up and left the lab. It was 7 a.m. and already light out. As they walked to their cars, none realized that deep in the recesses of the compound one light still burned dimly.

Cruickshank and Duesmann were once again watching the video of Elvis' revival. They were eating pig's feet from a jar and hard boiled eggs.

When the video ended, the two men looked at the clock and decided to go home. There were cracked egg shells on the floor and the jar was empty.

.   .   .   .

23

JUNE 5
IMB CRYONICS LABORATORY
ZÜRICH, SWITZERLAND

Upset with being delayed by bureaucracy, Hartmut Kell ordered the company security guard to telephone Dr. Verson in the cryonics laboratory with his request for an immediate visit. The late working Verson reluctantly approved. Hartmut rushed down the steep stairs to the laboratory. Out of breath, and without giving Verson an opportunity to say anything, Hartmut pointed at the dewar holding Jutta and asked, "How come my wife has no bandages on? What have you done to her?"

Verson was alone in the lab. He turned red. What could he say? He wanted to tell the banker the truth, but he felt he couldn't. Hartmut stared at him waiting for an answer. Finally Verson said, "Please calm down, Herr Kell. We've done nothing to harm your wife."

"Answer me. Why does she now have no bandages on and when she was first suspended you had her bandaged from her feet to her shoulders? She must have thawed out, and that would have killed

tissue." Hartmut was so upset his face turned a purplish color. "I want to know. Have you destroyed my wife's ability to return to life?"

Verson took a deep breath. "When we discovered the leak in her dewar, very little liquid nitrogen had escaped and we transferred your wife as rapidly as possible to the second dewar. During this process we put on a chemical solution to protect her and the solvent dissolved the bandages. They just fell off. No tissue damage was observed."

Hartmut sighed. "Oh, I'm so thankful."

"In our haste to get her into the liquid nitrogen of the second dewar, we felt it best we didn't take the time to re-wrap her in bandages," Verson said. "This way we can now observe her for any potential future freeze damage or fissures."

"I understand. But I do not like the idea that Jutta is now hanging naked for everyone to see. She is my wife."

"Only we doctors who work here will be viewing her."

Hartmut sat down heavily. "That is not true," he said. "There are always photographers here to take pictures for the newspapers and the journals. And what about the janitors and technicians?" Hartmut glanced at his watch. He interlaced his fingers in his lap as if praying, then took a deep breath. "Dr. Verson, I am old-fashioned. Jutta was shy. She would not like this. When I come back from my business in London next week, I will meet with your superiors and see if there is not a way we can bandage Jutta again."

.   .   .   .

24

PALMER LAKE
JUNE 6, 1987
3:00 P.M.

Eggs Benedict screamed. "JACKSON DID IT. JACKSON DID IT."

Nina walked over to his perch and reprimanded him. "Stop it, you evil bird. Jackson's coming up the driveway right now, so stop it immediately." She wondered who was teasing the poor creature.

The cockatoo raised his neck feathers and cocked his head at an angle towards Nina. His black eye stared at her as if he knew what he was talking about. He stayed silent as War Bird let Jackson in the front door.

Nina ran into his arms. She had no more tears left, but the hug felt good. "I got your telephone messages and I'm sorry you couldn't find me yesterday. I went to the burial ground at the reservation. I had to get closer to Wovoka and search for the truth."

"Did you find any answers?"

"Yes, Wovoka knows what happened."

"How about your belief in the church?"

Nina took a step back but didn't release her hold on Jackson's arms. "Come on. You know very well since our high school debates how I've always felt about Christianity," she said. "No bible thumper should ever preach their beliefs until they've read Twain's Letters from Earth."

"I didn't forget. I just know how much you respect Father Mc Queeny."

"That's different. I love his mind and his goodness. And I admit, I did go over to St. Mark's after I left the reservation."

"What's his opinion of the supposed suicide?"

"He's a priest who doesn't pass judgment on suicide. He hopes William has the forgiveness of God and won't linger in purgatory forever. But he doesn't believe William will return to life. That's too Christ-like for him." What Nina believed could not explained in words. She looked him in the eye. "What do you think really happened?"

Jackson pulled her closer. Nina had a musky bouquet. For years he had wondered if it was her natural smell or a perfume. Her eyes were swollen from her sorrow. Even with no makeup she was stunning. He brushed her hair from her face. "I don't know what to think. I need some time to look at some facts that don't add up yet in my mind."

"What kind of facts?"

"Sorry, but I can't share them at the moment."

Nina gently broke their embrace and walked away from him into the living room.

The room was filled with Will's mementos and hunting trophies. Giant elephant tusks lined the entrance. Zebra rugs were scattered before the fireplace. A twenty foot, man-eating, salt water crocodile covered an entire wall. A mounted polar bear stretched towards the high ceiling. Stuffed heads stared down from the walls—water buffalo from Central Africa, a ten-prong white-tailed deer from Virginia, an elk from northern Canada, it was a taxidermist's dream.

Jackson followed her and sat down next to her on a leather couch covered with leopard skins. He said, "Hey, I didn't mean to upset you. Let's take this slowly."

"That's okay. I'm just looking for some answers, that's all."

"I know. And I'm going to help you find them," Jackson said. "How are the kids doing?"

Nina took Jackson's hand. "They're fine. I left them with Red Cloud.

Following Will's wishes, Nina had waited until she was thirty to have children. She had wanted them immediately but Will said he needed to finish his M.D. When that didn't happen, it was then getting his business started before having kids. Nina waited. When Stirling arrived, a healthy nine pounds, Nina was ready. Sophie's birth only solidified her feelings. She doted on her children, didn't spare the rod, but spoiled them as much as possible. As with her own upbringing, the children knew both the white man's ways and the Indian's ways.

Stirling, whom Will named after his favorite Formula One driver, was nine. He might have inherited Moss's genes, as he could already out drive War Bird and his mother on the farm tractor. Sophie Chase, whom Nina named after her mother, was seven, actually seven and a half as she told everyone. She loved acting and was always putting on airs and staging plays in the barn.

Nina rang War Bird on the intercom. "Bring us some tea and snacks, would you."

"Do you think the kids comprehend what's happened?"

"Not really. They can't believe their daddy's gone. He was their world. So I keep telling them he'll be back soon."

"Nina, 'soon' to children is tomorrow. Maybe you should have them talk to Father McQuenny. Hell, even if this cryonics works, it's way in the future. Maybe fifty or a hundred years from now. Aren't you being a bit unfair to them?"

Nina fingered a claw necklace that hung to the middle of the tan, fringed buckskin dress she wore. Her ruby wedding ring sparkled in the dim light. She stared at the floor. "I don't know what's fair anymore. I can't believe that cryonics is so far away. And I don't care what the church says. Wovoka says William's coming back soon. I have to believe that or I'll go nuts. I want the kids to believe that, too. My God, if it weren't for them, I'd join William in suspension."

Jackson touched his mole. "You know, I believe you would." He drew in a deep breath. "Why do you think Will was murdered when everything points to suicide?"

"Maybe it's just a woman's intuition. Do you know George has a hunch William was murdered?

"Yes, I was over at his office earlier and he told me he was bringing in everyone for questioning tomorrow who might have a motive to have Will out of the picture. As executor of his estate, I suppose he'll be calling me soon."

"I guess so." Nina shifted nervously on the sofa. She got up and fiddled with a picture that wasn't crooked. She suddenly turned around and said, "Jackson, will you answer me something honestly? Whatever you say will always remain between us."

"Okay. Shoot."

"Did you have any prior knowledge of William's death?" She sat back down on the couch and looked at Jackson for an answer.

"None," said Jackson, "I've been surrounded by death a lot in my life, and let me tell you, nothing came as more of a shock than when Lenny phoned me about Will's suicide." He scrutinized her for a moment. What was she thinking? Was he some kind of suspect in Will's death in her mind?

Nina's eyes were moist. "I'm so sorry I asked that. But why would he kill himself? If he wanted to be suspended while he was still young, don't you think he would've shared that with me?"

"I'm not sure. Will was pretty stubborn and tightlipped."

"I don't think I can live in this house without him."

"Nina, we both know Will did a lot of crazy things in life. It was sort of his M.O. Why don't we start with two questions to each other. One, if Will killed himself, why? And two, if he was murdered, who?"

War Bird entered the room carrying a tray of freshly brewed Earl Grey tea, crispy biscuits and a wheel of Edam cheese. He set it down and departed as silently as he had entered. Jackson wondered how the white man ever defeated the Indians. They could sneak up on their own shadows.

Nina sliced red wax from a piece of yellow cheese, put some on a biscuit for Jackson, and poured him a cup of hot tea. She said, "There was no way William killed himself, so who would want to murder him?"

The perfumed tea had a sweet taste and Jackson took his time in swallowing it. He nibbled on his cheese and biscuit. "Nina, I disagree with you. Will very well could have committed suicide. He lived for solving the unknown. Can you imagine the thrill and the attention he'd get if he were to be the first human being to return from suspension—from death?"

"Yeah, that would be just like William. He'd love the glory and discovery. Especially if he was the first one." A glowing smile lit up Nina's face. "Is it really possible they're that far along in the technology over at Mankato that he'd take such a chance?"

"That's one thing I'd like to know. I need to go over to the Foundation and see just how advanced the medical world is in cryonics. I'm willing to bet Will knew everything that's been going on the past few years that the public knows nothing about."

Nina set her tea down. "Didn't you promise to help me find out if William was murdered? You gave me your word."

"You do have my word," Jackson said. "But if I'm going to solve this equation, first I'll have to rule out the possibility that he committed suicide. I'll go over to Mankato and do as much research as I can. If they're as far from reviving someone as we're led to believe, then I'll pursue your murder theory. But if there's some new discovery being held secret, I need to find out if anyone at Izor was in cahoots with Will."

Nina stood. "I'm going to start on my murder theory today with George, then I want to go to Mankato with you. You know, there were a lot of people who hated William and were jealous of him."

"Maybe you can give me some names?"

"Later. Right now I've got to get over to the reservation and pick up the kids. I'll see you tomorrow at the memorial service." Nina started up the stairs to her bedroom. She turned around half way up and said, "Oh, and Jackson, don't ever die before I do."

"Why's that?"

"I need you here."

Jackson looked at the tea leaves on the side of his cup. They augured bad luck.

Jackson headed for the front door. A wooden grandfather clock quietly chimed four o'clock. War Bird stood towering at the door, stone-faced, as usual. He stepped aside as Jackson passed.

Eggs Benedict whispered to Jackson from his perch, "kris catlin did it. kris catlin did it."

Who the hell was talking to this bird? Jackson looked at the silent Indian.

Not a muscle moved in War Bird's stern, weathered face.

Jackson left without saying a word.

.   .   .   .

25

JUNE 7, 1987.
PALMER LAKE
10:00 A.M.

Chief George Winter had a shiner. His left eye was black and blue and practically shut. The previous evening he had been pounding nails in two-by-fours at his house so he could hang the macrame plant hanger Polly had given him when the telephone rang. He couldn't get down in time to get the call. His answering machine automatically picked up.

A garbled voice said, "George, if you know what's good for you, Will Chase committed suicide."

He started to hop off the ladder, but the big claw hammer lurched back from a nail he had just struck and the metal butt hit his eye. "Goddamit."

By the time he got to the telephone, the caller had hung up.

Polly whistled when she saw George in the morning. "Chief, what happened? Looks like somebody got the best of you."

"Oh, it's nothin', babe, just a little tussle last night out on the reservation. Hell, you should see the other guy."

"Sorry I missed your performance last night." Danny, who *had* been at the reservation, looked up from his desk and winked at George. "I got Bobby Joe Baker, Red Cloud, and Rising Coyote coming in this afternoon."

George sponged his eye with a damp hankie. "Good work. I'll go speak with Jackson and Nina. How 'bout Kris Catlin and that boozo, Terry Potter?"

"Well, Potter is still in Colorado. The Denver police picked him up for drunk driving without a license the night of Will's suicide. And this dickhead Catlin is playing hard to get. I'll have to take a drive over to his house again and bring him in personally." Danny pointed at George's eye and gave him a wry grin.

George took the hankie from his eye and peeked in a mirror next to his desk. "That's a beaut all right. Damn good thing I still got a great right cross. Listen, Danny, when you pick up Catlin, I want you to stop by the twins' houses and politely tell 'em I need to have a word with 'em before Will's memorial service."

Danny was putting his hat on and heading for the door when George added, "Also, don't forget to tell Freddie to bring along Big Bertha."

During lunch George suffered through the usual guffaws about his shiner from the crowd at Donna's, especially when he ordered the daily special, which was liver and onions with black-eyed peas. Polly smiled and said nothing.

Back at the police station, they found the office crammed with: a handcuffed Kris Catlin, who had a bloody nose and cut lip; Danny standing next to him smiling; Woody Chase sitting on a long wooden bench; Bobby Joe Baker, with a *Walkman* strapped on his head, and his wife, MaryBell; Red Cloud, dressed in a feathered tribal costume; and Rising Coyote and his attorney.

Towering next to George's private office door was a glaring Big Bertha, her arms crossed across her chest.

Freddie cowered behind her. Big Bertha, and the Catholic church, which Freddie had fanatically converted to years ago, were his only defenses in life.

Big Bertha had on a bright yellow track suit and white and yellow Nike running shoes. She said to George, "If you don't want a matching black eye, you'd damn well better tell me what this intrusion is all about. You've got Freddie half scared to death." She yanked him by the arm to face George. "Ain't that right, Hawkeye?"

George tilted his cap back with his thumb and turned to Polly. "Shit, it's so crowded in here it looks like the Legion Hall when they're givin' away free beer on the Fourth of July."

There were some nervous smiles from the crowd on the bench but Big Bertha wasn't smiling.

"Come on in, Bertha, an' bring Freddie with you," George said. "I'll get to the rest of you just as soon as I can. Thanks for comin'."

Big Bertha and Freddie had each other as their alibi. Freddie looked at Big Bertha and fidgeted with his sweater. He told George, "We watched television all night, right Mama?"

"That's right."

"An' you went to bed right after that, I suppose?"

"Yes we did," said Freddie, "Cause I fell asleep during the middle of *Mary Poppins*, and then Mama carried me to bed. Didn't ya, Mama?"

"That's right." Big Bertha winked at Freddie.

George didn't trust Big Bertha. She was nuts. Of course, what did that make Freddie?

"I don't know what you got up your sleeve, Georgie boy," she said. "But I ain't leaving this room until you've questioned all these people. I don't want to get pinned for something I didn't do."

To make her happy, George decided she could remain. Maybe her hulking presence would flush a clue out of someone. "That's okay Bertha, just stand there an' be quiet. Freddie, will you please wait in the other room."

Next, Bobby Joe Baker nervously explained that he was playing poker with the boys until the wee hours of the morning. His new wife, MaryBell, didn't know of this nocturnal event. She kept tugging at her oversized T-shirt that had "CHECK-OUT-THESE-HOOTERS" printed on the front. Her tight Bermuda shorts revealed ungainly cellulite flapping around her thighs and buttocks. They left the room arguing.

George figured if Bobby Joe was going to murder anyone, it would be MaryBell.

"That woman dresses like a damn tramp," Big Bertha said.

"Bertha, if you want to stay in here, keep quiet." George wondered who the hell her couturier was.

Rising Coyote's public defender, Knut Ronning, told him to say nothing until George gave them a reason for his incarceration.

George excused them for the time being since Danny had been told Rising Coyote had been at a whorehouse the night of Will's death. He'd check that out. But if it were true, George was envious; he hadn't been alone with Polly for a week.

Woody Chase claimed he and two buddies had bowled most of the early night and one of them had stayed and shot the breeze about the stock offering of MICROMED until four in the morning.

Likely story, thought George. The fags might have balled all night, that was more like it.

Just as George was starting to question Kris Catlin, who was dressed in a maroon polyester suit with bell-bottom trousers, and had a frizzy, white-man's Afro, Carl Chase barged in the office.

"Sorry to butt in, George, but I've been hearing some crazy rumors around town. Why in hell do you have Woody and Freddie down here?"

"Hold on, Carl. Have a seat. I'm jus' following a hunch, that's all."

Carl walked behind George's desk, sat down and folded his arms across his chest. Big Bertha stood in the corner glaring down at him. He scowled up at her.

George guessed Catlin to be about five-eleven. A stocky, tough, big punk. He asked, "Kris, I jus' want to know your whereabouts from midnight to six o'clock the night of Will Chase' suicide."

"Shit, George, I don't know where I was. It ain't none of yer business nohow."

"Well I can make it my business. Answer me this, do you have a military fatigue jacket?"

"Yeah, I got all my old Nam garb."

"So where's your jacket?"

"I don't know where none of that crap is nomore."

"An' you're sure you can't tell me where you were the other night."

"Nah, I can't."

"Come on, Kris, this's not a rocket scientist question."

It appeared Catlin had no alibi. "If the rich prick killed himself, what are you buggin' me for, George?"

Carl jumped up from his chair towards Catlin, but Danny grabbed his arm and cut him off.

George said, "Maybe you'd better come back later Carl. This's police business."

Carl pointed at Catlin. "Don't talk about my brother like that if you know what's good for you."

"Ya ain't my commander nomore, 'member I got kicked outa the army, thanks to you, asshole." Catlin gave Carl the finger.

Carl jerked his arm from Danny's grasp and left the room.

Big Bertha said, "That little shit never would have broken my grip, Danny."

"Shut up, Bertha," George said. He continued with Catlin, "Just answer my questions, smart ass. I'll ask you one more time, where were you that night?"

"I can't remember. But I sure as fuck know a couple of guys that wanted that stuck-up, rich asshole dead."

"Like who?"

"Like Joey Gabrel...Oh, fuck you, that's for me to know, and for you to find out."

George had nothing on which to hold him, although he was going to get a warrant and search every inch of his house. He had to let him go. But he knew this guy could be a murderer. And why'd he start mumbling about that dead creep Gabrelli?

Red Cloud had plenty of witnesses to testify, if needed, that he was on the reservation all night.

George didn't care. He knew Red Cloud wasn't a murderer, so he and Red Cloud went over to Donna's and had a coffee together. They both loved the Minnesota baseball team and George had wanted to be a ballplayer ever since he was a kid. He never had the talent and it bothered him that someone like Jackson, who could have played baseball professionally, gave it up to join the air force. Hell, when Jackson was at university he could throw a fastball well over 90 mph. Major league stuff. To George, pissing away this talent was inexcusable. He said to Red Cloud, "I wouldn't be surprised if the Twins win the World Series this year."

"That's possible," said Red Cloud. "The division's weak and Kelly's got those guys playing like a team. No big heros out there."

They drank their coffee and dissected the team lineup.

Weary, but undeterred, George was now back at square one in his murder theory.

Big Bertha and Freddie passed Huey Goey Loo's restaurant. They could smell cooked garlic. Freddie looked up at his wife and asked, "Aren't you glad I didn't tell George that when I woke up during *Mary Poppins* you were gone?"

Big Bertha lifted Freddie off the sidewalk and held him in front of her face. "Hawkeye, if you ever tell anyone that, I'll break your skinny neck."

Smiling, she gently lowered him to the ground.

Freddie felt horny.

1:30 P.M.

The telephone was set on the low ringer. It rang six times before a gloved hand reached out and picked it up.

The caller's voice was but a whisper. "I'm worried. George's asking everybody where they was when Will killed hisself." There was a short chuckle.

The recipient said, "I've told you never to call this number. It's private and it's only for emergencies."

"This's an 'mergency. I'm worried."

"There's nothing to be worried about. We just put him to sleep, and now Nina's going to freeze him until they wake him up."

The caller's voice lowered to a murmur. "When'll they do that? 'Cause that's what worries me."

"I don't know when they'll do it. Probably not in our life-time."

The caller was breathing hard. "Okay. But it was kina fun wearing my gas mask agin. Weren't it fun when we held Will down in the front seat of the ol' car in Ingrid's garage? Kinda like the ole days, huh?"

"Yeah, that was a lot of fun, but listen—"

"Heck, he couldn't breathe and we could. Drunk as he was, he sure did look surprised, din't he?"

"Yes, he sure fell for our trick, didn't he?" said the recipient, "But listen to me closely, did you tear your military jacket during our operation?"

"I don' know. I'll have to look."

"Well if you did, you'd better hide the evidence from the enemy."

"I sure will. Ya know, ol' Will didn' just act like he was drunk, he sure acted surprised."

The caller didn't know the recipient had shared and drunk with Will a half-quart of boiled peyote buttons before Will went to Ingrid's.

"I'm not going to repeat this order. Don't ever call here again. You can never tell anyone about this. I've told you that before. It's our secret. And remember, if the police ever find out, George will have you hanged like one of those barbecued ducks at Huey Goey Loo's."

"Don't worry, Commander. They kin torture me all they want, but I'll never tell."

"Nobody's going to torture you, you stupid moron. Just keep quiet."

The line went dead.

.   .   .   .

26

⌣⌣⌣

JUNE 7th
Le DEZALEY RESTAURANT
ZÜRICH, SWITZERLAND

The lederhosen clad waiter took the orders of Hartmut and the director of the IMB cryogenic research laboratory, then poured them each a tankard of dark beer and departed for the kitchen. Hartmut wasted no time in getting to the point of the luncheon. "Before I left for London last week, I stopped by the laboratory and noticed that when you moved my wife to the new dewar, you left off her bandages."

The director, who was quaffing his brew, put his pewter mug down.

Hartmut went on. "As a concerned husband, I do not want my wife hanging naked upside down like this for the world to view."

"Herr Kell. Let me assure you of the privacy of—"

"No, I've heard it all before, and I want Jutta re-bandaged. Immediately."

"That will be very difficult, Herr Kell," the director said. "I'm not happy with the prototype dewars that we've been using. The first one should not have leaked from the rivets and I'm reluctant to open the second where your wife is now suspended. I don't want any further accidents."

"Couldn't you get one of the large dewars they're using in America moved here and put Jutta in that?"

"*Perhaps in a few years. However, each time we move a sus-pended patient we're taking a chance for damage to them. For example, when we had to move your wife, I peeled the bandages from her one by one so I could be assured there would be no damage to her tissue.*"

Hartmut was hunched over the table listening. He sat up quickly. "Didn't you use a chemical solvent to remove the bandages from my wife?"

"*Absolutely not. What ever would give you an idea like that? Any solvent would immediately destroy frozen tissue. I assure you, I removed the wrapping myself with the utmost of care.*"

The waiter put down the steaming raclette, cheese fondue, and fondue Bourguignonne.

Hartmut wondered why the director was lying to him.

Back in 1982 Jutta Kell went to Central Africa to do humani-tarian relief work. It had seemed such a romantic idea that she and Hartmut would get married, then she could finish her life's dream in Uganda while he completed his banking career in Zurich over the following two years. They would then retire to their chalet in St. Moritz, raise a family and travel the world.

Jutta worked for over a year in Kampala with a Suisse Red Cross unit that helped the local hospitals in their daily efforts. Al-though she had been immunized for malaria, cholera and various other African diseases, she seemed to be constantly sick. She was always exhausted with flu-like symptoms. After a year she found that she missed Hartmut and the change of seasons in Switzerland. She decided to go home.

Two weeks before Hartmut was to arrive and pick her up, Jutta was feeling so bad she took a short break from the hospital and went to the village of Jinja on the shores of Lake Victoria for a visit with a tribal medical man she knew. As the hospital's treatment of antibiotics was not working, she felt possibly he would have some remedy for her constant exhaustion and nausea.

The medicine man put Jutta in a small, dank and dark thatched hut and gave her a mixture of yohimbe and goats blood. Yohimbe is an herb usually associated with sexual stimulation, however, the medicine man knew it could restore energy in most cases of fatigue.

On the second day Jutta's fever rose. The shivers started and she couldn't get out of bed. She noticed the first crimson spot, about the size of a nickel, on her right bicep. Soon she became hot and achy. Her throat became raw, her lips cracked, and her mouth was so swollen that she could barely speak. As a physician Jutta knew about Trypanosoma brucei, sleeping sickness. She was so weak it was all she could do to communicate to the tribesmen that they must send someone to Kampala and notify them of her condition.

Death is swift among victims of East African trypanosomiasis. At the turn of the century sleeping sickness had killed over half of Uganda's six million people in less than a year. The disease is insidious. Twice as big as the house fly, with predatory mouth parts and scissorlike wings, the tsetse fly breeds in dark, moist niches.

The flies swarmed over Jutta in the humid hut and bit her everywhere her flesh was exposed. They laid eggs in the folds of her skin in hopes they'd become maggots. She knew their bite caused creeping inflammation of the brain, which would quickly lead to seizures, stupor, coma, and then death.

The medicine man built a fire in the center of the hut and created smoke to drive out the evil spirits instead of the flies.

For a week Jutta lay in her own sweat. Red welts soon covered her body. Her lips became so inflamed she couldn't close her mouth. The tsetse flies crawled in and bit her tongue. She was too weak to even scream.

Trypanosomes have a wicked way of dealing with the body's immune defenses. Wave after wave of them breed in the blood of a victim. Each wave represents a new generation with altered surface proteins. This new coat triggers a fresh host of antibodies. The an-

tibodies work at first, then fail in the face of yet another wave of reconfigured parasites.

These new parasites glutted Jutta's bloodstream, her own immune system became her enemy. She developed severe anemia, malfunctioning kidneys, and an inflamed heart, all due to her own antibodies attacking her own tissue. Trembling shivers racked her body. Her fever soared. She thought, if only I had some Ciprofloxacin. There's a cure to sleeping sickness if caught in time. But would someone rescue her in time? Once her fever reached 108 degrees F. she realized no one could help her. Her last memories were of the thick smoke, the thatched roof and the constant buzzing of the flies.

Hartmut arrived in his private jet. He had with him a team of Suisse physicians to look after Jutta. They immediately injected her with melarsoprol, an arsenic-based parasite poison. But it was too late—she died that morning.

Jutta was taken to the Kampala hospital and her body was sterilized and cleaned up. The Suisse physicians did a total body washout and then packed her in a container of dry ice. When they were finished, Jutta didn't look as if she'd been sick, she looked more like a sleeping angel when they flew back to Switzerland that afternoon.

.   .   .   .

27

JUNE 7 - 5:30 P.M.
PALMER LAKE COUNTRY CLUB

Blooming pink rhododendron bushes bordered the golf course. In a field about half an acre away, a swaybacked horse munched on grass, his stomach nearly touching the ground. For years he had watched people chase after little white balls. He didn't bother to look up anymore.

Jackson and Bernard, both smoking cigars, were driving a covered golf cart from the apron of the par five eighteenth green towards the clubhouse. Jackson had on his usual all black outfit, Titleist cap, and black shoes. Bernard wore a beige silk/cashmere sweater, white visor, brown pants and brown and white golf shoes. Jackson had won their match and a bottle of beer for his efforts.

Balthasar, whom Jackson used to retrieve out-of-bounds and lost balls, loped beside the cart. This caused much dismay to some of the members, as dogs were not allowed on the course.

However, since Will and Jackson were the main benefactors of the club, there was a tacit agreement among the members to turn a blind eye.

Bernard hadn't mentioned Will once all afternoon, but now he started where they had left off at lunch. "If the coroner found an overdose of peyote in Will's blood, a garden hose connected with duct tape from the exhaust pipe to the back window of an idling car, and no sign of foul play, why is Nina questioning his suicide?"

"Because she feels it incomprehensible that he'd kill himself." Jackson exhaled a cloud of cigar smoke. "She loved the guy more than life itself. Why don't you ask her tonight at the service?"

"I will. How about you? Do you find it impossible that your best friend committed suicide?"

"I have my own theories because Will thought and did some strange things. He was capable of most anything."

"So you think he killed himself?"

"I didn't say that. Don't put words in my mouth."

"But you *were* aware Will was a frequent user of drugs?"

As they neared the clubhouse, Jackson looked Bernard straight in the eye, and his tone brooked no contradiction. "Yes, I knew Will and Nina used pot and peyote in the privacy of their home and at Indian religious ceremonies. But they never hid it. They felt it was their legal and spiritual right to do so."

"Did that bother you?"

"I had no argument with it. They were productive people. Funny, isn't it, that most of the people bitching loudest in the world against pot are the very ones that should be using it."

"Right on," Bernard said.

The two men laughed and slapped a high five.

"By the way, does it bother you that many of your fellow TV entertainers use drugs for recreational purposes?"

"Touche', Jackson."

They parked the golf cart beside the clubhouse. Budding Virginia creeper draped a stone building designed after St. Andrews, but much larger. Jackson and Bernard walked Balthasar to the parking lot. Their metal spikes clicked on the pavement. Jackson opened the back of the Bronco and the dog reluctantly hopped in. His sad, watery eyes followed the twosome as they entered The Nineteenth Hole for a drink. They were the last ones on the course that day. Paintings of all the golf greats hung in the room, from old Tom Morris to Jack Nicklaus. The tenth annual MICROMED Open had been won the previous year by none other than the master himself.

The bar was crowded. Numerous people turned around and waved to Jackson. They stared at Bernard. There were not a lot of black people in South Dakota and the club members' curiosity overcame their normal good manners. Many of the men sat at tables with their wives having a drink before dinner. The male uniform was blue blazer, club tie and grey slacks, while the women, hair tinted and lacquered, wore pearls and print dresses. Laura Ashley seemed to be the designer of choice.

Jackson ordered a *Hamm's* beer and a bowl of peanuts from the waiter, then said to Bernard, "What'll you have?"

"I'll have a Charlie Lindbergh."

The tux-clad waiter, who had a Bogart-like overbite, glided over to the bar station and put in the order.

"Hey, don't think you're going to fool the bartender here with your order," Jackson said. "Old Lucky Lindy was born right across the border in Little Falls, Minnesota."

Without fanfare, the waiter placed the drinks on the table.

Jackson picked up his beer, ignored the frosty glass, and took a swig from the long-neck bottle.

Out of the corner of his eye Jackson could see Woody Chase

sitting alone watching *Jeopardy* in the corner. He was munching on a bowl of popcorn.

Big Bertha came stomping into the bar in a pair of laced, black and brown hiking boots. She wore a lime-green track suit with a matching bow in her fulvous hair, and a string of pearls.

Freddie, dressed like an undertaker in a black suit two sizes too big, dutifully trailed behind.

They sat at a table next to Woody, who said, "Well if it isn't the commander in chief and her troop."

"Watch your mouth, you skinny little fruit. I'm only going to be nice to you because we're going over to your brother's memorial service together. Isn't that right, Hawkeye?"

Like a blinking-eyed Hawaiian hula doll in the rear window of an East L.A. stud car, Freddie bobbed his head in approval.

Up at the bar, Carl Chase walked in and ordered a Mexican Sunshine. He had just dropped a bundle at the casino but didn't want anyone to know. He talked to no one and stared at his reflection in the mirror, a face surrounded by brightly labeled liquor bottles from around the world.

One of his former Green Beret buddies walked by and said, "Cheer up, Commander, it might never happen."

Carl only nodded.

"There sure are a lot of commanders in this town," Bernard said.

"Yep, there sure are." Jackson drained his beer. "Want another?"

"No thanks. One's my limit." Bernard was finishing the peanuts on the table.

Jackson signaled the waiter for another beer.

"I guess you want to talk more about Will."

"If you don't mind. That's what I came over here for."

"Sure. What else do you want to know?"

"Can we just be frank with one another?"

"Yep. Fire away."

Bernard asked, "First of all. With you now having control of the world's largest private fortune, are you going to continue Will's generous ways?"

Jackson leaned back in his chair, put his hand in his pocket and jingled his change and car keys. He mulled over Bernard's question. Only he, Will, Nina, and Kirby Borg knew the specifics of Will's will. Jackson was *not* just the executor of the estate, he had inherited all of Will's assets and stock in MICROMED. Kirby handled a small trust for Nina and the children. Will loved Nina but never found her responsible with money, an area where he trusted Jackson implicitly. It was an unusual legal arrangement, and now, possibly an incriminating one.

"Bernard, as to my wanting to continue Will's generous ways as executor of his estate, yes, as long as Nina and the kids are taken care of, I'll do what I think he'd have wanted to for Palmer Lake."

"How about society in general? There's lots of problems out there that money could help solve. Why just help Palmer Lake?"

"Hell, where would I even start?" Jackson said. "Man's always been inhumane to fellow man, whether there's prosperity or poverty. Look at our own backgrounds. My ancestors are still killing each other every day in Northern Ireland. Your Ethiopian ancestors have been slaughtering each other's tribes for centuries. It seems it's always been that way. I just want to help my neighbor and see if Will's seed of goodness will grow and spread from here. I guess that's why Palmer Lake comes first."

"I get your point, but how'd you know I was of Ethiopian decent?"

"I did my due diligence."

"You must have. I thought only my mother knew that."

"I even know that your mother's name is Miniferd, but you call her Minnie," said Jackson with a grin.

"Maybe the wrong guy is the investigative reporter here." Bernard smiled back. He knew he was dealing with no fool. This man, whom he was starting to like, was a calculating thinker. And he smoked pot. He had to be alright. "When you were growing up with Will, did either of you ever dream you'd be billionaires?"

"You gotta remember, neither of us *ever* grew up. We just got older. And I'm not a billionaire, although Will was."

"Well, I did some checking around too, and I've heard you're now in complete charge of Will's monetary estate. So, you *are* a billionaire." Bernard flashed a knowing look. "Surely you realize people might consider you the ideal suspect in Nina's murder theory. People have killed for a hellava lot less than four billion dollars."

Jackson frowned. Who in his inner circle had talked? Probably no one. More likely a supposed trusted secretary somewhere along the line had opened his or her mouth. But he was starting to bond with Bernard. This was a man he could trust.

Actually, Bernard's question had haunted Jackson for the past few days. What did Papa Loo think? What did Ingrid and the twins think? What about Carl and Dixie? And the others? He could imagine the gossip at the Donut Shoppe, but he didn't care about that. Most of all, what did Nina really think?

Jackson swallowed the last of his second beer from the long-necked brown bottle. "You're right about the money and people killing one another for less than that. I know, I've been to war."

.   .   .   .

28

~.~.~.

SISSETON INDIAN RESERVATION
JUNE 7, 9:30 P. M.

A blazing bonfire lit up the black sky. Dry wood had been piled high as a tepee and spiked flames roared towards the heavens in blazing orange and blue streaks. From beneath the pile, a tiny but deadly white scorpion crabbed its way to safety under a cool obsidian rock. The reservation was surrounded by millions of milkweed plants, the sustenance of the fragile looking Monarch butterfly that flies three thousand miles from the Midwest to the mountains of Michoacan, Mexico, to breed and reproduce every year. Indians in colorful regalia danced glassy-eyed around the fire.

Drums pounded in Bernard's ears. The thumping became louder and louder. He had never attended a Pow-Wow, or Wacipi, before, but he had covered a story on the Masai in Africa and he knew these celebrations could be noisy.

Bernard saw Nina among the dancers. She was chanting and

singing around the flaming debris in a sheer, see-through feathered costume. As she hopped and weaved among the trancelike
Ghost Dancers, he could see a multi-colored tattoo of a hawk
that spread across her brown buttocks. She moved towards him.
He could almost smell her. She moved like a seductive animal,
the fire sparkling behind her, as if she were taunting him. Then
he realized she was in a trance, but so was he, and she held him
captive while she slithered through the motions of the Ghost
Dance.

Weathered old Red Cloud shuffled over to where Bernard
and Jackson were standing. He took them between his arms
and led them to a quieter area where they could share a drink
and talk.

He sat on a large chopped log, then offered a space to Bernard. Red Cloud lit up a feathered tribal pipe. "Do you understand the meaning of the Ghost Dance?"

"No, I don't know the meaning, but I've heard of the dance,"
Bernard said.

Jackson, still standing, had heard the coming tale numerous times before. "Better arm yourself with a couple of beers,
this's a long story." He handed Bernard two beers.

Bernard took a long swig of one of the warm beers. Brown-
ish fizz foamed over his hand when he set the bottle down.

"I'll start my story way back in 1889," Red Cloud settled
back into a Y of the log. "That was the year Wovoka got sick
with fever and saw a vision that our ancestors would come back
to help the Indian in their fight against white soldiers. In his
dream our warriors wore shirts they believed the soldiers bullets couldn't penetrate."

"That faith seems unbelievable today."

"It may seem unbelievable to you, but some Lakota credit
the Ghost Dance with helping them preserve our ancient reli-

gious traditions over the last century. Others have found it a workable blend of Christianity and the old religion."

"I've heard the dance was drug induced so no one would be afraid of the white man's guns," Bernard said.

"I'm a good Catholic," Red Cloud said, "but I also smoke the pipe."

Bernard gave a knowing nod of his head.

Red Cloud took a drag from his pipe. "My grandfather said that when the last of the warring plains bands had been gathered into reservations, we Indians had nothing left but our dreams. Within a few years those dreams led to a last brief conflict. Then Wovoka told everyone that an Indian Messiah was coming. He said he'd bring back the Indian dead and even the vanished buffalo, the white man would disappear, and the Indians would once more be masters of their land."

Red Cloud took another deep toke from his pipe. He offered it to Bernard.

Bernard inhaled the noisome ingredients and passed it back.

With smoke drifting around him, Red Cloud went on. "Then Wovoka called upon his followers to perform a trancelike dance called the Ghost Dance. The cult soon swept across the West and gained many followers among the Sioux. But the government, afraid of more fighting, tried to stop the dance and disarm its practitioners. At the height of all this tension, Sitting Bull was killed. Then, in 1890, a misunderstanding between soldiers and Indians waiting to surrender at Wounded Knee Creek touched off a massacre of some 300 Sioux men, women and children. But who knows if this's true."

"At least the fighting ended," said Bernard.

"As a fellow minority, you must understand, something more than the fighting ended at Wounded Knee. The Indian's spirit and hope died there, too, escaping like a puff of warm breath into the bitterly cold air of a winter day."

Bernard took a long drink of beer. He put an arm around Red Cloud's shoulder. "I'm sorry. But believe me, I understand."

Red Cloud offered him another hit from the pipe. Bernard took it, inhaled, and then handed the pipe to Jackson.

Jackson took a long drag, exhaled, and took another. That was for Will. He walked away from the crowd; he wanted to be alone for awhile.

The drums became quiet, a red fox barked in the distance, and a low hum of chanting rose from the people now bowing to the ground in front of the fire. Other than Bobby Joe, Kirby, Jake, and Pietro, there were few townsfolk among the throng. Notwithstanding Will's suspension, they had paid their respects at the Methodist church and at St. Mark's Cathedral.

Rising Coyote and Kris Catlin sulked by the fire drinking beer.

Bruno stood by, happily mumbling to himself. They didn't dare fool with him.

Stirling and Sophie were sitting quietly with some Indian children beside the fire.

Carl, Dixie, Ingrid, Woody, Freddie and Big Bertha, all keeping a respectful distance from one another, represented the immediate family.

Nina was the only one standing, her arms stretched upward, as she spoke in a quivering voice. "My people. Nothing lives long, except the earth and the mountains. You come here tonight to remember my husband and the father of my children. We thank you, but Wovoka tells me William will return soon."

Most of the bowed heads rose to look at Nina. Dozens of wide, brown eyes lit up beside the fire.

"I believe that. My children believe that," she said.

A female voice said, "We believe you, Nina. We believe Wovoka will bring William back."

A mantra of, "WOVOKA, WOVOKA, WOVOKA" from the crowd filled the cool night air.

Nina brought her arms down. Her hands were clasped together in prayer. "One of our great warriors once said, `tears unshed are stones upon the heart.' So I grieve with you until my husband returns."

Tears rolled down her cheeks and she joined the others, bowing down in optimistic hope before the fire.

Jackson had not been out to the reservation in years. Whatever was in the pipe had made his head swim. His mind floated somewhere in space. Oblivious to Red Cloud and the mourners, he picked up Bernard's small duffel bag full of golf clothes, and walked away from the pounding drums and blazing fire into the darkness of the night. Several people watched him leave. Kris Catlin sneaked after him.

Jackson could see the outline of the desolate prairie, the vastness of the land and sky, while in the distance a herd of black buffalo crested over an undulating knoll. Images of Will, Johanna and his dead son danced before him. Waving, frolicking and laughing, they appeared to be riding the bison.

Will's voice came through the mist. "I'll be back sooner than you think, Commander."

"I miss you, Daddy," came the cry of Jackson, Jr.

Johanna stood on the back of her buffalo. "I'm so sorry my darling. I loved only you."

Jackson wailed into the soft spring breeze, "Please come back with Will. I'm so lonely. I love you all so much."

A slight drizzle had dampened Jackson's hair. He shook his head. There was no clarity, only illusion. Was this just another of his nightmares, or was this a reaction from Red Cloud's pipe?

How could she have killed herself and Jackson, Jr. that cold morning on the lake? Didn't she think he could understand and forgive her affair with another man? She was young and beautiful. Good God, he'd been gone for over four years. He was supposedly dead, killed in action. Besides, it had made no difference to him that the boy was not his blood son. He loved him as his own.

On that morning he saw a canoe tip over on the lake. He didn't know that it was Johanna and Jackson, Jr. Out of neighborly concern, he called the police and started rowing out to help. It took him almost thirty minutes to reach the overturned canoe, which he quickly realized was his. There was no one on the surface and he dove under the clear water to find out what had happened. On a weed-infested bottom he saw Johanna and Jackson, Jr. lying there. His one hundred and twenty pounds of workout weights were bound and tied with yellow nylon rope around their legs. There was no sign of life.

He surfaced for air. He could hear the wailing of the police boat's siren as it raced towards the overturned canoe. He frantically waved to them, grabbed a fish knife from the bottom of his rowboat, and dove under the water again. He cut the rope from the bodies and they popped to the surface, arms splayed and face up. Gasping for air, he shot towards the underside of the canoe, only to have his thigh get hit by the propeller of the police boat. Blood spread on the surface of the lake, floating on the waves like coagulating jello around Johanna and Jackson, Jr.

She had left nothing behind except the tear-stained, wrinkled poem he had written for her engagement, her wedding rings, and a note on the bedroom dresser that said:

I'm sorry I lost faith in your being alive while you were captured and I'm sorry I lost faith in my love for you. I can't live with my shame. This was not the son I promised you. He belongs with me. But I do love you, FOREVER.

Jackson suspected George Winter knew the truth, but he never said anything to Jackson, or to anyone else. He and Leonard ruled the deaths a boating accident.

The evening mist formed perspiration on Jackson's face. Broken clouds floated by. He looked up through them at the hazy moon, and in the distance the trio on the buffalo waved goodbye as they disappeared over the horizon.

Like a lone wolf on the prairie, a howling cry of desperation came from Jackson's guts.

"JOHANNA!"

Kris Catlin was drunk and feeling sorry for himself. He had groggily watched Jackson freak out over something up on the hill. Kris laughed to himself, then walked down to a hollow and sat on the dead branch of a big sycamore tree that had been felled in a hail storm. He knew Will hadn't committed suicide, and he was sure he could get to the bottom of his hunch—then maybe a little blackmail money to put him on easy street. Kris had heard strange rumors from a buddy when Will died. He hated everything that Will stood for. The rich, lucky bastard. He was glad he had said what he did to George in the police station. Fuck what Carl Chase thought. The rich little prick. Vietnam hero. Commander of the Green Berets. Hell, Joey was the one doin' the goddamn dirty work all the time. He was the one who blew away all those gooks and saved Jackson in Nam, not Carl. An' Carl's nothing but a no good fuckin' gambler. Nothin's changed. I always get the crap. Now that shithead Palmer is goin' to inherit all that Chase bread. The stupid fuck. Standing up there in the middle of the night yellin' into the wind for his dead wife. What's he got that I don't got?

A rustle in the brush behind Catlin caught his attention. He grabbed a piece of dried wood from the ground and stood. There were lots of night predators prowling the reservation; large, big-eyed owls, rattlesnakes the thickness of a man's arm, an occasional black bear, raccoons, possums, and the ever present coyote. He threw the wood in the direction of the noise. "Fuckin' critter, ya ain't scarin' me."

The wood landed harmlessly in the brush and the vast prairie became still. The night noises momentarily disappeared. With his head spinning from too much beer, Catlin went to sit down. As his butt hit the oak log, a thin rope quickly came over his frizzy hair and tightened on his throat. A gloved pair of hands squeezed the noose, while a knee was braced inside his back. Catlin was then yanked back, his bell-bottom trousers flailing as he kicked his new Nikes in the air at his attacker. He tried to fight. His eyeballs popped out and his mouth made gurgling sounds, but the killer was strong. The rope made cutting sounds. Whoever this was had done it before. Gagging, his head flipped backwards, Catlin recognized his assailant. He tried to call out a name, but nothing but a gasping sound came from his mouth.

Catlin was dead within minutes.

Before the sun rose, the fire ants had attacked the corpse. They liked the soft flesh around the eyes, ears, mouth, and anus.

PALMER LAKE
MIDNIGHT

The telephone rang softly four times. A gloved hand reached out and turned down the T.V. On CNN a muted rerun of a Larry King interview with Sean Connery kept playing. A citizens band radio tuned to the Palmer Lake police frequency buzzed static in the background. The telephone rang two more times before the gloved hand put down a steaming cup of coffee and picked up the receiver. A nervous voice said in a whisper, "Commander, I know you said not to call 'cept for 'mergencies, but I can't find my fatigue jacket nowhere. I'm worried."

The recipient of the call answered, "Don't worry. I took care of it for you. Now, I repeat for the last time. Don't ever call here again or I'll freeze you like Will and you'll never come back."

The line went dead before the caller had time to respond.

.   .   .   .

29

JUNE 8th
11:00 A.M.
THE MINESHAFT
PALMER LAKE AIRPORT

A huge metal crane hung over the mineshaft where Joey Gabrelli's plane had crashed. It looked like a hundred foot tall tinker-toy with a long wire cable and a giant bucket attached to it. The crane's operator had removed tons of crushed granite from the shaft over the past couple of days. He hopped out of the machine and carrying a rolled up map, approached George Winter.

"Chief, we've gone as far as we can," said the crane operator. "There ain't no body down there. Only a burnt out hull of the plane. And when we pulled it out, the sides of the shaft collapsed again to cover where we was. I want you to take a look at this map of the mine and the tunnels leading away from it and see if you agree with what we think happened."

George spread the map over the hood of the police car. The yellowed mining map was dated 1888. "Holy balls, from what I think you're saying, is that punk Joey's body somehow got pushed out of the plane and it's now buried in one of these tunnels."

"Yes sir, that's what we think. But there's no way to get it and there ain't no way in any of them tunnels after the sides of the mineshaft collapsed. There's tons of rock that's buried every goddamn one of `em. Besides, according to this here map, there ain't one of them tunnels that goes anywhere. They're all dead end!"

George tilted his cap back and took one last look at the gaping hole in the ground. "Tell your boys that it's too dangerous to go any further," he said. "I guess Danny was right, any evidence we might have found on Joey is buried there forever."

1:30 P.M.
IZOR LIFE EXTENSION FOUNDATION
MANKOTO, MINNESOTA

The city of Mankato was experiencing a tornado watch. The sky was a dark, grey pewter and the atmosphere was still and sticky. Twisters tore through the Minnesota plains with great regularity during the early summer when the cold Canadian fronts met the hot, humid, cumulus clouds being blown in from the south.

After a choppy flight, Jackson, Bernard, and Nina were happy to have the MICROMED King Air turboprop land safely at the airport. A black Cadillac limousine waited for them on the tarmac. The chauffeur sped through the countryside trying to get them to their destination before the storm. Within twenty minutes he was at the entrance of the Izor Foundation. They stepped from the limo into air charged with energy. Flowering purple hydrangeas glowed eerily against the side of the building. Flashing streaks of lightning blasted into the earth nearby.

Jackson thought they were much too close for comfort, plus he was still queasy from last night's pow-wow.

Peter Sayers held open a glass door and welcomed them. "Come on in before the bad weather hits. Kary and Neville are waiting for us in the basement."

Thunder boomed and vibrated within the building. Hail and silvery sheets of rain suddenly started pouring from the sky.

"The basement sounds like the safest place to be," Nina said nervously. "Where're the stairs?"

Bernard forced a laugh. "Isn't it odd that tornados seem to avoid downtowns but love suburbs and mobile homes?"

"I think it's more of a fact," Jackson said. "And, might I point out, we're in the suburbs and we just passed two mobile home parks on the way here. Let's get hustling."

"Follow me." Sayers led them down three steep flights of stairs into the bowels of the foundation's storage and preparation area.

They entered a spacious cavern surrounded by stainless steel railings. Below, in the center of the room, prep vats and dewars emitted steaming vapors, and the air smelled sterile. White-overalled workers dollied tanks of liquid nitrogen through the corridors. Sounds of whirring equipment echoed from the walls. They gazed down upon fifty huge containers—each housed three suspended people—a hundred and fifty hopeful souls.

Nina had a tormented look on her face. She knew Will was in one of the dewars, his sarcophagus until he returned to her one day in the future. Her eyes teared and she grabbed Jackson's arm and clutched it.

Before Jackson could say anything, Kary Duesmann popped out from an office door. His white smock was food stained, his beard tobacco stained, and his unlit pipe was hung upside down from his mouth. "Glad you made it," he said. "We were getting a little worried. Come on in."

Duesmann and Cruickshank's private laboratory was enormous, at least three thousand square feet. The ceiling was twenty feet high with hundreds of mercury vapor lights. Hypofilters hummed and quietly purified the room. Exotic machines, dripping with wires, made groaning sounds, and blinking bulbs of yellow, green, red, and blue popped on and off periodically. Bunsen burners cooked chemicals that emitted an odor smelling strangely like Lysol. The south wall contained a scientific library, and in a connecting room to the rear, a dog whined.

Jan Elton sat at a long rectangular metal table in the center of the main lab. Coffee, juices, fruits, toast, and sweet rolls were laid out on the table. Jan gave Bernard an inviting smile and extended her hand. "Nice to see you again, Bernie."

"Thanks, you too. Are we going to have some brunch while we discuss what we came over for?"

"Yes. Help yourself."

The entire group sat around the table and started polite conversation, everyone being careful not to say anything that would offend Nina. Jan passed around the sweet rolls and toast.

Neatly turned out in a blue blazer with matching polka dot tie and hankie, ever the reporter, Bernard asked, "How long before the tornado hits, or if it doesn't, when do they lift the alert?"

Cruickshank scratched his scalp through his wiry hair. "We've never had a tornado chock-a-block this area before. But they buried the dewars and us underground with our machinery just in case. Usually the alert lasts for less than two hours."

"Did you have a comfortable flight over?" Jan asked Nina.

"A bit bumpy, but thanks for asking." Nina was pouring Jackson steaming coffee from a metal pot.

Jackson took a sip of the dark brew. He hated small talk. Nina *knew* the flight had been a nightmare. Damn, why couldn't people just say what they felt? He put his cup down. "How about we get started. We're here for a couple of reasons. One, to find out just how far advanced cryonics is today and what Will knew about that. Two, Nina has a theory that her husband was murdered and didn't commit suicide."

Sayers looked over at Jan for help. She stared back at him. Sayers began, "First of all, Kary and Neville can bring you up to date on cryonics and their personal relationship with Will. If there is any part of the perfusion procedure you want to see, you may, for as you know, we film every suspension; although it's unusual for the family survivors to want to watch it."

Everyone at the table was silent and they could see Sayers struggling with what he wanted to say next. Finally he spoke. "The thought of anything but suicide is, I respectfully say, preposterous. We examined Will and filmed—"

"But Wovo—" Nina started to say.

"Why don't we let him finish what he has to say," Jackson said. He knew she was fuming inside. But he hoped she could be patient.

Nina gave him a dirty look.

Sayers started again. "I know this is difficult, Mrs. Chase, however, we not only filmed every bit of the suspension and perfusion for your or any authorities' benefit, but there was not one single physical sign that would indicate anything but suicide. I'm sorry."

Once again, everyone at the table looked at one another in silence.

Then Bernard said, "Nina, I was there too. My crew videoed every step of the suspension procedure. There were at least six to eight professionals working on your husband at all times. No one ever said anything but suicide was possible. Do you have any other proof?"

"Yes, I do," Nina said. "The strongest proof possible—a woman's intuition. There were so many people jealous of him.

No one in Palmer Lake thinks he committed suicide, only the professionals."

Jan put her half-eaten apple down on the table. "Mrs. Chase, that's not entirely true. We have a police report and Doctors Bookner and Tragus both signed the death certificate as a suicide."

"They're just like you here at the Foundation, they're professionals. You all have your own reasons for suicide. You see this in a way to help your own causes, not from any other viewpoint." Nina's eyes were misting again and her hair was falling over her face. She combed it back with her hand. "Can't you see that William had no reason to kill himself? We were so much in love. And Stirling and Sophie. He lived for those kids. Please believe me, my husband was murdered and I'm going to prove that."

As sympathetic as everyone at the table was, clearly no one from the Foundation believed her. However, this *was* the benefactor's wife; she couldn't be easily dismissed.

Cruickshank, who had seen plenty of his own apparitions in his past drug life, said, "I understand your intuitions, Mrs. Chase. Is there anything scientifically we could show you that would put your mind to ease regarding our belief in Will's suicide?"

"I don't want to look at the suspension being filmed, if that's what you mean."

Duesmann laid his pipe into a ceramic holder. He handed Nina a two-inch stack of papers encased in a manila portfolio. "The film isn't necessary to watch, but I'd like you to take copies of the county coroner's report, the police report, and our medical reports on the suspension and perfusion procedure. Read them tonight and call me tomorrow if you have any questions."

"I'd like to do that," Nina said softly. "Do you think I could tour the Foundation while I'm here today?"

"Absolutely. We could spend the balance of the day showing you the facilities."

Nina puffed the lustrous scarlet hankie in the pocket of her black pants suit. With a quick twist of her head, she threw her mane of hair back over her right shoulder, then said, "I'd like to see where William is now."

Sayers wiped his brow with the back of his hand and stood. "Jan and I can arrange that. Where the dewars are located is a bit cramped for space, so possibly Jackson and Bernie could stay here and talk with Kary and Neville."

Jackson said, "Let's do that."

Bernard walked the trio to the door.

.   .   .   .

30
~.~.~.

JUNE 8
IMB CRYOGENIC RESEARCH LAB
ZÜRICH, SWITZERLAND

It had been a draining work day. Ralf Verson had worked from eight in the morning until late evening. There were still so many questions that he wanted answered regarding Jutta Kell's mysterious revival. He was dozing face down at his lab desk when he heard the sound of knocking. Groggily, he got up and walked over to the entrance of the lab and opened the door. No one was there. He looked down the hall. Maybe one of the night janitors was playing a prank on him. Verson returned to his desk and gathered his papers into his briefcase. He was exhausted.

The knocking started again. The noise rang like metal. It was coming from the far side of the room. It sounded as if it came from the new dewar Jutta was in. Chills shot down Verson's spine. The red night light in the lab was dim. He slowly walked around the dewar and peeked into the Plexiglas window. Jutta was frozen as solid as a piece of stone. She was also smiling and one arm was banging on the side on the stainless steel pod.

Verson fell to his knees. Her arm was moving. The knocking continued. My God, what was he witnessing? This was beyond comprehension. He knew what he had to do. He struggled up and wobbled to his desk. He retrieved his Polaroid camera and took four quick pictures of Jutta. Then he picked up the telephone and dialed Hartmut Kell's home number.

.   .   .   .

31
~:~:~:

IZOR FOUNDATION
2:30 P.M.

Jackson jumped right to the point, and said to Duesmann and Cruicksank, "As I'm now in charge of the future of this Foundation, I need all of the help I can get regarding Will's death."

Duesmann and Cruickshank glanced knowingly at each other.

"I promised to find out for Nina if there was any possibility of murder, and to learn as much as possible about cryonics and what Will knew that I didn't. So—do either of you feel there's any chance whatsoever that Will was murdered?"

Duesmann relit his pipe. "None that I could see. How about you, Neville?"

"Anything's possible, mate. But unless I'm shown something concrete regarding this issue, it's more than remote. You see, Will spent a considerable amount of time with us trying to find out just how soon he could be revived if he were to die young. He studied everything. He even took medication to help preserve his brain tissue."

"You mean that horrible tasting mannitol gum?"

"Yes, among other things," Duesmann said. "And he always wanted the latest update on what might help preserve tissue. In fact, he seemed obsessed with being suspended one day and his obsession grew when he saw the results we've gotten recently reviving animals. He came at least twice a month to be updated. But we just thought it was out of curiosity, not out of his wanting to be the first to be revived using cryonics."

"Do you mean to tell me you both think Will might have actually committed suicide so he could be the first human to be revived?" Bernard said. He knew this could be a major story.

"I want you two to think about this for a minute." Duesmann fondled his dirty beard with his left hand. "It wasn't that long ago that men, and I'm talking about good family men with kids, were lined up to sacrifice themselves to space travel. They had no idea if it was suicidal or not. They wanted to be the first to do it. Time meant nothing, they spent their entire lives devoted to finding out the unknown, then strapped their healthy bodies into a cramped metal space capsule to be shot off into space, knowing full well the dangers of never returning. They wanted to be the first on the moon. The first to come back to Earth from somewhere else. The first to experience it. And don't forget the glory they received. With that in mind, it's not so far-fetched that Will did this purposefully. But only time and Will can tell us that."

Bernard asked, "How much time do you think that would be?"

"It's sooner than you think," said Cruickshank. He grinned and winked at Duesmann, then sighed, "Sooner than you think."

Knowing Will as he did, Jackson was becoming convinced

this was a purposeful act on his friend's part. "Could you bring Bernard and me up to date on your work with cryonics?"

Duesmann's and Cruickshank's faces lit up.

Cruickshank said, "It'd be a pleasure. Come on in the back room and meet Elvis Presley."

As they walked to the back lab Jackson and Bernard didn't know what to expect. Secretly, Jackson hoped that they had dug up some DNA and reproduced one of his favorite entertainers. But he wasn't about to admit that.

Duesmann walked them to Elvis's cage.

Cruickshank opened the locked door to let the beagle out into the lab. "Come on out, matey." He bent down and petted the wiggling dog. "Here's Elvis, the first large mammal ever revived from being completely frozen in liquid nitrogen.

"You mean to say this dog was suspended just like Will is now?" Jackson said.

"Yes. But the whole thing was an accident. Elvis is my dog and he fell in Kary's liquid nitrogen vat last year. Kary revived him only a couple of months ago. When it happened, he videoed all of the revival process, and of course, showed it to Will. We can show you the same results if you like."

"Can we start today?" said Jackson. "Bernard has to get back to New York tomorrow."

"We can," Duesmann said. "But, Bernie, as a newsman you'll have to sign a waiver of confidentiality. We keep them on hand. You know, lab secrets and all that." He dug in his desk drawer and handed Bernard a document and a ballpoint.

"It's against everything I've been taught, but I'll do about anything to find out more." Bernard signed the paper with a Hancock flair.

Elvis, in his excitement at being released, knocked over a large, empty beaker sitting on a work table. It was plastic and it bounced on to the floor in every direction like a punted football. Scared, the dog ran back into the protection of his wire cage. Cruicksank reached in, patted Elvis gently and then replaced the lock-bolt on the door.

Duesmann tapped the burnt contents of his pipe into a dirty ashtray. He looked over at Jackson and asked, "Where would you like to start?"

"Let's work backwards with the dog's suspension."

Back in the main laboratory, Cruickshank set up a large screen and they watched Elvis' revival.

Jackson could see that he had been frozen solid before being revived. The video held him spellbound.

Bernard shifted gears into the reporter mode. "How normal is the animal now?"

"His tissue is completely normal and his memory appears intact," said Duesmann. "But due to possible ischemic injury during the freezing process, we won't know for some time whether his long term memory has been affected."

Cruickshank was fiddling with his frayed collar. "You must understand that the damage most commonly associated with freezing is that caused by ice."

"You mean like when water pipes explode in the winter?" Bernard asked.

"Bloody well not," Cruicksank said. "Contrary to common belief, freezing doesn't cause cells to burst open like pipes in the winter. Quite the opposite, ice formation takes place outside the cells in the extracellular region."

"What Neville is getting at is that present evidence supports but doesn't prove the hypothesis that memory loss doesn't occur for at least a few hours following the onset of ischemia, which means maybe we can save long-term memory with present day suspension methods," said Duesmann.

Bernard looked up at Duesmann. "Meaning if you freeze people soon enough after they die, then they'll save their memory?"

Jackson was deep in thought. He pushed his fingers against one another like two five-legged spiders making love. He asked, "Did Will know all of this?"

"Absolutely," Duesmann said. "Being trained as a physician all those years ago, he was as informed about cryonics as any individual I've ever met."

Cruickshank added, "Will once told me that if human memory is stored in a physical form that is obliterated by freezing, then cryonics suspension won't work."

"So why would he commit suicide if he thought he might return without a memory?" asked Jackson.

"In layman's language we told Will that his tissues could be restored to normalcy and that he could retain his memory if frozen," Cruickshank said. "We showed him Kary's assembler, which should be able to restore damaged tissue of any kind. And Will was frightfully aware that freezing wouldn't cause him to lose his memory."

Nina's theory of a premeditated killer appeared less and less of a possibility as the conversation went on. Jackson asked, "Kary, do you really think Will did this on purpose?"

"Without implying that we had anything to do with this act, yes, I think he did." Duesmann fidgeted with glasses and smock. Jackson and Bernard stared at him.

"Will's quite a dreamer," Duesmann said. "Look at what he accomplished so far in life. He's a real visionary. He understands that future molecular repair is right around the corner."

Jackson limped as he moved closer to the two scientists. That damn leg. He leaned on the corner of a desk. "How about you give us a rundown on what you know, and of course what Will knew, about actually coming back to life."

"Sure," Cruickshank said. "I know this must be shocking for you because you knew Will better than we did. But use Kary's earlier analogy—treat this act of Will's as a form of space travel, a personal and spiritual search for knowledge, one where he's on a long journey and he'll be returning to friends and loved ones when the proper technological spacecraft can bring him back to Earth. A lorry in the sky, as it were."

"Do you have a name for your spacecraft?"

"We call it nanotechnology."

Bernard smoothed his jacket lapels. "Any chance you could show us some of this technology?"

"Just wait until you see Kary's ETM," Cruicksank said. "This machine can fabricate materials according to complex atomic specifications. Unlike the simple static materials used in technology today, materials engineered by Kary's ETM in full molecular detail could incorporate a myriad of active microscopic components. These components, like cells in living tissue, could confer novel properties to materials, such as muscle-like movement, self-renewal, and even abilities to metamorphose."

"Not so fast, Neville," Duesmann said. "I think I'd better explain the synthetic arthropoda perfusate process I'm working on that had Will so fascinated. Then we can show them the ETM."

"Is Neville saying you could not only revive someone one day, but also solve a paraplegic's problem by rebuilding his system?" Jackson said.

"It won't be long before people won't have to be crippled for the rest of their lives, and of course, short of being brain dead, they'll be able to be revived from what we now know as death." Duesmann tapped his pipe in his hand. "Come on over to my work area where I can give you a demonstration."

Down below in the storage area, Jan hugged Nina as they viewed the container Will was suspended in. Nina had gone to the limo and retrieved a potted geranium plant with bright red blooms, which she placed at the base of Will's dewar. It was his favorite flower. He had once told her that the plant needed little care, could tolerate most any hardship, and still survive—just like him.

Other than the hissing vapors and the whirring of the equipment, there was silence.

Nina prayed to Wovoka, not Jesus Christ.

.   .   .

4:00 P.M.

The ETM machine crackled as it spit blue-green streaks of piezoelectric crystals within its glass cage. A white lab rat lay dead inside the machine on a metal table. Jackson and Bernard watched the fiery display.

Holding a 50 cc syringe filled with liquid, Duesmann said, "I'll let the ETM warm up while I explain my synthetic arthropoda perfusate." He pushed in the plunger of the syringe with his thumb and a thick, pink fluid sprayed in the air. "A perfusionist like Jan Elton injects this fluid into the body of the patient, or in this case as we already have with the rat in the machine who's died from carbon monoxide poisoning. It's nothing more than an antifreeze for the body during suspension, similar to the *Prestone* you put into the radiator of your car to protect it in the subfreezing temperatures in the winter. I'd like you to know, my perfusate seems to work better than anything science has come up with so far."

"Did it work on Elvis?" asked Bernard.

"Good question. We found no freezing damage to Elvis' tissue when I used it after his accidental suspension. Nor have we found any damage to any other subjects we've used it with."

"Did you use this perfusate when you suspended Will?" asked Jackson.

"You betcha," Cruickshank said with his proper British diction. "When Will arrived here we replaced the glycerol cryo-protective fluid that Jan had perfused into him over at Palmer Lake with Kary's synthetic perfusate."

Bernard unloosened his tie. "So what you're saying is that science is closer than we think to reviving someone that's been suspended?"

"A lot closer than anyone can imagine, Bernie, which you and Jackson will see when I show you how the ETM works. But we're here to discuss Will, so let's use him as an example."

Duesmann opened a small cellophane bag of salted Planters peanuts with his yellowed teeth. Without offering any to the others, he emptied the contents of the bag into his mouth. A few pieces lodged in his beard and he kept talking with his mouth full. "Will wanted to know the most efficient way for a person to die and be revived. He wondered what it would be like to come back the same age as his children. And of course, what an older Nina would think of him. I told him that was an emotional judgment I didn't think his kids would have a problem with, however, his wife was another story and one we felt he had to discuss with her. I also told him drowning in icy water at a young age would be ideal for suspension. But he told me he wouldn't choose that because of personal reasons."

Jackson knew what those reasons were. "Did he ever imply that dying from carbon monoxide might be close to drowning in ice water?"

"In hindsight, I think he did."

Murder was the furthest thing from Jackson's mind at the moment. What could Nina be thinking? He said, "It's now 1987, less than twenty years after we've sent men to the moon and retrieved them. I know science is moving quickly, but in all honesty, how soon do you think you can revive a human from suspension?"

Cruickshank said, "In my opinion we'll be able to do it around—"

"One second, Neville," Duesmann said. "Jackson should know there are huge moral, religious, and legal obstacles we have to overcome before such a revival can take place, or even be attempted."

"I'm aware of that," Jackson said. "All I want to know is, with all the obstacles aside, what's your personal belief in the ability of science to revive a human being after being suspended in ideal conditions?"

Duesmann wiped his palms on his lab jacket. "I calculate in around twenty years."

Jackson pondered if it were possible Will could be the first subject. Jackson would then be sixty-three, and oddly, Will would still be forty-three.

Bernard wondered where he would be in twenty years.

"Kary, the ETM is ready," Cruickshank said. "Let's show them just how far advanced we are."

"Okay." Duesmann inserted his hands into two gloves that protruded into the machine, and started manipulating two levers over the body of the lab rat. The metal tips zapped voltage through the rat onto the surface plate of the machine. "This is the most remarkable tool in the microtechnology arsenal today. It can accomplish in a single step what science assumed would require a lengthy series of developments."

"Do you mean to tell me this machine can clone that rat?" Bernard said.

"No, that's another side of medicine where one grows a single body cell of its parent that's genetically identical to the parent," Duesmann said. "My ETM can repair cells and rebuild tissue to an original or pristine stage. It can literally bring one back to life. Watch what it does to this animal."

Jackson was now caught up in what he was hearing. He knew

what Leonard had told him caused Will's death. "Can you re-pair damage done to that rat's lungs and brain?"

"I believe the potential of cell repair technology is so vast that it might be easier to ask whether there's anything that this technology couldn't fix," said Duesmann.

Cruickshank added his two cents. "Not only can Kary's ETM see individual atoms, it can also physically manipulate them. In-deed, it'll provide a vehicle by which engineers can both perform and monitor construction tasks involving even single atoms."

Duesmann again ran the metal tips slowly over the entire body of the rat. The rat moved. It twitched and opened its pink eyes. It tried to stand, fell, and then stood on wobbly legs.

"Did I just witness some sort of trick or a miracle?" Bernard asked.

"What is before your eyes is the future of medicine and of mankind," Cruickshank said.

His excitement palpable, Jackson asked, "Can this machine repair the damage done to Will?"

Duesmann looked up at Jackson and Bernard while remov-ing his hands from the machine. He coughed and held onto his belly with two hands like a pregnant woman does at eight months. "Yes and no. It's possible to imagine instances of repair so extensive that the healed patient would no longer be the original patient. Specifically, this will occur when injuries be-gin to impinge on a patient's brain. Although my cell repair technology appears capable of reversing any injury, it won't be able to restore brain information lost during injury."

"So what happens if someone you revive can't remember anything?" Bernard asked.

"In my estimation brain information loss will pose a funda-mental limitation for future medicine, and the ultimate divid-ing line between life and death. To answer your question, he'd be dead."

"So how do you know if Will suffered any brain damage?" Jackson asked.

"It can't be known. But as long as some brain structure remains, it'll always be possible to reconstruct a patient's brain and body on the basis of persisting information. Remember, Will was placed in biostasis only a few days ago."

"What's that?" Jackson asked.

"It's a condition in which an organism's cell and tissue structures are preserved, allowing later restoration by cell repair machines," said Duesmann, "It's similar to anesthesia when operating on a patient. Anesthesia interrupts consciousness without disrupting the structure of the brain, and biostasis procedures must do the same, but for a longer period of time."

Bernard was taking notes on a little pad. "In a case like Will, what kind of success do you think you might have?'

"We won't know for some time, but the success of such reconstruction on a patient like Will would depend on how much memory and personality could be salvaged by the repair process," said Duesmann, "But just know that biostasis is only an interruption of life, not an end to it."

"So Will may not be dead as we know it and we can hold out hope he'll return?"

"Maybe."

"Are you saying he knew everything about your ETM and research work?" Jackson asked.

"Yes, he knew of my cell repair technology. But most important, he knew the basic structure of his brain would still be intact because of the carbon monoxide poisoning, and he also knew cell repair devices could be deployed throughout the body to repair cellular injuries caused by the hours of absent blood flow."

"In other words, there's no question in your mind that this was anything but a suicide and one day you might revive him?"

"No doubt in my mind whatsoever," said Duesmann, "One day in the future, I feel that after several days of repairs conducted at deep hypothermic temperatures, staged restart of metabolism could be performed by selective unblocking of metabolic enzymes as Will is warmed. He'd then emerge from his coma in perfect health, with perhaps mild amnesia as the only remnant of what had happened."

.　　.　　.　　.

32

ىىى

SISSETON INDIAN RESERVATION
2:30 P.M.

George Winter had received a telephone call regarding a dead body being found out at the reservation. Leonard Bookner picked him up in the coroner's wagon so they could examine the evidence and bring back the body. As much as George would have liked to use the siren on his squad car and go blasting out there, death meant there was no necessity.

Leonard picked up George within thirty minutes. As George got into the van, Leonard said, "What a lovely azure sky. Too bad whomever we're going to pick up can't luxuriate in it."

George slammed the door. "You're a bald, wordy snob, do you know that, Lenny."

"Just remember, the more hair I lose, the more head I get."

George laughed. He wondered if Leonard finally wanted to come out of the closet. "I'm sure *that's* true. Come on, let's jus' git goin'."

Leonard drove out of the Palmer Lake city limits.

"We haven't had a murder here in over ten years an' now there might be two in a matter of weeks," George said. "What'n hell is goin' on?"

"For God's sake, Will wasn't murdered. I'm sure this unknown body can be explained."

"You got an answer for everythin', Mr. Edjewcation." George checked his teeth in the overhead visor mirror.

The van's tires droned on the pavement as they slowly made their way further into the plains.

After about ten miles Leonard pulled the black wagon off the highway and into a rutted, two-tire marked path. Prairie grass grew up the center of the path and it pinged on the oil pan of the van. They drove a mile up and down the rolling knolls, stopping in a tree-laden hollow where eight Indian men stood around a blanketed body. A quintet of black turkey vultures roosted optimistically in a dead cottonwood nearby.

One of the men walked over to the van and said, "It's Kris Catlin, Chief."

George and Leonard walked over to the body. George grunted as he bent down. He lifted the multi-colored blanket. "Well, I'll be damned. Who did society a favor an' killed this creep?"

Leonard sat on one knee and superficially checked the dead man. After a second, he recoiled back in a knee-jerk reaction. "Good God. He's been garroted."

"What? Who the hell kills anybody that way but the Mafia."

A pair of noisy blue jays squawked in the scrub brush.

One of the Indians said, "They taught us that in Nam, man."

George quickly turned around. "Are you telling me that this was a common way of killin' the enemy in Vietnam?"

"Yeah, man. It was taught in survival training so you wouldn't get captured."

George looked at the crowd of men and bit his lip for a second while he thought. He hitched up his polyester issue pants with a tug. "Look, I appreciate you guys callin' me, but Lenny an' I need to examine the body an' any evidence left here by ourselves. You'll have to leave. Did any of you move anythin' or take anythin'?"

In harmony the group answered, "Nope."

As the Indians walked away Leonard said to George, "Look at this, there's a little saprophytic matter growing on his forehead."

George removed the quilt from the rest of the body. "I can't see anythin' but a little mold. Is that what you mean?"

"Yes."

"Lenny, I keep tellin' you. Stop it with the Greek, will you? Just say the creep is rottin' around the head. I'll understand."

"It's Latin, and I can't help it if your entire education took place in the back seat of a car, *homme moyen sensuel*."

"If that's a put down, go screw yourself." George started wrapping the blanket around the body. He noticed Catlin's clothes were the same that Danny said Joey Gabrelli had been wearing on the day he died—a military fatigue jacket and new Nike basketball shoes—plus Catlin had big feet, also like Joey, and both had a motive to kill Will Chase. "Lenny, somethin' don't smell right in the kitchen. I think someone's tryin' to mislead us."

"What an imagination you've got. This body has nothing whatsoever to do with anything."

George noticed the fatigue jacket had a hole in the upper right shoulder. He didn't say anything to Leonard. He would remove the jacket once they got to the morgue.

The air moved just enough to bend the spacious, green fields of spring wheat. The only sign of humanity was four silver-topped grain silos on a distant knoll. Red ants were crawling everywhere as Leonard and George put Catlin in a bodybag.

.   .   .   .

33

JUNE 8, 10:15 P.M.
HARTMUT KELL'S RESIDENCE
ZÜRICH, SWITZERLAND

After Verson's phone call, Hartmut sent his driver to fetch him. Now Verson sat across from Hartmut in the latter's study with cups of black coffee. Verson's hands shook so badly he couldn't add cream to his cup. He hardly knew where to begin. "Herr Kell, a while back, Jutta came back to life for a short time."

Disbelief came over Hartmut's face. Tears welled up in his eyes. "Please, what you are saying sounds crazy. What are you telling me?"

"It's true. I can't explain it to you medically. I can only tell you what happened and that the Director covered it up. I also lied to you, too. I'm sorry."

Verson then told the incredulous Hartmut the bizarre tale of what had transpired on June 4th.

"I knew someone was not telling the truth, but I did not know why," Hartmut said. "I beg of you, give me every detail of tonight. This is the dream I have been waiting for."

Verson showed Hartmut the Polaroid pictures.

"See how she's smiling and her arm is against the pod? Whereas in the second photo it's half way to her side and by the fourth photo it's back at the side of her body. I'm telling you, Herr Kell, she was knocking a message on the side of the dewar."

"If this is true, we must return to the laboratory. We can take my car."

They cut through he center of town. There was barely a soul driving on the Bahnhofstrasse and they made it to the laboratory research center at close to midnight. The security guard duly noted the lateness of the hour on his time sheet, but with Verson's unrestricted pass, he had to let the two men into the building.

They rushed to the storage lab containing Jutta's dewar. Other than a dripping water faucet, there was not a sound to be heard. They both peered into the Plexiglas of the pod. Jutta no longer had a smile on her face, nor were her arms anything but frozen to her sides.

Verson broke the silence. "I don't know what to say, Herr Kell. You saw the photos. This's similar to when I found her the first time and she'd written you the message. First she was alive, then when we tried to remove her, she was no longer living."

Hartmut looked bitterly disappointed. "It's okay, Dr. Verson. You have given me hope, where I had none. I'll contact the director here at the lab after I call the Izor Foundation. I'll see if I can get Jutta transferred over to their facilities."

"Herr Kell, please, I don't want to lose my job."

"I assure you, you will not. As long as Jutta is in this laboratory, you will be employed here. And if there is any further movement or life witnessed by you, call me on this cellular number as quickly as you can."

.   .   .   .

34

10:00 A.M., JUNE 11, 1987
PALMER LAKE, SOUTH DAKOTA

Every day since Catlin's murder George had examined the military fatigue jacket with the hole in the shoulder. The torn patch of material from Ingrid's garage matched the hole in Catlin's jacket perfectly. Yet the jacket had been many sizes too big for Catlin. The jacket was big enough to fit Big Bertha, or Bruno for that matter, but neither one of those two had ever been in the military. It must have been somebody else's jacket, perhaps someone who had put it on Catlin after he was garroted. Who? Why?

George had heard rumors at the Donut Shoppe that Jackson and Nina had returned from their trek to Mankato. What were they chasing that pipedream for anyway? It was nuts. George figured the odds of Will ever coming back were about the same as Brigitte Bardot showing up in P.L. and giving him a quick fuck. Fat chance. He decided to give them both a surprise call in person. He hopped in the black and white squad car and headed first for Jackson's penthouse.

Nina, Leonard, and Jackson were sitting quietly in his living room looking out at the lake and St. Mark's Cathedral. The water was cerulean and calm. "Bruno's Beacon" was still twinkling in the sun on the steeple of the church.

Jackson broke the silence. "You've got to accept facts, Nina. Will did this act on purpose, and for some reason didn't want to tell us. Lenny and Doc Tragus concur with me. Maybe you should call Dr. Duesmann and have him explain to you what he thinks happened, the way he did to me and Bernard."

Nina smoothed the front of her long linen dress. She slowly turned the wedding ring on her finger, the gems glittering in the bright morning light, then looked Jackson in the eye. "I don't need to call anyone. I know in my heart William didn't do this on purpose. I don't care what any of you think. I'm going to find out who did this whether you help me or not."

"Come on," Leonard said. "You're not being rational. We're only trying to make this easier on you."

The intercom buzzed loudly next to Jackson. He spoke into the speaker plate. "Who is it?"

"It's George. Mind if I pop up and talk to you for a minute?"

"Not at all. Nina and Lenny are here. Come on up and we can all have a cup of tea."

"Sounds good. I'll be right up."

George entered the room with a broad smile. He removed his cap. His uniform was freshly pressed, his snakeskin and leather cowboy boots shined, and his white shirt was for once unwrinkled. He had a chaw of Copenhagen chewing tobacco stuffed between his lower gum and teeth. He chewed only when he was nervous—and today he was plenty nervous. "I'm sure glad you're all here. It saves me a trip to your places."

Balthasar's big, black head peeked over the top of the window on the balcony. He shook his ears and returned to his snooze on the warm terrace.

In the kitchen Jackson removed the plaid tea cozy Nina had given him for Christmas from a porcelain Chinese pot. He poured George a steaming cup of Ceylonese Darjeeling tea. "What can we help you with?"

George ignored the silver serving tongs and with his fingers dropped four cubes of sugar into the black tea. He turned his back to the group, and with his tongue, deposited his wet chaw into an ashtray. "Well, it's kinda personal, Jackson."

"I'm glad you're here, George," Nina said. "These two don't want to hear a thing about our thinking William might have been murdered. Why don't you try talking to them?"

Leonard sat on the couch, legs crossed. "Yes, Monsieur Poirot, why don't you give Jackson and me your newest theory on Will's murder?"

George glared at Leonard, then at Jackson. He decided to act calm. He said, "I guess Lenny's told you that we found Kris Catlin murdered out on the reservation."

Nina walked around the counter and stood next to Jackson. She restlessly ran her hand through her hair.

Jackson took a sip of tea. He glanced at the brown dregs in the bottom of the cup. They didn't tell him anything. "Yep, he told us. But how does that have anything to do with Will's suicide?"

"I think whoever killed Will also murdered Kris Catlin. I got to figure out who an' why."

Leonard stood up from the sofa. The small, blue veins in his temples showed. "Chief, I've no idea if you're drinking again, or if those kids at the wrestling classes over at the high school are squeezing your head too hard, but Will wasn't murdered, he suspended himself on purpose. Jackson told me what's going on over at the cryonics foundation and he doesn't believe there's any chance Will was murdered. Isn't that right, Jackson?"

Jackson nodded in agreement, then put his hand out to Nina, she took it and gave it a squeeze, but he aimed his answer at George. "I found out things in Mankato that can only lead me to believe Will did this act on purpose."

Nina let go of his grip. "But why?"

"They believe he wanted to be the first person to be revived from suspension. To explore the unknown. To be the first to take such a journey, like the astronauts. All the things that drove Will to be the person he was."

"Oh, come on. He loved life too much to take such a chance."

"That's my point," Jackson said. "I think life is a series of calculated risks especially if you want to be a winner like Will was. I know it's hard to comprehend, Nina, but everything he did was hard to fathom. The scientists over at Izor explained things so rationally and implied that Will was eager to be suspended. Even asking about your and the kids' feelings when he came back."

Like a blindfolded child with a stick waiting to club a piñata, George blurted to Jackson, "Could you tell me where you disappeared to the night of Will's memorial service? People told me you left early on foot carryin' a little black bag. That you walked right out into the reservation by yourself."

"I did. I had to get away from everybody that night."

"You got any witnesses to where you went?"

"No, I don't. What is this, George, am I a suspect in killing Kris Catlin or something?"

"Right now I don't know who's a suspect an' who ain't. I got the town folk askin' some tough questions."

Leonard asked, "Like what?"

"Like what was in that little black bag?"

Jackson flushed deep red. "This is ridiculous, George, that was just Bernard Grable's dirty golf clothes."

George shot back like a machine gun, "I'll tell 'em, Jackson. But they want to know how come you're now the world's richest man an' Nina's got to go through you an' Kirby to get any money."

"That's none of your busines—"

"I'd appreciate it if you don't butt in, Nina," George said. "People tell me Catlin was braggin' over at the Muni that he knew somethin' about Will dyin' an' he was going to get to the bottom of it. Is that why he was killed? An' I got a few clues that don't add up, an' one dead body—maybe two."

Leonard asked, "What kind of 'clues' are you talking about?"

"Sorry, that's police business. But Catlin was garroted by someone who'd killed this way before." George turned his attention to a stunned Jackson who was now staring at the ceiling. "When you were in Nam, were you ever instructed in how to garrote someone?"

"Sure. But so was everyone else."

"When you was shot down over there, did ya ever have to survive by killin' somebody this way?"

Jackson looked dejectedly at Nina. He said, "I'd rather not talk about it."

"I think you'd better talk about it," said George.

"Get off it, Chief," Leonard said. "Aren't you eschewing civility with what you're implying?"

"Knock off those big words, will ya?"

"You're hopeless," Leonard said. "For God's sake. Jackson wasn't just a war hero and a POW, but he was Will's best friend. You can't be thinking that he had anything to do with your farrago of insane theories are you?"

"I'm only tryin' to piece together some facts, that's all. I didn't mean to offend ya, Jackson. We were all proud of you over there in Nam."

"That's okay," Jackson said. "We know you've got a tough

job to do, but I think you and Nina had better talk to the people at the Foundation before you rush to any further judgments. And, for the record, I was no war hero."

George stood. He wanted to get back to the office and analyze his murder evidence. He contemplated taking back the soggy chaw in the bottom of the ashtray, thought better of it, and said, "Sorry for the intrusion. Best I be goin'. Thanks for the fancy tea, Jackson."

.   .   .   .

35

~:~:~:

JUNE 11 - 12:30 P.M.
IMB CRYOGENIC RESEARCH LAB
ZÜRICH, SWITZERLAND

It had taken Hartmut Kell three days to get an appointment
with the laboratory director. Hartmut was furious over the obvious
delay, as the Izor Foundation wanted him to transfer Jutta to the
States as soon as possible. During the interim, as the banker for the
IMB laboratories, Hartmut had made certain that Ralf Verson was
secure in his tenure at the Suisse company.

Upon seeing the director, Hartmut offered no handshake, only a
cordial nod of his head, then started right in. "I'm not accustomed
to such unnecessary delays. As you are aware, Dr. Verson has told
me everything that has happened to Jutta. Therefore, before I take
legal action, I want my wife moved from this laboratory to the Izor
Life Extension Foundation in America. And I want that done starting today. Do you understand?"

The laboratory director was a mousey little man with gray hair
combed straight back. He was dressed in a dark pin-striped suit
and gray tie. In a high-pitched voice, he tersely said, "Herr Kell, it

is you who doesn't understand. Your wife won't be moved from this laboratory. According to the contract you signed upon having her suspended, she's the property of this research facility."

"That cannot be true. I shall have my lawyers see to this."

The director sat behind a large wooden desk. He put on his pince-nez glasses and looked down his nose at Hartmut. "What I tell you is true, Herr Kell. Remember, you signed that contract because you thought you would be long dead by the time your wife might be revived, and as you have no heirs, you wanted the laboratory's administration to have full responsibility for her safe future."

"I am going to take you to court."

"You can take this to court if you want, but you'll find your lawyers can do nothing. Your wife is now the property of science forever. She's one day going to prove to the world cryonics works. We think she might be the missing link in discovering life itself."

"I, and Dr. Verson, shall expose what has happened. You will not get away with this. I want my wife moved from here, and I want that immediately!"

"Please be rational, Herr Kell. If you were to go to the media with this story, who would they believe? The laboratory, or an over-worked, under-paid employee who's been seeking public attention and making up stories for some time?"

"That is not true."

"Naturally, we'd have papers to prove that. And what kind of credibility would a desperate husband who is lonely and wants to believe this hallucinating employee have in the business world after this becomes public? After all, Herr Kell, your wife is still frozen solid in a dewar for any authority, or the media, to see." The director paused to let what he had said sink in. He then pointed his index finger at Hartmut and said, "If you try to expose anything that you think has happened, you will be the laughing stock of Europe."

Without saying a goodbye, Hartmut got up from his chair and left the building.

.   .   .   .

36
⌣⌣⌣

BEAU PALMER DAY
SEPTEMBER 30, 1987

July and August had been stifling hot and dry. South Dakota hadn't seen a drop of rain since the first week of June. Drought on the prairie brought wind, dust, and rolling tumbleweed. Plus plenty of heartache. Farmers never got used to it and on this day they were thankful a night time cloudburst had drenched their parched fields. Most had worked hard over the summer and were ready for a county fair and a parade. They came in pickups, old cars, and tractors, driving into Palmer Lake from many of the small towns in the region—Britton, Lake City, Sisseton, Eden, Roslyn, Peever, and Brown's Valley.

Ingrid and the other town women had cut late blooming flowers, abelia, purple Michaelmas daisy, celosia, and the hardy Canada goldenrod. The women made bouquets, tied them with bows of colored string, and put them on the gravesites of Beau Palmer and Huey Goey Loo.

Big Bertha and Freddie were in charge of the traveling circus. Being a former military expert, Carl usually administered the night's fireworks show. Bruno was always his assistant.

The Palmer Lake children, including Stirling and Sophie Chase back from summer holiday and already bored with the new school year, mixed with the Indian children from the reservation and made ingenious wooden floats for the parade.

The Wahpeton Sioux, led by Red Cloud and dressed in their tribal costumes, played flutes or drums for the ritual.

Dixie Chase, clad in a tight-fitting black sequin outfit, rode a handsome golden palomino along side the town's equestrian elite. The horses dropped dung everywhere and covered wagons pulled by huge Clydesdales dropped even more on the heretofore clean streets.

The American Legion Post #169 had a brass band that marched each year and, sobriety being unimportant, did not always miss the steaming ordure in the road.

The local Palmer Lake men drank beer and gossiped under the shade of Donna's tent awning, which was set up by the side of the parade route:

"He was murdered, sure as hell."

"Jackson did it and then garroted Kris. He must've had the rope in the black bag."

"Shit, man, Big Bertha hated both Will and Kris. She coulda handled either man."

"Hey, maybe Freddie and Woody inherited more than we know?"

"What the fuck do Carl and Dixie get outa this?"

"That jealous goddamn Rising Coyote was nuts enough to do it." *"And as I recollect, R.C. and Big Bertha were at Will's memorial service on the reservation."*

"Bullshit, the druggie bastard killed hisself."

"Piss off with all this talk about killing. The Twins look like they're going to win the pennant."
"Looks like George and old Red Cloud were right."

Most of the educated crowd, and that was anyone with a high school diploma, felt Will was an eccentric and had committed suicide. They gossiped outside of Burt's:

"Come on, be reasonable. Will simply was too strange for us to understand and decided to end it all."
"And leave behind billions?"
"How come no one seems to recall that Will's father, Ian, died in that same garage all those years ago under unexplained circumstances?
"What's going to happen to Nina and the children?"
"How about what Doctor Stampf said after he was down in Sioux Falls playing trombone at that jazz club? He said he saw Joey Gabrelli's look-alike working as a bouncer."
"That good-looking bone-crusher should stick to adjusting backs instead of playing jazz and hanging around all those dope heads."
"You seem to be forgetting that after the plane wreck, George had that Mafia punk sealed up in his mineshaft of a tomb last June."
"If there's any chance of foul play, it's Jackson."
"If Jackson had anything to do with this—it's the money, stupid!"

The Chase brothers, Carl, Freddie, and Woody, along with Ingrid, agreed with Doc Tragus and Leonard that Will killed himself out of stress and some kind of intellectual challenge connected with cyronics.

George and Nina's theories were considered emotional drivel, as George could find no foundation for his beliefs, but most everyone pitied poor Nina.

During the summer Jackson had attacked his new position of running MICROMED with an unrelenting passion. He revamped the board of directors, bringing on board Kirby Borg, along with Carl Chase. He gave them stock options for a half a million shares and a tidy sum for directors' fees each year. These two additions gave him the voting power to do as he pleased with the corporation. He purchased a Gulfstream IV for company business and personal travel. Which Carl secretly flew to the casinos in Las Vegas and Atlantic City once a month.

Jackson changed the direction of the corporation from Will's laser technology back to coronary balloon angioplasty catheters. He put in successful stock bids and purchased Chase's three largest cardiovascular competitors, then started developing a computer software division. Five hundred new employees were added to the payroll in Palmer Lake, another two thousand around the world. He, the stockholders, the directors, and the town were getting richer by the minute. None of this helped quiet the gossip that he had gotten away with murder.

Nina spent her time with Stirling and Sophie and her memories of Will. She visited him in his dewar in Mankato once a week, always taking along her baggie of blue Miracle Gro fertilzer to make sure his red geranium stayed alive. Was it really possible Will might be revived one day? She questioned Duesmann and Cruickshank to the point they started hiding when they knew she would be in town. George and she dined once a week at Donna's, discussing all the possibilities of Will's death and return. Red Cloud consoled her daily, and after a hit on the pipe, joined her in the Ghost Dance more than once. Rising Coyote hung around her like a puppy hoping for a handout. He got none. Nina spent numerous evenings in talks with Father McQueeny over at St. Mark's. However, each night she asked for Wovoka's guidance.

Over Pietro's pizza, George, Danny, and Polly discussed each potential suspect's profile and motive. Jackson stood out like a proverbial sore thumb. He had killed before in order to survive. He had garroted people. With Will out of the way, Jackson was now the world's richest man. Quite a motive by itself. He had no alibi the night Catlin was murdered, said he was just wandering around the prairie by himself talking to Will, Johanna, and his son, with someone else's golf clothes in a little black bag. Strange story…so bizarre it might be true.

George wondered if Jackson had imbibed something stronger than beer that night.

Danny reminded George that that old, big-footed War Bird always wore Nike sneakers.

Polly said that Jackson was already worth about two hundred million and what was the difference when you have that much money and what he was now worth?

George said, "About three and a half billion dollars, girl!" Yet they all agreed, no one as smart as Jackson Palmer would leave such an obvious trail.

Who else out there might be a multiple murderer?

Carl stood out. He seemed to hate the world. Was he in debt from his gambling? There were rumors. He certainly stood to gain financially from his brother's death.

George knew Big Bertha hated to be ridiculed for her looks, and Will and Catlin had both called her a freak. When Catlin had uttered his remarks to her in a bar, it took five men to hold her back. She had threatened one day to break his neck. Her husband, Freddie, gained financially by Will's death in receiving stock options potentially worth millions. Also, she had no alibi the night of Will's suicide, other than Freddie, who was scared shitless of her.

"Big Bertha's strong as an ox and crazy as a damn loon,"

George said. "I'm sure this nutcake is involved in some manner, but I can't get a handle on it."

Danny pointed out that Rising Coyote had more venom in his soul than anyone he had ever met. He was cunning. He was big enough and he could kill anything without the slightest bit of remorse. He and Catlin had once been in a fistfight over Rising Coyote catching Catlin red-handed trying to steal his CB radio. There had been death threats uttered by both parties. And for a lifetime without Nina, he certainly hated Will enough to kill him.

George thought he would step up his investigation of Rising Coyote. He also decided to do some checking on Woody Chase's whereabouts during all of these deaths. George believed all homosexuals were pathological liars, and Woody was not only a lying queer in his mind, but he had motives other than envy to want his brother and Kris Catlin dead. A few years back Catlin had beat him up one night at the Muni after Woody had supposedly made advances in the john towards him. The stock, money, and the promotions at MICROMED he might receive after Will's demise, were also mitigating factors.

Back at Ridgely Heights, Jackson had driven out to pick up Nina so they could go see the parade. He had on a suede jacket and a thin, blue pullover shirt and grey slacks. His country casual Polo clothes and soft leather Italian shoes fit him perfectly.

Nina was her usual ten minutes late and Jackson sat in the study and listened to Paul Harvey's midday news.

Just as Harvey was wishing his audience a "Good Day," Nina bounced into the room. She wore moccasins and a beaded leather dress, and her hair was tied back in a scarlet ribbon. Her eyes were red and glazed; a forced smile was plastered on her face. She sucked in a large toke from a well-smoked roach. "Damn, I miss William. Funny, but we always took the kids to this goofy parade together. I thought it was stupid, but I don't now."

Jackson saw that she had a tear in her eye. He hugged her close. "Hey, I know it's no fun being lonesome, but let's go show everybody a happy face."

"Okay. Do you want a hit before we leave?"

"That's not a bad idea if I'm going to have to watch the parade and listen to that marching band." Jackson finished the joint and butted it in an ashtray.

As the Bronco drove down the tree-lined driveway, Eggs Benedict screamed after them. "WAR BIRD KILLED WILL. WAR BIRD KILLED WILL."

The stone-faced, towering Indian, clad in his black hightop Nike basketball shoes, scowled menacingly at the squawking cockatoo.

Jackson walked Nina over to a sidewalk table in front of Burt's. The gossip about Will stopped. Jackson said, "Order me a cherry coke, will you? I haven't had one of those in years. I'll walk over to Pietro's and get us a pizza."

"I'll have one of those cokes with you. Could you get a large sausage pizza? I told Stirling and Sophie to meet us here and they'll be starved."

"I'll get two. See you in a jif."

"Say hi to Pietro."

Jackson noticed George sitting by himself when he walked into Pietro's. "Hi, Chief. Mind if I join you while I'm waiting for my pizza?"

"Naw. Sit down. Polly and Danny just left. What's up?"

Jackson fingered his mole. No good luck hair yet. "I brought Nina down to see the parade. Thought it would do her good to get out."

"She's still mopin' about Will, huh?'

"Yep. But you can't blame her, can you?" Jackson said. "Look, ever since the day you came by my house I've wanted to stop by and talk to you about some theories of mine but I've just not made the time."

"Shoot," George said, tilting back his cap.

"Remember the day after Will's suicide when you told me you had some strange evidence you found in Ingrid's garage?"

"Yeah, but that's confidential."

Jackson put his elbows on the table and got close to George's face. "I want you to know, it doesn't make sense to me, yet I think Will did commit suicide. But I promised Nina I'd do everything I could to see if it was possible he was murdered. She thinks you also believe Will was murdered. So if you've got some evidence that could help me out, I'd appreciate it."

George stared at Jackson for a moment. The garroted Kris Catlin came to mind. Was this friend or foe? But he liked Jackson. "I ain't got much. Some material I found in the garage on a nail and a plaster of paris mold of some big footprints. And a hell of a lot of hunches."

"Do you think I could come over and see them sometime?"

George's suspicion was now aroused. Why was Jackson now starting to play detective? Especially if he believed Will croaked himself. Something wasn't kosher here. "Naw. I think it best if Danny and I see what else we can find. Thanks anyway."

Pietro yelled from behind the counter. "Ah two large sausage pizzas to go, Jackson."

. . . .

Palmer Lake
Thirteen Years Later

37

ددد

DECEMBER 24, 2000
6:00 P.M. CHRISTMAS EVE,
PALMER LAKE, SOUTH DAKOTA

Nature heeds no holiday, and howling winds filled with opaque snow buffeted the leaded windows of Ridgely Heights. White drifts formed like sculptured sand dunes around all immoveable objects on the property. A severe prairie blizzard had swept in from Canada and down through North Dakota during the afternoon. Fortunately, all of Nina's house guests and family had arrived before the long road to the house became impassable. War Bird could use the old green John Deere tractor to plow them out in the morning. The family lounged around the heat emanating from a colossal stone fireplace in the rotunda. A twenty-foot-high Russian spruce, brightly decorated in white lights, silver tinsel, and blue and red bulbs, centered the living room. Under the tree, piles of presents waited to be opened. Louis Armstrong's gravelly voice sang Christmas carols from the stereo speakers in the corners of the ceiling, while Eggs Benedict tried his best to sing along. The fragrant smell of

Nina's roasted turkey wafted through the house, and faithful War Bird, now stooped with arthritis, wordlessly served hors d'oeuvres and champagne to the chattering guests.

Twenty-one year old Stirling Chase was a rising star on the Formula One circuit in Europe and, as an heir to billions, one of the world's most eligible bachelors. He stood beside his mentor Jackson Palmer, who had an arm around his godchild, TV sitcom actress Sophie Chase. *People* magazine had recently announced her separation from heartthrob Brad Pitt.

In 1988, Kirby had shocked the community of Palmer Lake by marrying Beverly Loo, Papa Loo's eldest daughter. Beverly had retired as a midwestern opera diva. Kirby was now the U.S.'s most successful investment manager according to Barron's. He, Beverly, and Papa Loo sat on a leather sofa talking about the stock market.

Papa Loo, now one hundred years old, and prone to repeating himself, kept reminding Kirby that China was the best new country to invest in. "Buy China Fund. Buy China Fund. Get all companies in one."

Carl, Dixie, Woody, and Freddie, who was dressed as an elf, and Big Bertha, who was dressed like Santa Claus, were now comfortable around the fire. They raised their glasses and toasted Ingrid, who had died during the year at the advanced age of eighty-two. Until the day of her death, her roses were still the best each year at the Ortonville flower show.

Ironically, Red Cloud had died a week after Ingrid, but Nina had been so devastated that she still couldn't bring herself to talk about it. He wasn't interested in being suspended over at the Izor Foundation. He wanted to meet Wovoka and the rest of the spirits and, following his last wish, she had him cremated and spread his ashes upon the reservation.

Leonard Bookner, who had visited Fire Island and San Francisco bath houses one too many times, was sick and skinny with AIDS. He sat alone in the library, in a regal Louis XIV chair, reading a copy of the Bible in Latin. Unknown to the others, painful purple lesions of Kaposi's sarcoma covered his legs, feet and toes.

Sophie went in to the kitchen to help her mother baste the turkey.

Nina popped out of the kitchen and cornered Jackson in the study. She gave him a hug and a kiss on the cheek. "Just a private Merry Christmas." Her hair was still majestically black. She wore it long in the back with bangs, a hairstyle more suited to a younger woman. However, since she hadn't aged a day since she was forty, it fit her personality well. Her figure was fuller, but no one ever noticed as she dressed daily in her Indian costumes. She trailed her long fingers down Jackson's back, tracing each muscle. "Don't you ever just get horny?"

"What's that old saying, is a whore nervous in church? Sure I get horny. But if I ever had another affair, I'd want it to be with you."

Nina broke the embrace. She held Jackson by his firm biceps and smiled up at him. "Me, too. But I'm still waiting for William." She threw her hair back, laughing. "Come on, let's join the others and watch Bernie. We can catch up on the news before dinner."

After his successful TV documentary on cryonics in the late eighties, Bernard Grable had been at the right time and place in Moscow when Russian president Mikhail Gorbachev signed bills promoting *glasnost* and *perestroika*, and again when President Reagan had his summit conferences with the communist leader. Bernard's on-the-spot commentary vaulted him to the top of the reporting world and, in 1989, right after he covered the opening of the Berlin Wall, he had become the nightly news anchorman for NBC.

Bernard had maintained his friendship with everyone in Palmer Lake over the past decade. He and Jackson played golf together at least four times a year somewhere on the globe, and he and his new wife, Dr. Jan Elton, called Nina each year on the anniversary of Will's suicide and wished her well.

Bernard's fascination with cryonics had never diminished. He and Jan had done two follow-up shows after Will's suspension. He traveled twice to Switzerland to cover the trial of banker Hartmut Kell, who was trying to get his suspended wife moved from Europe to the States.

Over the years, Bernard, through Jan, had stayed in close touch with Kary Duesmann. In 1995, when Duesmann, on his fifty-eighth birthday, won the Nobel Prize for medicine with his development of the scanning tunneling microscope or STM, Bernard had covered the ceremony in Stockholm. At the time Duesmann brought Bernard up-to-date on the progress of cryonics and cloning. Science was very optimistic on both techniques.

The following year Scottish scientists had cloned Dolly the sheep and Bernard was there to tell the world about it. He had reported that mankind was closing in on the ability to solve its medical ills and lengthen its lifespan. Maybe one day soon, even to revive the supposed dead.

Jackson tuned in the news with the remote control on the giant Sony screen. Bernard had interviewed Pope John Paul II that morning and was in the process of finishing his newscast from the Vatican.

The group watched for a few minutes and then Stirling yelled into the kitchen. "Do you think there's any chance of an early Christmas dinner?"

A head popped out the open door. "Absolutely, we'll eat in fifteen minutes," Sophie said.

11:00 P.M.

Across town, the static on the CB radio buzzed loudly. One could barely hear the voice of the State Highway patrolman making an emergency call to the Palmer Lake police department. The blizzard was still raging. Danny Whistle could then be heard responding to the officer about the interstate accident outside of the city. The static became louder and a gloved hand reached out and turned the volume down. On the TV, Charles Dickens' *A Christmas Carol*, with Alistair Cooke, was playing in black and white.

.   .   .   .

38

CHRISTMAS DAY, 2000
DR. RALF VERSON'S HOME
ZÜRICH, SWITZERLAND

Verson was spending the day alone listening to holiday music and reading. He had come down with a bad cold and didn't want to risk infecting others. A roaring fire spit sparks into a metal screen. Verson glanced above the mantle of the fireplace and saw Hartmut's Christmas card. Over the past decade, Hartmut had never forgotten his birthday, nor the Yuletide holidays. They had a social dinner once a year, with Hartmut always reminding Verson that if anything unusual ever happened again with Jutta, to call him immediately.

When Verson recalled the front page photo of Hartmut in last month's Neue Zürcher Zeitung, he was saddened. Hartmut had lost his thirteen-year battle with the cryonics research lab. The court had decided the frozen Jutta must stay in Switzerland. No mention was ever made in the trials of her having come back to life years ago. Hartmut only wanted her moved, he didn't want to create a sensation. The photo of Hartmut showed him gaunt and haggard.

At the laboratory, Jutta was still hanging, unbandaged, in the same position she had been in for the past fourteen years. There was a slight hissing sound at the riveted base of her dewar.

. . . . .

39

~~~

2:30 P.M.
NEW YEAR'S DAY 2001
JACKSON PALMER'S HOME

In 1992 Jackson had purchased the entire condominium unit his penthouse was in. He converted the building to the largest private home in America. Including Papa Loo's apartment, there were sixty-eight thousand square-feet of living space in the main house.

Papa Loo would never allow his space to be refurbished. He liked it the way it was, so it stayed that way.

The garage in the basement contained the world's finest collection of antique cars—racing Ferraris, Cobras, Porsches, Benzes, Renaults and Dusenbergs.

The first floor was devoted to a massage room, gym and indoor pool, and Papa Loo.

Walter Belsky, now retired from the Country Club, worked for Jackson full time. Besides his daily massages, he did the cooking. Jackson had sent him to Paris for a year to be trained as a chef, but Walter now spent the bulk of his time driving Papa

Loo to wherever he wanted to go. It seemed there were many places Papa Loo wanted to see and make up for all the years he walked everywhere.

The second floor was for guest bedrooms, lavishly furnished and reserved for the world's elite.

The third floor contained kitchens and staff quarters. Running Fawn was in charge of the housekeeping.

The fourth floor was Jackson's living room, dining room, and ballroom.

The master bedroom, library, and business office covered the top floor of the five story home.

Jackson stood talking on his cell phone and looking out the picture window, his Ben Franklin wirerim bifocals glinting in the sun. His reflection in the glass showed his hair greying at the temples and his build still firm and lean. He fingered the mole on his right cheek. It seemed to have grown over the years, but it grew no hair.

Once when Jackson was microwaving a cup of tea, Papa Loo had said, "No wonder no hair in mole, you use machine for tea, bad luck. Pee-pee no work and hair no grow."

Palmer Lake was frozen solid. The wind had blown away most of the snow and the ice was cloudy in color. The sun glared from the surface. Ice fishing huts dotted the lake. Cars drove out to the little houses, which had smoke coming from their chimneys. Most of these huts were outfitted like a normal home—TV, laptop computer, stove, beds and the other amenities of modern life. They furnished a good excuse to get away from the wife and kids—just fish, watch football, and drink beer. Jackson had planned on spending the holiday in much the same manner, only in his own home, with his pal, Kirby Borg.

About a mile past the church steeples, Jackson could see the construction of a new Wal-Mart going up by Interstate 29.

It was hard to believe, but Palmer Lake had grown to over sixteen thousand inhabitants.

A half mile farther to the west was the blinking sign of the Indian casino, which stayed open twenty-four hours. When Carl wasn't working, you could always find him there, sitting at a card table in his stiffly starched white shirt.

Over the past few years the tribes had become affluent because of the gambling. The councilmen wore Minnesota Vikings football T-shirts, and baseball caps with ponytails sticking out the back, and drove new BMWs. The reservation now had government-controlled housing and had bureaucratic buildings to accommodate every form of social ill. Those who chose not to work in the private sector stayed on the dole. Welfare checks became a way of life. Sadly, the towns within the reservation remained poor and many were now abandoned. Only the Catholic missions remained the same.

The big-screen TV in the library contained four separate squares of bowl games that were being played simultaneously. Jackson sat down in his worn Lazy Boy recliner. He could keep track of all of the games and at the same time have the Internet running on his PC. His email file was always full and his cell phone rang constantly. With his police radio and CB he could pick up activity throughout the state. He was never out of contact wherever he was. Even his two new corporate Gulfstream V jets were outfitted with the latest equipment that could keep him in touch with home and office anywhere in the world. He had become an electronic addict.

MICROMED software products and creative innovations led the medical and computer world. The company now had forty-five thousand employees around the globe and was expanding rapidly. The corporation had become one of the Dow Jones thirty industrials on the New York Stock Exchange. MICROMED was the fastest growing of all the components.

Even with the recent plunge in the stock market, Jackson's personal worth was approximately sixty-five billion dollars. *He* now appeared on the cover of *Forbes* and *People*. He played bridge with Buffet down in Omaha. He was about to bid on purchasing the Minnesota Vikings football team. The Hollywood "in" crowd came to his golf tournament every year. He spoke before Congress when asked, played tennis with the head of the Federal Reserve, and had the ear of the new President. South Dakota's Jackson Palmer had become one of the world's most powerful men. However, none of his detractors complained much since they, too, were all becoming filthy rich.

The intercom buzzed. Kirby Borg's round body flashed on the security screen. The investment counselor, a former Yale man, still had his hair cut by Bollie, Ivy League style: short on the sides, parted on the left, and long on the top and the front. He hadn't changed this since his days as a National Guard commander. Jackson let him in electronically and then watched the camera follow him to the elevator. There an armed guard waved him on.

Kirby proceeded to the top floor where another guard was posted who recognized the rotund guest. He was then let in the penthouse by Running Fawn.

"Hey, Palmer, you old fart, where are you?"

"In the library watching the games and talking to Tokyo on the telephone. Come on in."

Flatfooted but nimble, Kirby waddled through the living room, snatching candy from dishes along the way. He looked at the photos on the fireplace mantle. A huge portrait of Balthasar stared at him. The Great Dane had lived to be fifteen, an unheard of age for a dog that size. Jackson never replaced him, but three years back he had received two black and white male kittens as a gift from Nina. He named them Puss and Tiger, and they had become his new family, having free rein of the house as if they were watch dogs. Knowing they were probably in for a handout of some sort, the cats greeted Kirby with a rub on the leg as he entered the library.

Jackson was grateful to see Kirby on the holiday. "Hey Big K, how ya doing?"

"Not bad for a guy my age and weight class. Who's winning?"

Kirby swallowed the last of his purloined candy and dipped his hand in a bowl of popcorn sitting on the coffee table. With any kind of food around he was like a Roman at a bacchanal.

"Do you mean the football games or the contract deal I was competing against Sony for?"

"The Tokyo deal, naturally." Kirby munched a mouthful of popcorn. "We can watch football anytime."

"I knew there was a reason I admired you. Yep, we beat out those Sunnyvale snots and got the contract with Mitsubishi. A billion a year for ten years."

"The stock should open strong tomorrow."

Jackson switched one of the TV channels to the start of another ball game. "Yep, I'd imagine the stock will have a strong opening. Just think, with your profits you could finally build Beverly her dream opera theater over by Pickerel Lake."

"You know, you're right. But I think it's about time you and I had a talk about me stepping down from the board at Micromed. Handling your personal finances takes up almost all of my time, and I also want to travel the world with Beverly and build her dream Wolftrap before its too late."

Football forgotten, Jackson turned to Kirby. "I'd certainly miss you at the board meetings, but can't I talk you into staying on? I mean, we've had quite a run, haven't we?"

"That's an understatement. I'd have been perfectly happy just managing my little growth fund fifteen years ago. Now look at me. I'm the number one man in my field, with you as my best friend, and Beverly as my wife. Other than getting too fat, I couldn't have planned it any better if I tried. But now I've had enough."

"Well, I guess I'll have to accept reality. But let's not forget, all of what you mentioned was possible because of Will. It was his vision and inventions that got us all started, not mine."

"I've never forgotten that. Nor can I forget that he knew what he was doing when he made you executor of his estate and not Nina or his loser brothers," Kirby let out a huge breath of air. "Just think what a happy camper he'll be if cryonics works in fifty years. Hell, with compound interest on his money, he'll own half the world."

Both men laughed. Jackson knew Kirby thought the chance of anyone coming back to life during his time on earth was non- existent.

"I sure hope it works sooner than that. Kary Duesmann over at Izor tells Nina that he still believes it'll happen in her life-time. I'd sure like to see Will again before I'm suspended my-self."

In the hope of making cryonics a reality, and in memory of Will, Jackson had donated over one hundred million dollars to the Izor Foundation in 1994 and now sat on their board. He had planned to be put in a dewar with Will and Nina when his time arrived.

"Me, too," Kirby said. "But lemme change the subject. Beverly and I were thinking, maybe you'd step down at Micromed at the same time I do. After all, you're fifty-six years old and in perfect health." Jackson sat up in the chair and started to say something, but Kirby continued, "Hear me out. You have everything any human could possibly want, and we'd like to see you enjoy the rest of your life, maybe even meet the woman of your dreams to share it with. Why not turn the corporation over to Carl and join me in early retirement?"

Jackson let the recliner down to a relaxing position, then folded his hands on his lap. His long fingers were slightly chapped, and there were small liver spots on the back of his hands. "It's a wonderful thought, Kirby, thank Beverly for me. I'm sure she put you up to this. I love you both. But my work *is* my life. And I always thought you knew I have no desire to share my life with another woman. Johanna was the woman of my dreams, my one true love."

Jackson paused momentarily to recall the memories. "You know, for years I didn't know where I was going in life, until one day I realized I was already there. The only silly dream I have anymore is that someone would give me a copy of next year's *Wall Street Journal*."

Kirby chuckled. "Can you get two copies?"

"I'll sure try," Jackson said. "But I'll tell you this, if Will came back, he'd suspend me over at Izor if I ever put Carl in charge of the company."

"Why's that?"

"He never wanted his brother involved with the corporation, it was me that talked them all into hiring Carl in the first place."

"I never knew that. But as Beverly always says, you're a bit of a mystery sometimes."

.　　.　　.

JANUARY 1, 6:00 P.M.
WOODY CHASE'S APARTMENT
PALMER LAKE

"W.O.C. calling F.A.C. W.O.C. calling F.A.C. Do you read me?" These were the code names Woody and Freddie had long ago established for their CB communication. Woody was tired of waiting for Freddie to answer. Afraid Big Bertha might get on the line and start an argument, he switched his set off. He hated that freak. How could his brother ever make love to that? He was trying to reach Freddie to tell him that he was bailing out of MICROMED stock during the upcoming week. He'd finally be worth a few million in cash. Why not have Freddie join him and start their own company somewhere else? Jackson had gotten too big for his britches, and besides, Will Chase and his real brothers had started the company, not him. The arrogant prick. Maybe he should garrote Jackson, like Catlin got it.

The air outside was frozen and still. Crystal icicles hung from the apartment balconies. Sidewalks were glazed, hard and slippery. Car exhausts looked like steam engines. It was minus ten degrees Fahrenheit, and Woody bundled up with coat, scarf, and hat. He put on leather gloves and headed out his front entrance to go visit Leonard.

In less than ten minutes a large figure with long hair opened the door to Woody's apartment, went in and switched on the CB, then changed frequencies. A voice spoke in the microphone. "Commander, it's me. I'm worried."

"Look, you moron, I told you if you ever called me again you were history. Frozen just like Will."

"I know you said that, but things ain't right. I got to talk to you, or else I got to talk to someone else. I'm hiding all these years and I'm worried I'll get caught."

"All right." There was static over the frequency before the voice continued. "You know where to meet me. Be there at nine thirty tonight."

The line went dead.

.　　.　　.　　.

40

FRIDAY, JANUARY 5, 2001
10:30 A.M.
IZOR LIFE EXTENSION FOUNDATION
MANKATO, MINNESOTA

Receiving the Nobel Prize and the million dollar gift that went with it did not change Kary Duesmann one iota. He paid for his kids' college, bought a new home, a new Chevrolet Suburban, took his wife to Bali for a month, and donated the rest of the funds to the Izor Foundation.

As Neville Cruicksank was so fond of saying, "Kary, you're the same old slob we've always known and loved."

Former administrator and surgeon Peter Sayers had lost his life in the 1988 terrorist bombing of the Pan Am flight over Lockerbie, Scotland. His place had been taken by Jan Elton-Grable. With the huge endowment bestowed upon the Izor Foundation by Will Chase and then Jackson, Jan had in the past twelve years advanced the research and development of cryonics by decades. Along with IMB's Switzerland nanocomputer research division, genetic engineering was far exceeding science's wildest expectations.

Duesmann's new scanning tunneling microscope (STM), a hybrid of his original ETM, had revolutionized the world of nanotechnology during the past five years. It now allowed science a way to build a cell repair machine, a device smaller than a living cell that could travel along capillaries to enter and repair living cells. It gave mankind the ability to heal disease, reverse the ravages of age, and make humans speedier and stronger than before. It allowed science to make machines reduced to the size of viruses, machines that could work at speeds heretofore unknown to man. Finally, man could replicate life. However, as is the case with many new medical products, drugs, inventions, and advancements, the law, religion, and bureaucracy kept much of this technology confined to the laboratories.

Kary Duesmann's basement office was cooler than normal. Under his desk, Elvis lay on a rug shivering, trying to find some warmth and comfort in his chewed up blanket. The dog amazed Duesmann and Cruickshank: he was now nineteen years old, almost double his life expectancy.

Neither Duesmann or Cruicksank had a scientific explanation for this phenomenon. Was it the liquid nitrogen? The arthropoda perfusate? Or the way he was frozen? What caused this death-defying aberration? Did this mean that human subjects frozen under the same conditions would double their lifespans, or more, because Elvis wasn't dead yet?

Duesmann reached under the desk and pulled the woolen blanket over Elvis. The dog stood, flexed its legs, circled the blanket and then snuggled into it.

"I don't think I'll ever be able to put old Elvis down and do an autopsy," Duesmann said. "I'm completely puzzled, why can't we find anything different in his blood or tissue?"

Cruicksank, horn-rimmed glasses sitting on top of his crimped hair, said, "Maybe it's about time we did some probing in Elvis' stomach and see if we can locate any abnormalities. There has to be some clue to his dormant cellular condition."

"You're right. When did he last eat?"

"Not since last night."

"Okay. No time like the present. Come on, Elvis. This won't hurt," Duesmann said.

One of Duesmann's many inventions was a molecular machine directed by a nanocomputer. It combined sensor programs, and molecular tools to form systems able to examine and repair the ultimate components of individual cells. Duesmann decided to use this machine in his analysis of Elvis. He put the dog on an operating table and gave him a general anesthesia of thiopentol. He kept him stable with the inhalant halothane.

Both Duesmann and Cruickshank then fastened fiberopticscope glasses on their foreheads and started the probe. What they found was the potential key to human revival. Like the xray, the discovery of penicillin, and many other medical miracles, Duesmann had accidently developed his key to future life with the use of his arthropoda perfusate. It seemed to act as an agent to interrupt metabolism completely for hours, days and years, creating a condition of perfect biostasis.

"My, God, Kary. You might get another Nobel for this."

"It does appear that we hold the key to future life right here in the laboratory."

Life. The ability to create life. Playing God. One would think Duesmann and Cruickshank would be shouting to the world. However, their excitement was tempered by reality, the work they knew would lie ahead in bringing this news to the scientific community, and the months and years of tests, compiling data, and proving the merits of the technology.

Cruickshank straightened up from the table. He had a knowing smile on his face. "Imagine, if we'd injected this into astronauts a fortnight before they were to leave. We could shoot them off into space for decades and then revive them once they got to their destinations. There'd be no worry about boredom, sex, aging, defecation, food, and sickness. Kind of like one-way time travel."

Duesmann took off his surgical equipment and sat down in a chair, his white smock food stained and dirty with paw marks. He was a practical man. It would take the revival of an individual or the actual reproduction of life to excite him. "You know, it appears to me we can reverse unconsciousness by simply washing the bulk of the perfusate out of the patient's tissue, then injecting a combination of whole blood and my perfusate."

"Probably true. But how much do we wash out, and what's the right mixture of blood and arthropoda perfusate for a human?"

"I'm not certain, since we never monitored that in Elvis," Duesmann said. "But we can rectify that with a few tests on our other frozen animals. But think of it, I can enter one of our patient's tissues with my cell repair machine, remove the packing from around the patient's molecules, and replace it with water, then remove the cross-links, repair any damaged molecules and structures, and restore normal concentrations of salts, blood sugar, ATP, and so forth. Finally, I can unblock the metabolic machinery. The interrupted metabolic process resumes, the patient yawns, sits up, and returns to everyday life."

"Cheers, mate. I love it," Cruicksank said. "But if you recall, as far as I know, there's only one human patient that the arthropoda perfusate has been used on."

Jointly, a name came to mind.

"WILL CHASE!"

.   .   .   .

41

_∴∴∴_

SATURDAY EVENING
JANUARY 6, 2001
IMB CRYOGENIC RESEARCH LAB
ZÜRICH, SWITZERLAND

Ralf Verson was driving home from a restaurant on a frosty night when he thought he would stop at his office and retrieve three bottles of champagne he had left in his lab refrigerator after the company New Year's party. Other than the guard, the Research Lab was deserted. Verson chatted with the chubby security man for a few moments and then went downstairs.

Verson turned on the bright light in his office, leaving the dewar and storage area of the lab bathed in a dim red light. A large stand-up fan was humming in the center of the room and there were the usual night sounds of the hissing of liquid nitrogen tanks. He walked over to the refrigerator and removed the bottles of champagne, putting them into a plastic bag. He thought he would give the guard one of the bottles for a New Year's gift.

Verson switched off his office light and started walking towards the main door of the laboratory. Something moving in the far cor-

ner of the lab caught his eye. He turned towards the movement, his eyes straining to see through the reddish light. He made out a figure in the Plexiglas window of the dewar.

It was Jutta Kell.

Was the impossible happening again? She was not hanging upside down, nor frozen. She was standing in the metal container waving at him. He dropped the bag of champagne and the bottles exploded on the floor. Verson ran to the dewar. There was no liquid nitrogen in the tank. Once again the rivets of the prototype had failed. A two foot crack in the Plexiglas ran up from the bottom of the dewar. The fans must have dispersed the foul odor of the gas.

Jutta smiled at him and mouthed, "Bitte, hilf mir!"

Verson didn't know whether to get the Polaroid or try and help Jutta from the dewar. She started crying and pointed to the top of the pod. He grabbed a hold of the stainless steel ladder attached to the metal cylinder and climbed to the top. A screw-top hatch needed to be undone in order to open the lid. It contained six threaded bolts with turnable hand cranks. Verson twisted them as rapidly as he could. There was a whooshing sound as the last of the bolts came undone. Whatever gas was left in the dewar had escaped. It took all of his strength to lift the lid back on its hinges. Finally it opened. He hoped he had not once again returned Jutta to a state of unconsciousness.

The dewar was seven feet deep and Jutta was reaching up to Verson. His excitement soon overshadowed any fears he might have had. He was on his knees on top of the pod and lowered his arm into it to touch her. Their fingers met and intertwined. It seemed medically impossible, but she was alive. A tremor shivered through his body.

A booming voice from the entrance of the main door of the lab filled the room. "Doctor Verson. I heard an explosion. Is everything okay in here?" It was the security guard.

"Yes. Yes, it is. I just dropped the champagne, that's all. I'll clean it up and meet you upstairs in a few minutes."

There was a long pause, which to Verson, seemed forever. Then the guard said, "Okay. I've got to get back to my post anyway."

Jutta was still holding on to Verson's arm. She mouthed something to Verson, but no sound came out.

"Let go of my hand and take my jacket to keep warm," he said. "I'm going to leave you here for a few minutes until I get your husband on the phone."

She took the clothing.

Verson climbed down and went to his office and dialed Hartmut's cellular number.

Hartmut drowsily answered. "Yes." He must have been sleeping.

Verson whispered into the phone, "Herr Kell. I'm at the laboratory. Hurry, this is beyond an emergency. Jutta is alive."

"What?"

"Yes, believe me, she's standing in the dewar right this minute. I don't know what to do. You must help her. Meet me here in the laboratory as soon as you can. I'll think of something to say to the guard so you can get in. Please, hurry!"

Verson hung up and telephoned the security guard upstairs. "I've made quite a mess down here and it'll take me awhile to clean it up."

"I'll be right down to help."

"No. No. Everything is okay. I've got it under control. Listen, I've called my dinner companion, Herr Kell, on his cellular and told him to meet me here in the laboratory on his way home. My car's battery is dead and he's bringing some jumper cables to get me started. Please tell him to come down to my office when he arrives."

"Will do, Dr. Verson."

Fifteen minutes later Hartmut ran down the stairs to greet

Verson, who was waiting for him at the main entrance to the storage lab. They shook hands and Verson walked Hartmut over to the dewar containing Jutta. Hartmut stared at her through the Plexiglas window. He couldn't believe it—she was alive! Tears ran down his ruddy face.

Jutta put her lips to the glass window.

Hartmut did the same.

Jutta had Verson's large woolen jacket draped over her naked body.

Verson pointed out the ladder leading to the top of the dewar to Hartmut. "Herr Kell, I have no medical answers for you, I only know that you two deserve to be together. Monday's a holiday, so there'll be no one in the laboratory until Tuesday morning. At least you'll have that much time to see if Jutta will stay alive and for the two of you to spend it with each other and decide what you want to do. You have my home telephone number if you need me or if anything happens to Jutta. I'll stall the guard for the next thirty minutes. You must be gone by then."

Hartmut embraced Verson.

Jutta mouthed, "Danke, Dr. Verson."

.   .   .   .

42

~:~:~:

MONDAY, JANUARY 8, 2001
10:30 A.M.
BRUNO TOMACELLI'S HOUSE

A neighbor had called George Winter because she hadn't seen Bruno in over a week. Bruno Tomacelli was the largest man George had ever met in person. A man that size, of that sheer volume, couldn't just disappear. *Couldn't.* How could anything that big just vanish? Someone must have seen Bruno. You really can't miss a six-foot, eight-inch, three hundred and twenty pound man, especially if everyone knows him. So George assumed that Bruno was just home, sick in bed. Or maybe on vacation...but where would he go?

The snow that Bruno was supposed to have shoveled from the sidewalks was still there, and the children had made a walking path through it. All of the electrical appliances he had taken home to repair had not been returned, and little seven-year-old Sally Myers, whom he walked home from school each day, was heartbroken. People were worried, as the gentle giant hadn't missed a day of work in twenty-five years.

George sent Danny Whistle over to have a look through Bruno's dilapidated house out on the far end of Ballard Street, on the other side of the tracks from the offices and homes of the MICROMED executives. It was a one story, one bedroom, one bath home covered in wood shingles and peeling tan paint. It was isolated from the rest of the neighborhood by twenty acres of trees. On the roof a ten foot high metal TV and CB antenna was held in place with four guide wires anchored to the corners of the house.

When no one answered the back door, Danny tried the handle and the door opened. A stench flew out into the open air. Danny slowly made his way into the filthy kitchen. Someone had the thermostat turned up to eighty degrees. Danny reached over and turned it down to seventy.

Dirty pots and pans were lying in a cracked sink. Open cans of peas and carrots sat on the linoleum counter. A dark brown Hefty bag full of rotting garbage was jammed under the sink. The smell was noxious. Two cockroaches scurried into a crack in the floor.

Danny quickly made his way to the junk-crammed living room. There were mountains of broken furniture, buckets of used razor blades, parts of automobiles, bicycles, lawnmowers, and cardboard boxes full of defective light bulbs. It was mostly discarded junk, worthless to the world, but obviously a treasure to Bruno. In one corner of the room Danny found a vinyl-covered folding table that Bruno used as a desk. A wooden rocking chair sat alongside it. The table was piled with newspapers, letters, periodicals, junk mail, a tape recorder, and an old citizens band transmitter and receiver, next to which a pair of brown leather gloves lay neatly folded. Pencils and pens were strewn about the table and floor. A metal bendable lamp sat on the edge of the table. A handwritten letter lay open underneath the light.

Danny picked the letter up and gasped. The letter read:

"To Daddy an Mama an Jeorge Winter,

This is goodby. I kilt Will an Kris. I tought it wuz
only a war game I wuz playin wit Jacksin. The
cumander helpd me an says we culd freez em an bring
em back later. When we didnt bring em back the kidds
at skool tol me dat it wernt no game. I'm sorrie it
happend an its best I'm doin what I'm doin. Goodby
agin.
                BRUNO"

This, thought Danny, was no good. He was so nervous that
he forgot to radio in the news to headquarters. Instead, he turned
on the siren of the squadcar and roared back to talk with George.
He ran up the steps of the police building. Huffing, he handed
him Bruno's handwritten letter.

"What in hell's name have we got here?" George was tugging at his bad ear so hard it turned purple. "Wooie, Danny.
Ain't this somethin'? An' to think all these years I always thought
it was that loony Big Bertha. Jackson an' Bruno. Well, I'll be
damned."

Danny asked, "Don't you think we should find Bruno before
we believe this letter?"

"You're right, as usual. Say, doesn't Bruno keep a fishin' house
out on the lake every year with Risin' Coyote an' Bobby Joe?"

"He sure does. They always put it out past Bailey's Cove
where the big Northerns are."

"Well, if he ain't at home an' this here letter means anythin',
we might find him there. Let's git goin'."

BAILEY'S COVE, PALMER LAKE
11:45 A.M.

The wind had made the frozen lake as smooth as if someone had taken a Zamboni to the ice. George and Danny drove across the glistening surface to the other side of the lake. When they saw the ramshackle fishing house, George spun the steering wheel and did a fourwheel slide into a small pile of snow next to the hut. They jumped out and entered the hut through a floppy wooden door. The structure was nothing more than a tar-paper shack made up of two-by-fours for framing, a corrugated tin roof, two-by-twelve planks for a floor, and sheetrock walls, with newspapers stuffed in every crack to keep out the howling wind and snow from the barren lake.

Inside were the basic amenities: a wood-burning-potbellied stove, two beds, a metal table, four folding chairs, a radio, and a blue plastic cooler to keep food fresh. The walls and ceilings were covered with photos of nudes from *Playboy* and *Hustler* magazines. In the south corner of the room, someone had sawed a large hole about four feet in diameter in the wooden floor and chiseled another through the ice. A pair of boots and two legs pointed towards the ceiling from the middle of the hole. Frozen upside down two-thirds of the way in the water was the body of Bruno.

George was the first to get to him. "Holy shit."

"Quick, let's get him out of there."

"What's your hurry? The poor bastard's frozen stiffer than Bill Clinton's pecker."

Next to the ice hole George picked up a partially frozen rag. He squeezed it and a fluid ran down his wrist. It smelled of chloroform and he quickly held the cloth at a distance from his face. On the table sat a glass bottle with a red and yellow biotoxin skull and crossbones label on it.

"It looks like the dumb shit held this rag full of dope over his nose an' jumped headfirst down that ice hole tryin' to kill hisself."

"Well, it appears he did a pretty good job," Danny said, wiping his runny nose on his sleeve. "Come on let's drag him out of there. It gives me the creeps to see him like that."

The ice had frozen the body and clothing to the sides of the ice hole. It was stuck solid. Danny took a six-foot-long iron ice probe from the corner of the hut and started chipping Bruno out.

Once he had the body free it bounced up and down in the hole like a giant fishing bobber. Since Bruno weighed over three-hundred pounds the two men decided to push the body down as far as they could in the ice water and when it shot back to the surface they would pull him out in one big heave. It worked, and the huge frozen corpse lay face up on the wooden floor like a block of ice. The fish had eaten off his ears and parts of his nose. But it was Bruno, no doubt about that.

Gasping for air, Danny said, "What do we do now?"

George sat down on the edge of the bed and lit a cigarette. He sucked in a huge puff. Smoke billowed from his mouth. "First of all I'll radio Lenny. He can drive out here with the coroner's wagon an' meet you. Take Bruno to the morgue an' wait for me, then while you're there, call Risin' Cloud an' find out where he was last night. Okay?"

"Roger. Where you going?"

"First, to search Bruno's house, an' then go over to Klay Bond at the D.A.'s office an' get an arrest warrant for Jackson."

"On what charges?

"Murder one."

George drove slowly back across the ice, the snow tires crunching underneath like someone cracking open peanut shells. How was he going to arrest Jackson Palmer quietly? The town would be a lynch mob within hours. People loved the guy, yet envied and despised him the same way they did Will when he was alive. Money was certainly a powerful motive to hate and kill.

George reached over and fumbled with the glove box. He got it open without spinning the car on the ice. Inside was a large roll of yellow police-line tape. He'd have to yellow-tape Bruno's house, and within hours probably get more tape and do Jackson's house. A lot of tape. That house was bigger than an Arab's palace. The curiosity seekers and reporters might cross the line anyway. After all, this was the world's richest man, and he'd killed people to get to where he was in life. Quite a story. Possibly the trial of the century comin' up right here in Palmer Lake. Certainly bigger than that O. J. Simpson fiasco out in L.A. a few years back. He'd have to post extra men all night. Maybe even call in the National Guard.

George turned right off the lake and on to Ballard Street. Bruno's house loomed eerily ahead. George was willing to bet Bruno had never had a visitor in his life.

George parked under a rotting porte cochere and went in a side door. He walked through the dirty kitchen and into the living room. He glanced at the untidy desk in the corner. He didn't know where to start. Out of frustration he went into the bedroom. The bed was unmade and the blankets and quilt were piled in the center of it. He opened a chest of drawers and started rifling the contents. It contained underwear, socks, T-shirts, red and blue patterned cowboy handkerchiefs, and work pants. He opened the clothes closet and found only a few items hanging there, mostly overalls, one tattered dark blue suit that Bruno had always worn to church.

George went into the living room and put the tape recorder and C.B set in a cloth valise. He decided to take one last look around the house. He walked over to a second bedroom and looked in. Strange, the TV was on with no sound. The Jerry Springer show. An old CB set sat in the corner on a desk. And someone had been sleeping in the bed. From the size of the indent in the mattress, a very large person had slept there. There was a pair of cheap black lace panties lying in a corner behind the bed. Who would be visiting Bruno? Did Bruno use this room for hookers? Naw.

George walked into the bathroom and saw a woman's bottle of cheap cologne, White Flowers; a tube of Revlon pancake makeup; a small, gold coke spoon that was usually worn around the neck; some used shaving equipment and a messy can of Gillette Foamy on the lavatory. The toilet's bottom seat was down and the upper rested against the white tank. The bowl hadn't been flushed. Bruno, or this other person, had left the house in a hurry. What had Jackson said to entice him, or her, to leave the house in such a rush? It must have been Jackson who chloroformed Bruno and stuffed him down that ice hole. But he would've needed help. The perfume. Was it Big Bertha sleeping here? No way, she was so weird she'd be sleeping *with* Bruno in *his* bed. Or, did Risin' Coyote help him? Was that Bruno's mysterious visitor? George just knew that jealous bastard Rising Coyote was the other key to this mystery. Jesus Christ, Jackson and Rising Coyote. Risin' Coyote loved whores and he was sleeping here with one and helped Bruno. Damn, George knew his theory of two killers had been right all along.

The smell in the small bathroom was overwhelming. George flushed the commode, then realized he might have just removed evidence. Damn, damn, damn. Goddammit.

He opened the second bedroom's closet. There were two wigs lying on the floor—one blonde and one brunette. Oddly, at the far end of the closet was a cluster of Wal-Mart brand womens clothing. He looked at the size tags. Extra large!

George slid back a plywood door to a closet full of fetid old shoes and boots. He started sorting them on the floor. One pair grabbed his attention—black, hightop Nike basketball shoes. The sides were practically worn out, but the soles still had tread on the bottom. Bruno, or his guest, must have saved everything he had ever owned.

George wrapped the shoes in newspaper and put them under his arm. There must be plenty of proof lying around that Big Bertha or Rising Coyote was here. Fingerprints, hair samples, blood, anything to connect the bastards to these crimes. He'd have Danny come over, do a thorough search and dust for prints.

George went back in the living room for the valise, dumped the shoes in, then headed out the back door. He yellow-taped the property under the curious eyes of the neighbors who had gathered once they saw his police car parked outside; although he told them nothing of finding Bruno dead. He radioed for help, gave the officers instructions, and left for his office.

George sat in his office wondering how he was going to arrest Jackson, when Polly Byrd-Winter bounced in and kissed him on the cheek. George had married her in a Las Vegas chapel back in 1990, and after all these years, he knew he had made the right choice. Unlike George, Polly hadn't matured quietly— she still wore her girly taffeta skirts and red lipstick, and still snapped her gum, although George now found it almost endearing. Almost.

Polly's hair was a mess and she pushed it up on her head with her fingers. "Wow, you look like you've seen a ghost."

George nodded. "I have."

Polly's eyes widened.

George liked impressing his wife. Although to be honest, it wasn't that hard. "Bruno's dead. He...Danny and I found him in his fishing shack this morning. He'd drowned." George didn't know if he could easily explain how they had found him, and certainly couldn't explain how they had gotten him out.

Polly snapped her gum. "Really? How could anyone drown in the middle of January? Even in a fishing hut?"

George shut the door to his office, then sat down on the edge of his desk. "Polly, babe, I got to tell you something, but you gotta promise you're gonna keep it quiet, okay?"

Polly nodded, her eyes still wide.

"It seems that Bruno and Jackson were the ones who killed Will. And Kris Catlin. And now Bruno's dead, too, which can only mean that Jackson had somethin' to do with his death."

Polly stopped chewing her gum.

"I got some tennis shoes out of Bruno's house, and I'm going to match them to molds I made back in '87. If I'm right, and I think I'm right, we're going to have to go bring in Jackson this afternoon for murder one."

Polly's eyes were wet, and she started blinking wildly. "Are you sure? Oh, George, Jackson wouldn't *do* that. He just *wouldn't*. He's the nicest man—"

"I know you have a place in your heart for Jackson, Polly. We all did. But we're the law, and Jackson's a murderer. There's nothin' more to say. I'm sorry, babe. I guess some of us were wrong."

Polly stared blankly at George. "How can you...how can you be so cold?"

"Honey, listen—"

"No, I won't listen. You're just being mean, that's all you're being."

"Okay, look. I want you to take these shoes and see if they match the molds we made. Call me on my cell phone when you know. Oh, I almost forgot. Have Danny go over to Bruno's house, do a complete search and dust the kitchen and bathrooms for prints."

Polly snatched the shoes away from George angrily, and he walked out the door.

"Don't forget to call me!" he yelled over his shoulder.

Polly slammed the door in his office, just to have something to slam.

George grabbed the military fatigue jacket Kris Catlin had on the night he was murdered, the one with the hole in the right shoulder. He rubbed the area where the Green Beret insignia used to be on the arm, then headed out the front door for the county morgue.

Polly grudgingly dropped the shoes off at the lab, then started walking slowly back towards George's office. He didn't understand, she thought. She couldn't bear it for Jackson to have another thing go wrong in his life. Just this morning she saw that Jackson's Mercedes was towed into the police lot for being illegally parked in Judge Ronning's private space over at the courthouse. She was sure that it was a mistake—the new meter maid was a strict adherent to the book, and there was no way she would have known this was Jackson Palmer's car.

Jackson's car.

Polly stopped in her tracks and thought for a second. Surely there would be something in his car that would indicate that he hadn't been with Bruno when he was killed. And the car was in the impound lot. She knew exactly where it was.

There was not a soul around when Polly opened the door to the black Mercedes. The car had that wonderful new-car smell that she had never been able to have herself. She sat in the driver's seat and just breathed in the leathery air. She glanced around and looked at what he had left in the car—Gucci sunglasses were over the driver's visor, a red, rosewood cigar holder was in the door recess along with a South Dakota state map. Nothing out of the ordinary. She reached in the glovebox, but there was nothing there but the car manual and the registration and the proof of insurance. She saw the trunk button and pushed it. It was already popped. Odd? Maybe there'd be something in there.

The only thing in the trunk was a set of old golf clubs. Maybe, she thought, maybe there's a score card or something with a date on it. She was sure there was no way that Jackson had been with Bruno when he was murdered. She unzipped the top pocket of the bag. Only tees, balls, markers, and a glove. The back pocket contained a pair of brown and white golf shoes with rubber cleats, a blue sweater, and below it a wooden-handled wire of some kind. Almost like a short jump rope. She drew it out.

A tiny jump rope? She looked at it more closely. That wasn't a jump rope, it was a garrote.

"Polly, what are you doing?"

Polly gasped and spun around, dropping one of the golf balls that she still had in her hand. It bounced under the car and rolled against the back wheel. "My God, Danny." she let out a big sigh. "I thought you were with George and Lenny. What are you doing here?"

"What are *you* doing here?"

"I'm...it's...Jackson's car got towed this morning, and look." She showed him the garrote. "It was in the golf bag."

Danny scratched his forehead with one finger and winced. "Okay, Polly, put that down. We don't want any fingerprints on it. I'm not even sure we're allowed to touch it, so let's just...put it down, and go talk to George."

"But—"

"Polly, look. George is gonna get himself all worked up in a tizzy if he sees that you were in here without a warrant. What you did is good, it was real good, and we might be able to use it to trap Jackson, but for now, just put it back in the bag, and we'll go find George."

As Polly was zipping the bag back up, she could only imagine how horrible she would feel if she had been the one to find the evidence that put Jackson in jail forever...or worse.

"Okay, Polly's sorry, chief," Danny said. "She's real sorry that she went looking in there without a warrant, but she *did* find the murder weapon, and that's big news."

"Sorry? Hell, she didn't do a damn thing wrong! That car was in our impound lot, we had every right to search it!" George ran his thumbs along the inside of his waistband. "The murder weapon is great news. Now, of course, Polly, you gotta stop tryin' to help us. You did good this time, and I appreciate it, sweetie, I really do. But next time we might not be so lucky. You don't know what you need to know to do what we do."

Polly bit her lip and sat down. "Just think, if Will's really been murdered, Nina's been right all along."

"Babe, she sure was." George turned to Danny. "The shoe prints matched. Bruno was the one inside Ingrid's garage back when Will was killed."

"We don't know that yet, you only know those shoes were inside the garage that night," Danny said quizzically.

"That's a good point, but there ain't many other size fifteen's around town. So, that's the good news. The bad news is that I went over to the reservation to see if Risin' Coyote has been around these last few days, but unfortunately he's been out in Wyoming." George shook his head from side to side. "I would have loved to nail that scum for this."

"Here's something even odder," Danny said. "There were no prints in Bruno's house but his. No other evidence whatsoever. But I got a bag full of fiber and hair yet to analyze. But even all the stuff in the second bathroom had only Bruno's prints on it. Whoever else was there musta wore gloves."

"No shit. That don't make no sense. No prints?"

"No prints. What about the jacket?" Danny asked.

"I took the jacket over to the morgue, and it fit Bruno like a glove. Bruno musta been in that garage, and it seems Jackson was behind the whole thing. We got to go get him now, and bring him in. We've got ourselves our killer. Finally."

Danny nodded. "It makes sense, chief. It really does. That's a lot of money."

"Money does strange things to people," George said. "If I've learned anythin' at all these past years, it's that. But for now, let's go get Jackson and bring him in."

.   .   .   .

43

∴∴∴

1:15 P.M.

Across town, Jackson and Judge Lars Ronning were finishing their walleye and salmon. Judge Ronning had been eyeing the newly released Mercedes out at the dealership but had to have his name put on a waiting list to receive one, so he had spent the lunch hour talking Jackson into selling him the one Jackson had recently purchased. Judge Ronning was so sure he could convince Jackson to sell him the car, that he had asked him to leave the Mercedes in the judge's private stall back at the courthouse.

The lunch was wonderful. They had discussed their golf games and the success of the MICROMED stock, and eventually Jackson and the judge agreed on a suitable sum for the car. Neither one of them particularly cared about money, but the bargaining always entertained them both.

After the waiter took away their plates, Jackson reached over and raised his glass of wine. "Alright, Judge, sixty thousand it is. It's a steal, and I can't believe you convinced me, but for a friend, I'll do it." Jackson winked. "Here's the keys."

"Skoal." Judge Ronning clinked his glass against Jackson's. "And it's not that much of a steal—you'd have had to drive all the way to Minneapolis to trade it in otherwise. I'm doing you a favor."

"A favor?" Jackson chortled. "That car only has eight thousand miles on it!"

Judge Ronning had sad, watery eyes, and the wrinkled skin of a Chinese Shar-Pei. He smiled and leaned back in his chair. Over the years he had grown closer to Jackson, not just because Jackson was responsible for the judge's small fortune, but also as a golf partner, hunting companion, and all-around friend. Jackson's generosity never ceased to amaze the judge, and he appreciated his candor. "So I'll just have the money wired over to your account later this afternoon."

"That's fine, I'll have my secretary courier over the title in the morning." Jackson thought for a second. "I need to make sure my golf clubs are out of the trunk—I left it open for Gordy to pick them up and have them re-gripped. I guess I can have Walter pick me up after lunch."

"You trust everyone, don't you?" the judge grinned.

"I guess I do. If a person can't leave his trunk open in a place like Palmer Lake, it's time to leave," said Jackson. "Then again, it's not my car anymore. That's your car sitting wide open in the courthouse parking lot!"

They both laughed.

"Another sixty thousand dollars for you—it must be small change by this point."

"Well, any money helps. Your sixty thousand is going to the Izor Foundation to help them in their research."

"Really? You don't still think—" the judge checked himself, then began again. "Does Nina still hope they'll be able to revive Will while she's alive?"

"Of course she does, Lars. We all do," Jackson said. "We'd all love to have Will back, and of course to know that research has advanced far enough to achieve such amazing heights."

"Oh, sure, theoretically we all hope it's true, but really, what's the possibility?"

"A damn good one," Jackson said. He looked at the judge squarely. "Quite a good one. And I'm not going to give up on it."

"Of course, of course." He nodded. "Here come George and Danny. It looks like they want a word with us."

George strode over to the table, obviously uncomfortable with his surroundings. George was more of a Donna's patron. "Good afternoon, gentlemen," George said. "We need a word with Jackson, if that's alright."

"That's fine, sure. The judge and I were just about to have dessert and maybe a cigar. Why don't you join us?"

George shifted his weight back and forth between his feet. "Unfortunately we need to have a private word with you right now."

"What's the problem, gentlemen?" Judge Ronning's authoritive voice came out clear and even.

Danny tried to mitigate. "We just need to talk alone to Jackson, Judge, that's all."

"Well that's fine, but Jackson and I were just enjoying lunch, and we're not finished yet. You can either join us, or wait half an hour and he can talk to you then."

"I'm afraid that's not going to work, your honor," George said with as much deference as he could muster. "We have some questions for Jackson regarding his Mercedes. It's been towed to the impound lot for being parked in your *spot*, Judge."

Jackson lifted his glass towards his lips. "Well, boys, it's not my Mercedes anymore. You'll have to take it up with the judge, he's the rightful owner now." Jackson smiled and drank the rest of his wine. "It seems you've towed the judge's car from his own spot." He laughed.

Neither George nor Danny cracked a smile. George turned to the judge. "Sir, do you have the title of the car yet? Is it in your rightful possession?"

"What's with you two? You're acting like imbeciles. I'm not answering any questions while I eat lunch." Judge Ronning finished the sentence with such finality that George knew there was only one way that this was all going to work out.

George lowered his voice as much as he could, but he still had to proceed. "Jackson, I'm sorry, but we have a warrant for your arrest for the murders for O. William Chase, Kris Catlin, and Bruno Tomacelli. You're goin' to have to come with me."

"What?" Jackson almost jumped out of his seat. "You've got to be kidding me!"

People at the next few tables turned to see what the commotion was.

"I know, we didn't want to do it like this, Jackson, but we've got to take you in." George turned to Danny. "Cuff 'em and read 'em his rights."

"Oh, this is just enough!" Judge Ronning said. "If you're going to be so inept and so ignorant as to think that you can just arrest this man with no evidence that we have even heard of, then the least you can do is treat him like the gentleman he is. There'll be no hand-cuffing at the Radisson Hotel! Treat this man with some dignity!"

"Sir—" George started, but Judge Ronning would not let him finish.

"This man is an upstanding citizen of society, and he's always been a friend to me and to the two of you. I'm ordering you to take him downtown in a civil manner."

George opened and closed his mouth a couple of times, then turned away from the table. "Alright, then, let's just git goin'." George led, followed by Jackson.

Danny brought up the rear.

As the men stood, the country club couple leaned back in their chairs and whispered to six friends sitting at the next table.

Jackson slowly made his way out of the hotel, trying to quiet the questions in his head. Did the police *really* think he had committed these crimes? What possible evidence could they have? How could anyone think that he, Jackson, the man who loved Will Chase from their childhood, could really have killed him in cold blood thirteen years ago? And Bruno—Jesus, Jackson didn't even know he was dead! Kris Catlin didn't even register on Jackson's radar as someone to give the time of day to, nevermind bother to kill him. This was preposterous. This was insane. What was George doing? Jackson looked to Danny but the deputy wouldn't even return his gaze. It looked like he was going to have to go down to the station and clear everything up there. What a way to ruin a lunch.

Judge Ronning came outside to meet the threesome. "I signed for lunch, and I'm coming downtown with you. Here." He handed Jackson his cell phone. "I think you'd better call Thor and have him meet us at the station."

Jackson touched the mole on his right cheek and nodded.

Thor Ronning, the judge's first cousin, had been Jackson's personal attorney for the past twenty years. He would know how to make this go away quickly.

.   .   .   .

44

MONDAY, JANUARY 8, 2001
2:00 P.M.
THOR RONNING'S LAW OFFICE
PALMER LAKE

Ronning and Ronning was one of the most prestigious law firms in the Midwest. It had offices around the world to handle the legal work of MICROMED. Every office had on display a massive leather bound legal library, and each day fresh flowers were arranged in blue and white Japanese vases sitting on tables in the entry halls. Thick red and gold carpeting, dark oak paneling, teak desks, and oil paintings of the Impressionist era tastefully adorned each room.

Style and quiet elegance were Thor Ronning's trademarks. His expensive lifestyle was paid for by the long relationship between Ronning and Ronning and MICROMED. The law firm had represented Will since the seventies when he had started MICROMED, and they had grown along with it. Now seventy-two, Thor still had a full legal and social calendar.

Thor replaced the telephone in its cradle and leaned back in his black Italian leather chair. Contemplating what he had just heard from his client, he removed his thick horn-rimmed glasses and cleaned them.

Murder!

Jackson had just told him that he was going to be arrested for the murders of Will, Kris Catlin, and Bruno Tomacelli. How was this possible? In his mind, Jackson Palmer was no killer. Other than the President, and Michael Jordan, this was possibly America's most recognizable man. What would happen to MICROMED? Besides, Thor didn't want to represent a murderer. None of the firm's lawyers were defense attorneys, per se. The only murder trial Thor had ever been involved with was years ago representing jealous old Merton Peabody when he had chopped up his wife in their barn. That trial was a town joke. It had lasted only a week and the male jury found him innocent in less than an hour. Although Thor was batting one-hundred percent in this legal area, he knew he was going to need help, and the best defense lawyer in the United States was his eccentric, Montana-cowboy colleague, Gerry Brewster. Thor buzzed the front desk's switchboard.

"Ruth, I have to go over to George Winter's office right away. Please put in an emergency call to Gerry Brewster. If he calls back and you can't reach me, tell him to be on the next plane to Palmer Lake."

.   .   .

4:30 P.M.
PALMER LAKE CITY JAIL
GEORGE WINTER'S OFFICE

Youthful district attorney Klay Bond had been informed that Gerry Brewster was on his way from Montana to represent Jackson Palmer. News like this made him realize why he had be-come a prosecutor.

Jackson Palmer. The world's richest man. Gerry Brewster. The world's greatest defense attorney. Bond's heart was beating as if he were putting for the Masters Championship in a sudden death playoff with Tiger Woods.

Bond had met Jackson but once in his life. That was two years back when Jackson had given a speech at a Rotary Club luncheon over at the Palmer Lake Country Club. Bond was impressed. He had never met Gerry Brewster. He couldn't wait.

Bond was an indolent dreamer from the 1993 Tulane law class. He had graduated dead last. His fantasy of trying a major murder trial was possibly in the making. He took a deep breath and picked up the felony complaint from his desk. He read from it to Jackson, Judge Lars Ronning, and Thor Ronning, who sat opposite him.

"Item 1. Will Chase was found dead by his mother Ingrid in the garage in 1987, a supposed suicide; Jackson had no alibi for that night, he claimed he was home by himself.

Item 2. Kris Catlin was garroted out on the reservation after the memorial service for Chase. Jackson was seen that night leaving the service with a black bag going out into the reserva-tion, supposedly carrying Bernard Grable's golf clothes in the black bag. We believe a garrote was in that bag. It was common knowledge that Jackson was well trained during Vietnam in how to garrote someone.

Item 3. We have Jackson's fingerprints on what we believe is the murder weapon in one of the crimes. Garroting Kris Catlin.

Item 4. Bruno was found dead in his ice fishing hut—an-other supposed suicide. We think Jackson chloroformed him and then drowned him. Bruno also left a note implicating Jack-son in a murder conspiracy."

Bond looked up at the men and cleared his throat. A strand

from his blonde hair hung down his forehead. "Jackson has claimed he was home by himself each of the nights I've described. For such a busy man, it seems odd that there were no calls, records, or witnesses to indicate his whereabouts during the time of death of Will and Bruno."

"Klay, this is all circumstantial," Thor said. "Can you show us the note you claim Bruno wrote that would implicate Jackson, or can we see this supposed murder weapon with my client's fingerprints on it? We need to see some proof he was in any way responsible for these deaths."

"Normally this type of discovery is revealed at the arraignment, but I happen to have a copy of the note with me. You're welcome to have a quick read."

Bond handed the paper to Thor.

Thor and Judge Ronning read the note and frowned at one another. The atmosphere in the room grew tense.

Thor looked regal. He wore a colorful cravat, a pin-striped gray suit, and had his daily red boutonniere gracing his lapel. It was not his habit to appear rattled. He calmly handed the note to Jackson.

Jackson scanned the paper. "I had nothing to do with these murders," he said. "What would make Bruno write such a thing? I'm telling you, it's a fake. Somebody must have put him up to it."

George and Danny believed the letter and followed their plan. "I don't know why Bruno wrote what he did, nor do I know if sumbody put him up to it," George said. "But Jackson, I got a lot a dead people to account for, an' all the evidence points to you." He turned and looked at Danny.

"You'll have to come in the next room and identify the items we've taken from your car while it was impounded," Danny said.

"Sure."

The fivesome walked into the adjoining room. Piled on a table were his designer sunglasses, a roadmap, a wooden cigar case, and his old set of golf clubs.

"Would you go through everythin' to make certain it's all yours and nothin's missin'," George said.

An overhead heater fan in need of a squirt of WD40 squeaked in a four-beat time. Jackson picked up his sunglasses and put them in his inside coat pocket. He fingered the smooth surface of his rosewood cigar case and opened the top. Inside were two, six-inch Arturo Fuente Opus X's. He sniffed them and handed the case to the Judge. "You might want to smoke these while we're straightening this mess out."

Judge Ronning nodded. He had a worried look on his wrinkled face as he put the cigar case in the flap pocket of his navy blue blazer. George turned to Bond and asked, "Is that okay or is that seegar case some kinda evidence?"

Bond was trying to stay calm. He snapped his purple suspenders nervously against his white button-down shirt. One strap covered the Le Coste alligator emblem. He didn't want to screw up this arrest.

"Under the circumstances, with all of us being here, I think it's okay."

Jackson rolled over the golf bag and started emptying the contents of the upper pocket. Four used Titleist balata balls, markers, tees, a white glove, some change, and a silver divot repairer were all that the pocket contained. From the large zip-down pockets on the side of the bag, he removed a blue sweater, a brown and white pair of golf shoes, and a dirty towel. Inside the towel was a hard object. He unrolled the towel and spilled the wooden handled, wire garrote onto the table. His mouth fell open.

Judge Ronning and Thor stood transfixed looking at the object.

"Gentleman, it's a garrote," Bond said. "We found traces of dried blood on the wire and we've dusted the handles for fingerprints. We'll have the blood work back in a couple of days, and the DNA back in a few weeks, but we ran the prints through the F.B.I. about an hour ago. I'm sorry to say, they match Mr. Palmer's. I'm afraid we have no other option but to place him under arrest for these murders. George, please read Mr. Palmer his rights while his attorney is present."

"This is some kind of set-up," Jackson said. "I've never seen this thing before in my life. It was planted there by someone."

"Just like your fingerprints were planted, Jackson?" said George.

"That's enough speculation, George," Thor said. "Let Danny read Jackson his rights, get him booked, and we'll see if we can set bail for him." He looked worriedly at Judge Ronning. "Do you think we can get bail set as soon as possible?"

"I'll have to see the charges, counselor."

"Judge, the charges will be for two counts of the first degree murders of Kris Catlin and Bruno Tomacelli," Bond said. "Also, for one count as an accessory to the murder of O. William Chase." Bond was gaining confidence. "I don't think you'll be able to set bail."

While Danny read him his rights, Jackson felt like an individual facing imminent death. His past started rushing before his eyes. This accusation was a guillotine slicing him off from reality. Fifty-six years of an honorable, successful life. Of living through the pain of loved ones dying, of surviving war. Was he about to confront a hostile jury of his peers? He was well aware that South Dakota still had the death penalty. Who was behind these murders? There was a madman out there, someone he knew, someone who hated him enough to frame him and kill three innocent people in his insanity. He couldn't imagine he knew such an evil soul. He searched Thor Ronning's face for answers, but saw nothing but a confused stare. He remembered Papa Loo once telling him that no matter how good, honest, and productive one was, every second, minute, hour, day, month, and year one was here on earth, one was that much closer to death. It was a zero sum equation. One loses life in the end.

Danny tugging on his arm broke Jackson's train of thought. "Come on," Danny said. "We've got no choice but to book you, get you some jail garb, and then get you a cell."

By habit the boxer muscles in Jackson's biceps tensed. There was no escaping the inevitable. "Sure, let's get it over with." He turned to Thor. "Would you call Nina and Kirby? Tell them I'd like to talk with them before they pass any judgments on me."

"I'll take care of that. But first I'll try and get bail set and get you released in the morning to my custody. For now, cooperate with George, but don't say or sign anything without me being present."

Judge Ronning's eyes misted as Danny led Jackson to jail.

.   .   .   .

45

~:~:~:

5:45 P.M.
NBC NEWS, ROCKERFELLER CENTER
NEW YORK

The biggest news of the day appeared to be that the Dow Jones didn't top 11,000 again, and, were we really starting a bear market? Bernard Grable was digesting the move in the averages of the day when a newsman handed him a wire flash from the A.P. It read:

Jackson Palmer arrested in Palmer Lake, South Dakota, on dual murder charges. Palmer, reportedly the world's richest man, was charged with two felony counts of murder for the first degree slayings of two Palmer Lake men. He was also indicted as an accessory to murder in the death of O. William Chase, his former business partner.

Bernard looked at his watch. "Do you have any more? I'm on in ten minutes."

"Sorry, Bernie. Nothing more. I'll brief you as soon as any-thing else comes across the wire."

"Get me Nina Chase at this number."

Bernard's mind was numb as the assistant punched in the number on his cell phone. It seemed like yesterday that Jackson had worriedly asked him after Will's perfusion procedure, "Was there any sign of foul play?" Was something sinister possible? Maybe Jackson's question at the time wasn't so naive. Bernard stopped his train of thought. Boy, reporting the daily news could make a cynic out of anyone. But no way could he make himself believe the story. A make-up woman was doing the finishing touches on his face when Nina answered the telephone. "Nina, it's Bernard. What's happened? I just heard Jackson was arrested for murder. Is it true?"

"Yes, they arrested him this afternoon, but he would never do such a thing, you know that." Nina started to cry. "I don't know what's going on. Can you come right away?"

"I'll be on the first plane right after tonight's broadcast. See you as soon as I get there."

Across town, an editor over at the *National Enquirer* was already setting the type for his morning headline, which read:

"IS AMERICA'S RICHEST MAN A SERIAL KILLER?"

. . . . .

46

TUESDAY, JANUARY 9, 2001
ZÜRICH, SWITZERLAND

The afternoon edition of the Neue Zürcher Zeitung screamed
the headline:

"FROZEN BODY DISAPPEARS FROM IMB CRYOGENIC
RESEARCH LAB."

The follow up article went on to say:
Jutta Kell, suspended Suisse physician, was missing from IMB
Laboratory when workers arrived early this morning. The local
police and Interpol are searching for the whereabouts of Dr. Kell's
husband, billionaire banker Hartmut Kell, along with his suspected
collaborator, former IMB Cryogenic Research physician Dr. Ralf
Verson. Police think that the most probable cause of the theft of the
body was Hartmut Kell's recent court loss in a thirteen year old
trial to have his wife moved from the IMB cryonics laboratory in
Zürich to the United States.

Interpol police assume Kell and Verson will attempt to re-sus-pend Dr. Kell. They report that two first-class, one way tickets to Rio de Janeiro, Brazil, along with a large, stainless steel cargo con-tainer, were purchased by Dr. Verson. Interpol also confirmed that the cargo container, Hartmut Kell and Dr. Ralf Verson were on the Swissair flight to Rio on Sunday.

Next to the Izor Life Extension Foundation, in America, and the IMB Cryogenic Research Laboratory in Switzerland, the Quest Center in Brazil is the third largest cryonics facility in the world.

Verson had injected Jutta with a huge dose of Valium for the flight to Brazil. She lay hidden in the cargo container in the hold of the 747 as if in an MRI machine. She was close to being claustro-phobic. She seemed to be able to remember certain things. But they were only long term memories. She couldn't recall how, or why, she supposedly died and was then suspended. A thatch hut and insects, what was that thought about? The valium was strong and she lay back and fell asleep.

.   .   .   .

47

WEDNESDAY, JANUARY 10, 2001
7:00 A.M.
PALMER LAKE, SOUTH DAKOTA

The rosy sunrise gave off enough light so the flotilla of commuter planes and private jets streaming into the small Palmer Lake airport could land with visual flight rules. Anxious MICROMED shareholders, lawyers, TV and radio personnel, and reporters from around the world hopped off planes bundled in hats, gloves, and heavy overcoats. They huffed little white vapors of breath into the crisp, cold, morning air as they scurried towards the terminal like flotsam spinning within a tsunami. Each came equipped with their own cell phone.

Entrepreneurial newspaper vendors hawked the *Palmer Lake Pride* and the *Minneapolis Star* inside the terminal. Their headlines blared the incredulous scoop. Indeed, Jackson Palmer had been arrested for the murders of Kris Catlin and Bruno Tomacelli.

Nattily attired in a felt fedora, a white silk scarf and a camel cashmere topcoat, Bernard Grable handed a newsboy a dollar, grabbed a local paper and headed for his waiting limo.

Defense attorney Gerry Brewster, with his flowing, swept-back gray hair, was already vainly working the press. Dressed in his usual fringed buckskin jacket and black wool turtleneck, he stood talking to a CNN interviewer while the TV cameras from every major station in the country whirred. He knew there was going to be more coverage of this event than the Gulf War.

The out-of-town board members of MICROMED, all blandly dressed like Secret Service agents, rushed to a company bus sitting on the tarmac. They were whisked to the corporate offices for an emergency meeting. In Jackson's absence, Kirby would now be in charge. The board hoped to stem the tide of sell orders of MICROMED stock flooding the market during the pre-opening in New York. The stock was set to open down dramatically from the previous day's close. This likely event was going to cost investors billions of dollars and prevent the Dow from reaching its new pinnacle in January.

Across town, at Donna's Donut Shoppe, the local pundits were finally vindicated. They had known all along the rich, arrogant prick Jackson Palmer had killed Will for his money. They erupted with the red-hot lava of new gossip.

Neither Kirby, Jake Schwartz, or Pietro joined Bobby Joe for coffee and banter.

The Indian crowd sat in silence. For years there had been rumors on the reservation, and they were still certain Big Bertha and Rising Coyote had a hand in these murders.

The Germans and Scandinavians, drinking their hot chocolate, felt the Mafia had somehow set up Jackson as the fall guy.

The waitresses, most of whom had a crush on Jackson at one time or another, were heartbroken. Donna had never thought Chase had killed himself, and certainly didn't think Jackson had murdered him either. She decided to keep her opinions to herself.

An unknown factor was the mysterious prowler and burglar who had been spotted at least once each year over the past ten years. The Big Boogie, as the town kids called him, or maybe her, as some distant witnesses claimed they'd seen a large woman running from the crime scene. The town became infected with the syndrome, bogyphobia. He, or she, was indiscriminate in their robberies and break-ins, though whomever it was had broken into Burt's pharmacy more than once, stealing drugs each time. But George and Danny were never able to catch or identify the Big Boogie, much less think it had any thing to do with the killings. Unless, of course, it was Big Bertha or Rising Coyote!

At the Drug Store, Burt, who was now eighty-two, wore an ill-fitting hearing aid. He had nothing to say until he had heard all of the facts. In his usual acerbic manner, he threatened to physically remove any customer who would pass judgment on Jackson until all of those facts were in.

Dr. Tragus and skinny, coughing, Leonard Bookner sat in a corner booth, quietly discussing the arrest.

Neither Judge Lars Ronning nor the Chase brothers occupied their daily booths, but all of the white-collar regulars from MICROMED ordered breakfast and whispered their opinions to one another.

At the Palmer Lake Country Club, the breakfast crowd was like a pack of jackals circling a potential meal, yelping and yapping to get a fair share of the carcass. It seemed everyone knew something about Jackson that someone else didn't know. Malicious rumors flew around the room like Dorothy in the tornado. TVs were on in every corner. Mouths hung open as people watched the updated news of their fellow member. A few know-it-alls left the room and went to the exercise room.

.   .   .

PALMER LAKE JAIL

For his protection, Jackson had been isolated in a cell at the end of the hallway in the jail. The cell was small, eight by twelve, with a toilet, a wash basin, and a single bed—all stainless steel. The concrete walls bore the intaglio of many former prisoners' initials. It was damp and cool. Jackson had been issued a pair of orange jail overalls, which he slept in. A black and gray stubble of beard sprouted on his face.

A breakfast of two over-easy eggs, burnt toast, grits and stewed prunes had been served at the crack of dawn. He couldn't eat and his full tray sat on the concrete floor. He wished he could somehow give the food to someone else, as he had listened to his fellow inmates down the hall wolf down their meals, tin forks scraping on their tin plates.

The Palmer Lake police station sat next to the Great Northern Railway tracks. The pungent smell of creosote, painted on the old wooden bridge directly behind the jail, along with a cold draft, drifted in the cracked open, barred window.

Jackson sat on the edge of the bed, his chin in his hands, pondering his fate. He felt he was too old to be afraid, too rich to be worried, too compassionate to be vindictive, too experienced to be angry, and too intelligent to be confused.

But he was.

.   .   .

7:00 A.M.
RIDGELY HEIGHTS

War Bird had served Nina breakfast in her bedroom. She ate two soft-boiled eggs and melba toast. Then she dressed and sat in a chair next to her bed drinking tea. She was mesmerized by the morning news on TV. CNN already had live coverage from downtown Palmer Lake. They were interviewing neighbors about Jackson's guilt or innocence. The spires of St. Mark's Cathedral and the United Methodist church gleamed in the background. It was a living nightmare. She channel surfed each time a commercial came on, watching only the reporters discussing Jackson's arrest.

Bernard's driver pulled into the entrance of Ridgely Heights and started the ascent up the tree-lined driveway. Bernard had told his superiors that he would not report on his friend Jackson Palmer until he had the opportunity to gather all of the facts behind the arrest. The limo stopped at the front door.

Eggs Benedict cawed. "JACKSON DID IT. JACKSON DID IT."

.   .   .

8:00 A.M.
THOR RONNING'S OFFICE

Thor sat behind his ornate desk reading the instructions for his new Palm Pilot. Framed legal degrees and various awards hung on the wall praising his intellect, yet he felt stymied by his new electronic device.

He stood to greet Gerry Brewster. "Good morning. I appreciate you coming on such short notice, but as you can see, we've got some problems with my friend Jackson Palmer."

Normally a shoehorn was needed to get both Brewster and his large ego into a room at the same time. On this morning he seemed truly humble. He loved playing the dumb, country hick. Once people fell for his act, he amazed them with his analytic deductions and brilliant observations. His simple clothes made him appear just one of the folks. He was too politically left for most of the farmers in the area because he didn't believe in the death penalty. But he did support farm subsidies. He could charm a snake out of its skin with his quick wit and down home humor. Notwithstanding his love of the spotlight, he was a good, decent man, one of uncompromising integrity, and a loving family man. His greatest asset was that he could weave facts into a web of homespun reality that juries seemed to understand. He was perfectly suited for the twelve hardworking South Dakotans who would be trying Jackson Palmer.

Brewster sat down in a cushy leather chair. A well-endowed brunette secretary brought in a tray of cups, a pot of coffee, and an assortment of donuts.

"I wouldn't have missed this upcoming trial if I'd been hogtied in a hayloft," Brewster said. "Here's where I'd like to start." Brewster took a business card from his wallet and handed it to Thor. "I need the best private detective money can buy. Call this fellow out in Los Angeles, get him all the data you can asap. He's as good as they come and I trust him. Next, I want the best lawyer on South Dakota law—that's Professor Harold Chapman over in Pierre. We also need someone in the background who knows constitutional law."

Thor thought his old Harvard law school roommate was the perfect man for the job. "I'll handle that."

Brewster, like a hungry barnyard animal, sniffed the aroma of the coffee and donuts sitting on the table. "I'm flying in a criminalist buddy of mine, Chris Fremstad, from Norway tomorrow. He's absolutely the best in the world."

"Is that the young fellow who worked with Interpol over in France and did all the crime work that found Carlos the Jackel guilty?"

"That's him. He had that madman in the Bastille in no time." Brewster reached over the coffee table and grabbed a chocolate donut. "You know, Thor, my old football coach used to tell me that sometimes the best defense is a quick striking offense."

"If that's true, then I'd like to try getting Jackson released on bail as soon as possible."

Brewster poured himself a coffee and stirred in some sugar. "We'd have to have an act of God for that to happen, or a local judge you could pull some strings with. He could set bail, and then recuse himself from the trial. Do you have any pull with God, or do you have someone else in mind?"

"Judge Lars Ronning should fit the bill perfectly." said Thor.

.   .   .

8:00 A.M.
CARL CHASE'S HOME

White smoke curled from a red brick chimney. The deep snow on the sloped roof of the home, and the blinking Christmas lights on the outside that Dixie never removed until the end of January, gave it the look of a decorated gingerbread house.

Dixie was childless and grand-childless, and she was lonely. She sat on a sofa talking on the telephone to her brother-in-law, Woody. "...and to think all of us trusted him. My God, Will trusted Jackson with everything, his money—really our money, if you know what I mean—and his life. It makes me sick to think of it. The only good thing to come of all of this is that Carl will now get his proper place as head of Micromed."

Woody was sitting in the executive office at his newly formed company. "What can I say, Dixie. I never liked Will and I liked Jackson even less. The bastard stole everything from me—my father and mother's love, Will's love, and he stole my family's money. I hope they hang the son of a bitch. That way he'll get what's coming to him, and we'll get what is rightfully ours."

"Woody, that's cruel."

Woody was bored by Dixie. Besides, she was not a Chase. With his free hand, he punched the TV remote and watched the update of Jackson's arrest. Klay Bond, tugging on his suspenders, was telling a newsman the reasons behind it. Woody said, "Tell Carl the first order of business should be for him to be in complete control of Micromed, just the way Will would have wanted it."

"That's a great idea. I'll tell him when he gets home tonight."

"I've got to go, Dixie. I'll call you later when I have some more news."

Woody hung up the phone.

Dixie listened to the dial tone for a moment, then hung up. Who could she call next?

.   .   .

8:30 A.M.
MICROMED, INCORPORATED
BOARD ROOM OFFICES

There were normally seven members sitting on the board of directors for MICROMED; sans Jackson, there sat six: Kirby Borg, Carl Chase, one tall ex-president of the United States who had flown in from Texas, a black, know-everybody, ex-urban league legislative attorney from Washington, D.C.—who didn't like being called an African-American, the renowned ex-chairman of the board of Citicorp, and a former Federal Reserve regional officer.

Jackson's legal assistant acted as recording secretary for the meeting. She had the sniffles and a red nose.

Kirby gravely brought the emergency accord to order. "Gentlemen, obviously we have a crisis. Before we start any discussion, let's take a look at what's happening to the opening of Micromed." He pointed to a flat 72" digital TV screen hanging on the north wall. His dream of building Beverly her dream opera house was fast disappearing before his eyes.

CNBC's financial news service reporters filled the screen. The New York Stock Exchange was about to open. An attractive Italian woman newscaster stood on the floor of the exchange at the trading post of MICROMED stock. It was a wild frenzy of chaotic activity. She shrilled into a microphone. "Due to the news of the arrest of Jackson Palmer, the chairman of Micromed, the stock has an order imbalance and will have a delayed opening. The floor quotes are for an opening of between fifty-two and fifty-five dollars. The stock closed yesterday at one-hundred and ten. This could be the largest one day percentage and dollar loss for a Dow stock in the history of the market."

Brokers and traders, pencils and pads in their gesticulating hands, and dressed in jackets that looked like they belonged in a butcher shop, shoved the petite reporter out of her place at the trading post. She shouted up at the camera. "It's out of control down here, back to you in the studio, Mark."

Kirby made the first order of business a motion that Carl take over as the chief executive officer and run the day to day operations of MICROMED. The ex-president seconded the motion and the rest of the board approved.

Carl gently stroked his salt and pepper goatee. The arm of his white shirt crackled.

.   .   .

48

8:30 A.M.
IZOR LIFE EXTENSION FOUNDATION
MANKATO, MINNESOTA

Jan Elton-Grable stared at the television in disbelief. "How can he be charged with murder when Will isn't dead? He's only suspended in a state of biostasis."

Kary Duesmann and Neville Cruicksank stood in the middle of the room watching the debacle of Jackson Palmer's arrest unfold. Duesmann wiped his grimy hands on his white smock. "I was watching the news at breakfast and I think the murder charges are pertaining to the murder of two other guys. Plus, you have to understand, Jan, that it's only us at the Foundation that don't think Will is dead."

"What say?" said Cruickshank. "Jackson didn't bloody well appear to be Jack the Ripper."

Jan absorbed the next ten minutes of reporting like a child engrossed in cartoons. She broke from her TV trance. "Isn't it tempting to call your friend Governor Ventura and get his permission to try and revive Will? Then maybe we could find out the truth behind these accusations."

Ignoring the no-smoking signs, Duesmann put a match to his pipe and took a deep draw. "I might just do that. When I was the physician in Jessie's Navy Seal unit, we used to shoot the bull about being suspended one day. I'll tell you, we never thought cryonics might be used as a deterrent to crime. But I'd be willing to bet he could now see the possibilities. Imagine reviving Sam Sheppard's wife or Lee Harvey Oswald years later and hearing their stories."

"Or solving the riddle of O. William Chase," Jan said.

A boiling kettle whistled on a burner across the room. Cruickshank hustled over to the small stove and turned the gas off.

"Coffee anyone?"

"Yes please, and some cream," Jan said.

Cruickshank put a teaspoon of instant coffee and creamer in two styrofoam cups and poured hot water over the granules.

Jan blew on the steaming coffee through red lips. "I suppose I need to call an emergency meeting of the board. You know, make sure Jackson's arrest doesn't change our financial structure, or destroy the board."

"We'll be all right," Duesmann said. "I'm sure we're financially secure in any crisis. But call a board meeting and see."

"If he's guilty, what if he's given the death penalty and it's carried out and he's sent back here? Do we suspend a convicted killer?" asked Cruickshank.

"I guess there are a lot of questions the courts are going to have to answer about cryonics," Duesmann said. "As of now, Jackson Palmer is innocent until proven guilty."

.   .   .   .

49

9:00 A.M.
ROBERTS COUNTY COURTHOUSE
PALMER LAKE, SOUTH DAKOTA

A grand jury was impaneled and began hearing testimony. Witnesses were scheduled to appear for the next two days— Thursday and Friday—and then the following week. If the grand jury handed down an indictment, there would be no preliminary hearing. Gerry Brewster knew he would ultimately have access to the grand jury transcripts. However, he didn't want this, he wanted the information right away. A preliminary hearing was vital to his lightning attack strategy. He and his defense team would be able to see immediately what the other side had and could cross-examine prosecution witnesses. Brewster was not about to lose this first battle.

By midmorning not a room could be found within fifty miles of Palmer Lake. Any rental house was taken by the media at exorbitant prices. The chain motels were all booked. Every bed and breakfast room was double occupied. The Radisson's penthouse suites were taken by Gerry Brewster and his incoming staff. The local restaurants had never done such business before. They were working double and triple time.

10:00 A.M.
PALMER LAKE POLICE STATION

Sides were already being drawn regarding the guilt or innocence of Jackson. TV cameras whirred as protestors with placards pronouncing their preference marched outside the jail. This was a God-fearing, hardworking, moral community, and most people weren't about to tolerate murder, not from a local, nor from the world's richest man. Many were already demanding the death penalty.

George Winter's inner office was filled with friends of the accused. No reporter except Bernard Grable was allowed inside the compound. Kirby, Beverly and Papa Loo, Nina, Judge Lars Ronning, Lenny, and Bernard all had patiently waited while Thor and Gerry had briefed Jackson during the previous hour. There wasn't much conversation among Jackson's friends; they were lost in their own thoughts, but they couldn't wait to hear what he had to say.

As the attorneys were being ushered out of the police station, a haggard and worried looking George, who hadn't slept but three hours the night before, asked the waiting group, "Who wants to go in next?"

It had been agreed beforehand that Kirby, Beverly, Papa Loo, and Nina would go into the holding room first.

They almost didn't recognize the person sitting behind a glass partition. Jackson was unshaven, his eyes were swollen and red, his face puffy, and his hair matted. COUNTY JAIL was printed, along with a series of black numbers, across his orange denim suit. His hands and feet had been shackled. His eyes misted. He spread his hands and put them up against the glass partition. They all touched fingers against the see-through barrier, sharing an indivisible bond of friendship. Everyone cried except Papa Loo. He knew Jackson was innocent.

Jackson, head hanging, slid his hands down the glass. "This is pretty damn humbling. Thanks for coming. It means a lot to me."

"We're here for you," said Kirby, "Have you got any idea what this's all about?"

Jackson rubbed his eyes with his sleeve. He looked straight at Kirby. "Not a clue. I'm more shocked than any of you over these charges. I haven't slept. I spent the night going over and over what I've been accused of and I don't know what they're talking about. Not to mention the supposed evidence against me.

I can only ask you to believe in my innocence and understand that there's someone very sick out there who's murdered three people and framed me."

Nina, her hair held in place with a colorful beaded headband, blew her nose into a Kleenex. "Red Cloud warned me years ago that powerful people like William would always have lots of enemies. Now I see what he meant. You're in the same position he was when he was murdered. But just remember, we love you and somehow we'll find out who's behind all of this."

There was a short silence. Everyone looked at one another, realizing that for fourteen years Nina had been correct in her intuition.

Papa Loo broke the moment. He asked Jackson, "What lawyers say?"

"Thor turned me over to Brewster since he's considered the best defense attorney in the country. Brewster stressed that there'd be no polygraph test, even though I want to take one. He said that he never lets clients take the witness stand in their own defense. Hell, at this point, I don't know what to think. But in fairness to him, he's never lost a murder case. I told him I'm innocent and I don't want to get off on a legal technicality. I want to be exonerated." Jackson managed a smile. He tried to tidy up by running his shackled hands over his matted hair.

Kirby hastened to say, "Don't be so self-righteous. We know you're innocent and we want you acquitted under any terms."

"I couldn't live with myself if I were released on a legal technicality. I need to find out who the hell's responsible for these heinous crimes."

Beverly pushed back the jet-black hair that had fallen across her face. "Wouldn't it be easier to find the perpetrator from outside a jail cell than inside one?"

"I agree on that point," Kirby said. "The important thing is that you get the best defense you can muster, then find out who's behind these murders."

Danny then popped in the door and said, "Sorry, folks. That's all the time there is for today. We have others waiting to see Jackson."

Papa Loo stood as straight as nature would allow. He leaned forward on his cane and looked Jackson in the eye. "My number six son, Papa Loo have tea ready when you get out."

As the four friends walked out the front of the jail they saw the placards demanding the death penalty. The demonstrators booed their appearance on the front steps.

Kirby shouted at them, "Go home, you gossipy perverts." He turned to Beverly and said, "I'm going back in and visit a few minutes with George. I'd like to see if I can get this picketing nonsense stopped. See you back at the house."

Walter held open a limo door for Papa Loo and Beverly.

Bernard, Judge Ronning and Lenny marched into the holding room. Bernard turned around from view and dabbed his eyes with a crisp white hankie. He knew in his heart Jackson was no killer. Judge Ronning and Lenny greeted Jackson with timorous male compassion.

Lenny choked back a cough. "I just wanted to give you my support. I know you couldn't have done this."

"Thanks. It was nice of you to come."

Bernard also had a job to do, and he said, "Jackson, as a newsman I'm supposed to be impartial, but if you want me to present your side of the case to the public, I'll ask NBC to do a special interview with you."

"From what I've seen of Gerry Brewster, I would be remiss in not asking him to sit in on any interview with me."

The group shared a laugh.

Judge Ronning had but one question for Jackson. "I hate to ask this, but I have to hear it from you. Did you kill or in anyway whatsoever have anything to do with these murders?"

It would have been easy to take umbrage to such a question, but Jackson was well aware of Judge Ronning's position. He answered, "No. None whatsoever."

"That's all I needed to hear. We'll take our leave now, but you can rest assured I shall do everything in my power to see you get fair treatment and that the real culprit is brought to justice."

Judge Ronning walked defiantly from the cell. He knew exactly what he was going to do for his friend.

.   .   .   .

50

JANUARY 10, 2001
IPANEMA BEACH
RIO DE JANERIO, BRAZIL

Hartmut and Jutta Kell sat at a table by the pool of the Hotel Meridien drinking frosty pina coladas. It was a humid eighty-two degrees. Although Jutta couldn't get enough of the warmth, they were in the shade of a white umbrella with a multi-colored Cinzano emblem on top. Her memory was still muddled and her voice had not returned. She handed Hartmut a written note:

> *"My Darling,*
> *Do you think ten million dollars is enough money to have put into the trust fund for Ralf after all he has done for us? He did leave everything behind to come with us. He seems very lonesome, don't you think?*
> *P.S. I love you more this time around..."*

Hartmut gave Jutta a broad smile. He put his hand on hers. "Yes, I think the money is enough. It is also a payment to stay with us as your doctor in case anything happens to you. I'm sure he'll be homesick, but I think if you look out at our blue-eyed Ralf on the beach with that young lady in the bikini, you will see that a handsome man like him will not be lonely for long."

Jutta smiled back. She put both her hands on his.

Hartmut squeezed them gently. "And I, too, love you more than life itself."

Jutta patted Hartmut's cheek. She stirred the mushy ice drink with a straw and slurped what was on the bottom. Why did the bees swarming around her sweet drink bother her so much? Flying insects seemed to make her head hurt. Especially flies.

Then Hartmut said, "My dearest, we must start giving some thought as to where we want to settle. Soon, people will be looking for us. They can do nothing to us in Brazil, but the publicity would be horrible to live with. This is a big country. Maybe a small village up the Amazon? Or a major city like Sao Paulo?"

Jutta wrote on a napkin: "What's your hurry? After all, no one can extradite us."

Hartmut grinned and showed her a copy of the morning's International Herald. The lead story was not about their escape from Switzerland as in previous days, but of the trial of Jackson Palmer. While Jutta read it Hartmut looked up and admired the blue water of the Bay of Botofogo and Sugar Loaf Mountain in the background. He said, "It hardly seems possible this fellow Palmer, who was Chase's best friend, a war hero, the world's richest man, and one who has been such a benefactor to cryonics, could have killed these innocent people. If only they could revive Chase and get to the truth."

Jutta penned: "I was revived, wasn't I?"

. . . .

51

~:~:~:

10:30 A.M. THURSDAY, JAN. 11, 2001
ROBERTS COUNTY MUNICIPAL COURT
ARRAIGNMENT FOR JACKSON PALMER

District attorney Klay Bond and his assistant, Sasha Maki, sat below the judge's colossal wooden bench. They were both scribbling notes on yellow legal pads regarding the judge's public statement to allow TV in the courtroom.

Sasha, of Finnish lineage, was notoriously stubborn. In 1994 she had graduated near the top of her law class from Hastings, but it was more out of tenacity than intelligence. Bond had appointed her deputy district attorney during his first year in office. Rumor had it that the tall, high-cheek-boned Sasha and Bond had a romantic thing going after office hours. It wasn't true. She thought him unqualified for his position, and a tedious dolt to boot. Furthermore, she planned on leading this prosecution effort herself.

Sasha was an idealist and her scale of justice tipped in an unbalanced fashion towards judicial naivete. She approached the trial of Jackson Palmer as the touchstone of her brief but promising legal career. To her the upcoming event was David versus Goliath, but in reality it was the Little League world champions against the Yankees. She and Bond were two wet-behind-the-ears recent law school graduates about to go head-to-head with America's best trial lawyer financed by the world's richest man.

Criminal procedure for murder requires two arraignments before trial in Superior Court: one after the arrest, a second after the preliminary hearing. Today was the first arraignment and Jackson was disheveled. He was scruffily dressed in a wrinkled suit and white shirt. Thor and Brewster had assured him that in spite of the evidence they would be able to present a case that would exonerate him.

The legal teams appeared before the presiding judge of Roberts County Municipal Court, Lars Ronning. Judge Ronning was ready for retirement and he wanted to end his career on a positive moral tone. Therefore he was about to set an unprecedented legal course of action in a murder trial.

It was reality time. The TV cameras all focused on the accused.

Jackson stood.

Judge Ronning asked, "Mr. Palmer, are you ready to enter a plea at this time?"

"Yes, Your Honor."

"How do you plead to counts one and two? Guilty or not guilty?"

"Not guilty, Your Honor."

Dramatically, Gerry Brewster stood, his cowboy boots making him appear taller than he was. In a booming voice he said, "Your Honor, for the protection of our client, we are requesting bail be granted by this court, for it is our contention that he will be in physical danger if held in jail during his upcoming trial."

Judge Ronning flexed his jaw ruminatively. He stared down

from the rarified heights of his bench at the defense attorney and the two seated prosecutors, then sucked in a large breath of air. Exhaling, he said, "Due to the exceptional circumstances of this case, and the reputation of the accused, I am hereby granting bail. Mr. Palmer is to be confined to his home under guard and kept under electronic surveillance twenty-four hours a day. Bail will be set at one hundred million dollars."

A gasp could be heard throughout the courtroom. No one moved, nor uttered a word. The judge solemnly looked over at Jackson, then shifted his gaze to Bond. Sasha rose from her seat holding her yellow legal pad. The most bail she had ever heard of was one hundred thousand dollars, and she had *never* heard of bail in a double homicide. Her face was white. She tersely said, "We object to this ruling."

"Objection overruled."

Sasha put her hand over her mouth. Her glare shot rockets of spite up at the judge. She then plopped back down into her chair. Brewster immediately stood. "Your Honor, we would like to set a date for the preliminary hearing today."

Judge Ronning asked, "And what day would that be?"

"This coming Monday. That is January 15th of the year 2001."

Bond jumped to his feet. His legal pad and clipboard clanged to the floor. His hands were shaking. With his pencil, he pointed the eraser towards the judge. "We object, your honor."

"Objection overruled."

Sasha grabbed the stunned Bond by the hand and yanked him to his seat. The duo had hoped time would be their ally.

Brewster nodded to Thor and a slight smile formed on his lips. Thor sniffed the red boutonniere in the lapel of his dark, gray suit.

Brewster received the copies of discovery from the prosecution. The felony complaint, the police reports, photographs, diagrams, and the coroner reports. A large binder called a "murder book" was also exchanged. As the trial and investigation continued, and as the police and the D.A. got their supplemental reports, they would be added to the book.

The learning curve had started.

.　　.　　.

FRIDAY, JANUARY 12, 2001
GEORGE WINTER'S OFFICE

George had his feet up on his desktop. He and Danny had just finished lunch at Donna's. George took a toothpick from his shirt pocket and started picking his teeth. "Damn, Danny," he said. "It's somthin' aint it? First the Judge gives Jackson bail and we got to put an extra man over at his house just in case he tries to flee. Now I just talked to Klay Bond and he tells me this Brewster fellow is goin' to try an' get this case to trial before we can gather any more evidence. How long before you'll get word from those hair and fiber people?"

Danny put his coffee mug on George's desk. "I'm not sure. Besides the hair and fiber, I also gave them some toenail cuttings I found in the second bathroom at Bruno's. But if we want DNA results to find out exactly who that person is, we got to wait some time."

"What kind of time?"

"Months, I'm sure. And even then, who do we match it up to?" George stood and removed his hat and jacket. "I don't know who, but I want hair and blood samples from Bruno's body, Risin' Coyote, Big Bertha, Woody, Freddie, Carl and Jackson. Somethin' just don't add up yet."

"You don't think Jackson's guilty, do you?" Danny asked.

"I ain't a hundred percent certain yet," George said. "Say, Brewster's got a private eye from L.A. here helping him. You know the defense's job is to get Jackson off, not find another killer, so maybe you can give this P.I. a hand and we can find out if there is another killer out there."

.   .   .

SATURDAY, AFTERNOON
JANUARY 13, 2001
JACKSON'S HOME

Jackson, Gerry, Thor, and Kirby sat upstairs watching an NFL playoff game on FOX.

Jackson laughed as the football analysts Terry Bradshaw and Howie Long clowned around for the audience during halftime, but Jackson was stiff and sore from being cramped in the jail cell and he decided he would rather use the time to work out in his private gym. He did a few leg stretches in front of the full-length mirror. The electronic monitoring ankle device chafed his skin. He started his daily ritual of twenty repetitions of the "Five Rites" on a large padded mat. These were yoga-type exercises developed by Tibetian monks centuries ago, which Jackson had learned as a POW in Vietnam.

Once finished, he went to his locker to get a jump rope. He couldn't find any hanging in their normal places. He snooped in the bottom of the locker, a locker that hadn't been cleaned out in years, and opened a smelly duffel bag. There was a rope at the bottom of the bag. He pulled it out. The handles were missing. Jackson grabbed the worn rope and ran upstairs.

Thor, Gerry, and Kirby were yelling encouragement to a defensive back who was running an interception back for a touchdown.

Jackson grabbed the remote, turned it down, and said, "Look! Someone's cut off the handles of my jump rope. Now I know how they got my fingerprints on the handles of that garrote."

The trio looked stunned. For a moment they were speechless. Gerry Brewster was the first to respond. "Hold your horses, Jackson. And be careful not to touch that rope any more than you already have. The real killer's fingerprints may be on it somewhere, although it seems a little stupid that someone would leave this for you to find. More than likely it's been planted wherever you found it."

"Nobody that stupid is behind these murders," Thor said.

"Where'd you find the rope?" asked Brewster.

"It was in my duffel bag in the gym."

"Do you keep it there all the time?"

"No, I carry the damn thing around in the truck and the car to the gym at the club and sometimes over to the Y to work out with the kids." Jackson dropped the rope on the floor.

Thor took a handkerchief from his jacket pocket and picked the rope up by the frayed end. He said to Jackson, "Have Running Fawn bring up a freezer Baggie. We'll get this over to the criminalist first thing Monday morning and check for prints."

The football game had ended and Brewster explained to Jackson the legal ramifications of his find. Jackson thought he had found how the killer got the handles of the garrote that was in his golf bag. But the D.A. would simply say Jackson had made the garrote from his own jump rope.

Suddenly a local TV station started a news broadcast which silenced even Brewster. The baby-faced announcer excitedly said, "We have breaking news on the Jackson Palmer murder case. Mr. Palmer was arrested and accused of killing Will Chase, Bruno

Tomacelli, and Kris Catlin. An audio tape made by Bruno Tomacelli was anonymously mailed to us today. We feel, as a community service, compelled to play the tape in its entirety. The following, as verified by the Tomacelli family, is the voice of their son Bruno:

> "*Mummy and Daddy. I left ya all a note of why I'm doin' what I'm doin'. But in case it gets lost or sumthun' I'm recordin' dis tape fer ya both to hear.*" Still photographs of Jackson, Will, Bruno, and Kris were shown in the background as the scratchy sounding tape played. "*I didn' mean to kill Will, I tought we waz only playin' war games, dat's what Jackson tol' me. I wore a gasmask an' held Will down in the ol' tank in Ingrid's garage. I taught we waz gonna freezin' 'em an dey wuld come back later an play wit me agin. But da kids at schul tol' me dey waz dead an culdnt ever come back. So I'm gonna go be dead wit 'em, too. I'm sorry I waz a bad boy, an it's best I'm doin' what I'm a doin'. See ya both in heaven. Bye from Bruno.*"

The crew-cut announcer came back on the air when the audio was finished. "This station has no further comment until we have an interview with Palmer Lake District Attorney Klay Bond or Mr. Palmer's attorneys, and possibly Jackson Palmer, who's been released from police custody on bail. We'll attempt to arrange for that as soon as possible. This is Rudy Fortensky at WBBC."

Thor was the first to speak. "My God, Jackson, what was that all about?"

"I honestly don't know what the hell's going on. I never committed these crimes and I don't know who's trying to frame me. Why would Bruno make such a tape?"

Gerry Brewster had both hands on the back of his neck. He leaned back in his chair, putting his feet up on an ottoman. "Bruno wasn't too bright. He was a lot like that horse, Boxer, in the book *Animal Farm*. I think he was being used by someone and got killed for telling those school kids what he knew. I have a hard time believing he could think of leaving a note and making a tape before planning a suicide." Brewster flexed his arms behind his head. "Since we know he was murdered, I think he was cajoled by someone to do it so people would think Jackson guilty. You know, one of those dual suicide pacts where one party talks the other into going first, and when the first person commits suicide, the second party doesn't. Or—we got *two* other killers."

"What?"

. . . .

52

MONDAY, JANUARY 15, 2001
MUNICIPAL COURT
PALMER LAKE, SOUTH DAKOTA

Thor Ronning asked the court for a five day delay in Jackson's preliminary hearing due to the airing of the Bruno Tomacelli tape by the local television station. The prosecution was temporarily relieved when the delay was granted.

After hearing the incriminating tape, Thor and Gerry felt their client's rights to a fair trial had been violated. It was possible the entire potential jury pool of Palmer Lake residents had heard the tape. Brewster made a bold move. He asked for an *ex parte* meeting, that is, a private meeting with the judge that excluded the prosecutors because privileged information would be discussed.

The following morning Thor and Brewster found themselves before a Superior Court Presiding Judge. The judge read a statement saying he had conducted a personal inquiry into the matter, in response to the concerns of District Attorney Klay Bond. The grand jurors, he concluded, might have heard potential evidence not officially offered by Bond's office. To protect Jackson's due process rights and the integrity of the grand jury process, the judge was recusing the grand jury. This would mean no more incriminating evidence could be produced by the prosecution from a grand jury.

Brewster was pressuring his criminalist, Fremstad, and the other scientists at the same time. He wanted to know if they could complete their work by early spring. His surprise plan was to go to trial within sixty days. He had every legal right to do so.

Chalk up the first win for the defense.

Brewster left the courtroom with Thor. The first thing he noticed was that the East coast contingent of writers, magazine reporters, and wannabe authors had invaded Palmer Lake.

People magazine, *Talk*, and *Vanity Fair* had sent reporters. Steve Forbes came personally to represent his magazine. Jackson had been a large campaign contributor when Forbes ran for President.

Fortune and *Money* magazines had writers there. This was big financial news.

Simon & Schuster and Random House had assigned biographers to the upcoming trial. The publishers wanted an "instant book" on the stands before trial's end. A Jackson Palmer/Will Chase book would be huge. Potentially millions to be sold in hardback. Possibly a movie deal.

Brewster said to Thor, "The parasites have arrived. They look like a bunch of wiggling lampreys on the back of a lake trout."

Vanity Fair's Nicky Funne approached Brewster. Funne was a pint-sized dynamo, known as a snobbish sycophant, who had sacrificed his Princeton education and razor-sharp mind for the fame of writing gossip. His beady-brown eyes bulged behind round, black-wire-rimmed glasses. Smiling from ear to ear, Nicky said to Brewster, "I'm assigned to cover the trial from inside the courtroom. I do hope you'll put in a good word for me with the judge who grants such favors."

Brewster thought the little writer a giant pain-in-the-ass, but he didn't want anything negative written about himself in a national gossip column. So he said, "I'll certainly see what I can do."

Chief George Winter was sitting at his desk, perplexed. He knew he had inventoried a portable tape recorder when he cleaned out Bruno Tomacelli's house. George had never found the time to check out the recorder, nor whether there was a tape in the machine or not, but he thought it odd that a tape recording of Bruno had been mailed to the local TV station, then played, and now Bruno's recorder was gone from his desk drawer where he had stored it. He trusted his staff implicitly. Who else had been visiting his office in the past two weeks? Half of Palmer Lake, that's who.

.   .   .

FRIDAY, JANUARY 19, 2001
PRELIMINARY HEARING
ROBERTS COUNTY COURT HOUSE

The protestors with their placards still paraded in front of the courthouse. In the holding cell next to the courtroom, Jackson waited nervously. He had on a dark business suit and tie. He knew he was innocent and he felt he was ready. A sheriff's bailiff knocked on the door and then escorted him to the courtroom.

Brewster was ready to start his blitzkrieg. If he moved quickly, he felt the prosecution would be rushed into mistakes. He wanted to keep them off guard.

Harold Chapman, his Dakota law expert, felt the defense had a chance to get the garrote evidence excluded by filing a motion to suppress evidence against the police.

In a deposition, Polly Byrd-Winter had testified she found the garrote in the golf bag of the trunk of Jackson's Mercedes before he identified the bag and its belongings to be his property. The defense motion claimed there was no search warrant obtained and that the police illegally searched Jackson's car and finding supposed evidence, identified it, replaced it, and declared it, in their minds, "the murder weapon."

The judge denied the motion, saying the court and prosecution had only received the paper work from the defense that morning—also, that the car legally was no longer Jackson's, it had been sold to Judge Lars Ronning earlier in the day. He was not willing to delay the motion to a later date.

Bruno's handwritten "suicide" note was admitted as evidence, as was the audio tape made by Bruno and played by the local television station.

Then the Roberts County criminalist dropped a bomb on the defense. He testified the blood found on the handles of the garrote contained traces of Kris Catlin's *and* Jackson Palmer's blood. This was determined by PGM subtype serology tests. (Phosphoglucomutase enzyme in human blood.) Brewster and Fremstad knew PGM subtyping was ancient science compared to DNA testing, but the results pointed in a dangerous direction.

Under oath, Fremstad, the Norwegian criminalist, had to testify that less than one-half of one percent of the population had the combination of enzymes shared by Jackson and the killer. One in over two hundred people. It wasn't unusual for defendants to be convicted on such evidence.

The judge felt the district attorney showed ample evidence the defendant might have committed the crime and ruled that he "held the defendant to answer." Which meant the trial was going to Superior Court in two weeks, Friday, February 2th.

Brewster objected to the prosecution wanting Jackson's bail revoked because of the audio tape of Bruno's that had been played on television. Brewster also objected to the prosecution's request for more blood to be taken from Jackson. The defense let it be known to the prosecution that they would be fighting for everything. The prosecution didn't seem to mind. They were happy with what was accomplished that day

The judge called for an adjournment.

The first victory for the prosecution.

.   .   .   .

53

SATURDAY, JANUARY 20, 2001
GOVERNOR JESSIE VENTURA'S HOME
ST. PAUL, MINNESOTA

Jessie Ventura had stunned the political world by winning the governor's race in Minnesota on the Reform Party ticket in 1998. Ventura was an ex-Navy Seal and ex-heavyweight professional wrestling champion who, with little financial help and with few so-called political skills, had bucked the system and revamped the way voters think today in electing an individual to higher office. Jessie was for real. And if you didn't believe it, you could always ask him.

The governor was a life-long friend of Dr. Kary Duesmann. Therefore when Governor Ventura's aide mentioned that the scientist had called twice during the week regarding an emergency personal meeting, Ventura had him call Duesmann and set aside time for a luncheon meeting on Saturday.

The duo met in as much privacy as the highly visible governor could offer, the den of his home. Ventura was not about to miss the Minnesota Viking football game that afternoon. Emergency or no emergency, this was playoff time.

Duesmann drove his wife's new Chevy Suburban up from Mankato through a driving snow storm. The weather caused him to be late and the football game, which the Vikings lost, was over.

Ventura was pacing the room talking on a cell phone to Donald Trump when Duesmann arrived. Ventura hung up and greeted his old Navy pal. He picked him up in a bear hug, put him back on the floor like a doll, and held him at arm's length. "Doc, how ya doing? It's been a long time, eh? I saw ya on television when ya won the Nobel Prize. We were proud of ya over there with them Swedes when ya got it."

"Thanks, Jessie. We felt the same way about you when you were elected. We're very proud of you down in Mankato."

Ventura pulled Duesmann towards the dining room table. "Enough of the bull. Come on an' eat, Doc. It's gettin' cold. Ya must be starved. Why don't ya tell me what the emergency is all about while ya refill your tank, eh? The First Lady made ya a Cornish game hen, carrots, an' mashed potatoes."

By the time coffee and the strawberry shortcake dessert were served, Duesmann had told Ventura all about the predicament he and Nina Chase were in regarding their desire to revive Will Chase. It was the reverse of asking for a governor's stay of execution in a death penalty case—which the state of Minnesota didn't have, and according to Ventura, thankfully so. Yet, by law the Izor Life Extension Foundation needed the Governor's approval. Ventura listened intently. He was fascinated by what he was hearing. If Duesmann and Nina Chase were correct in their belief that Jackson Palmer did not murder anyone, then the only sure way to prove he was not guilty before the murder trial was over—where possibly an innocent man would be sentenced to death—was to attempt to revive Will Chase and get the truth from him.

Duesmann explained just how close medicine was to bringing someone back to life, and how the STM worked. He told Ventura of Elvis' revival, and all the potential benefits just over the horizon, even reminding him that cryonics might be a possible deterrent to crime, especially murder. The worst case scenario would be that the revival process didn't work and they would have to re-suspend Will. Ventura was nodding. This situation might change the world as we know it. Medical miracles bigger than the Internet.

"I'm all for it, Doc. I'll have to ask the State Attorney General how long this will take. How much time do ya think we've got?"

"I'm not sure, maybe two months. But if the newspapers and TV are correct, the defense team for Jackson Palmer is trying to get the trial started as soon as possible."

"Well, Doc, these here politicians an' their system move as slow as molasses in January. But I'll try an' speed up the process an' get back to ya as soon as I can, eh."

.   .   .   .

54

SUNDAY, JANUARY 21, 2001
PORTO ALEGRE, BRAZIL

Before leaving Rio de Janiro, Hartmut had used his Swiss banking connections to hide his wealth in numbered accounts around the world. His only worry was of somehow losing Jutta to the authorities, or to the scientists in Zurich. Therefore, he, Jutta, and Ralf Verson were visiting the mysterious city of Porto Alegre to secure forged identification for their futures. For a price, diplomatic passports, drivers licenses, birth certificates, and local Brazilian photo I.D.s were known to be available in the back alleys of this bustling seaport. It turned out to be a large price. An attorney billed Hartmut a total of three hundred thousand U.S. dollars. That was for a complete set of documents for each person, which were untraceable and as good as any legal set of identification in the world.

The Swiss authorities were still searching for the missing trio, calling them "fugitives." However, they were only guilty of violating Swiss law, not any international laws.

*The IMB Cryogenics people wanted to find Jutta for future re-
search. The press wanted to find Jutta because of their morbid curiosity of why a billionaire husband and a physician friend would
run off with a frozen body, as they still didn't know Jutta was alive.*

*The three had kept a low profile since leaving Europe. Both the
men had grown mustaches, and Verson a beard, which had small
patches of gray in it. Jutta dyed her golden hair black. With a little
extra make-up, she was not recognizable. Photos of them had run
every now and again in the International Herald, which is probably why Hartmut had to pay so much for their new identification.
But no one seemed to notice or bother them in Brazil, not even the
authorities.*

*While the documents were being made, the trio waited a week
in a hotel surrounded by tall, thin, swaying coconut palms. The
weather was hot and humid, and the wooden, white-shuttered hotel
sat not far from a foul-smelling bay. The trio stayed in their air-
conditioned rooms, ordered room service, watched television and
read newspapers and travel brochures. The news of the Jackson
Palmer murder trial in the States was discussed at length every
night. Jutta wanted to know everything she could about Will Chase's
suspension.*

*The three Swiss each had a personal desire to live in various
locations around the world. All seemed to want a large city—one
far from Switzerland. Jutta suggested Sydney. Hartmut liked
Montreal, and Verson fell in love with the brochure from San Jose,
Costa Rica. After much debate, they decided upon Buenos Aires as
their new home. The Paris of South America. The city of beautiful
boulevards, quiet sidewalk cafes, and European architecture. The
land of Evita, excellent wine, tango, gauchos, beef, Pampas, and
the spectacular Andes mountains.*

*At the end of the week, with their new names, and black diplo-
matic passports, they boarded a plane for Buenos Aires to embark
on a new life.*

.   .   .   .

55

MONDAY, JANUARY 22, 2001
PALMER LAKE, SOUTH DAKOTA

Waking up without William beside her in the mornings was tough on Nina. She often masturbated at night dressed the way he used to make love to her, in sheer thigh-length stockings and covered with Kama Sutra powder and nothing else. She had done this the previous evening after staying up late and watching a re-run of *Out of Africa* on TV. She woke up exhausted.

Nina had been tired since Jackson was arrested, as if it were sitting in her mind and physically weighing her down. She was smoking more, retreating back into herself more each day, but every day she became more determined that Will would be revived. The vision of a supposed dead person rising up out of the miasma from a metal tube was implausible to most people. But not Nina.

The window panes of the bedroom were lined with starry patterns of crystallized frost. Nina put on a robe and stood in her stockings looking out over Ridgely Heights. It had snowed and was so bright outside that it hurt to look. The vegetable garden was frozen over and ravens swooped down looking for food. The ravens never went away. For most of the winter Nina had seen the ravens sweeping over the property looking for food. They never gave up. Nina hadn't either. If Governor Ventura were to grant approval for the revival attempt, she just knew that Dr. Duesmann would be able to do it. Modern science was going to return her husband to her. Plus, Wovoka would help. She kissed her wedding band for good luck.

The roar of a snowmobile illegally sledding through Ridgely Heights sent the ravens flapping into a barren oak tree. Nina's tranquil morning ended as the machine skidded to a stop in front of the house. It was occupied by two young newsmen covering the trial. They had a television camera mounted on a tripod on the back of the snowmobile and were shouting into a microphone while pointing up at the house. They were also about to learn some midwestern prairie justice.

War Bird picked up his double barrel twelve-gauge shotgun and stepped out the front door. He pointed the gun directly at them.

Eggs Benedict screamed from his perch, "WARBIRD SHOOT. WAR BIRD SHOOT."

The snowmobile quickly sped off towards the public road. Nina crawled back into the warmth of her bed. The kids had gone to school. She spread her legs, put her hand between them, and pointed the toes of her sheer stockings towards the ceiling.

.   .   .

THE BASEMENT OF
CARL AND DIXIE'S HOUSE

Dixie had twenty minutes to kill before her ride came to pick her up for the horse show. She thought she'd go down to Carl's office and shooting area in the basement to snoop around. She was certain he was hiding papers about his gambling debts somewhere down there. Why were they always so broke?

It was pitch black as she entered his office and silent as a coffin. She clicked on a small, high density desk lamp and started quickly going through the papers on his desk. She had barely begun when she found what she was looking for. A small ledger with a rubber band around it. She cautiously opened it. Was it possible? It contained Carl's past year's betting history. Jesus Christ, they were millions in debt.

Dixie heard the door behind her creak. Before she could move, it closed. She couldn't see beyond the ray of light given off by the lamp. Gradually a large shadow loomed over the blotter on the desk. There was someone in the room. Dixie froze as the shadow grew in size, the outline appeared to be that of someone huge with long hair. She tried to call out but couldn't. She could see no weapon to defend herself. She heard her heart pounding under her breast. Her knees were ready to buckle. Fear shot through her like pain. My God who was it? It couldn't be Carl, he would have just yelled at her and then beat her to a pulp. Was it Big Bertha? In panic she spun around in the dark and ran for the closed door. A large hand came from out of the blackness and grabbed her. She tried to scream but the other hand covered her mouth. Before she fainted, she recognized her assailant.

The Big Boogie thought of strangling her, then heard a car honking in the driveway. Dixie was dropped on the floor and the Big Boogie ran out the basement door into the woods.

. . .

THE IZOR LIFE EXTENSION FOUNDATION

The staff at Izor was excited at the news that they might be allowed to attempt to revive Will. Jan Elton-Grable was sitting in her office with Duesmann and Cruickshank. An Andrea Bocelli CD, *Sogno*, was playing in the background.

"The governor called this morning and told me the wheels of bureaucracy move very slowly, but he's all for our attempt to revive Will." Duesmann smoothed his rumpled white smock with tobacco stained fingers. "He urged us not to speak to the press. He wants this done quietly. He hasn't mentioned our name to the State Attorney General, nor what we'll be attempting, only that he's finding out legally what his rights as governor are to grant this approval. He wants to do this on his own, with no publicity."

"How long do you think we have to wait for an answer?" asked Cruickshank.

"The governor didn't know, but I stressed that time was of the essence."

Jan added, "We'll need at least a week to revive Will."

. . .

JACKSON PALMER'S HOUSE

Jackson was having his morning cigar and tea in the den. He stood and looked out the picture window. The ice on the lake sparkled in the noon sun. It was a work day, so only a few fisherman dotted the cold landscape. The wind swirled the snow in low, feathery patterns, brushing the surface of the lake. It looked so peaceful.

Jackson turned and walked across the room to a small window overlooking Birch Street. The road running in front of his mansion now had the atmosphere of a circus carnival. Bleachers had been set up on a vacant lot across from the house. Gawkers, bundled in overcoats, gloves, and caps, occupied every available seat. TV cables, looking like snakes slithering across the road, ran every which way. Vendors sold T-shirts printed with colored pictures of all the principals involved. Someone sold aluminum Will Chase coffee mugs shaped like dewars. Temporary flood lights were strung up and directed at the property each night. Three wooden stages were covered by a heated plastic bubble that was normally used for the indoor tennis court out at the Hyatt hotel. All the major networks and cable news shows had representatives covering the event. They sat inside their temporary shelter communicating with the rest of the world. Every trivial piece of information regarding the crimes, the town, the people involved in the trial, and their families was talked about, written about, and examined under the media microscope.

NBC had assigned Bernard Grable to Palmer Lake for the trial's duration. He even did the nightly news from the bubble. It was a media zoo. This was already being called "the trial of the new millennium."

Gerry Brewster decided to use Jackson's house as the headquarters for the defense. Each time he visited his client, the press mobbed him. He loved it.

Harold Chapman, the South Dakota law expert, was an academic and nervous in front of the cameras. He always entered the house through the back door garage.

Thor Ronning found the pack of reporters bothersome, so he avoided saying too much.

To keep some semblance of order, Brewster decided to give

a daily press conference and update the journalists in their plastic tent. He loved that, too.

At the Roberts County Courthouse, the scene was just as chaotic. Klay Bond and Sasha Maki were inundated with requests for interviews. George Winter, his wife, Polly, and Indian Danny Whistle, along with the breakfast crowd at Donna's Donuts, were some of the journalists' favorite subjects.

Out-of-towners were everywhere. There were license plates from most every state in the Union. Horns honked constantly. A person couldn't even jaywalk without looking anymore. Restaurant tables occupied for decades by the same people, now were filled by strangers. At night, the bars and muni were crammed with opinionated drunks using cell phones. Most seemed to be prejudging Jackson guilty of murder. They were certain the prosecution would ask for the death penalty. They didn't care how good Gerry Brewster was, his client was guilty.

The locals were on edge. A few fights broke out between them and the visitors. The circadian rhythm of this small town was being upset. Everyone knew of MICROMED, Jackson Palmer and Will Chase, but now Palmer Lake was being put on the world map and they didn't like it. They wanted their privacy back.

.   .   .   .

TUESDAY, JANUARY 23, 2001
DOWNTOWN, PALMER LAKE

The recent midwestern cold spell had not abated.

Carl and Dixie were walking through the wooded park in the middle of town. They had just had a spat at the house over the discovered gambling debts. Why hadn't he told her of all of this? Plus, although Dixie had a large bruise on her forehead, Carl claimed he didn't believe her story of the Big Boogie. He had hit her where it wouldn't show and told her to just keep quiet.

"While I go over to Bollie's for a haircut, why don't you walk over to Olsen's and get us some pastries for later?" Carl said.

His warm breath looked like curling smoke in the chilly air.

"Okay. But I'll just walk in the park for a while first. I've got to think about what's just happened and what I'm going to do about it."

"Yeah, you do that."

They separated. Dixie hadn't strolled too far before a pushy television reporter, microphone in hand, stopped her. She had been asked one too many times for her viewpoint on Jackson's innocence or guilt. "Please, for the last time, let the court decide whether or not Jackson did this. The facts seem to speak for themselves. I don't want you to bother me ever again."

Dixie didn't realize what a prophet she was with that statement. She turned around, hoping to avoid any further contact with the press, then popped into the street heading for the bakery. At the same time a big van was barreling down Walleye Lane. It was no contest. Dixie was three steps into the street before she saw the van. It was too late. The truck struck her, knocking her twenty feet back onto the sidewalk. Dixie hit her head on the cement curb and died instantly.

The van never stopped. Almost all of the witnesses rushed to aid Dixie and no one got a license number of the vehicle. One couple said it was a white Ford Econo van, but another said it was a Chevy Suburban. Though they both thought it had South Dakota license plates.

"Sioux Falls county tag, I think."

"The poor woman was killed by a hit and run driver."

"He didn't even try to stop."

"Where're the police when you need `em?"

The morning of the funeral, the county judge made an exception to his ruling that Jackson had to be isolated in his home until the trial was over. As long as he was monitored, he was allowed to be in attendance.

Dixie was buried in St. Mark's cemetery on a blustery afternoon. Father McQueeny gave the eulogy, a poem by Margaret Bruner:

"Death takes our loved ones—
We are bowed in grief. For whom?
Are we not selfish?
A mourner weeps for himself,
The dead know nought sorrow."

Jackson, whose arms were shackled, looked over at Carl and said, "I'm sorry, Carl."

"You should feel sorrier for yourself. You didn't have to come, you know. Or were you just looking for more attention?"

"After all that's happened together in our lives, you've still got that damn chip on your shoulder. I came because I wanted to. I always liked Dixie."

"I think I've got a right to be pissed. The law says you killed my brother."

Jackson knew it was no use explaining his innocence.

The two men stared at each other in the blowing wind as Dixie was lowered into the ground.

.   .   .   .

56

JANUARY 28, 2001
SUPER BOWL SUNDAY
JACKSON PALMER'S HOME

After the men watched the Ravens beat the Giants, they adjourned to the dining room to have coffee. Gerry Brewster wanted to go over his list of likely killers. At his meeting were Jackson, Kirby, Harold Chapman, Thor Ronning, and criminalist Chris Fremstad.

Brewster said, "Gentlemen, as we all believe in Jackson's innocence, we need to find the real killer, or killers." Brewster looked Jackson straight in the eye. "Some of my theories may offend you, my friend, but we're going to look at all possibilities. No emotional outbreaks, only a logical evaluation of what might be. Is that agreed?"

Jackson returned Brewster's stare. "Agreed."

"Harold, take out the chart we worked on and go over it with everyone."

The law professor unfolded a paper and put it on the dining room table. "Gerry, Chris, and I worked out some motives and theories for the following individuals. We'd like your comments."

The list read as follows:

"—POSSIBLE SUSPECTS—

—Carl Chase, Woody Chase, Freddie Chase, his wife, Big Bertha, Rising Coyote—all had motives—all had holes in their alibis. Maybe some parties were connected and framed Jackson."

Harold had written in, "THE LOCAL MAFIA. They could easily frame anyone. Motive—Indian gambling rights—territory —Bruno Tomacelli and Joey Gabrelli, both dead, both connected to mob?" Fremstad had added, "why are so many people close to this case dead?"

Gerry had capitalized and circled, "WAR BIRD and Nina CHASE."

Jackson immediately violated his promise to stay calm. "There's no way on earth that Nina's involved," he said. "And if she were, I'd rather suffer the consequences than stay alive and know that."

"She couldn't be involved," said Kirby.

"I agree with Jackson," Thor said, rubbing his red eyes. "Nina Chase is not involved in this in any way. I think you should cross her off the list."

Brewster removed his buckskin jacket and put it over the back of a chair. "I thought adding her name might stir up some controversy among you. But I'm happy to hear such positive support for her. She was never a suspect in my mind either. So I'll remove her from our list, but I'm leaving War Bird on."

Fremsatd said nothing. He read the faces of all the men in the room. He didn't think Jackson guilty, but he knew the DNA was going to implicate him in the Kris Catlin murder. How was he going to explain that? That someone stole Jackson's jump rope, cut off the handles, which he had bled on, and then made a garrote out of those same handles? Not very plausible. Was there possible police contamination? And if the DNA were not incriminating enough, the prosecution had informed the defense that the bottle of chloroform found in Bruno's ice fishing hut belonged to Jackson. Jackson had explained that he did have a bottle of chloroform in his gardening shack. He used it in fertilizing his roses in the spring, it was part of his secret recipe. Bruno, as his gardener, must have taken it.

Fremstad had Jackson's fingerprints on the handles of a garrote that murdered one man, and his fingerprints on a bottle of chloroform that was used to kill another man. Fingerprints could be explained in court, extenuating circumstances could be shown. Fremsatd had been involved in many murder trials and people lied all the time. He could usually spot them. Unless Jackson was the world's greatest actor, he didn't see that in him. However, a few billion dollars and the power and prestige that went with it were certainly powerful motives for murder. The jury was going to believe that. That's why he had become a criminalist, to find truth. "I think we need a handwriting expert right away. I promise, the prosecution will have one for Bruno's `suicide' letter."

Thor said, "I'll take care of that tomorrow."

"We know someone out there killed three people. Carl, Big Bertha, and Rising Coyote stand out like sore thumbs. But there's something strange I just can't put my finger on," Brewster said. "Are there any other suspects you can think of?" No one said a word. "If not, I'm going to have our P.I. bring in some assistants from California and investigate every angle we can on each suspect we have on our list and any others not on our list."

. . . . .

FRIDAY, FEBRUARY 2, 2001
ROBERTS COUNTY COURTHOUSE
SUPERIOR COURT
SECOND ARRAIGNMENT

Upon entering the courtroom, the first thing Brewster noticed was Nicky Funne sitting in the front row of seats, not far from where a jury was soon to be sitting. Although now sixty-nine, Funne was dressed in his usual Ivy-league outfit—club-tie, Oxford shirt, blue blazer, gray slacks, and penny loafers. He nodded toadyishly at Brewster. He had received Brewster's requested "favor" from Judge Lars Ronning.

According to the other networks, Bernard Grable had been granted unfair access by Judge Ronning. Nicky and Bernard were the only journalists represented in the courtroom. Television, the Internet, radio, and newspapers on the outside would cover the rest.

Brewster's second observation was somewhat curious. The Chase family—Carl, Woody, Freddie and Big Bertha, along with Rising Coyote—were all sitting together on one side of the room. Nina, Kirby, Beverly, Papa Loo, Lenny, Judge Ronning, and War Bird all sat together on the opposite side of the room. It appeared sides were being drawn.

An unarmed bailiff approached Papa Loo.

"Excuse me, sir. But there's no smoking allowed in the courthouse."

"Papa Loo no smoking. Cigarette only in mouth. Heh, heh, heh."

It stayed.

Jackson was dressed in a navy business suit, freshly pressed white shirt, and blue silk tie. He was ushered in and appeared upbeat. He once again pleaded not guilty to the charges. The presiding judge, who had huge ears that stuck out like cabbage leafs, accepted this and allowed the present bail to stand. He told Klay Bond that he had sixty days within which he must bring the defendant to trial unless the defendant "waives time." To the shock of Bond and Sasha, Brewster stated he was prepared to go to trial in sixty days.

That being the right of the defense, the presiding judge announced that Judge Barbara Hawk was being assigned the trial in Superior Court unless the defense team or prosecutors wished to object. She was no-nonsense—tough, smart, and fair.

Thor and Brewster made a quick decision. They could do worse.

Thor stood and said, "Judge Hawk is acceptable to us, Your Honor."

"Judge Hawk is also acceptable to the prosecution, Your Honor," replied Klay Bond.

The stern judge nodded his approval. "I shall set a pre-trial date for thirty days hence. That would make the pre-trial date Monday, March 5th of this year. If the defense wants to enter a 995 motion, please be prepared to do so at that time. If there is no further business from either the defense or the prosecution, I shall adj—"

"Excuse me, your Honor," said Sasha, jumping to her feet, "but there's one further piece of business the prosecution wants on record at this arraignment." Sasha had outfitted her leggy frame in a tailored brown pantsuit from the Gap, white blouse and a strand of imitation pearls.

"Yes, Ms. Maki, and what's that?"

"The State of South Dakota will be seeking the death penalty in this case."

Aghast, Bond now jumped to his feet. This was not the time for that to go on the record. "Just a second, Judge. I want—"

Sasha pulled him by the arm to his chair. She smiled impishly and sat down next to him.

There was an immediate buzz in the courtroom. Commotion broke out among the spectators. Jackson couldn't believe
what he was hearing. Brewster seemed to know it was coming,
albeit not this soon. Nina gasped. Kirby touched her arm. Papa
Loo didn't move, he kept his hands folded on top of his ivory
handled walking cane. Lenny started coughing uncontrollably.
Judge Ronning had a tear in his eye. War Bird stared straight
ahead. The Chase brothers and Rising Coyote all smiled. Big
Bertha, in her excitement, farted. Nicky and Bernard stood as if
to exit. This was a story.

The judge pounded his gavel, the sound echoing in the small
room. "Order in the court. Ms. Maki, the court so records the
State's request. Court adjourned."

The press went into a feeding frenzy over the unexpected
death penalty news. The attorneys had a difficult time getting
through the horde of cameras and newsmen waiting for them
on the courthouse steps. Only Brewster stayed to talk.

Jackson needed a police escort. They sneaked him out
through a tunnel under the old stone courthouse. He was
whisked away in a cruiser.

Later that evening, TV cameras recorded Jackson's silhouette in a window shade of his home.

Know-it-all Nicky Funne appeared on the Geraldo Rivera
television talk show that same evening. He couldn't say enough
about his belief in Jackson's guilt. He felt this man was going to
have a very difficult time escaping the death penalty. He never
mentioned cryonics.

Bernard and all of the other reporters had their nightly news
story. The world couldn't hear enough about the murders in
Palmer Lake.

57

~~~

MONDAY, FEBRUARY 5, 2001
IZOR LIFE EXTENSION FOUNDATION
MANKATO, MINNESOTA

In his excitement to get to the ringing telephone, Duesmann tripped over Elvis, who was lying beneath his desk. The dog let out a yelp. Duesmann gave him a quick pat on the back with his hand, which smelled of peanut butter from his recent sandwich snack.

Elvis wagged his tail.

"Doc," said Governor Ventura on the phone, "Listen, I read about the prosecution over there in South Dakota asking for the death penalty of your friend Jackson Palmer. The papers say the trial will start in sixty days, so I got ta thinkin' maybe we got ta hurry up this revival attempt of yours, eh?"

"We'd certainly like to get started as soon as we could. We have no idea what problems we're going to be facing."

"Okay. Here's what we'll do. The State Attorney General says it's completely in my right ta grant an approval for something like your plan. Of course, he wants ta know why I want ta do that. But I haven't told him a thing about Izor. I'll Fed Ex ya a signed and notarized authorization ta proceed with a revival attempt on a mammal. No one can know about this but us. As ya told me, the worst case is that ya don't succeed and Mr. Chase stays suspended the way he is."

"Thanks, Jessie. We'll start our attempt as soon as your letter arrives. Remember, you'll always have three votes down here in Mankato."

"Good luck, Doc."

Duesmann called Jan and Cruickshank up to his lab to share the good news and discuss where to start. The trio thought the best place to begin would be to thaw Will gradually. After that was accomplished, perfuse back into him the five pints of his whole blood that had been frozen when he was suspended. Then have Duesmann use the STM and molecular assembler to repair all the cellular damage done by the carbon monoxide poisoning to his blood and tissue. When that procedure was completed, Cruickshank would use CPR and electrical shock to attempt to revive him.

"I know the knowledge of this procedure isn't supposed to leave the laboratory, but I think we should have Nina here in case we're successful," Jan said. "The man should have some reference to the past when he wakes. Do you think we could have her here?"

Duesmann was nodding his head in agreement. "I don't think Jessie would be upset over that medical decision. You call Nina when you think we're ready for her."

They hoped the governor was sending the letter via Overnight Federal Express.

. . . . .

58

WEDNESDAY NIGHT
FEBRUARY 28, 2001
JACKSON PALMER'S HOME

Gerry Brewster's birthday was cause for a small celebration. The rest of the group, Jackson, Harold Chapman, Chris Fremstad, Thor, and the grouchy private eye from Los Angeles, who had been holed up together for almost ten days, ordered beer and pizza from Pietro's and a large chocolate cake from Olsen's. The men were grateful for the change, as Brewster had ordered Chinese food every other night from Huey Goey Loo's.

"That hit the spot, Gerry," Harold said. "But I hope you have your future birthdays under better circumstances. Now let's get back to business. We have an important decision to make. Starting tomorrow, we have only six days before pre-trial. I don't think Judge Hawk is going to go for a 995 motion. She'll deny it as sure as we're sitting here. So, do we continue finding a defense for Jackson, or do we consider offering a plea bargain?"

No one knew what to say. Did this mean Harold Chapman thought Jackson guilty? Brewster started to offer his viewpoint.

Jackson cut him off. "I appreciate what you're trying to offer me, Harold, but I'm innocent of these charges and I'll fight them myself if any of you aren't convinced of my innocence. I've said from the beginning, I'll willingly take a polygraph test and I'll take the witness stand. There's nothing I won't to do to prove my innocence."

"Hold on to your britches, Jackson," Brewster said. "I think everyone in this room believes in your innocence. What Harold was trying to say was the law is a strange animal, and it's sometimes best to test all alternatives before a judge instead of a jury. That's part of what the pre-trial is all about."

Brewster rocked back in his chair, hands behind his head. He believed Harold thought Jackson guilty, which was not a good sign. Thor broke the tension. "If it meets everyone's approval, let's go over the evidence and our alternatives one more time."

All heads nodded in agreement.

"Gerry, would you start?" Thor said.

"It would be a pleasure, counselor. Let's start with what we think the prosecution is going to throw at us. Jackson, you have no alibi the night of Will's suicide/murder. Is that correct?"

"That's correct."

"They have a letter from Bruno stating you helped him gas Will. Even our own handwriting experts concur that Bruno wrote that letter. Correct, Chris?"

"Correct."

"And we know their expert will also verify this. They also have an audio tape of Bruno giving testimony that you were in collusion with him. That tape has been played on public television, so most of the jury is going to have heard it. Then the prosecution will bring up the fact you were the executor of Will's estate. And they'll remind the court you knew of this. They'll also remind the court you're now the world's richest man, worth about sixty billion dollars." Brewster noticed Jackson glaring at him. Brewster continued his outline. "In the case of Kris Catlin, they'll tell the jury you wandered onto the reservation in the middle of the night carrying a mysterious black bag, and of course, they'll supply witnesses to attest to that fact. Next they'll remind the jury Mr. Catlin was garroted that night in the middle of the reservation. Then I assume they will have military records to prove you've killed men this way before in a time of war. The blood serology on the handle and the noose of the garrote already matches yours, and you admit you probably bled on the handles of the jump rope at some time in the past, which means the DNA will come back against you. The fingerprints of both you and Bruno will be on the handle of the garrote."

With a bright flash, the TV flood lamps were turned on across the street from the house. The reporters were looking for any sign of life in the house. The sudden light scared a large Snowy owl who had been hooting from a tree in the back yard. He took flight and silently glided by the picture window. Brewster stopped talking momentarily to watch him. What was it that War Bird had told him about the owl in the moon?

Brewster took a drink from his flat glass of beer. "Next the prosecution will tell the jury you had no alibi the night of Bruno's drowning. They'll point out the bottle of chloroform found in the ice fishing hut belonged to you. Then they'll inform the jury that both yours and Bruno's fingerprints were found on the bottle. In closing they're going to talk about greed, power, and jealousy. And they'll probably finish by having that young assistant D.A., Sasha Maki, stating to the jury that this is the most open and shut murder case she has ever seen. Although this is her very first."

"Look, I know it looks terrible," Jackson said. "But dammit, I didn't kill anyone and we have to prove that. What's our defense going to be?"

Thor took a stack of papers from Fremstad and some from the P.I. He arranged them around the top of the desk and read. "First, as Harold pointed out, we could plea bargain in good faith. Find out what the prosecution's willing to settle for. We'd stick with our not guilty plea under the grounds we could delay the trial for years until we found the real killer. That's if they would agree to you being out on bail for the duration."

"That's ridiculous," Jackson said. "They're only looking for the death penalty."

"Probably, but Thor is just trying to give you all of our options," Brewster said.

"Please, Jackson, bear with me," said Thor.

"Alright, sorry."

Thor took a long drink from a glass of water. He cleared his throat. "Originally we thought by rushing the case to trial, the prosecution and the police would make enough blunders that would allow us a legal way out of a trial. That hasn't happened as yet. But in court, it probably will. They're young, they've never tried a murder case before, and they don't know what they're doing most of the time. Remember, there're numerous legal motions that can be applied for in Superior Court, which would give us more time to find the real killer. Once Gerry's in the courtroom, he can cross examine witnesses, the police, the county coroner, question the evidence, the time frames, explain your side of the story, and your relationship with Will. He can use your witnesses, including Nina who believes completely in your innocence. There are technicalities that could be brought up to have this case dismissed—blood and fingerprint evidence and how it was gathered and tested—even the garrote itself. Autopsy procedures followed on the victims, witness tampering, police mishandling of information, possible alibis you haven't thought of yet."

"I'm telling you for the last time, I don't want to get off on a legal technicality. I want to be exonerated."

"It's going to be tough, but Gerry's never lost a murder case yet and that's because his real expertise is in the courtroom," Thor said. "The jury has to convict without doubt. If there's reasonable doubt proven, one is acquitted. We have a great deal of evidence to put that doubt into the minds of the jurors. For example, Chris found traces of fingerprint swirls on both the garrote handles and the chloroform bottle that are inconsistent with both your fingerprints and Bruno's. The swirls aren't enough to identify someone, but they do establish that someone else handled those items besides you and Bruno. George Winter will testify that someone else was living in Bruno's house, but they can't prove who it was. All of this's going to establish doubt." Thor stopped and took another swig of water. He looked over at Jackson. He now had his attention. "Our P.I. found out that your masseur, Walter Belsky, thinks he remembers talking to you the night of Bruno's murder. Nina is certain she spoke with you the night of Will's death. Possibly we can pin these down with telephone records, but these were local calls and it could take forever to trace them. Yet just using them as witnesses will create even more doubt in the jury's mind. I assure you, Gerry can convince a jury of your innocence and that there's another killer out there." Thor wiped his brow.

"Or killers," Brewster said. "And, of course, if all else failed, Jackson, we would give you a polygraph test for proof and call you to the witness stand in your defense."

Gerry Brewster truly believed his client an innocent man, but for the first time in his legal life he wondered if he was about to lose a murder case.

.   .   .   .

59

IZOR LIFE EXTENSION FOUNDATION
MANKATO, MINNESOTA

Governor Ventura had air-expressed Duesmann a grant of approval for the "medical research procedure to attempt to revive a mammal."

Duesmann's team now had limited time in which to get Will revived before Jackson's trial. If the procedure worked, it would probably take some time for Will to return to normal behavior—both psychologically and physiologically.

The team had spent ten days going over every computerized formula they had developed for the revival process. They had to be sure they wouldn't harm Will if they were not successful.

For maximum privacy, the procedure would be done behind locked doors in Duesmann's laboratory. No one in the organization but he, Jan and Cruickshank were aware of their plan.

Early in the day they started unthawing the frozen body. This entailed removing the liquid nitrogen from the dewar, then placing the frozen body in a pressurized warming chamber—a device similar to the one used by the Navy to prevent divers from getting the bends. It took five hours to get Will's frozen body temperature of minus 320F to plus 78 degrees Fahrenheit.

Jan removed the protective layers of material from Will, then drained the synthetic arthropoda perfusate from his system. She replaced it with the five pints of his own whole blood that had been frozen when he was originally suspended.

Duesmann had thawed this blood. Then he repaired all implosion damage done to the cells by freezing with the cell repair machine he had. This blood carried molecular devices to tissues, where they enter cells. Duesmann would block the molecular machinery of metabolism, in the brain and elsewhere, and tie structures together with stabilizing cross-links. He went through the carotid artery in the lower neck, with his STM, and worked inside the heart. Next, he went through the bronchus into the lungs to repair all cellular damage done to the interlobar fissures by the carbon monoxide poisoning. He also used the molecular assembler to repair all surgical openings and stitches in the head and outer chest from the suspension surgery. After the enlightening experience with Elvis' revival, Duesmann had decided in advance to do nothing to Will's brain tissue. Duesmann knew he didn't have all of the answers for what he hoped would take place in the morning.

Finally Will was put back in the pressurized chamber to keep him at 78F until the next day. The last piece of business was for Jan to call Nina in Palmer Lake and have her be at the Foundation in the morning.

It was late, around nine p.m., when the scientists left the laboratory and walked rapidly in the cold night towards their cars in the dimly lit parking lot. Halfway to the lot, they were greeted by two men and a woman. The woman's face was half covered and she was bundled in a fur coat with a high collar. One man was large, with a thick beard, and was dressed in a military type overcoat. The other had a mustache, a handsome, ruddy face, and the same type of bulky coat. Was this a robbery attempt? There had been a spate of them in town during the past month. Who were these people? Protectively, Duesmann and Cruickshank stepped in front of Jan.

The man with the mustache spoke. "Good evening. Please excuse our rude intrusion. My name is Hartmut Kell. This is Dr. Ralf Verson and my wife, Dr. Jutta Kell."

The Izor scientists were stunned. They knew who the Kells and Ralf Verson were. The story of the Swiss physician who had helped Hartmut remove his suspended wife from Zurich was almost as big with the press as Jackson Palmer's arrest. Were these really Swiss fugitives? How could Jutta Kell be alive? She was supposed to be suspended somewhere in South America.

"That's preposterous," Duesmann said. "Who are you and what do you want?"

The man was calm. He smiled. "I am sorry to have startled you, Dr. Duesmann. We were great admirers of your work when we lived in Switzerland."

Cruickshank muttered in Duesmann's ear. "Blimey. I think the chap's telling the truth. He knows who you are."

Hartmut reached inside his overcoat and retrieved an envelope. He handed it to Duesmann. "These are letters from O. William Chase that he wrote to me years ago. I would like you to read them. Mr. Chase was a benefactor of cryonics in Europe as well as America. He would want us to meet."

Duesmann opened the envelope and held the letter towards the light in the parking lot. He read for a few moments. "I don't know what to say. This borders on the incredulous. Why are you here?"

"We think we might be able to help you revive Mr. Chase. Have you thought about trying to do that?" asked Hartmut.

None of the Izor scientists knew what to say. They stood speechless, looking at one another.

Hartmut started speaking again. "According to what we've read in the papers, we think his testimony might be needed in the murder trial of his friend, Jackson Palmer. Dr. Verson would be happy to fill you in on the medical details of how my wife is with us today. If there is some place warm to talk, I think we have much to discuss."

Jan could see Jutta was shivering, almost as if she was ill. Duesmann also took notice. He didn't know why, but he suddenly believed. Human emotion took over from scientific logic. "Dr. Kell, would you like to come into my laboratory and have a hot cup of coffee?"

Jutta nodded.

Hartmut said, "Unfortunately she hasn't regained the use of her voice since she was revived, but we would like that very much. Thank you."

Jan crossed herself and softly uttered under her breath, "Holy Mary, Mother of Jesus. It really is Jutta Kell."

They hurried into the warmth of the building. At this hour no one was around but the security people. Once inside Duesmann's laboratory, Cruickshank locked the door and plugged in the electric coffee pot.

In Duesmann's office the scientists noticed the visitors all had nice tans. Cruickshank hung their coats in a closet.

For a few minutes the group sat silent. Then they grinned at one another—six people who were aware they might share the secret of life.

The bubbling of the coffee maker brought them out of their preoccupation. Cruickshank got up and poured everyone a cup of steaming coffee.

Verson spoke for the first time. "We're here to help, but no one must know we're here."

"Why not?" Duesmann said. "Dr. Kell's the most famous piece of medical information we have to work with. Madam, you're possibly the missing link."

"That may be true, but we're traveling with false documents we purchased so we might live our lives out in privacy and obscurity," said Hartmut. "That's why we did not call in advance."

With this simple statement of honesty there was somehow an instant bond of empathy between the group.

"We understand," Duesmann said. "Obviously, we can use your help, and your timing is perfect. Can you tell us how Dr. Kell was revived?"

Verson spent the next hour explaining to the mesmerized scientists the complete story of Jutta's revival.

Duesmann realized this was quite the opposite of what they were going to attempt in the morning.

Cruickshank then spent the next hour telling the Swiss how they had accidently revived Elvis.

Jutta laughed but no sound came out. She and a dog were the first living things, other than Christ's arguable resurrection, to return to life.

By now it was after midnight, but no one thought of sleep. Duesmann lit up his pipe, filling the room with smoke after exhaling a deep puff. "Dr. Verson, your method is quite different from ours. Would you be willing to assist me in our revival attempt of Will Chase?"

"When would you like to start?"

"Tonight."

"Okay by me."

"Then let's get started," Jan said. "First of all, I'll need blood samples from Dr. Kell so we might make an exact percentage match for Will of the synthetic arthropoda and the whole blood perfusate in her system."

The group left Duesmann's office and went into his laboratory. Will was lying in the refrigerated vat set at a temperature of 78F. The first thing Duesmann noticed when he reached in to touch Will was that rigor mortis had set in.

"Don't worry," Verson said. "That's the same thing that happened to Jutta when we perfused her with her own whole blood. Did you do that yet?"

"Yes, about six hours ago."

"If Mr. Cruickshank will help me, we can put Mr. Chase back into the warming chamber and restore his normal body temperature. This will take a couple of hours. Then we can perfuse the mixture of synthetic arthropoda solution and Chase's whole blood back into him. From there, it will be a combination of our revival methods to see if we can bring him around."

Jan drew five c.c.'s of fluid from Jutta's arm and checked the mixture at the lab bench—it was one-fifth whole blood and four-fifths synthetic arthropoda perfusate.

Duesmann couldn't believe this possible. Years ago he had sold a few gallons to the IMB lab in Switzerland with the idea they would use it on animal test subjects. And now this. It was unbelievable. However, he had living proof right in front of him that it worked on animals and on humans!

It wasn't long before the first rays of daylight were brightening up the city of Mankato. But none reached the windowless basement of the Izor lab. The group had worked the night away. Jutta lay sleeping on the sofa in Duesmann's office. The scientists were now ready to perfuse the mixed solution of synthetic arthropoda and of Will's own whole blood into him. Jan thought this would take up to three hours by her drip method.

They kept Will's body temperature stabilized in the warming chamber. Only his arms and head were visible on the gurney.

Jan agreed to stay with Will while the others took a break in Duesmann's office. Jutta woke upon their entrance.

They all looked up at the clock on the wall. Seven a.m.

They were beat. It wasn't long before they all were asleep in chairs.

Jutta went out and sat next to Jan in the lab with Will.

At ten a.m. Jutta and Jan woke up the sleeping men. They had coffee and discussed the upcoming revival attempt. Cruickshank would apply CPR and Verson and Duesmann would use electrical stimulus. Jan would monitor all life signals. Hartmut and Jutta would stay in the office for the duration.

By eleven a.m. they had tried almost every procedure they knew, but to no avail.

Duesmann didn't want to give up hope. He decided to try his own theory. He took his machine and entered Will's heart and lung tissues, removed the packing from around Will's molecules and replaced it with water. He removed the cross-links, repaired all the damaged molecules and structures he could find, he restored Will's normal concentrations of salts and blood sugar. He then unblocked the metabolic machinery. Still, there was no sign of life. Nothing. Absolutely nothing.

Duesmann made verbal notes of the exact procedures he had followed into his tape recorder. He then called to Jan. "I've done everything I could. I think you should perfuse a fresh five pints of synthetic arthropoda into him. We'll probably have to get the techs over here and re-suspend him within the next couple of hours."

The group was crestfallen. They decided to take a break and go over the computer printouts. Possibly they had overlooked something. Maybe Verson was tired and had forgotten exactly what it was that revived Jutta. For the moment they decided to leave Will in the warming chamber.

The telephone rang in Duesmann's office. It was the direct line to the security station. Exhausted, Duesmann answered, "Good morning, cryonics lab."

"Good morning to you, doctor. We saw your cars were left all night, so we assumed you and your crew were up to your old tricks again and did an all-nighter."

"That we did."

"The reason we're calling is that Mrs. Chase is here and she said it's urgent she get in to visit with you. So we thought we'd better contact you."

"Send Mrs. Chase down immediately."

Duesmann turned around to Cruickshank and said, "My God. We forgot about Nina Chase. She's here now. I hope she'll understand what happened."

Jutta wrote a note and handed it to Duesmann. It read: *"Don't give up hope. I'm here. I'm proof for her this will soon work. Let my husband and me be with her."*

Nina had just finished praying to Wovoka when she entered the room. She could see immediately that all was not right by the look on the faces of the people in the room. "Something's wrong, isn't it?"

Jan took hold of her hand and Jutta took hold of the other hand. Nina thought it very cold.

Cruickshank had tears in his eyes. "I'd like you to meet Dr. Jutta Kell."

The two men Nina didn't know looked downcast.

Duesmann said, "I would also like you to meet Dr. Ralf Verson."

Verson nodded.

"Also Hartmut Kell, Dr. Kell's husband," Duesmann said. "You may have heard of these people lately in the news."

"Yes, I know who they are," Nina said. "But how did Dr.

Kell get revived? The newspapers have always said she was still suspended in Brazil."

The two women sat down on the sofa together, still holding hands. Hartmut explained to Nina how they happened to be there and how Jutta was revived. Nina perked up.

Duesmann then said, "Nina, I'm sorry, but we forgot about you in our haste to work on your husband last night. We wanted you here, really we did. We tried this morning to revive him. We did exactly what was done to Dr. Kell, but I'm sorry, it didn't work. Will is still in a state of biostasis. We're going to have to re-suspend him."

"Where is he?" Nina was implacable. "I'd like to see him."

Jutta handed her a note. It read: *May I go see your husband with you?*

Nina gave a nod. She held on to Jutta's hand as the two women stood from the sofa. "May we see William now?"

Duesmann led the two women into the sterile laboratory.

Will was lying in the warmer chamber in the middle of the room. Tubes for the perfusate were connected to both arms. His black screened respirator monitor registered nothing but a flat green line.

Duesmann said to Nina, "Take your time. We'll wait in the other room."

Once Nina saw her husband, tears flowed down her cheeks. She and Jutta walked slowly over to where he was lying.

Jutta brushed the tears from Nina's face with a lace handkerchief. A fly buzzed above, circling the ceiling. How did he get in this sterile setting?

Nina touched Will's hand. It was warm. Just like when he was alive. She softly cried. "William. I love you so. Oh, please come back to me. The children are grown now."

She knelt down, not letting go of his hand. She prayed again to Wovoka. The room was still. A clock ticked. The respirator gasped soft sounds. "Please. You've got to come back, even if it's only to save Jackson."

Then a weak voice moaned. "Nina?"

Nina saw the systolic and diastolic green spikes jumping on the monitor. She bolted up. Was it possible that her husband spoke to her? That Wovoka didn't let her down? That the synthetic blood miraculously worked? That Duesmann's STM machine really worked? She bent over, stroking Will's forehead.

"Is that you, Nina?" said Will, barely audible.

"Yes, my darling, it's me."

She could feel Will trying to squeeze her arm.

"Oh my God, you're alive. I love you, I love you." Nina started sobbing. She couldn't talk.

A single tear ran down Jutta's cheek. She saw the joy in Nina's eyes. She tried to mouth something to her. A gurgling sound was all that came out. Jackson had come back to life just as she had. Why? How? Somehow and someday she would help find the medical explanation. It wasn't just a miracle.

Nina was shaking in sobs next to her and hugging Will.

Jutta watched the fly on the ceiling soar down and land on her arm. Tsetse flies. Africa. A medicine man fanning smoke inside a thatched hut. The flies not leaving the hut and biting her tongue. Her horrible death. Her memory came back. A sound rose in her throat. She coughed mucus into her hankie. And then a hoarse voice pleaded. "Dr. Duesmann, come quickly. He's alive! He's alive!"

The men ran into the laboratory.

Will still had hold of one of Nina's hands, and Jutta had hold of the other. Will's eyes fluttered but he didn't open them. He was trying to say something. He gently moved his fingers around Nina's. "I love you, too."

He then drifted into a state of unconsciousness.

60

MONDAY, MARCH 5, 2001
PRE-TRIAL FOR JACKSON PALMER
SUPERIOR COURT
ROBERTS COUNTY COURT HOUSE

On the drive to the courthouse, Judge Barbara Hawk noticed colorful crocus were peeking through the snow on the ground and white pelicans were on the Red River. A good sign for an early spring. However, she thought a premature thaw meant a raging river. This was worrisome. The town didn't need a repeat of the horrible flood of 1997.

The judge was also angry. What was the big rush to get into the pre-trial? She wasn't going to listen to any 995 motion from the defense. They knew she would deny such a move. There was plenty of evidence against Jackson Palmer. Maybe the district attorney was going to offer a plea bargain? If not, she'd set a quick trial date, summon jurors for *voir dire*, and get on with it. And as for the television presently in the courtroom, it had to go. The media circus going on in Palmer Lake was about to come to a halt. She would not allow them to make a mockery of her courtroom.

This was going to be a quick, equitable, and efficient trial. One about murder. No histrionics from the famed Montana cowboy lawyer would be tolerated in her courtroom. No sidebar jawboning every thirty minutes. No lawyers being held in contempt or fined. No interviews with the judge. She was going to be in charge, and today she would let them know it.

As the limo driver pulled into the courthouse parking lot, reporters and television cameras descended upon the car like sharks circling a sinking sailboat. Unknown to the judge, the courtroom was already packed with spectators. Even George, Polly, and Danny were in there.

The Jackson Palmer murder trial was the biggest news in the world. It hogged national and international headlines on television, radio, periodicals, the Internet, and newspapers. The world's richest man appeared guilty of multiple homicide. No detail of the event was too small to report. Normally, the pretrial was a procedural process between prosecution and defense lawyers, with occasionally a judge being present. The coverage on this day was as if the Super Bowl and the World Cup were being broadcast simultaneously. One would have needed a machete to cut a swath through the throng of curiosity seekers. It was chaos.

Inside the courthouse, while waiting for the judge to arrive, Nicky Funne sat gossiping with anyone who would listen to his viewpoint. Bernard was busy typing on his laptop.

The television cameras swept the room.

The Chase family had arrived and assumed what they felt were their rightful places. Carl, Woody, Freddie, Big Bertha, and Rising Coyote were all on one side of the aisle.

Oddly, only Kirby, Beverly, Papa Loo, Lenny, and Judge Ronning sat on the other side of the aisle.

Where were Nina and War Bird? This caused a great deal of

whispering among the Chase family, for there was a strange threesome, two men and a woman with her face partially covered, sitting in their places. No one had ever seen them before. Woody thought they looked European.

A great hush fell over the crowd as the attorneys for both sides were ushered in.

A bailiff escorted Jackson to his seat. Jackson also noticed Nina's absence.

Everyone rose as the notoriously tough Judge Barbara Hawk strode into the chambers. With her black robes flowing, and with an angry scowl on her white-powdered and red lipsticked face, she resembled a legal Morticia.

She took her seat at the bench. "Ladies and gentlemen, please be seated."

One could hear scraping and shuffling of chairs, coughing, and murmuring as the packed group sat back down. The noise built into a small crescendo.

The judge whacked her gavel on the bench. "Order in the court. I will have order in this court immediately, or the bailiff will show you all to the door. Is that understood?" There was instant silence. No one wanted to miss this pre-trial. "Thank you. I'm going to commence these proceedings with a few words of warning to both the prosecution and the defense. Whatever you have to say today, I shall arbitrate, but the issue before this court is two counts of murder, and those charges will be tried in Superior Court at a later date to be determined after today's hearings. Now, as to my personal warnings to the prosecution and to our esteemed colleague from Montana, Mr. Brewst—"

A huge commotion in the hall directly outside the courtroom doors interrupted the judge. Every spectator in the room turned to see what was happening. They could hear a loud woman's voice. "Open the door. Open the door!"

The door to the room opened, the small bailiff in charge of

the door unable to prevent Nina and her entourage from entering. War Bird was pushing a wheelchair containing Will into the room, followed by Kary Duesmann. The gawking spectators broke out in boisterous chatter.

The judge started banging her gavel once again. "Order in the court. Please, order in the court. What's the meaning of this intrusion into my courtroom? Bailiff, get some help in here immediately."

Gasps could be heard throughout the room. Nicky Funne's mouth dropped open, his face looking like the tormented soul in Munch's painting of The Scream.

Bernard stared at Nina. What was happening before them was surreal. Would he be writing fact or fiction?

Rising Coyote looked as if he had seen a spirit.

Big Bertha had to hold back a sudden gas attack.

No one in the Chase family moved; they were frozen in shock.

Judge Lars Ronning started laughing.

Lenny, skinny as a skeleton, was ecstatic, and almost gagging, trying to suppress a cough.

Kirby, Beverly, and Papa Loo grinned at one another.

Nina, Kary Duesmann, and War Bird, were now wheeling Will towards the judge.

Nina said, "Your honor, please forgive us. If you'll have the courtesy to hear from my husband, I'm sure there won't have to be a murder trial for Jackson."

Whatever scientific experiment or medical phenomenon was transpiring, it was way beyond Judge Hawk's experience. But the individual in the wheelchair, to the best of her recollection, certainly resembled the O. William Chase she had known. "Bailiff, help Mr. Chase to my bench."

Sasha and Bond bumped each other as both tried to stand and get the judge's attention.

Gerry Brewster motioned for them to sit down. He wanted to see this scenario play itself out. They would all have plenty of TV time when this was over.

The television cameras panned into a closeup of Will. He looked like a man just out of surgery. His complexion was pale and he looked weak. But when he gazed up at his wife, her hand on his shoulder, he looked like a man in love.

Every romantic in the world watching the news would remember forever where they were at that moment. Newspaper editors put an immediate stop on their previously planned daily editions. Newscasters scrambled to their stations, the TV and sound engineers in the trucks outside the courtroom were showing hundreds of images of Will on their monitoring screens. They shouted instructions into microphones to the television world that was holding its collective breath to hear what Will Chase was about to say.

Judge Hawk asked, "Are you, in fact, O. William Chase?"

Will bent his head back. He looked up at the judge from his wheelchair. "Yes I am, your honor. And I'm here to testify in behalf of my friend, Jackson Palmer."

After regaining her composure, the judge peered down from the bench. "You're supposed to be dead, or at least frozen. Now you're in my courtroom to testify on the behalf of the accused. Good Lord, I think all in these chambers would agree, what's happening is most unusual. However, since this is just a pretrial hearing, we'll proceed. But before we go any further, are any of you other individuals standing before me in a position to identify this man as O. William Chase?"

"I'm his wife, your honor," said Nina.

Although they didn't socialize, Judge Hawk already knew that.

Untidy Duesmann approached the bench. "I'm Kary Duesmann, a scientist from the Izor Life Extension Foundation, and I can verify that this man is indeed O. William Chase."

Judge Hawk also recognized the modest Nobel Prize winner. "All right. The two of you may have a seat. Mr. Chase, what is it you have to tell the court?"

Will had been facing the judge, with his back to the spectators. He had War Bird rotate the wheelchair so it faced the courtroom. Will looked directly at Jackson, smiled and gave a thumbs up sign. Then he turned to Judge Ronning, Kirby, Beverly, and Papa Loo, and Lenny. He smiled again. He slowly turned his gaze upon his brothers, Big Bertha, and Rising Coyote. He wasn't smiling when he said, "Carl, why did you and Joey try to murder me?"

George said to Danny, "Joey? What 'en hell happened to Bruno?"

Leonard went hysterical. He jumped up and ran across the room and started slapping Carl. "You fucking BRUTUS—you bastard. We were your frie—"

A bailiff grabbed Leonard from behind.

Carl seemed frozen in his seat.

Leonard slapped him one more time before he was restrained.

Carl slowly stood. He started to speak. "You might as well know Joey's still—"

Suddenly through the open rear doors of the courtroom burst someone whose head was covered in a black hood. The person jumped into the courtroom and pointed an automatic pistol towards Carl with both hands. The gun barked four times.

The first round struck Leonard. Mortally wounded, he slumped into the arms of the bailiff. The stunned bailiff dropped to the floor clutching Leonard.

A window pane shattered with the second round.

The third and forth rounds hit Carl. He fell face forward, blood streaming from two gaping holes in his right temple.

The gunman moved fast. He pointed at the bench.

336 ~ PALMER LAKE

Judge Hawk scrambled under her desk, her robes billowing in the space she just vacated. Bullets thudded into the back of her empty leather chair.

War Bird and Nina draped themselves protectively over Will in his wheelchair.

Bond grabbed Sasha and ran behind the sidebar.

Brewster and the rest of the defense team huddled behind chairs.

Nicky Funne hid behind Bernard, using him as a shield.

The others in the courtroom dove to the floor.

George whirled, fell to one knee, took aim, and fired his 9mm PPK Walther at the assailant. The shot entered directly into an eye hole of the black hood and the man lurched backwards, his gun spraying bullets into the ceiling as he fell.

The man lay still. Blood spurted, then slowly bubbled, from the eyehole in the hood. His gloved hand twitched, still clenching the automatic pistol.

Danny, his pistol drawn, imitated a hunting cat, and ran hunched over on all fours to the body. He took the pistol from the man's hand as George walked over beside him.

George was shaking. He bent down on one knee to brace himself, then pulled the hood off the dead man. "Jesus H. Christ. It's Joey Gabrelli."

"So that's the Big Boogie," Danny said.

The room was strangely silent. Judge Hawk's head popped out from under her desk.

Will was gasping for air and Nina was kissing him. "Are you all right?"

"Yes."

In all of the turmoil, Papa Loo had tried to make his way over to protect Jackson. He had only made it half way to the defense table. He leaned on his ivory handled cane gasping, his cigarette dangling from the corner of his mouth.

Jackson, tears streaming down his face, hobbled over in his leg shackles, and hugged him. Then they made their way towards Will.

Hartmut, Jutta, and Verson walked past the commotion. Once outside the building, they disappeared into the crowd.

.   .   .   .

Epilogue

Will's supposed suicide, Catlin's, Bruno's, and Dixie's murders, and the shooting of the others, was all about money, power, politics, greed, gambling, the mob, and stupidity.

An autopsy showed Joey's body was full of crack cocaine and Oxycontin. He was stoned the day of the courthouse shootings. He was no different from those postal workers who crack up over something no one else can comprehend and drive off to work with a car full of guns to shoot all of their pent up goblins, who, sadly, always seem to be in the form of their former workers and employers.

In the thorough search of Bruno's house and property, Danny found a makeshift diary of Joey's. It told of Joey's thirteen year travels between Sioux Falls and Palmer Lake. The frayed, spiral ring notebook documented his escape from the airplane crash into the mineshaft. Joey had a few broken bones, mostly ribs, some superficial head wounds, but when the granite rubble buried the plane, it pushed the crushed frame upside down to the bottom of the shaft and the cockpit into an abandoned tunnel. The sloping tunnel ran for over a mile under the airport and towards a wooded gully at the south end of the lake. It was the only tunnel that had been dug with an escape outlet. It was filled with dripping water, muddy puddles, snakes, ginkos, rats, and rumbling echoes. The outlet was hidden by a hundred years of ground cover, thick vegetation and roots. The tunnel was dug and blasted by the Chinese coolies and wasn't very large, only five feet by five feet. Joey was able to extricate his duffel bag from the wreck, and between a few chocolate bars and lots of cocaine to ease his pain, he was able to crawl to the one crack of light he could see in the tunnel.

He had hidden at Bruno's until he recuperated and again whenever he was in Palmer Lake, and hid at his mobster uncle's when in Sioux Falls. The mob used him as a hit man once he was certified as being dead. Joey hated that. He was always being used. So he worked as a bouncer in a jazz club. But he got lonely for his thug pals in Palmer Lake that he had gone to school with and worked with out at the dump; they had been his only friends in life, and he would return and break into homes or Burt's for drugs. He became the Big Boogie. It tickled him each time he read the nickname in the newspapers. Over the years it became a game with him not to get caught and to keep the name and mystery in the papers. He felt he really had them confused when he dressed up as a woman during some of his robberies.

None of Joey's garbage hauling pals were a problem, they were all employed by the Tomacellis. They didn't dare gossip, although there always seemed to be gossip spread at the Muni. Following one of those rumors, Kris Catlin came out to the dump and ran into Joey and threatened to blackmail him. Joey garroted him out by the reservation with Jackson nearby. Joey then planted his Green Beret jacket on Catlin as evidence. He later put the garrote in Jackson's golf bag on Carl's orders. Joey had almost been discovered cutting the handles off the jump rope and had dropped the rope in Jackson's gym bag by accident.

Joey thought Bruno became dangerous when he started talking to the school kids and telling them he knew who the "Big Boogie" was. Joey and Carl figured he had to go. It was no problem to get Bruno to write the note implicating Jackson, nor to make the audio tape implicating Jackson. They just told Bruno it was a big game and they were only teasing Jackson and would tell him the truth after the game was over. Bruno was so harmless and stupid that he even assisted in his own demise. They sat around the ice fishing hut smoking dope and then told him they were all getting stoned on the chloroform in the rag and he had to go first. Which he did.

When Joey couldn't reach Carl any longer on the telephone or by CB, he had run into Dixie in her home when he had snuck in the basement. He and Carl decided she had to have an accident.

Joey had no idea that Will had been revived. It was only when he thought Carl might either rat on him during Jackson's trial, or worse, that Carl might have him killed because of what he knew, that Joey flipped and decided to kill Carl at the courthouse. Leonard was just an unfortunate accident.

By the end of the summer of 2001, most of the facts of what transpired over the years came to light.

Carl had left a log as neat and thorough as a ship's captain. George and Danny discovered it behind his shooting targets in the basement. The diary documented Carl's huge gambling debts over the years. Much of the truth of what happened would never be known, but to the best of their abilities, George and Danny assumed Carl had killed his own father in order to collect his share of the family insurance policy on Ian's life. Carl then paid off his debts with the funds and became an even bigger gambler in hopes of matching Will's business successes. By the time he was over five million dollars in debt to the mob, it was a matter of them killing him, or Carl killing Will. He decided to get rid of Will. He assumed he would either collect a portion of Will's fortune, or be in a corporate position with new stock and options, to pay off the debt. He needed help and he went to his old high school wrestling and Green Beret buddy, Joey Gabrelli. Joey leapt at the chance to have all the coke he wanted, cash, and the praise of his former commander.

Papa Loo had kept his promise to Jackson and had the pot of tea waiting upon Jackson's release from jail. But Papa Loo did not get to see his 102d birthday. Walter found him dead one morning in the garden, his cigarette dangling from the corner of his mouth. Papa Loo died tending his beloved vegetables. Heh, heh, heh, as he would have put it. He was buried next to Beau Palmer and Huey Goey Loo.

After fourteen years Big Bertha finally gave Freddie his surprise. She had been secretly converting to Catholicism and on the night of the supposed murder of Will, she had snuck out to a catechism class. She was another of life's lonely souls, searching for a belief higher than what her daily life had to offer. The murders and being a suspect made her accept her new faith. She and Freddie were planning to move to the Black Hills and run a church orphanage.

Woody tested positive for HIV and left Palmer Lake for San Francisco. He drove out of town giving the finger to the offices of MICROMED.

George publicly apologized to Jackson. That summer, George and Polly decided to retire to Ajijic, Mexico on their pension monies. George had on a sombrero and his cowboy boots, and a stewardess noticed Polly was chewing her gum vigorously as they boarded a *Mexicana* plane in Minneapolis.

Kirby decided to stay in Palmer Lake as Will and Jackson's personal finance manager and finally started the construction of Beverly's dream opera house out by Pickerel Lake.

Indian Danny Whistle was made the chief of police. He didn't care if anyone called him Chief. He ordered new radios for all of the town's squad cars.

Klay Bond quit as district attorney and Sasha Maki replaced him.

Gerry Brewster returned to his ranch in Montana and wrote a book about his involvement in the arraignment and his views on cryonics in the area of law and crime. He is now appearing weekly on nationwide talk shows.

Duesmann and Cruickshank were inundated with new requests for future cryonic patients. Duesmann was nominated again for a Nobel. Cruickshank was nominated for the presidency of Izor pending the announced retirement of Dr. Jan Elton-Grable.

Bernard quit as NBC anchorman and started his own show on another network. He and Jan bought a new penthouse on Central Park West in New York. Jan became a pregnant housewife.

Hartmut and Jutta decided the privacy of Argentina was where they wanted to spend the rest of their lives. Jutta told Hartmut about her experience in Africa and that she had no desire to return. There was a large German community in South America and they felt at home. Plus Jutta wanted a baby. Many babies. They bought a ranch on the pampas facing the snow-covered Andes and started raising a family.

Ralf Verson took the ten million dollars Hartmut had given him and purchased a few vintage racing cars and decided to travel the world on the old timers racing circuit.

Will and Nina returned to Ridgely Heights, where War Bird listened to Eggs Benedict shout, "WILL'S BACK. WILL'S BACK." Will turned MICROMED over to the board of directors, who hired an executive from G.E. to run the corporation.

Will wanted to dedicate his life to cryogenics and the suffering in Africa. He and Nina donated a billion dollars for the fight against diseases on the continent. The news media ran the story day after day. Will volunteered each year for testing at Izor so they could follow his medical progress. He seemed in perfect health and loved to tease Nina about her now making it with a younger man.

Stirling was a favorite to win the 2002 Formula One series. And Sophie finally landed a movie role in an upcoming James Bond film.

Jackson's first priority was to return his stock to Will and the billions that had been accumulated during Will's suspension. Will, through Kirby and Ronning and Ronning, split the monies with Jackson, leaving them tied as the two richest men in the world. Jackson had no further desire to be at Micromed, nor to serve on the board. He decided to buy a large motor yacht and spend a few years sailing the world. When he arrived in Greece at the shipbuilding yard of Paul Neofotis, he bought a two hundred and eighty foot yacht that had been built for Onassis. During the summer in Greece, he hired a crew, learned about the ship, and traveled the islands on the coastline of the Aegean Sea. On his return to the shipyard he met Aphrodite Neofotis, the owner's daughter. It was love at first sight for both of them. Aphrodite was forty, she had been married once and lost her husband in an airplane crash in the Philippines. She had no children. Jackson courted her for two months, but as with Johanna, he knew this was the woman for the rest of his life. They were married at the end of October on the island of Corfu.

The wedding was the event of 2001. Business leaders, politicians, friends, and celebrities from around the world came to the wedding. Will was the best man. Bernard, Kirby, Judge Ronning and Governor Jessie Ventura were the four groomsmen. Beverly sang with a Greek chorus at the reception. Nina and Jan were maids of honor. Verson came, although Hartmut and Jutta declined. The wedding made the covers of most of the world's magazines, including People and Vanity Fair. Nicky Funne did the lead story, claiming he knew Jackson was innocent all of the time during the murder arraignment. He ended by saying:

"And wasn't this just the perfect fairy tale."

.　　.　　.　　.

Acknowledgments

I am deeply indebted to Jane Rafal, Rafal & Associates, Scottsville, Virginia, for her final editing of my manuscript. I am grateful for the thoughtful editorial suggestions from Patricia Cottey, Kate Webber, and Denny Strole for his insights into Vietnam. My thanks to Shawn Chapman for her assistance in legal information regarding a criminal trial.

It is to be hoped my novel is taken as a tongue-in-cheek, far-fetched version of a fictional cryonics suspension today. I believe so strongly in the science behind cryonics and its ability to one day revive man, that I have become a cryonicist. The science of cryogenics holds many benefits for the future good of mankind. Therefore I hope the reader will consult experts around the world, and not use this novel as a guide to the science of cryogenics, but only as an introduction to what one day might be.

In asking the reader to understand my personal decision to one day be suspended in a cryonics facility, I suggest one read books on the subject of cryonics such as: *Engines of Creation* by K. Eric Drexler; *The Prospect of Immortality*, and *Man Into Superman* by Robert C. W. Ettinger; and articles that have been published and written by such individuals and scientists as Ralph C. Merkle, R. Michael Perry, Tanya Jones, Thomas Donaldson, Max More, Steven Harris, M.D., Peter Mauzer, Linda Chamberlin, and Brian Wowk.

My special appreciation goes to my many friends and loved ones who tolerated my eccentricities during the writing of this novel, especially Brett Bauman, who was there when I needed him. And I thank my young son, Tim, whose love and inspiration were a constant reminder of why it is so wonderful to be here on Planet Earth.

For specific and up-to-date information on cryonics one might contact: Cryonics Institute
      24355 Sorrentino Court
      Clinton Township, MI 48035
      810-791-5961 (phone) 810-792-7062 (fax)
      www. cryonics.org